the Falconer

the Falconer

ELIZABETH MAY

GOLLANCZ
LONDON

First published in Great Britain in 2013 by
Gollancz
An imprint of the Orion Publishing Group
Orion House, 5 Upper St Martin's Lane,
London WC2H 9EA
An Hachette UK Company

A CIP catalogue record for this book
is available from the British Library

ISBN 978 0 575 13040 1 (Cased)
ISBN 978 0 575 13041 8 (Export Trade Paperback)

1 3 5 7 9 10 8 6 4 2

Typeset by Deltatype Ltd, Birkenhead, Merseyside

Printed in Great Britain by Clays Ltd, St Ives plc

The Orion Publishing Group's policy is to use papers that are natural, renewable and recyclable products and made from wood grown in sustainable forests. The logging and manufacturing processes are expected to conform to the environmental regulations of the country of origin.

www.elizabethmaywrites.com
www.orionbooks.co.uk
www.gollancz.co.uk

Mr May, this one's for you.
Thanks for all those midnight strolls.

Chapter 1

Edinburgh, Scotland, 1844

I've memorised their every accusation: *Murderess. She did it. She was crouched over her mother's body, covered in blood.*

Behind me, several ladies are gathered close, gowns touching, heads bent as they murmur. A common sight at every ball I've attended since coming out of mourning a fortnight ago. Their comments still sting, no matter how often I hear them.

'I heard her father caught her just after it happened.'

I jerk away from the punch-dispenser. A panel opens on the gold cylindrical device's side. A metallic arm extends, takes my porcelain cup from under the spout and returns it to the table.

'You can't believe her responsible,' another lady says. She's standing far enough away that I only just catch her words above the other discussions in the crowded ballroom. 'My father said she must have witnessed what happened, but surely you don't think—'

'Well, my brother was present at her debut last year and *he* told me she was completely covered and elbow-deep in ... Well, I shan't go on. Too gruesome.'

'The authorities insist it was an animal attack. Even the Marquess of Douglas said so.'

'He couldn't accuse his own daughter, now could he?' the

first replies. 'He should have sent her to the asylum. Do you know she—' Her voice dips too low for me to hear the rest.

I grip the fabric of my dress. If not for the thick silk, my nails would have bitten into skin. It's all I can do to keep myself from pulling out the pistol hidden beneath my petticoats.

You're fine, I tell myself. *You're not angry. They're just a bunch of ninnies not worth being upset over.*

My body doesn't listen. I clench my teeth hard, releasing my dress to press my thumb against the quickened pulse at my wrist. One hundred and twenty beats later, it still hasn't slowed.

'Well?' a voice next to me says. 'Are you going to take some punch or glare at the contraption for the rest of the evening?'

My friend Miss Catherine Stewart regards me with a reassuring smile. As usual, she looks absolutely beautiful in her rose-pink silk gown. Her blonde curls – all perfectly in place – shine from the overhead lights as she leans in, plucks a fresh cup from the table and passes it to me.

My breathing is a bit ragged, audibly so. How utterly annoying that is. I hope she doesn't notice. 'Glaring at inanimate objects has become my new favourite pastime,' I say.

She scrutinises me slowly. 'Oh? I thought you might be listening to the chatter at the other end of the refreshment table.'

The gaggle of ladies gasp collectively. I wonder what transgression they have made up for me this time – other than the obvious one, of course.

No, best not to think about it. If I do, I might resort to threats of bodily injury; I might even pull out my pistol. And if I do that, I'll *really* be put in the asylum.

I place the cup under the spout and shove the machine's button much harder than necessary. Steam spurts from the top and punch pours out, filling my cup almost to the brim. I remove the cup and sip.

Dash it all. Not even a hint of whisky yet. Surely someone

has sneaked in a flask to save us all from the tedious chatter. Someone always does.

'No witty rejoinder?' Catherine asks with a click of her tongue. 'You must be ill.'

I glance at the gossips. Three young ladies are garbed in near identical white gowns, each decorated with various-coloured ribbons and flowered adornments. I don't recognise any of them. The one whispering has dark hair pulled back from her face, a single ringlet resting on one shoulder.

Her eyes meet mine. She quickly averts her gaze and whispers to her companions, who glance at me for a moment before turning away. Just long enough for me to see the distress in their features, along with a touch of malice.

'Just look at them,' I say. 'They're about ready to draw blood, wouldn't you say?'

Catherine follows my gaze. 'If my eyes don't deceive me, her claws have most certainly come out. Did you happen to hear what she said?'

I exhale a bit louder than necessary and try to calm myself. There's a place for my rage inside me, a hollow I've carved to bury it deep. That daily control allows me to feign a pleasant demeanour and an incandescent smile, complete with forced bubbly laughter that's a touch vapid, even stupid. I can never let the real me show. If I do, they'll all realise that I'm far worse a woman than they imagine me to be.

With all the poise I can muster, I sample more punch. 'That I am the very picture of grace,' I say sarcastically. 'You know very well what she said.'

'Wonderful.' Catherine smooths the front of her gown. 'I'm off to defend your honour. Expect me triumphant upon my return.'

I step into her path and say bluntly, 'No. I'd prefer you didn't.'

During my year in mourning, I've apparently forgotten the

fine art of the polite insult. The old Aileana Kameron would have sauntered over to that group of ladies and said something amiable and utterly cutting. Now, my first instinct is to reach for one of the two weapons I have with me. Perhaps the solid weight of the blade in my hand would be a comforting thing.

'Don't be silly,' Catherine says. 'Besides, I've always disliked Miss Stanley. She dipped my hair in an inkpot once during a French lesson.'

'You haven't had a French lesson in three years. Goodness, but you can hold a grudge.'

'Four. My opinion of her has not improved with time.'

She tries to manoeuvre around me, but I'm too quick. In my haste, I bump into the refreshment table. China cups clink together and a few saucers teeter close to the table's edge. The group of ladies take note and whisper even more.

'For heaven's sake!' Catherine stops. 'Are you really going to stand here and drink punch while that harridan falsely accuses you of—'

'*Catherine.*'

She glares at me. 'Say something, or I will.'

None of them – including Catherine – realises that the rumour isn't inaccurate, only understated. I've committed murder exactly one hundred and fifty-eight times in twelve months. My tally now grows almost every night.

'And what would you have me do the next time?' I ask. 'Shall I confront everyone who says the same?'

She sniffs. 'It's ridiculous, old gossip that's soon to become stale. People like Miss Stanley refuse to let the topic die because they've nothing else to discuss. No one actually believes the horrid rumour.'

I shift from the table then. The Hepburns' ballroom is crowded with groups of people milling about, enjoying refreshments before the next round of dances begin.

A crystal chandelier hangs in the middle of the room, newly outfitted with electricity since the last time I was here. Floating lanterns drift about just below the ceiling, each glass casing decorated with its own distinct, ornate design. Their inner mechanisms hum as they hover above the crowd. Shadows from the tinted glass play along the floral-patterned wallpaper.

As I study the groups of people in their fine dresses and tailored suits, more than one head swivels in my direction. Their gazes are heavy, judging. I wonder if those who were there for my debut will always see me as I was that night – the blood-soaked girl who couldn't speak or cry or scream.

I brought misfortune into their tidy, ordered lives, and the mystery of my mother's death has never been solved. After all, what sort of animal slays as methodically as the one that killed her? What daughter sits next to her mother's corpse and doesn't shed a single tear?

I've never spoken a word to anyone about what happened that night. Never displayed any outward signs of grief, not even at my mother's funeral. I simply didn't respond the way a guilt-less girl should have.

'Come now,' I murmur. 'You've always been a terrible liar.'

Catherine scowls in the direction of Miss Stanley. 'They're just being hateful because they don't know you.'

She sounds so sure of me, certain that I'm innocent and good. Catherine did know me, once. The way I used to be. Now there is a sole individual alive who truly understands me, who has seen the destructive part of me that I conceal – because he is the one who helped create it.

'Even your mother suspects me of some involvement and she's known me since I was a bairn.'

Catherine smirks at me. 'You do little to improve her opinion of you, what with you disappearing at every assembly she escorts us to.'

'I have headaches,' I say.

'A good lie the first time, but suspicious by the seventh. Perhaps try a different affliction next time?'

She sets down her empty cup. Immediately, the dispenser's arm picks it up and places it on the conveyer that returns dirty dishes to the kitchen.

'I'm not lying,' I insist. 'The headache forming at my temples right now was caused by Miss Stanley.'

Catherine rolls her eyes.

The orchestra at the back of the room strikes a few practice chords on their fiddles. The strathspey is about to begin, and the dance card that hangs from my wrist is surprisingly full. Aristocrats are nothing if not hypocritical. They have invented a crime and condemned me for it, yet the business of our acquaintance continues uninterrupted. My dowry is a draw many gentlemen won't ignore.

The result: not an empty spot for a dance, and hours of inane conversation. At least I enjoy the dancing.

'Your Lord Hamilton is leaving his companions,' Catherine observes.

Lord Hamilton manoeuvres around a group of ladies near the refreshment tables. A short, stout man about twenty years my senior, Lord Hamilton has a receding hairline and a penchant for cravats of unusual design. He also has an unfortunate habit of patting my wrist – which I suppose is meant to comfort me, but makes me feel all of twelve years old.

'He's not *my* Lord Hamilton,' I say. 'Good heavens, he's old enough to be my father.' I lean in and whisper, 'And if he pats my wrist again, I shall surely scream.'

Catherine lets out an unladylike snort. 'You're the one who agreed to dance with him.'

I cast her a withering glance. 'I'm not a complete boor. I won't turn down a dance unless someone else has claimed it.'

Lord Hamilton stops before us. Today's cravat has mauve, green and blue dye splashed in a strange pattern on the silk. Ever the gentleman, he smiles politely.

'Good evening, Lady Aileana,' he says, then nods at Catherine. 'Miss Stewart, I trust you're well.'

'I am indeed, Lord Hamilton,' she says. 'And may I say, that is quite a ... *striking* cravat.'

Lord Hamilton peers down at it fondly, as though someone has complimented his greatest achievement. 'Why, thank you. The dyes form the outline of a unicorn. Part of the Hamilton crest, you see.'

I blink. If anything, it resembles a sea creature of some kind.

Catherine, however, simply nods. 'How wonderful. It suits you very well, I think.'

I remain silent. I'm so terribly out of practice with social niceties that I might actually tell him the mauve splashes look like tentacles.

The orchestra strikes a few more chords as couples move to the centre of the room and take their places for the dance.

Lord Hamilton extends his gloved hand. 'May I have the pleasure?'

I place my fingers in his palm, and – hell and blast – he pats my wrist. I distinctly hear Catherine's stifled giggle as she is led off by her own suitor. I glower at her over my shoulder as Lord Hamilton and I walk to the dance line. He deposits me at the end and stands across from me.

But just as the orchestra begins to play, an odd taste sweeps across my tongue from front to back. Like a volatile mixture of sulphur and ammonia, hot and burning as it trickles down the inside of my throat.

A vile swearword almost escapes my lips. There's a faery here.

Chapter 2

I close my eyes and try to swallow the faery's power. The chemical tang in my mouth is so sharp that I want to cast my accounts over the ballroom floor. Heaving once, I lose my footing and pitch forwards.

'Oof!' I careen into the lady nearest me. The wide skirts of our dresses collide and we almost topple onto the marble tiles. Just in time, I grip her shoulders to steady myself.

'My apologies,' I say, my voice hoarse.

I look up at the woman then. Miss Fairfax. She regards me with well-controlled mild distaste. My eyes dart to the other dancers. Many couples in the strathspey crane their heads to see the commotion. Though the jaunty music plays on, everyone – *everyone* – is staring at me.

Some of them whisper, and I catch their accusations again. Or I think I do. *Murderess. She went mad. The marchioness's death was—*

I pull myself away from Miss Fairfax. It takes every ounce of effort to tamp down the memories that threaten to surface, to stay where I am and not run. I know what Father would say. He would tell me that I am the daughter of a marquess, and I am responsible for representing the family name at all times.

'So sorry, Miss Fairfax. Lost the count,' I say.

Miss Fairfax merely straightens her skirts, pats her mussed brunette hair and lifts her chin as she rejoins the dance.

'Lady Aileana?' Lord Hamilton says. He appears quite concerned. 'Are you all right?'

I force a smile and speak without thinking. 'I'm terribly sorry – I must have tripped.'

Oh, dash it all. *I feel faint,* I should have said. That would have been the perfect excuse to get up and leave. How could I be so stupid?

Too late now. Lord Hamilton simply smiles, grips my hand and guides me back to the line. I avoid the prying gazes of my peers and swallow down the last remnants of power on my tongue.

I have to find the blasted creature before it lures its victim. My instincts tell me to leave the dance, find the faery and slaughter it. I spare a glance towards the exit. Dash my reputation and the idiotic notion that a gentlewoman shouldn't cross a ballroom – or leave it – unescorted.

I feel the dark part inside of me stir and rise, desperate to do only three things: hunt, mutilate, kill.

Oh, I want to, more than anything. The faery is nearby, just outside the ballroom. I step out of the strathspey and head towards the door. Lord Hamilton intercepts me and asks a question. I can't hear it over the pounding need, my murderous thoughts.

Responsibility, I remind myself. *Family. Honour.* Damnation.

I reply to Lord Hamilton's question with a simple, 'Of course.'

He smiles again. I feel sorry for him, for all of them. They think I'm the only monster in their midst, but the real danger is the one they can't even see. Faeries select their victims and compel them with a small push of mental influence, then feed from them and kill them.

Five minutes. That's all I need to find the creature and shoot a capsule into its flesh. Only a little time unobserved to—

I grip Lord Hamilton's hand hard. I've been out of society so long, and the hunt has become second nature. I have to hush my barbaric thoughts or I'll act too soon and lose myself. My etiquette lessons repeat in my mind. *The daughter of a marquess does not charge out of a ballroom. The daughter of a marquess does not abandon her partner in the middle of a dance.*

The daughter of a marquess does not hunt faeries.

'—don't you agree?' Lord Hamilton is asking, pulling me back into the dance.

I shake myself. 'Of course.' I actually manage to sound reassuring.

Lord Hamilton pats my wrist and I grit my teeth against a violent response as we circle another couple.

The strathspey seems to go on for ever. Left foot hop, right foot back, left foot into second position. Instep, third position. Right knee bent, second position. Over and over again. The music doesn't register any more; it has become a background of screeching strings, and the dance is only halfway over.

My hand brushes the side of my blue silk dress, right over the spot where my lightning pistol is hidden. I envision myself hunting in the corridors, taking aim—

Calm, I tell myself. I study the fine details of the room again, the mosaic lanterns that continue to float over our heads. Above them are the clicking brass cogs and wiring along the edge of the ceiling, all of it connected to New Town's electricity system.

I focus on the clicks, on mentally reciting my lessons. Propriety. *Click.* Grace. *Click.* Smile. *Click.* Kill. *Click.*

Hell and blast.

The fiddles screech on. Lord Hamilton says something else and I manage to smile and give a non-committal nod.

I try again. Politeness. *Click.* Modesty. *Click.* Civility—

At last the music stops, and I turn to Lord Hamilton. He

offers his arm without comment and leads me to the perimeter of the ballroom. I eye the door again.

'I say,' Lord Hamilton murmurs, 'where is Miss Stewart? I shouldn't leave you alone.'

Thank heavens Catherine is nowhere to be seen. She is one less person I have to excuse myself from.

'You're forgiven,' I say in that charming voice I hate. 'If I might beg your pardon, I must take my leave to the ladies' parlour for a few minutes.' I touch my temple lightly. 'A headache, I'm afraid.'

Lord Hamilton frowns. 'Tch, how dreadful. Do allow me to escort you.'

Once we reach the double doors that exit into the hallway, I stop and smile. 'There's no need for you to leave the ballroom, my lord. I can find the parlour on my own.'

'Are you certain?'

I almost snap at him, but force myself to breathe deeply and regain some composure. My desire to hunt is pounding, unrelenting. If it consumes me, politeness won't deter me. I'll want nothing but blood and vengeance and release.

I swallow. 'Indeed.'

Lord Hamilton doesn't appear to notice a change in my behaviour. He simply smiles, bows from the waist and pats my wrist again. 'Thank you for the pleasure of your company.'

He turns to leave and I step into the hallway, breathing a sigh of relief. *At last.*

As I tiptoe down the corridor, away from the ballroom and the ladies' parlour, my mouth tingles when the faery power returns. My body is growing more used to the taste after its initial violent response, and I recognise the particular breed it comes from. A revenant.

I have only ever killed four revenants, but never on my own, so I haven't yet grown as accustomed to the potent taste of their power as I have to that of the other breeds of fae I kill more often. In my limited experience, they have three vulnerabilities: an opening along the thoracic cage, just over the left pectoral; an abdominal cavity with a slight soft spot in otherwise impenetrable skin; and rather sub-par intelligence.

Revenants make up for their weaknesses with solid muscle, which makes them difficult to kill. Then again, I do love a challenge.

I reach into the small pocket sewn into the folds of my ball gown and pull out a thin, plaited strand of *seilgflùr*. A rare soft thistle nearly extinct in Scotland, *seilgflùr* gives me the ability to see faeries.

The thistle was almost entirely destroyed by faeries thousands of years ago to prevent humans from learning the truth – that the plant is a faery's only true weakness. Oh, they all have some spots on their bodies that can be punctured by an ordinary weapon, but that would still only injure one of them. *Seilgflùr*, though, is deadly enough to burn their fae skin and even inflict a mortal wound. I use it in the weapons I make to hunt them.

I tie the *seilgflùr* around my neck and start forward again. My muscles are ready, relaxed, honed from twelve months of gruelling training with Kiaran. My techniques have improved during the nights when I have slaughtered faeries without his help. Kiaran claims I'm not ready to hunt on my own. I have proven him wrong a dozen times. Of course, he doesn't know I've been disobeying his direct order not to hunt alone, but I have a distinct tendency to disobey him when the opportunity arises.

The taste of the faery's power leaves another strong pulse against my tongue. It must be somewhere around the next corner. I stop abruptly. 'Brilliant,' I mutter.

The corridor leads to the bedrooms. If I'm caught inside, there would be no preventing the ensuing scandal. My reputation is intact only because the rumours about me haven't been proven. Being caught nosing around the Hepburns' private quarters would be a real issue my already questionable reputation can't afford.

I shift on my feet. Perhaps if I'm very quick—

'Aileana!'

I whirl. Oh ... *hell*.

Catherine and her mother, the Viscountess of Cassilis, stand in the corridor behind me by the double doors leading into the ballroom. As they approach, Catherine stares at me with surprise and confusion, and her mother – well, she regards me with blatant suspicion.

'Aileana,' Catherine says again when they reach me. 'What are you doing over here?'

Both women share the same shining blonde hair and wide blue eyes, though Lady Cassilis's gaze is shrewd rather than innocent. She has the keenest ability to notice even the smallest infraction in propriety. Nay, even the merest hint of disgrace.

Dash it all. This is bad, being caught heading in the direction of the Hepburns' private wing. This isn't where a respectable woman would be. Or, at least, she wouldn't get caught here. That's the important bit.

'Catching my breath,' I say hurriedly, breathing hard for emphasis. 'Lord Hamilton is very quick on his feet, you know.'

Catherine looks terribly amused. 'Oh? Well, for a man of his age, I suppose.'

'*So*,' I say, narrowing my eyes at Catherine, 'I'm here to relax a moment. That's all.'

'My *dear*,' Lady Cassilis says with heavy emphasis, 'you should relax in the ballroom, which is *this* way.' She inclines her head towards the doors down the hall.

The faery power leaves a distracting pulse against my tongue – it must be extending its powers again to draw someone in.

My body tenses in response. 'Oh, aye,' I say. My voice sounds strained. 'But—'

'*Yes,*' the viscountess corrects. '"Aye" sounds so *terribly* unsophisticated.'

Lady Cassilis is among the small but growing number of Scottish aristocracy who believe that if we speak like the English, Scotland will be considered a more civilised nation. It's a load of rubbish, if you ask me. We're perfectly urbane as we are. But I'd rather not debate the matter in a hallway while there's a bloodthirsty faery on the loose.

'Aye, of course. I mean, *yes,*' I respond. Heavens, isn't there any way to gracefully extricate myself from this conversation?

'Mother.' Catherine inserts herself between us. 'I'm certain Aileana has a reasonable explanation for … loitering here.' She turns to me. 'I thought you promised this dance to Lord Carrick.'

'I have a headache,' I say, trying to sound as innocent as possible. 'I was searching for the ladies' parlour to rest.'

Catherine raises an eyebrow. I return it with a glare.

'Well, do let me come with you,' Catherine says.

'Ah, the ever-persistent headache,' Lady Cassilis says. 'If you intend to nurse it in the ladies' parlour, you'll find that at the *other* end of the corridor.'

The viscountess narrows her gaze at me. I have no illusions that if she had proof of my ill behaviour, Catherine would have been barred from spending time with me long ago. Lady Cassilis might be my escort to formal functions, but only because Catherine asked her to, since the viscountess and my mother were friends. I can't imagine what on earth they had in common.

'Regardless,' Lady Cassilis says, 'a lady ought never to leave a ballroom unescorted. As you well know, Aileana. Need I remind you that this is yet another breach in etiquette, being alone in an empty corridor?' She sniffs. 'I fear your mother would be quite aggrieved, were she still with us.'

Catherine sucks in a sharp breath. I clench my fists and gasp. Grief rises briefly inside me, quickly replaced by rage and the overwhelming desire for vengeance. For just one kill to bury the painful memory of my mother's death once more. Even my careful control has its limits – I must find that faery before my need consumes me.

'Mother,' Catherine says deliberately, 'if you could wait for me in the ballroom, I shall be there directly.' When Lady Cassilis opens her mouth to protest, Catherine adds, 'I won't be long. Just let me see Aileana safely to the parlour.'

The viscountess studies me briefly, lifts her chin a notch and strides to the ballroom.

Catherine sighs. 'She didn't mean that.'

'She did.'

'Aileana, whatever you're planning – be quick, or I may be unable to visit for elevenhours on Wednesday. Mother—'

'I know. She thinks I'm a bad influence.'

She winces. 'Perhaps not the best.'

I smile. 'I appreciate you lying for me.'

'I never lie. I merely embellish information if the situation calls for it. For example, I intend to tell Mother that this *headache* of yours is severe enough that you may miss a few dances.'

'How very tactful of you.' I pass Catherine my reticule. 'Would you hold onto this for me?'

Catherine stares at it. 'I do believe the ladies parlour allows reticules.'

'Aye, but carrying the reticule might make my *headache* worse.' I press the purse into her palm.

'Hmm. You know, someday, I'm going to ask questions. You might even answer them.'

'Someday,' I agree, grateful for her trust.

She flashes a smile and says, 'Very well. Go off on your mysterious adventure. But at least think of our luncheon. Your cook is the only one who knows how to make proper shortbread.'

'Is that really the only reason you visit? The blasted shortbread?'

'The company is also quite agreeable … when she isn't having "headaches".'

She departs with an unladylike wink and saunters through the double doors into the ballroom.

Freed at last, I advance down the corridor again. My skirt rustles, its deep flounces fluffed by three stiff petticoats. Since I began training a year ago, I've become keenly aware of how limiting a lady's wardrobe is. The adornments are all beautiful – and absolutely useless in battle.

As I round the corner, the faery power returns in force. I let the burning tang wash over my tongue; I thrive on the anticipation. This is one of my favourite parts of the hunt, second only to the kill itself. I imagine myself shooting it again, feeling the calm release at its death …

Then, all at once, the taste tears out of my throat so fast, I bend over and gag.

'Damnation,' I whisper. The abrasive absence of its power means the revenant has found its victim and is drawing in human energy.

With another muttered oath, I gather my bulky skirts and petticoats, slip the stole off my shoulders to tie around my waist – propriety be damned – and bolt up the stairs. I glance about in dismay when I reach the top. So many doors. Now that the power has gone, I have no way to tell which room the faery is in.

I walk quickly down the hallway. The corridor is quiet. *Too* quiet. I'm painfully aware of every swish the fabric of my dress makes, every floorboard creak beneath my satin slippers.

I press my ear to the nearest door. Nothing. I open it to be certain, but the room is empty. I try another door. Still nothing.

As I palm the next handle, I hear a low gasp. The kind of

breath someone takes with only scant moments of life remaining.

I consider my options carefully. I have but a single chance to save the revenant's victim. If I charge in, the faery might kill the person before I shoot.

Quietly pushing my petticoats aside, I draw the lightning pistol from my thigh holster. I grip the handle of the weapon as I nudge the door open to peek inside.

Next to the four-poster bed in the corner of the room, the revenant's behemoth form is bent over its victim. At nearly seven feet tall, the muscled faery resembles a rotting troll. Stringy, limp dark hair hangs in patches around its scalp. The creature's skin is the pallid shade of dead flesh, speckled with decay in some places and peeling off in others. One cheek is open and gaping, exposing a jawbone and row of teeth. Faeries can heal most injuries in less than a minute, but this is the natural state of revenants. They are utterly disgusting and corpselike.

The faery's fingertips are sunk deep into the chest of a gentleman I immediately recognise as the elderly Lord Hepburn. His waistcoat is soaked through with blood, and his skin has a bluish cast.

When a faery feeds from a human's energy, they are both enveloped an astonishing white light. Lord Hepburn isn't that far gone yet, but almost.

I hold my breath and ease up the lightning pistol until the sight is level with the revenant's pectoral, just over its thoracic opening. My grip tightens, my thumb tracing the ornate carvings on the handle of the pistol in a soft caress.

Move, I think to the revenant. *Just a bit, so I don't injure my gracious host.*

The faery doesn't move and I don't have a clean shot. Time to intervene.

I lower the pistol and step into the room, shutting the door behind me with a loud click.

The revenant's head snaps up. It bares two rows of long pointed teeth and gives a low, rumbling growl that makes the fine hairs on my arms stand straight up.

I smile sweetly. 'Hello there.'

I detect some small movement from Lord Hepburn and I relax slightly. Still alive, thank goodness. The revenant's black gaze tracks me as I move to stand near the velvet settee, but it stays where it is, still greedily drinking the poor man's energy.

I need to force its attention to me again. 'Drop him, you ghastly thing.' The beast hisses and I step forward. 'I said drop him. *Now.*'

My grip on the pistol tightens again as the creature releases Lord Hepburn and rises to its full height. Now that the faery has stopped feeding, the ammonia and sulphur flavour is back, scorching. The creature towers over me, muscled and dripping with some repulsive clear substance I would rather not inspect closely.

I'm filled with a familiar rush of excitement as the faery snarls again. My heart pumps faster. My blood rushes and my cheeks burn.

'Aye, that's it,' I whisper. 'Take me instead.'

The faery leaps forward.

Chapter 3

I aim the pistol, but the faery is much faster than I expect, a blur of movement. It knocks the weapon from my hand before I can shoot and slams me into the wall. Wallpaper tears. A vase on the shelf next to us falls. Over the sound of shattering glass, I hear the pistol skid along the floor somewhere. *Hell and blast.*

The creature opens its mouth. Its saliva drips onto my silk bodice. The rancid stench of decay, with a hint of bare earth, invades my nostrils. I can't help but gag.

Snarling, the faery pins me against the wall. My legs dangle. Claws scrape my middle and fabric shreds. I struggle.

I have to free myself before the revenant can take my energy, but I'm caught between the wall and its massive chest. The faery's muscles bulge as it tries to keep me still, slicing through my dress and undergarments into my skin, leaving small cuts that burn as though they've been cauterised. Then it sinks its claws into me.

The faery breathes in and rips energy from me. Pain blossoms within my chest and fans outwards like needle pricks. Thousands upon thousands of tiny, agonising jabs all over my body.

'Falconer,' the revenant growls, and those dripping teeth

widen into a hideous grin. 'Falconer.' The word is guttural; I only just understand it. Blood scorches under my skin. The pain is almost unbearable.

The faery's eyes are shut, its body growing ever more still as my strength leaves me.

Stop struggling, I tell myself sternly. *Focus.*

I let myself slacken in the faery's arms. It drags me closer until my forehead rests against its slick neck. I pretend to give myself over, to appear close to death as I desperately slither an arm from between us, a fraction at a time. It falls to my side, a dead weight. My body has become rock where it should be bones and flesh.

In that moment, my blood goes from hot to the most numbing kind of cold. My teeth chatter. In shock, I realise my breath is visible, as though the temperature in the room has dropped.

I clench my numb hands into fists. If I'm going to die, I'll die fighting. Never at the mercy of any faery – not like my mother.

Strength resurging, I let out a fierce scream and slam a fist into the revenant's soft spot, its abdomen.

The creature howls and staggers.

I drop to the floor and crawl to put some distance between us. I try to stand, but stars dot my vision. My dress – the blasted, impractical, smothering dress – catches under my toe and I stumble.

I look up just as the faery recovers. It launches itself at me again, and I manage to roll beneath its body.

My temples are pounding, but I ignore the headache. I shove my petticoats aside to grip the handle of the *sgian dubh* snug in its sheath along my other thigh just as the faery rears back on its haunches, then jumps. I spin low to the ground, and have but a moment to aim for its soft spot again.

I won't have another chance to surprise it. I sink my blade into the front of its massive torso.

The faery screeches and flails, knocking over what must have been an exceedingly expensive mahogany chair.

The *sgian dubh* will only distract the revenant for seconds before its wound heals. Where in the blazes is that lightning pistol? My eyes dart around the room in search of it, ranging across carpet and furniture and—

There! I spot the steel glint of my pistol underneath the dresser.

Beside me, the faery rises and gropes for the knife thrust in its stomach. I dive for the pistol, grabbing it as I roll onto my back to take aim. The pistol's generator hums as conductor spines rise along the top of the barrel. At the pistol's mouth, bluntly pointed core rods open like flower petals.

The faery yanks the blade out of its flesh with a yelp. It drops the *sgian dubh* to the floor and pulls back its lips, baring sharp teeth. A low, reverberating snarl escapes its throat and it rushes me again.

I aim for its pectoral and pull the trigger.

The capsule of *seilgflùr* in the pistol releases first, a split second before a strong bolt of electricity is pushed through the core rod. Both hit the creature square in its muscular, oozing chest.

The revenant claws at the wound. A fernlike Lichtenberg figure forms rapidly at the point of entry. I watch it bloom as the *seilgflùr* is released into the creature's body.

The massive faery crumples to the floor at my feet, gasping.

Breathing hard, I wait for the moment I treasure most. For the faery to take its last breath.

When it does, its power slides into me, smooth and hot and soft like silk across skin. I shiver as the ammonia and sulphur taste in my mouth ebbs, leaving the heat of power around me.

I feel. I *feel.* Strong and untouchable and capable. An exquisite glow of joy fills me up and extinguishes my anger. For this instant, I am whole again. I am not broken or empty. The shadow-self inside me that compels me to kill is silent. I am unburdened. I am complete.

All too soon the power fades and so does the relief. And as always, I'm left with the familiar ache of rage.

Chapter 4

'Lord Hepburn?' I pat his cheek once. 'Wake up.'

His injuries are worrisome. A younger person might survive them, but Lord Hepburn is two and seventy. He could handle the small amount of energy he lost, but the cuts on his chest are so deep that he's bleeding all over the place. I must attend to them quickly.

Lord Hepburn mumbles something. I take this as an encouraging sign.

'My lord,' I say deliberately, trying to keep my voice down. 'Do you have a stitcher kit?'

He groans.

'Confound it,' I mutter. 'Wake up!'

His eyes flutter open. 'Miss Gordon?' His eyes are glazed with pain as he squints at me.

Oh dear. *Gordon* is his wife's maiden name. Some faeries have mental abilities that can make people see things, deceive them into believing whatever the faery wants. It wouldn't surprise me if the revenant made Lord Hepburn think he was sometime years in the past, meeting his future wife here. 'Aye,' I say gently. 'It's Miss Gordon. And I would like to know if you have a stitcher kit.'

'At my bedside.' His voice is barely audible.

Thank heavens. Many wealthier families don't bother to keep one – they call a doctor to bring it for them.

I rush to the table beside the bed. Next to the lamp is a small octagonal gold box. I kneel by Lord Hepburn again and place the box flat against his chest, just over his injuries.

He gropes for my wrist and winces. 'I couldn't see …'

'Your attacker,' I finish for him, softly. 'I know. Now, this might hurt a bit.' I twist the brass key at the base of the box and sit back.

Panels at the top of the box slide apart and stitchers deploy from the small opening. The wee mechanical spiders crawl atop his chest, spinning fine threads of human tendon through his injuries. I watch as his flesh is stitched back together again in perfectly straight sutures.

It's not entirely painless. Lord Hepburn gasps and his thin body shudders, his hand clutching mine. 'Almost done,' I reassure him. I don't know why I say it; it's not as if he'll recall me being here.

He smiles slightly. 'Thank you.' Moments later, he faints.

I think of how I enjoyed the sensation of the revenant's death instead of immediately aiding Lord Hepburn. How I tracked it, more concerned with vengeance than anything else. Some hero I am. I don't deserve his gratitude.

The stitchers complete their task and return to the metal box. Once they are safely back inside, I remove the contraption from Lord Hepburn's chest and check his pulse. It's steady under my fingertips. Another encouraging sign.

I lift his torso and pull him up onto the bed. I doubt he will remember much when he wakes. If he does, I hope he has the sense not to speak of an invisible assailant.

I study myself in the mirror next to the clock and assess the damage. Heavens, I'm a walking fashion nightmare. Springy copper curls have loosened from my once-stylish chignon and the bodice of my dress and my corset are shredded, my skin visible underneath and daubed with blood. The revenant sliced me deep enough that I'll have to stitch myself, too.

I glance at the clock on the far wall and swear silently. The assembly is almost over and there's no time to stay and tend to my injuries; I'm sure everyone has noticed my absence by now. The best I can do is correct my hair and clothing, and perhaps cut one of the thick ribbons from the bottom of my dress to tie over the torn bodice before I return to the ballroom.

With a sigh, I step over the dead faery towards the door. No one will notice if I leave it here – faeries decay to nothing in about an hour. Even if someone discovers the slumbering Lord Hepburn before then, it's not as if the faery's corpse would be visible.

I nod at my sleeping host. 'Apologies, my lord. I would tidy up, but I have other matters to attend to.'

When I return to the ballroom, the last waltz has begun. Catherine stands alone by the long-case clock near the fireplace, her hair shining in the light from the lamp floating directly over her head. She shifts on her feet, watching the door, as though she'd rather be somewhere else.

I make my way to the refreshment table. The levels in the punch dispensers indicate they're all empty.

Humming the tune for the waltz, I settle next to Catherine, gathering my stole to hide any blood that might have seeped through the ribbon tied clumsily around my bodice. 'The headache's gone,' I say.

Catherine looks visibly relieved as she passes me my reticule. 'Thank goodness you're here. People have been asking after you and Mother has been pestering me about leaving. I didn't know how much longer I could hold everyone off.'

'You gem. I appreciate your efforts to keep my reputation intact.' I nod towards the couples. 'Why aren't you dancing?'

'You know my mother thinks the waltz is indecent.'

I watch the couples dancing. They spin around the room, bodies pressed together. Close, intimate. The way dances should be.

'Your mother would find the sight of a chair leg indecent,' I tell her.

Catherine sputters a laugh, a satisfyingly unladylike sound. 'Aileana!'

'What? I do believe the waltz has been acceptable for many years now.'

'Oh, do tell *her* that,' Catherine says drily. 'I should dearly love to hear my mother lecture someone else about it.'

'Where is the esteemed lady, anyway?' I scan the room. 'Using the opportunity to approach remaining gentlemen on your behalf?'

'I'm afraid my introductions have already been made.' Catherine nods to a place over my shoulder. 'She's, ahem, glaring at *you*.'

I turn. Lady Cassilis is surrounded by her friends, the other matrons of Edinburgh whose daughters are yet to wed. They have no doubt been discussing their plans to ensnare the poor, foolish men of Edinburgh, but the viscountess doesn't appear to be listening.

Heavens. She could scare off a revenant with that scowl. I survey my crooked bow. Perhaps I look worse than I thought. Lady Cassilis is probably wondering yet again why she let Catherine badger her into becoming responsible for me at formal events.

With a sweet smile, I wiggle my fingers at the viscountess. Lady Cassilis couldn't look more appalled if I spat on her.

'I take it she's angry with me, then?' I grin at Catherine.

'You missed five dances! Of *course* she's angry with you. I hope your headache was worth it.'

'It was,' I say.

Catherine studies my hair, my face, then the awkward state of my dress. 'Forgive me for being so blunt, but you look ghastly.'

Unconcerned, I wave a hand between us. Hair arrangement is not a great talent of mine. Nor, apparently, is tying ribbon over my dress to hide my injuries.

'That's a horrible thing to say,' I tell her. 'What if I'd just escaped a perilous situation?'

Catherine examines me from head to toe again. 'Barely, I assume.'

'Your confidence in me is inspiring.' I glance around. No one is paying us any attention. Some groups have begun to filter out through the doors, finished for the night. 'See, no one else has even noticed I look different.'

'They're all tozy from the punch. Someone must have emptied a considerable amount of spirits into it.'

So that's why the dispensers were empty. 'I can't believe I missed that,' I say. 'How very disappointing.'

'Don't change the subject. Tell me what happened.'

'Very well. It was a faery.' I decide to betray a bit of truth, just to see how she responds. 'An especially nasty one, like the one you used to be afraid lived under your bed.'

'Fine,' Catherine says drily. 'Keep your secrets. But I demand extra shortbread at luncheon in recompense for abandoning me half the night.'

'Done.'

After a few long goodbyes among Lady Cassilis and her friends, she, Catherine, and I take the air coach for the hour-long journey home from the Hepburns' estate in the country-side. Catherine attempts polite chatter, but eventually even her manners fail. Lady Cassilis stares austerely out the window the entire time. The only noises are the whisper of the engine and the flapping of the coach's wings as we slice through thick clouds.

The coach is still silent as we land in Charlotte Square. Lady Cassilis's coachman helps me onto the street and shuts the door behind me. Lady Cassilis pulls the window aside, inclining her head towards me in silent dismissal. Clearly she has not forgiven me.

I nod back and – petty creature that I am – smile only at Catherine. 'Goodnight, Catherine.'

'I'll see you at luncheon,' Catherine says. 'Sleep well.'

Lady Cassilis huffs and pulls the window shut.

The coachman and I step onto the pavement in front of my house. A tall, white building of neoclassical design, Number Six is the largest residence in the square. Nine windows grace its front façade – something my father is particularly proud of, despite how blasted expensive the window tax is in this country – with stone columns between the six upper ones. It's dark inside, except for the sliver of light between the curtains of the antechamber.

A cold breeze picks up and ruffles my hair. I shiver and tighten the stole around my shoulders as the coachman escorts me up the steps and deposits me at the door.

The door is always unlocked so I have no need to ring for a servant. 'Thank you,' I tell him. 'You can leave me here.'

The coach's engine starts with a shrill whistle and a chug as the wings along the side of the machine flap thrice. With a groan, it lifts off the cobblestone street. Warm steam blows towards me as the vehicle slowly ascends, disappearing into the thick rain clouds.

Chapter 5

Boisterous laughter erupts from the basement as I step into the antechamber; the kitchen staff must be relaxing after their duties. All the other quarters are empty, since my father is rarely at home.

A wee lantern on the far wall is lit, casting dark shadows around the hall. I flip the switch to turn it off and climb the staircase to my room, past the portraits of my ancestors. The painting of our family used to hang at the top, until my father put it in one of the other rooms after my mother died. The hook that held it is still there, stark against the light wallpaper.

In my room at last, I pull the lever by the door to turn on the lighting mechanism. Gears along the ceiling click and purr. Hanging lights attached to the overhead beams flicker, then brighten.

My room resembles the interior of a ship. The walls are panelled in teak, with small bulb lights between the wood panels. The helm from a Scottish schooner is mounted on the far wall, framed by maps of the Outer Hebrides and strung sea-glass my mother and I gathered from beaches on our various holidays.

The room has been built to my precise specifications. My mother used to sit for hours sketching the plans with me. This had been another of our projects, just one among many. It wasn't until after she died that I hired the crew to have it built, and even contributed a few hidden aspects of my own.

As usual, it's a mess. My current attempts at engineering weapons to kill faeries are littered on the mahogany work table in the centre of the room. The rest of my arsenal is hidden in a locked trunk next to the red velvet settee.

Wearily, I move to sit and pull off my slippers when there is a knock at the door. 'Aye?'

The door opens and my maid peeks inside. 'May I come in, Lady Aileana?'

'Of course.'

Dona closes the door behind her. My father hired her three weeks ago to dress and help prepare me for social events. No older than fifteen, Dona is a shy lass with light blonde hair tucked under a linen cap. A fair bit shorter than me, she frequently has to stand on her toes to comfortably reach the topmost buttons of my dresses.

I stand, and Dona slips behind me and immediately sets to work unbuttoning my dress. If she weren't here, I would be tempted to rip the intolerable thing off and toss it across the room.

'Did you say something, my lady?'

'Hmm?' God, did I speak aloud without realising? I rub my eyes. 'I'm just tired.'

'Did you have a splendid time at the assembly?' she asks.

Oh, aye. Killed a faery. My fifth this week.

I clear my throat. 'Quite.'

Dona unbuttons more, then pauses. 'Begging your pardon, my lady, but was this ribbon here before? I don't remember—'

'I added it,' I reply quickly. 'If you could undo my corset, I can remove the rest myself.'

In my exhaustion I had completely forgotten about the ribbon. Even the most discreet lady's maid might panic at the sight of my shredded bodice and injuries. I'm just lucky the blood hasn't seeped through. I am quite a skilled liar if the occasion calls for it, but even I would struggle to explain that.

Dona hesitates, but says, 'Very well.' She finishes with the buttons and begins unlacing my corset. 'I was wondering: have you noticed any mice about?'

'No. Do we have an infestation?'

'Not ... precisely.' Dona leans forward to whisper, 'I've heard scratching, my lady. From your dressing room.'

'Really,' I reply drily. If only that were mice.

'And I thought I heard singing,' she mutters, low enough that she might have been speaking to herself.

'Singing?' I go entirely still and cold crawls up my spine.

'It's nothing,' she says quickly. 'I'm sure I imagined it.'

I swallow hard. 'All the same, I'll have MacNab inspect my dressing room tomorrow.'

I'm tempted to give her a handful of notes – enough to last until she finds a new position – and tell her to get the hell out of my house and never come back to Edinburgh. Nay, Scotland.

Dona finishes unlacing my corset. 'Just watch for the faeries,' she says with laughter in her voice. 'My auld-mother used to tell me they sometimes reside in closets and dressing rooms.'

I heard stories of faeries myself when I was wee. No bairn in Scotland is raised without them, or without a healthy measure of superstition.

But they have always been presented as nightmarish tales, certainly never as fact. Catherine's brother used to tease us with stories, tell us to sleep with one eye open lest the faeries nab us from our beds. Eventually, I stopped believing in such nonsense. Until I learned that all the stories are true.

There are other Scots who still believe the fae to be real, but they're becoming fewer in number. Very few humans are able to perceive the fae, and believers have been whittled away by the

Church of Scotland's attempts to denounce beliefs they consider uncultured. Even still, faeries persist as children's stories in this country.

'What else did she say?' I can't help but ask.

'The fae will complete every task you've ever dreamed,' Dona says, 'in exchange for your soul. That I should always keep iron on my person, for protection.'

I swallow. I wish I could tell her that iron doesn't work, it never has. That I nearly died once because I believed it would protect me. 'Well, that's just silly, isn't it?'

'It is indeed,' Dona murmurs hesitantly. I've no doubt she half-believes her grandmother's tales. She steps aside. 'Will you be needing anything else?'

'No, thank you. Goodnight.'

I close the door after her and wait until her footsteps fade down the hall. 'Derrick,' I tell the empty room. 'Get the hell out of that dressing room.'

The door swings open and slams against the wall. The faint taste of spices and gingerbread settles on my tongue a moment before a ball of light, no bigger than the size of my palm, barrels out of the dressing room.

Chapter 6

'What a silly little baggage,' Derrick says. 'What would I do with a soul?'

Despite his size, Derrick's voice is as deep and masculine as a man's. He flies over my work table and settles on a piece of scrap metal. The light around him fades to reveal a small, handsome creature with an elfin nose, pale skin and a patch of dark hair atop his head. Thin, translucent wings stick out from his lawn shirt and frame his tiny body. A muslin bag hangs from his shoulder and rests on his hip.

Derrick resides in my dressing room, where he mends my clothes for the price of a bowl of honey a day. Although sometimes he does the exact opposite of *mend*. I recognise the fabric of his black trousers from one of the mourning dresses I neglected to throw out weeks ago.

'Her fears aren't completely groundless. Your faery brethren do appear to enjoy consuming—' I hesitate, not wanting to offend him. He's small, but he can make quite a mess if he feels insulted.

'Ugh! That's disgusting. Human souls taste like porridge, you know.' So much for offending him.

Lesser fae like Derrick don't actively hunt humans. They could take energy if they wanted, but it would never be enough to kill or even seriously injure a person. If they were as powerful as the others, I wouldn't have let Derrick live when I discovered him in the back garden a few nights after my mother died.

I incline my head towards the door. 'Would you care to explain that?'

'Wood panelling,' he says. 'Very solid. Smells nice.'

'You know what I'm saying. Dona can hear you.' He simply blinks at me, clearly not at all troubled by it. I groan. 'I thought only men had the Sight. You told me that.'

Derrick shrugs. 'She doesn't have it. She's just a wee bit perceptive, is all.'

'I gathered that.'

'No need to get huffy,' he says. He brightens and the halo around him glimmers gold. 'She can only sense me on occasion. Most other times, she's as ignorant of my presence as the rest of your kind are.'

'I don't care. How long have you known?'

He picks up a loose cog from the table and examines it. 'A sennight.'

'Seven days! And you didn't think to tell me?'

Derrick doesn't look the least bit concerned, as though I've asked him why he didn't bother to tell me about the fabric he uses to make his trousers.

I consider the worst possible situations. What if a faery ever follows me home? What if it realises my maid can occasionally sense the fae? Sensitive humans and Seers have more energy to take than a normal human. That lass is a walking target and she doesn't even know it.

'I didn't think it was important,' he murmurs, 'since I surely won't harm her.' He slips the cog into his bag.

'Put that back, thief,' I say.

'But—'

'*And* all the others.'

Derrick reluctantly pulls the part from his bag and tosses it onto the table. And another. And another. 'You won't release Dona, will you?'

'Of course I will,' I say. 'Good heavens, that poor girl should leave the country. I don't think they have faeries in the West Indies, do they?'

Derrick eyes me, as if to say, *You bloody wish they don't.* 'She cleans my home the *best,*' he whines, drawing from his bag a gold button that looks like it came from my father's wardrobe. 'She uses this rose-scented substance when she cleans. Makes me think of spring and waterfalls and lovely ladies.'

I roll my eyes. 'Am I to understand that you want me to keep my oblivious maid in a position of danger because you enjoy the scent of her cleaning solution?'

'Well.' He looks rather embarrassed. 'Aye.'

'At least you're honest about it.' I open the dressing room door and groan. It's a mess of frills and silk, skirts and petticoats strewn everywhere. 'And no wonder you want to keep her here. *Someone* has to tidy this.'

Derrick's wings buzz as he flies to my shoulder and perches there. 'I'd prefer she didn't. This is just the way I like it.'

'It looks hideous.'

'How dare you?' His wings flick my ear. 'That's my home you're insulting.'

His wings are starting to hurt me. 'Behave yourself or you'll get no honey from me today.'

Derrick calms and sits next to my neck. 'Cruel.'

If he wanted, Derrick could steal from anywhere. But it's my ready stock of honey and constant need of stitched clothing that keep him happiest. The small fae are menders, compulsively so. They've been known to steal worn clothing just to use their fingers – Derrick says it keeps his sword hand quick. Honey is simply what he requests for services rendered, even though I tend to provide it whether he sews or not. He adores it that much.

'I'm perfectly wonderful to live with and you know it,' I say. 'Now, if you don't mind, I'm going to borrow your home to undress.'

Derrick rises from my shoulder and flies back to the table. I assume he'll steal more parts while I'm distracted.

I shut the dressing room door behind me and press the button for the light. Hardly any dresses remain on the shelves. The scent of roses clings to the air. I grudgingly admit that Derrick is right – it does smell rather heavenly.

Deftly, I untie the bow around my chest. Blood sticks to the fabric and I wince as I step out of the many layers of petticoats and undergarments that have constrained me all evening. The thigh holsters securing my pistol and *sgian dubh* go next.

My inspection reveals five superficial cuts and four deep others, running across the freckled skin just below my bosom. The deeper ones will require stitching.

I brush my fingers along the healed welts elsewhere across my ribs. No one knows that underneath my beautiful dresses I hide a body that is scarred and cut and bruised. Old injuries are scattered across my thighs, my stomach, my back. They're my badges. My secret tokens of survival and victory. And vengeance. I can name the faeries that inflicted every scar, and I remember how I killed each one of them.

With a sigh, I pop open the lid of my trunk and pull out my stitcher kit. I lie amid my scattered dresses and twist the key at the bottom of the box. The tiny mechanical spiders crawl across my chest and abdomen, mending my torn flesh.

I close my eyes. I listen to their bodies move, the whisper of wee mechanical pieces interworking as tiny legs creep across my skin. They puncture me over and over, cauterising and threading gossamer tendon through my sensitive flesh. Finally I feel them finish and crawl back into the box.

The dressing room is silent when I open my eyes and place the kit back in the trunk. My midsection is smeared with blood around four stitched wounds that will become new badges.

I reach for fabric to wipe the blood away and draw an old, tattered tartan from beneath the dresses.

Then I can't breathe. My eyes are wet and my chest aches.

I shove the tartan inside the trunk and shut it with a loud thump, gasping for breath.

Derrick must have dug out the tartan from the back of the dressing room. I wish I could burn it, even if it is the last memento I have of my mother. I managed to salvage it before my father ordered her most personal belongings removed from the house. He said he couldn't look at them any more, as though their presence gave him some hope that she'd return.

I understood. Even this last reminder of my mother's life just makes her absence all the more glaring. So the tartan stays hidden, where I won't be tempted to hug it or sleep with it or wear it in a poor attempt to pretend she's still alive. The pretending would only make reality all the more painful.

I snatch a small handkerchief off the floor and dip it into the bowl of water Derrick leaves out for me next to my rows of slippers. He always anticipates that I'll come home with an injury that requires cleaning. He's always right.

I gently mop the blood from my skin and change into my nightdress. When I step out of the dressing room, Derrick is sitting cross-legged on my work table, sifting through metal pieces, no doubt choosing which to steal next.

'Get away from there,' I say, flipping the switch for the fireplace. A spark under the coals sends flames bursting upwards. I toss the bloodied fabric into the fire.

Derrick flies to perch on the back of the pink muckle chair near the settee. 'But they're just sitting there, all shiny and unused.'

'How about another project to keep your fingers busy?' I hold up my ravaged ball gown. 'See? It's completely destroyed, just the way you like.'

Light explodes around him. 'What the hell happened?' Derrick bursts out.

'Revenant,' I say. I toss him the dress and Derrick catches it easily by the sleeve. I know pixies are stronger than they look, but his effortless strength still surprises me. 'You're welcome to work on it.'

I've finally learned never to say thank you when he mends my dresses. Faeries take heavy offence to gratitude.

Derrick drops the dress onto the settee and inspects the damage. 'Almost had you, didn't he?' he murmurs.

'Almost.'

I press my fingers against my new badges. They all tell stories, each distinct and significant. One of them – the longest scar, the one that spans the length of my spine – is the first I ever earned. It tells the tale of a girl who had just lost her mother and nearly died when she went out into the world armed with iron. The girl who was later remade into a killer.

I sit in my work chair and pick up an old watch fob lying amongst the metal scraps. 'I shot it, of course,' I murmur.

'Well done,' Derrick says. He holds up my dress to inspect it and his wings flutter once. 'Did you take its head?'

He sounds hopeful. Small faeries truly loathe the larger fae for being so pathetic as to live off the energy of less powerful creatures. They consider it a weakness.

'Of course not. What on earth am I going to do with a revenant's head?'

He brightens more, skin glowing golden. 'Take it as a trophy, put it on a stake and display it in the back garden where everyone can appreciate it.'

'Derrick, that's disgusting.' I'm amused despite myself.

'Do you think so?' He removes a needle and thread from his bag. 'When I was young we showed off our trophies, danced around them and gorged ourselves on fruits.'

'I don't know how to respond to that.'

Derrick merely grins and begins to sew my dress. 'Ah, happy memories.' I shake my head, and as I lean to pluck the turnscrew off the table, he adds, 'I have news.'

I go still, my breath catching in my throat. *News.* When Derrick has something to share, it's always to do with the faery who killed my mother, her latest murders. He has a network of tiny faeries – brownies and will-o'-the-wisps and *buachailleen,* to name a few – who chatter, always willing to share information in exchange for honey. Lately, her kills have become more frequent, once every few days.

'Aye?' I try to sound calm, try to keep the ache of vengeance from rising. Every night, I hunt in the hope that the next faery I find will be her. It never is. The fae I kill are merely substitutes for the one I want most.

'Stirling, this time.'

'How many?' My voice shakes.

'One.'

I rise from the chair so hastily that it wobbles and nearly falls. I stride to the back of the room and stand in front of the mounted schooner helm. Embedded in the wood is a small, barely noticeable button which I press gently, fingers shaking. A portion of the wall presses outwards and twists to show a hidden map of Scotland on the reverse side.

Aberdeen. Oban. Lamlash. Tobermory. Dundee. Inverness. Portree. Dozens of places around the country, into the islands and the Outer Hebrides. I've marked each of them with a pin and tied crimson ribbons around them to count the kills at each location.

As far as I know, she is the last *baobhan sìth* in existence.

The murder pattern is always the same for her – no more than three victims in the same place. She never stays anywhere for too long. She finds her prey on a road at night – lured there either by her strong mental influence or her unearthly beauty. Once there, she tears open their throats and drains their blood. There is one exception to her pattern: my mother. She ripped out my mother's heart.

I screw shut my eyes against the memory. *Don't think about it,* I tell myself. *Don't think about it. Don't think about it. Don't think about it. Don't—*

'Aileana?' Derrick asks hesitantly.

Clearing my throat, I open my eyes and grab a pin and ribbon out of the leather bag hanging next to the map. 'I'm all right.'

I jab the pin into the map and knot the ribbon around it.

The map is awash with pins and crimson bows; so little land is left unaffected by her spree. One hundred and eighty-four kills in the last year. She's been busier than I have. I began tracking her a fortnight after my mother's murder. I could never catch up with her or find her before she moved to another place. I can't prevent any of her kills. So I've been biding my time, preparing for her, training for the day when I'll meet her again.

She's been toiling away in the Highlands for the last fortnight, moving closer and closer to the city. It's only a matter of time now. And I have become very patient.

Derrick lands on my shoulder, wings gently brushing my cheek. 'They tell me she's on her way here.'

'She is indeed.' I smile and press the button to hide the map from view.

I sit at my work table again and unscrew the fob's back casing. Once removed, I carefully lift out the middle section, with its tiny wheels and wires still intact.

Frowning, I study the three separate sections of the fob, how each part works and how they fit together. I slowly dismantle the mechanism, memorising the position of each component as I remove it. Some parts are so wee that I have to wear my brass magnifying spectacles to see them better.

Nearly every night I find a new project. When my mother was alive, she used to help me build little contraptions for the house. Lanterns that turn on and off with the snap of my fingers, a self-delivering tea service, a floating metal hand to grasp the books on the highest shelf in the drawing room.

I destroyed all of them when she died. I stopped making frivolous things. Now my scraps are turned into weapons, all from my own designs. Whenever one is destroyed, I build another.

I never know in advance what I'll create. Sometimes I sit down with little more than a notion and build through the night to turn it into something real. Anything to keep me from sleep for as long as possible. This time, it's in preparation for the *baobhan sìth*.

I reach inside a drawer and take out my journal. When inspiration strikes, I sketch until my fingers are black with charcoal, and soon I have designed the fob's parts and the additions necessary to turn it into a weapon. I do some calculations and write the quantities for sulphur, charcoal, saltpetre and *seilgflùr* on the corner of the sheet.

Derrick looks up from his mending. 'What weapon are you making this time?'

I smile. 'Oh, you'll see. It's going to be magnificent.'

When the *baobhan sìth* returns, I'll be ready for her. I'll make her regret all one hundred and eighty-four of her kills.

Chapter 7

The following night, I prepare for my hunt.

I dress myself in wool trousers and a white lawn shirt tucked in at the waist. My leather knife sheath is buckled and slung low across my hips. Boots reach to mid-calf, laced all the way up and secured with three buckles. I tuck my trousers into the boots to prevent them from catching on anything, and don a long, grey raploch coat to complete my ensemble.

'You're only taking the dirk with you?' Derrick says from the chimneypiece, above the cooling coals in the fireplace. Gold flecks fall from the halo around him and disappear before they reach the ground.

'Of course not,' I say.

'Good. Shouldn't bother taking it out at all, I say.'

I smirk. Derrick told me once the blade was useless because I couldn't even kill him with an iron weapon.

'It works best for distracting my victims.' I carefully pick up the altered watch fob from the table. 'And I'll be testing out this little beauty after I see Kiaran.'

A test to see whether the fob is the weapon I want to use to kill the *baobhan sith*. I'll only have one chance to get that right, to make it meaningful, and I have plenty of other devices to choose from if this one isn't quite right.

Derrick snarls some fae curse that ends with, 'Vicious bastard.'

He has never told me why he hates Kiaran, not even after Kiaran saved my life and trained me to kill the kind of faeries Derrick would see dead. I doubt he ever will. If I so much as mention Kiaran, Derrick responds with the kind of vitriol that would make the workers down by the Leith quay blush. Already his light has turned a deep crimson and sparks sizzle around him.

I place the fob in my pocket. 'Indeed, he is that,' I say. 'But I still have to go.'

Derrick crosses his arms. 'Fine. I'll take the bowl of honey in exchange for mending your dress now.'

'Half,' I say. He's being unreasonable and he knows it.

His halo begins to lighten. Faeries enjoy bargaining. And for Derrick, honey is the greatest reward he could receive. The only problem with giving him any is his intoxicated behaviour afterwards: him flitting about, shining and cleaning my belongings repeatedly, and then lying about, declaring hand movements to be fascinating.

'Full,' he says again.

'Half.' Since this could go on for ever, I add, 'And I won't release Dona from her duties, so you can continue your strange obsession with her cleaning product.'

'Deal,' he replies and flutters his wings.

'When I return, then,' I say.

I push the wooden panel next to the fireplace. It springs open to reveal a series of small steel levers. I pull one and, with a soft whoosh, a large, rectangular portion of the wall detaches and descends slowly into the garden. Gears tick quietly as the ramp lowers and finally settles into the grass below. This was an addition to the room I built while my father was away on one of his many trips – a perfect, silent escape route from the house.

As I descend into the garden, Derrick says, 'Do give Kiaran a message for me.'

'Let me guess – "I shall hurt you if anything happens to the lady whose dressing room I reside in. Also you're a nasty seven-letter insult that begins with the letter 'B'." Close enough?'

'And I plan one day to eat his heart.'

'Right. Wonderful. I'll tell him.'

I shove the lever hidden behind the tall hedges and the wall closes behind me. Then I lean down, spin the dial to activate the locking mechanism and slip through my house's private garden into Charlotte Square.

The streets of New Town are always empty past midnight. Every house is dark, my surroundings silent save for the patter of my footfalls as I dart across the road. The street lights cast long shadows over the grass as I cross the garden in the centre of the square. Soft rain dampens my hair and soil squishes beneath the soles of my boots.

I spare a longing glance at the flying machines parked in the garden square, one of them mine. The design I came up with and eventually built was an ornithopter inspired by a few of Leonardo da Vinci's sketches, his fascination with the physiology of bats. The spacious oblong interior and wingspan are meant to imitate the body and motion of a bat in flight. In its resting position, the wings are tucked in at the sides.

Of all my inventions, it remains my most prized. If I weren't meeting Kiaran, I would take it out and soar over the city, slicing through the misty clouds above Edinburgh.

But tonight, I run. I breathe in the chilly air and feel so alive with it that I could roar. The darkness inside me unfurls and takes me over, a consuming thing that pounds the simple desires for vengeance and blood together in a constant beat.

This is what I live for now. Not the tea parties or assemblies or picnics at the Nor' Loch, or the spine-straight, chin-up, shoulders-back polite conversation accompanied by fake smiles. Now I live for the chase, and for the kill.

Rain-slicked cobblestones shine in the lamplight ahead of me. I race down the street and my boots pound through puddles that soak the hem of my coat.

Electricity hums from within the clock tower as I sprint past it. Translucent glass lines the sides of the building, blazing gold from a system that lights the whole of New Town. I slide my fingers along the slick glass, watching the pulsing bulbs within. They're so bright I can see through the flesh of my palm to the metacarpal bones outlined beneath.

I only slow to a stroll when I reach Princes Street, crossing to the side closest to the park. Rain drips onto my face as I gaze at the southern part of the city.

The castle is visible from here, although thick clouds obscure the keep and the rocky ledge that forms its foundations. To me, the castle has always seemed carved from the very crag that looms over the Nor' Loch.

Though the loch has been drained and turned into gardens, I've only ever heard it referred to by its former name. Now flowers, grass and trees separate the Old Town from the New. In the dark, the green space looks vast, empty, so far below street level that the lights miss it entirely.

Beyond the park, the Old Town is scantly lit. Thick clouds surround the tall, cramped buildings clinging to the rocky crag. Flickering light spills from scattered open windows, from crude candles made of livestock fat. It's all those in Old Town can afford to illuminate their homes. They don't have electricity there – gaslights line the main streets, their glow dimmed by a thickening, dewy mist that wafts over the ground.

Faeries frequent Old Town more than any other place in Edinburgh. There are so many hidden and cramped closes between the buildings into which they can lure their victims.

When the bodies are finally discovered, the authorities think nothing of it. Many people here die of illness. Faery killings are almost always attributed to a plague, spread easily through Old Town's dirty, crowded quarters. Authorities ignore the residents' talk of vengeful spirits and faeries and curses, believing them to be backwards and superstitious. I know better.

I cross North Bridge, which connects New Town to Old Town. An occasional exuberant scream echoes from somewhere within the Old Town labyrinth. On High Street, a few people meander drunkenly across the cobblestones. A gentleman wearing an oversized coat is sitting under a gaslight, singing.

I edge along the side of a building to avoid them and continue towards the High Kirk. Rain clouds have settled low enough to obscure the top of the cathedral and the buildings in front of me. The thud of my boots echoes across the empty street with each step.

Then I taste it – a stark fae power I can't yet identify. I smile. My first victim of the night. I only wish it were the *baobhan sìth*.

The faery will follow me until it finds the perfect place to attack. Faeries love the hunt, which is all about power, control and dominance. Everything builds to that moment when they realise I'm not the prey after all. I'm the predator.

I'm about to double back to the gardens when the full taste of the faery's power hits me. My head snaps up and I briefly savour the sensation.

Honey and dirt and pure nature, a thousand flavours that are difficult to describe. The taste of the wild – running through trees with wind in my hair as my feet pound soft dirt. The sea on a misty morning with sand and water swirling around my legs. A taste that conjures images that look real and significant.

There is only one faery I've ever met with that signature.

Before the taste gets any stronger, I break into a run towards the castle. My breath rushes in strong, quick pants. The faery is silent behind me, but he matches my pace.

I grin and duck into a tight wynd. The walls enclose me and heighten the musty scent of earth and stone. I can't see or hear anything except my heartbeat, my rapid footfalls, but that matters little. I've memorised the endless steps and curves and passageways of the Old Town.

Another cramped wynd, this one in the vaults underground, beneath the buildings. My shoulders brush against the walls, but I don't slow. I count until I reach the stairs ahead – *one ... two ... three ... four ... five* – then I bound down the stone steps. Two more sharp turns and I explode from the underground. Gaslights illuminate the dark road as I sprint to another small close.

It's narrow enough to place each foot on either wall and climb up the passageway easily until I reach the top.

And I wait.

A dozen rapid heartbeats later, a tall figure dashes through the entrance. The faery pauses beneath me, his body still. His breathing is silent; he is not at all winded from our chase. He starts forward, slow, quiet.

Supporting my weight on my hands, I drop from the walls and launch myself at him. *Got you, Kiaran MacKay.*

Chapter 8

Kiaran jerks, startled, as I slide my forearm under his chin, pressing it hard into his neck, the only vulnerable place on his body.

'Yield,' I say.

But Kiaran twists, lightning fast, and flips me onto the ground. I land hard and the air whooshes out of my lungs. *Bloody hell that hurt.*

'Bastard.' I lift my boot and slam the bottom of my foot into his knee. It makes a hard crack, but not even a hiss of pain escapes his lips. He smiles.

Aye, he enjoys this as much as I do. I'm not about to lose or yield to him if I can avoid it. Some nights we fight until I bleed. Until I'm aching and heaving, and still haven't left a bruise on his fae skin. I haven't beaten Kiaran in combat yet, but that just makes me more determined.

I jump into a crouch and reach for the *sgian dubh* at my waist. I leap at him with the blade high. He blocks my attack easily, grabbing the scruff of my coat to shove me face first into the wall.

'That was clumsy.' His voice is like a feline purr, beautiful and melodic.

I grit my teeth. I *hate* it when he starts to critique me while we're fighting. I whirl and strike again – and slice nothing but air.

'Still clumsy.' He sounds annoyed. 'You know where I'm vulnerable to a mortal weapon, so what the hell are you doing?'

'Would you kindly stop talking?' I snap.

I pretend I'm about to aim high again and lash out my foot to distract him. With a quick swing, I arc downwards and swipe him across the throat – the one place on his body an iron blade will puncture his fae skin, even if it could never kill him. A thin line of blood spreads across his smooth, pale neck.

'Clumsy now?' I grin.

He rips the *seilgflùr* necklace off me and throws it away. I hear it fall somewhere at the other end of the close. I gasp and stare where he'd been standing. I can't see him without the thistle, not unless he wants me to.

'Now do it again.' His words echo around me. 'Without the thistle.'

'MacKay,' I say calmly. 'Don't be unreasonable.'

Of all my lessons, this one is the worst. I hate knowing my lack of Sight is my biggest weakness. If Kiaran wanted to, he could exploit it and murder me. I'd be dead before I could open my mouth to scream.

'I don't give a damn about being reasonable,' Kiaran whispers. His breath is soft on my neck, there for an instant and gone. I shove my hand out and find only empty air. 'Cut me again,' he says. 'If you can.'

'MacKay—'

His invisible hands grab me and slam me into the wall. My grip on the *sgian dubh* loosens and it clatters to the ground. Warm blood trickles from my mouth. I clench my jaw against the pain. I won't give in to it. That's a lesson of his I've actually come to appreciate.

I retrieve my knife, then spin to confront the empty close.

The still lingering taste of his power indicates his nearness, but I can't tell where. How can I win a fight with Kiaran if I can't see him?

Silence. Kiaran moves with a sly agility, skilful and quick; he makes hunting an art. Not even his breathing betrays him. Experimentally, I strike with the blade and hit nothing.

'What do you feel?' He's behind me.

I whirl, blade raised, but he grabs my arm and shoves me again. When I swipe at where he was, he's already gone. 'Annoyed.'

'Wrong answer,' he says in that disembodied echo. 'Tell me what you *feel*, Kam.'

The shortened version of my surname is supposed to be practical, a quick single-syllable thing to call me when we're in the throes of a fight – a name he has come to always use. Now it rolls off his tongue in a single breath, almost a whisper. A dare.

I search for some sign of his location but find nothing. I could be alone with only the rain pattering on the rooftops for company.

'Tell me.'

How can I tell him I feel little else but rage? That it allows me to live day to day and hunt nightly for the faery I want to kill most? Without it I'm a void, a bottomless crevasse. Empty.

Kiaran and I have little connection beyond our names. We battle, bleed and hunt together almost every night. He teaches me how to slaughter in the most effective, brutal ways possible. But I've never told Kiaran why I hunt, and he has never told me why he kills his own kind. This is our ritual, our dance. The only one that matters.

So I'm not certain what compels me to whisper, 'I don't feel anything.'

Kiaran doesn't respond. The air around me feels still, despite the rain. I jump when his warm, invisible fingers touch my hair and he pulls a damp tendril from my cheek.

'If that were true,' he murmurs, 'you wouldn't be here.'

I shudder as Kiaran's power glides across my skin in a single inviting stroke.

'I thought we were fighting.' I arch my neck to his touch without meaning to.

Faery power shouldn't feel this seductive. The strong taste of wildness that has been with me since our chase from the High Street strengthens as his aura surrounds me. I want to lose myself in it. Something about it makes me want to run barefoot through the forest, through thick ocean waves, and—

Kiaran drops my hair. 'You lose.'

I know it the moment he steps away. The warmth from his body is gone and cold seeps through my rain-damp clothes. Suddenly his tall, lithe frame appears in front of me.

'You cheated.'

His lips curve into a smile that promises so many things I'd rather not contemplate. 'Are you really going to try that argument?'

'You used your powers.'

I swear that I was nearly faestruck, an awful thing that happens to humans when they're in the presence of one of the *daoine sìth.* They become bewitched, lulled by power, and compliant enough to do anything a faery wants. I'd rather die than have that happen to me.

'Even so, I didn't manipulate you, Kam. You yielded.' He leans closer and whispers, 'Or did I misinterpret that neck arch?'

Confound it, my face is burning. How humiliating.

'Again.' I raise my chin. 'I challenge you again, MacKay.' I'll beat him without the thistle. I'll fight until I'm too tired to move if I have to.

Kiaran stares at me for the longest time. He says, 'Your lip is bleeding.' Then he turns and strides towards the other end of the close.

Damnation! 'Wait!' I wipe my mouth with my sleeve and start after him, but he doesn't slow. 'MacKay, we're not finished.'

He leans down and plucks the *seilgflùr* necklace from the ground. I hear his sharp intake of breath as he hands it to me. 'Here.' When I don't take it immediately, he frowns. 'You're sulking.'

'I'm *not* sulking.' Although that's exactly what I'm doing.

'Kam, take the bloody thistle before it burns a hole through my hand.'

I snatch the thistle from him. The seared skin of his palm is visible only for an instant before he stuffs his hands in his trouser pockets.

'If I were a cruel woman, I would have wrapped the thistle around your neck when I leaped on you.'

Kiaran's mouth twitches into an almost-smile. 'If you had, you might have won.'

We exit the close in silence and walk back to the High Street. I suppress a shiver. Now that the excitement has worn off, the winter breeze pierces my damp clothes.

The street is entirely desolate now, silent. A few of the gas lamps have been extinguished and the road in front of us is shadowed. A baleful howl of wind gusts through the cathedral as we slip down the stairs to the Cowgate.

'I don't like it when you do that,' I say quietly.

'What?'

'Take away the *seilgflùr*.'

He doesn't spare me a glance. 'I know.'

'Especially when I came close to winning.'

'On the contrary,' he says smoothly. 'That's exactly when you need it taken.'

I clench my jaw. I hate that without the necklace, I'm just as vulnerable as Lord Hepburn. Kiaran proved that back in the alley.

'You certainly enjoy reminding me that I can't see you without it, don't you?'

'Enjoyment has little to do with it. The day will come when you have to fight without the thistle,' he says. He looks at me with that ancient, alien gaze. 'And you shouldn't expect any mercy.'

Chapter 9

With his faery powers of mental influence, Kiaran could live anywhere he wants – even in a house in New Town, one more extravagant than mine. Instead, he chooses to live in the Cowgate, one of the worst areas of the city.

We walk between the cramped, tiny tenements. Nearly every home is filled to the brim with large, impoverished families. They must have so little breathing room.

The old buildings are in such disrepair that some are beginning to crumble. I'll never become accustomed to the ever-present stench of human excrement here. A few residences are still illuminated, even at this late hour. Inside one of them, a group bursts into laughter. A door slams in the distance. The sound of glass breaking echoes through the street, followed by a harsh scream. I wince.

Kiaran guides me up the narrow stairway to his dwelling. His place is clean, albeit barren. The only furniture in the room, aside from a few cabinets, is a small table and two wooden chairs. It's dark despite the candlelight, and so very cold. The winter air settles in these stone walls and never leaves.

I shiver, unable to help myself. My skin prickles beneath my coat.

Sometimes I'm tempted to ask Kiaran why he took up

residence among humans, but I never do. I've decided I don't want to know.

'Your coat is wet. You should take off your coat if you're cold,' Kiaran says, lighting what remains of a candle in the centre of the table.

'No, I'm fine.'

'You're shivering.'

It would be foolish to interpret his words as concern. Kiaran is *daoine sìth,* the most powerful breed of faery in existence, and they are not known for their empathy. Rather, they are infamous for being cruel, unfeeling, destructive creatures who crave power above all else.

I remember the stories from my childhood that tell of the *daoine sìth* slaughtering and enslaving humans for hundreds of years before they were finally trapped underground. Kiaran confirmed the truth of that. Many of our first lessons consisted of him describing and having me write down each species of faery, detailing their abilities, separating facts about the fae from centuries of lore passed down by humans.

Kiaran is the only *daoine sìth* left. The others lost a war many years ago and were trapped beneath what is now Edinburgh, along with the faeries who aided them. The breeds who fought in the battle were the strongest of the fae, all ruled by the *daoine sìth.*

The faeries I kill every night possess little power in comparison. They are the solitary fae unwilling to join the battle that entrapped the rest. So they've remained above ground, breeding and living on, free to feed on humans.

'I'm fine,' I say again. 'Just let me have a fresh bundle of *seilg-flùr* and we'll go.'

His shoulders tense when he reaches into a small cabinet and I try not to stare at him. In such a dark, enclosed space, it's difficult not to.

Kiaran's skin glows softly in the candlelight, smooth and pale. His inky-black hair sweeps forward to rest on his high cheekbones. His eyes are the colour of spring lavender, except not at all gentle. They are shrewd, fierce and unearthly. Fae or not, Kiaran MacKay is damnably beautiful. I rather loathe that quality in him.

He tosses me a raploch bundle tied with twine. 'This is your third bunch in a fortnight.'

Blast. Of course he's noticed. 'It's useless once it dries,' I say. *And you've refused me a plant to cultivate, you cad.*

Seilgflùr stays fresh for only about thirteen days in the wintertime. Longer if I keep my supply outside. Past that, it's no longer effective. Another lesson I learned the hard way – that's how I received my third scar.

I've tried to grow it myself, but all of my attempts were unsuccessful. I've even tried preserving and pressing it between airtight pieces of glass, but that doesn't work either. So now I'm dependent upon Kiaran to supply it, and I'm still not certain where he finds it. He won't tell me.

'I'm not a fool,' he says. 'Don't treat me like one.'

'I shall endeavour not to.'

His expression hardens. 'You don't need as much as you use. Are you giving it to someone?'

I don't even dignify that question with a response. I might have broken his rule about not hunting on my own, but this is one rule I've kept. No one should have to see faeries, or what they do to their victims. The Sight is a burden, and I pity anyone who has the natural ability.

'Kam,' he says, with exaggerated patience.

'All you need to know,' I say, 'is that it's for my protection.'

I open the wool bundle. Nestled in the centre are small stocks of thistle tipped with vivid blue flowers. The common thistle natural to Scotland is spiny, with sharp leaves and woolly hairs. This is different. It looks the same as other thistles – so untouchable, aggressive – but *seilgflùr* is silken. The hair along the stem is soft as down.

And if it hadn't been so soft and strong and lovely, maybe my mother would have used something different to plait into my hair when I debuted last year. I still don't know where she managed to find some. I wore white and the thistle was the only colour on me that night, just a pretty little adornment then. If my mother had chosen lavender, roses, or heather, I would never have seen my first faery.

The first faery. The *baobhan sìth*'s voice rises up from my memories, cheerful and musical as a spring bird at first, then edged with the sharp notes of malice. *Crimson suits you best.*

I suck in a breath and shove the wool bundle into my pocket. That memory is always there, always lingering, triggered by the slightest thing. I can't get rid of it no matter how hard I try.

'*Ciod a dh' fhairich thu?*' Kiaran asks. He pulls his chair to settle across from me.

'You know I can't understand you.'

'What's wrong?'

I smile slightly. Sometimes he almost manages to sound like he means it when he asks me that. 'Do you care?'

Kiaran shrugs. The closest he comes to betraying emotion is when he stabs something. He reclines in his chair and crosses his long legs in front of him. I try not to admire how magnificent he looks, how uncanny. I avert my gaze and focus on the shadows cast on the far wall by the flickering candlelight.

How inhuman, I remind myself.

'I don't, really,' he replies. 'But you looked like you were about to cry.'

'I don't cry, MacKay.'

I'm such a mess today. First that blasted moment when I almost gave in to his temptation during our fight, and now this.

Where is a good ditch to crawl into when I need one?

'If you say so,' he says, uncrossing his legs. 'A bit of advice, Kam. Until you can admit your weaknesses, you'll never beat me without that damn thistle.'

I glare at him. 'Shall we hunt, or would you prefer to waste time haranguing me?'

My words trigger something violent in that usually cold, detached gaze. If I weren't a killer myself it might frighten me. This time, his smile isn't wicked. It's feral, maybe even a bit ferocious. 'I'll get my weapons,' he says.

We leave Cowgate, and as we walk along South Bridge, Kiaran strides slightly ahead of me. 'There's a *caoineag* hunting in the waters near Dean Village,' he says. 'She's already killed one woman since she arrived.' He maintains his brisk pace as he speaks. 'Try to keep up, Kam.'

Try to keep up. His legs are far longer than mine and he insists we walk everywhere during our hunts, even to places as removed from the city centre as Dean Village.

I jog a few steps and still end up behind him. The rain has dampened the hair that clings to the back of his neck and his shirt hugs his lean, muscular body as he moves. Sometimes, I wish he'd put on a bloody coat.

'You're staring.' He doesn't look at me when he says it.

'Haven't you considered wearing a coat? It *is* winter.'

'No.'

We continue in silence. The rain slows to a soft mist that tickles my cheeks. Fog thickens between the old stone buildings. I hear faint laughter from one of the lit tenements at the far end of the street, then there's silence again. I breathe in the damp air and decide to stop ignoring the ever-lingering taste of Kiaran's power. I take this moment to savour it.

As we reach North Bridge, I study the waning moon that

peeks through the clouds. It's surrounded by a halo of bright red, the colour of oxygenated blood.

Blood. My need for vengeance exists because of the night I was baptised in it. I've always considered that to be my night of lasts – the last time I saw my mother alive, the last time I was a girl who had never seen violence.

Now the darkness inside me wants little else than to kill again. I can't help but wonder if this is all I have left: the nightly hunt, all for that singular moment of intoxicating, all-consuming joy at the end.

In my weakest moments after a kill, I want desperately to feel the way I used to. Happiness that came effortlessly and – sometimes – hope.

I break from our brisk journey to Dean Village to approach the bridge's balustrade. 'Do you ever think about your future, MacKay?'

Kiaran looks surprised by the question. He stops next to me, leaning his back against a stone column. 'No,' he says softly. 'I don't.'

'Never?'

'I'm immortal.' He turns and rests his elbows on the balustrade. 'You consider the future because one day you'll die.' He looks up at the moon, a pensive, almost sad expression on his face. 'I don't have that uncertainty. I'll be exactly the same as I am now, for ever.'

He says it so mechanically, not a hint of emotion. 'Exactly the same?' I ask. 'Hasn't anything unexpected ever happened to you?'

'Once in three thousand years.' His smile is small, perhaps a little bitter. 'Maybe twice.'

Oh, God.

Sometimes I forget faeries don't age. They simply exist, like trees, or rocks. They can be killed, but if left alone, they remain unchanged. Perhaps this is why Kiaran is the way he is. Thousands of years have scrubbed him clean, jaded him beyond measure.

Kiaran glances at me. 'Well? Tell me about your future.'

'I used to have plans for my life, but … but they don't fit any more. That isn't what I want now.'

I used to daydream about the wedding and husband I would one day have. I remember describing the most elaborate ceremonies to my mother while she helped me tinker with my inventions, hands soiled with grease, fingernails torn. My fantasies were full of ivory silks and pink rosebuds and a man who would love me unconditionally.

Now I no longer see marriage, or a husband, or children in my future. There's no love. I see the same onyx expanse that my painful memories are stuffed into, dark and empty.

'Perhaps they never fitted you.' His eyes meet mine then. 'We all have to find out who we are, Kam. One way or another.'

There's such a clear hint of understanding there that for an instant, I wish he would say some words to comfort me, useless though they might be. I almost tell him something else about me, something personal, just to see if he'll do the same.

The unexpected taste of witch hazel and iron spreads swiftly through my mouth. So sudden I'm left gasping.

'Kam?'

Something moves behind Kiaran – the stark glint of metal in the moonlight. I shove him out of the way, and a heavy war hammer swings right at me.

Chapter 10

I bend my knees and duck. The hammer sweeps over my head so fast that the metal whistles.

My assailant snarls, a low, reverberating sound. I look up and, for the first time ever facing a faery, I go cold with dread.

The massive creature towers above me, lean and sinewy, with thick, muscular arms and hands big enough to crush me with a single blow. Leathery skin stretches over the sharply angled features of its face. Covering its cheeks, eyes, and the upper part of its nose is a dirty demi-mask made from a human's facial bones. Through the hollowed-out eye cavities, it watches me with a dark, ferocious glare.

Something else attracts my attention. The thick, wet substance that glistens across the faery's forehead.

Blood. But that's impossible.

I glance quickly at Kiaran. He's standing in the middle of the bridge and doesn't look at all surprised. 'It's a redcap,' I say. 'You told me they were—'

The redcap charges me. It swings that hammer as if it weighs nothing, so fast that I barely have time to react. I spin my body and roll to the ground. The hammer smashes into the cobbles beside my head and stone splinters.

I push to my feet, *sgian dubh* already in hand, my pulse

racing. I'm not trained to fight a redcap. Kiaran told me they were trapped under the city with the *daoine sìth.*

The redcap advances with amazing speed. I try to retreat far enough to throw my dirk, but the faery is too fast. I dodge the hammer just in time.

Where the hell is Kiaran? I look over at the balustrade to see him leaning against it, still watching. After I kill this redcap, I plan to wallop him next, hard enough to bruise that unblemished fae skin of his.

'Could you please –' I duck the hammer again '– *help!*' Particles of rock fly into the air.

Kiaran remains standing there, his arms crossed. 'You look to me to save you? That is a mistake.'

'Damn you, Kiaran MacKay!'

I'm filled with rage. *Save* me? I never asked to be saved. I don't need it. I don't need Kiaran. All I need is this – anger that takes me over until I burn with it.

I run at the redcap, my feet sprinting hard across the broken cobblestone road. The redcap charges, too. Just before our bodies collide, I leap into the air with the *sgian dubh* still in hand, grabbing the creature's meaty shoulder to launch myself over its back.

I hit the ground in a crouch, dropping low to plunge the blade into the base of its spine, the only place on its body Kiaran told me iron can penetrate.

The redcap howls and hunches over in pain. I tear the war hammer out of its grasp. It's heavy and dragging in my grip, but I don't care.

I look over at Kiaran and smile. 'This is me saving myself.'

I swing the hammer back and slam it into the redcap's temple. Blood bursts at me, splatters warm across my face. And a single thought echoes in my mind: *More.*

The redcap staggers and spits blood. It falls to its knees on the cobbles and I see the first gleam of fear in its eyes as I approach. I swing the hammer again. The metal head strikes the faery's massive torso and it sprawls onto the street, coughing up more blood onto the destroyed cobbles. Time for this to end.

I throw the hammer to the ground and approach Kiaran. His gaze is bottomless, unfathomable. I lean in, indecently close.

'You underestimate me,' I whisper. 'And that is a mistake.'

Kiaran is entirely still as I slide his own weapon from its sheath at his hip and step back. The blade is long and curved, made from some kind of golden, glittering metal. From hilt to point, elaborate fernlike patterns of silver are embedded in the gold. An immortal weapon, made to kill faeries.

Kiaran says nothing as I return to the redcap. It's still gasping on the ground, though its injuries will heal soon. I have to kill it before it recovers.

I kneel next to the redcap and slit its throat.

The result is immediate. The redcap's power is so strong, it courses through my chest and fills the empty expanse inside me. I revel in the feel of rain on my skin and the energy sweeping through my veins. If only—

The blade is knocked from my grip. A colossal hand grabs me by the throat – another redcap. *What on earth*? It lifts me easily into the air and my legs dangle.

I gasp for air and the redcap snarls, baring glistening sharp teeth stained with blood, its breath foul with rot. It relishes this. It enjoys watching people suffer, like every other disgusting faery I've fought.

I plant my hands on its arms, using them to lever my body up and swing my leg in a strong, sure kick under the redcap's chin. It's surprised enough that it drops me.

As I hit the ground, my teeth snap together and I bite my tongue. The coppery tang of blood fills my mouth as I stumble.

The redcap swings its hammer again. I roll and it just misses me. More of the bridge's balustrade crumbles. Then I remember: the redcap may have a hammer, but I still have my watch fob. I reach into my pocket and simultaneously press the two buttons on the clock face to release its concealed retractable claws. The metal talons emerge with a soft click, sharp and ready.

The redcap surges towards me again, arms wide. Diving between its legs, I roll into a crouch and thrust the explosive device against the redcap's lower back.

The redcap howls and swings its body around. I move with it, using all the skill learned from hours of endless, boring dance lessons. Twisting my body, I grasp its arm to hold it still just long enough to push the buttons on the clock's face again, so the claws dig into its flesh.

I scramble to my feet and sprint to Kiaran.

'What are you doing?'

I grin. 'You'll see.'

I pull him along with me, urging him to run faster and faster as I try to calculate a safe distance from the explosion, based on the quantity of black powder I've packed into the fob watch. The redcap's heavy, pounding footfalls are loud behind us and my breathing quickens as I try to put more space between us and the faery.

Four. My legs pump harder and I shove Kiaran in front of me. *Three.* I throw myself at him, rolling us so his indestructible body protects me from the direct blast. *Two.* I hold my breath and press my palms over my ears. *One.*

Even my hands over my ears don't muffle the boom. Clouds of dust boil outwards as the blast lights the sky orange. The most remarkable part is that underneath the orange is a vivid blue in a shade I've never seen before. Oh, my. These must be the colours a faery gives off when its biological material reacts to the black powder. How interesting.

I frown at the falling debris. The device shouldn't have had that much power. Who knew faeries exploded so magnificently? I certainly don't want the faery who murdered my mother to die that quickly when I find her.

Kiaran is so still beside me, his heart a heavy, soothing rhythm against my cheek. I'm unable to hear it because of the blast, but I can feel it. I watch the dust settle across the street and my body calms. The rain patters around us.

Kiaran shifts his body away from mine. I awkwardly clear my throat and stand to stare at the massive, gaping hole where half of North Bridge once stood. My ears pop and my hearing returns, though still a bit muffled.

'Well,' I say, working my jaw to pop my ears again. 'I didn't expect that.'

'Coincidence. Neither did I.'

Kiaran's tone surprises me. Oh goodness, his eyes are glowing as he gets to his feet. He brushes the debris off his torn clothes – bits of smoking rock that might have severely injured me if I hadn't used him as a shield.

'Black powder is a light explosive,' I say defensively. 'I didn't factor in the redcap's reaction to the *seilgflùr* – are you angry?'

A snarl reverberates in the night.

Kiaran and I turn to the remains of North Bridge. Across the wreckage stands a third redcap. Oh dear. Three faeries in one night isn't at all normal.

My hands clench into fists as the faery jumps across the remains of the bridge, graceful despite its large body. It doesn't matter that I don't have an effective weapon. I will hit it until my fists are raw. I will bite and claw to survive if I have to.

The redcap runs towards me, snapping sharp teeth.

Kiaran steps between us. The redcap comes to a halt and stares at him in surprise. It's as if … as if the redcap recognises Kiaran. Neither of them speaks. Kiaran tilts his head in that inhuman way of his.

I never see him move. One moment, nothing. The next, he's holding the redcap's dripping heart in his hand.

I gasp in horror as the redcap makes an awful choking sound and falls to its knees. Blood slides thick down Kiaran's wrist and stains his white shirt. He's still holding the dripping heart. *Still holding the heart …*

And I'm struck with a memory before I can even think to suppress it. Blood soaking through my mother's dress. Slick and dark on her pale skin. Thick lashes frame her eyes as they stare wide at the sky, glazed over and dead inside.

I watch mutely as Kiaran plants his heavy boot in the centre of the redcap's massive chest and shoves the faery over the bridge's remains. He tosses the heart after it.

Crimson suits you best, a voice from my memories says with a laugh.

No. I thrust that memory away. I'm left with a rage that consumes me, brutal and destructive. I hate faeries. I hate them for what they stole from me, for what I am. For that night I spent so broken that I couldn't even mourn someone I loved.

I clench my jaw and stride over to Kiaran. He looks up as I approach, his eyes blazing with unnatural light, and that only makes it worse. He's one of them. He'll never understand what he just did to me.

'Kam—'

I slam my fist into his face so hard, it breaks my skin. My knuckles bleed from the impact, but he doesn't even stumble.

'Enough,' he says.

I hit him again. Again. The blows have no apparent effect. I'll keep trying until I see a mark, until something breaks.

He grabs my shoulders, fingers digging in hard enough to bruise. '*Enough.*' His eyes search my face, as if he can see that broken part of me. 'Kam? Are you with me?' He says it so softly, with a hint of humanity I've never heard from him before.

It makes me want to hit him again. I can't let him do this to me. I try to gain control over myself and my memories again, burying them deep down inside me where they belong.

'He knew you,' I whisper hoarsely. I won't explain to Kiaran what just happened, or that I'm horrified by what he did because it reminded me that he is one of *them*. 'That redcap *knew* you and you *lied* to me.'

The near-compassionate look is gone, and he's back to cold Kiaran. His grip is so tight on me now that I almost cry out. 'A *bhuraidh tha thu ann*.'

'I don't speak your bloody language.'

'I said you're a fool! Do you know what you've done?'

My breathing is quick and hard. 'Hit you.' I lift my chin. 'Killed redcaps. That's what you trained me for. I saved *myself*.'

'That –' he nods to the bridge '– was not something I taught you. Where the hell did you get that explosive?'

'I built it,' I say through clenched teeth. 'You always told me to do whatever was necessary to slaughter the fae, and I did exactly that.'

He taught me that was all that mattered. Hunt, mutilate, kill and survive. If I didn't already have the instinctual urge to murder, Kiaran would have taught me that as well. His hatred for them mirrors my own.

'Let go of me,' I say when he doesn't respond.

He doesn't release me. Instead, he only pulls me closer. I receive the full effect of his burning gaze and I shiver.

'You've been killing them, haven't you?' His voice is low. Emotions thicken his melodic accent and it surprises me so much that I'm not certain how to respond. He shakes me once. 'Alone. Without me. When I explicitly told you not to.'

I've never seen him so out of control before. Whatever emotions he might feel are always so carefully reined in, coiled tight.

'Aye,' I say. 'And I'll do it again whenever I want.'

'How long, Kam?'

I'm startled by the severity of his voice. 'Just over a fortnight.'

Just after the ball when I was reintroduced into society. I went hunting with Kiaran, and when we finished, he left me in one of the underground wynds with a dead faery at my feet. As I relished the last remnants of its power, I sensed another come in with its victim. I couldn't resist. And I couldn't resist killing on my own the night after that, and the night after that. My new ritual.

He laughs coldly. I recoil as he strokes my cheek with a long, graceful finger. 'I hope you have more of your little weapons,' he whispers, his breath kissing my lips. 'Because now they will never stop hunting you.'

I can't breathe any more. I flatten my hands against his chest and push him away. His smile flashes, more ferocious than ever. Then he turns and starts towards Calton Hill.

'And who might this innominate *them* be?' When it becomes clear that he has no intention of stopping, I move in front of him so he can't escape. 'You said the redcaps were in the mounds. I thought faeries couldn't lie.'

'*Sìthichean*,' he corrects. He hates it when I call his kind *faeries*. 'No, we can't.'

'Then how did they escape?'

'It doesn't matter,' he says, his jaw set. 'When we hunted together, I could disguise our kills as mine. Now you've hunted alone and she knows there's a Falconer in Edinburgh.'

Falconer. That word again. I remember the revenant's gaping smile as it ripped the energy out of me. *Falconer*.

'What does that mean?' I say.

Before he can answer, I hear voices behind us. Kiaran looks past me and I turn. People are hurrying towards Waterloo Place, chattering, calling back and forth. They're off to find the source of the explosion, I realise. It made a great deal of noise.

Dash it all. I'll have to take a long detour on the way back to Charlotte Square if I don't want to be seen.

'Just go home, Kam,' Kiaran says.

'But—'

'I'll tell you the rest tomorrow.' He pivots on his heel and walks down the road.

An hour later, I re-enter my bedroom through the hidden door. Derrick flies out of the dressing room. His wings are fluttering so fast they blur.

At the sight of me, he halts and lets out a whistle. 'I feel I must inform you: you look like hell.'

I shove the lever that brings up the door, then slam my palm against the wooden wall panel. 'Thank you,' I say drily. 'How very kind of you.'

Then I look in the mirror. My hair is in complete disarray, copper curls springing every which way. Blood peppers my face and clothes. My neck is bruised; tomorrow it will be deep purple. Derrick is right. I am an absolute mess.

'I finished the gown,' Derrick says. 'Payment, please.'

'Close your eyes.'

Dutifully, Derrick places his hands over his face and I open the cabinet where I hide the honey. A small panel slides aside to reveal a compartment containing a jar. I pour some of the contents into a wooden bicker and hide the honey again.

I set the bowl on the table. 'No dribbling, please.'

With a squeal of glee, Derrick zooms over to the table. His light shines golden as he perches on the edge of the bowl. He dips his fingers into the honey and – without any shame – proceeds to place his entire hand in his mouth.

I cringe and step inside the dressing room. After I remove my soiled clothes and slip on my nightdress, I study my hands. My knuckles are torn, swollen and already bruised from hitting

Kiaran. I kneel next to the washbasin Derrick has left out and slip my hands inside, hissing in pain.

I should never have let Kiaran see me that way. I need to keep better control over my rage. He'll see it as a vulnerability far worse than my physical limitations. A weakness. It's one thing to tell myself this. It's quite another to act accordingly in front of him.

'Damnation,' I whisper to myself as I dry my hands. I don't know what I'll do when I see him tomorrow.

By the time I return, Derrick is already half-finished with the honey. He flashes me a wobbly smile. 'How are you this fine –' he hiccups '– evening, you lovely human?'

'I thought you said I look awful.'

'Like hell,' he clarifies. 'Like splendid, magnificent, beautiful hell.'

I drop my clothes into the washbasin to clean them. The water turns dark with blood and dirt. 'Now you're just being silly.'

'*Diel-ma-care.*' He waves a dismissive hand.

I stare at myself in the mirror again. I wonder how my power would taste if I were a faery. Ash and sandalwood, I decide. Things that burn. Maybe a hint of iron, from all the faeries I've killed for my mother.

Using a cloth, I begin scrubbing at the blood still splattered dark across my cheeks amid the vast number of light freckles. I look like a murderess, like death personified.

Crimson suits you best.

With a growl, I scrub hard enough that my flesh reddens and aches. No more memories. No more. The one Kiaran triggered earlier was enough.

I force my thoughts to the redcaps. I have to find out where they came from, and how they slipped out of their prison before it happens again. There's no possible way I could manage to fight three in one night again. I already struggle with the solitary faeries I fight, and they weren't trapped underground for more than two thousand years. The fae that were must be angry, and very, very hungry.

I can't trust that Kiaran will tell me everything I need to know. What he doesn't reveal might be essential to my survival. I won't make the mistake of waiting.

'Derrick?'

'Hmm?' Derrick turns his head towards me; he's glowing brightly with rapture. He slips his fingers into the bowl again.

'Have you ever seen a redcap?'

Derrick grins with delight and laughs. 'Such hulking creatures. Slow as molasses. Do you know I once took my blade, danced around one and sliced it to ribbons!' He stuffs more honey in his mouth and sighs. 'Alas, nothing left for a trophy.'

Slow as molasses? The redcaps had swung their hammers and run faster than any faery I've ever faced. I'd love to see what Derrick considers fast. Or perhaps not.

I continue scrubbing my clothes. 'Do you know how it might be possible for some to escape imprisonment?'

'It takes time,' he sings. '*Tiiiiime.*'

Oh, for heaven's sake. 'Derrick, focus. Kindly articulate in complete sentences. What do you mean?'

He proceeds to lick his fingers. 'I can do that. I can speak sentences. What were we discussing?'

'The redcaps,' I say through clenched teeth. I try not to snap at him, but he is making this very difficult. 'How might they escape from beneath the city?'

'Oh, that's happening now? How interesting!' At my glare, he sits up straight and his wings fan. 'One can't have a functioning prison without a seal. Over time, the seal reaches the end of its life and begins to falter. Complete sentences!'

My stomach drops. 'What do you mean, the end of its life?'

Derek smiles gaily. 'Nothing lasts for ever. A good thing, considering the number of intolerable people about.'

The clothes slip from my hands into the washbasin and water splashes all over my nightdress. 'Derrick, this is serious!'

He raises his hands. 'Bright side! If the redcaps were freed first, whoever built your prison had a plan in case it failed.'

A glimmer of hope worms its way inside of me. 'Really?'

'Of course! It means the most power is being used to keep the strongest *sìthichean* inside the longest. So the least powerful are released first –' he gobbles more honey off his fingers '– and their enemies can kill them off more easily and reduce the army's numbers before the more powerful ones escape. Brilliant plan. Wish I had thought of it.'

My hope dies, as I should have suspected it would. Whoever built the prison thought *redcaps* could be killed easily? Frankly, that's the worst blasted plan *I've* ever heard. 'So let me see if I understand this,' I say carefully. 'The one thing protecting Edinburgh is a weakening seal and the current insurgence of evil faeries being let through is the *bright side?*'

Derrick looks a bit sheepish. 'Well. Aye.'

'But we don't have our own army to kill them off!'

Derrick blinks at me, his light dimming. 'Cor. When you state it like that it sounds rather depressing.'

'So where is the seal? How do we fix it?'

'Don't know. Never seen it. Pixies don't get involved in other *sìthichean* business.'

No wonder Kiaran didn't look at all surprised by those redcaps, the secretive bastard. How on earth am I supposed to blow them up if I don't know where they are? If we don't fix that seal, Edinburgh will fall. It is an utmost certainty. The faeries beneath the city were trapped there for a reason. If they rise, they will destroy everything in their path.

And there's something else Kiaran didn't tell me. 'Derrick,' I say. He glances at me warily. 'Have you ever heard of a Falconer?'

If I weren't watching for his reaction, I might not have noticed his entire body go rigid. That isn't the normal response of a pixie drunk on honey. Derrick has never looked more sober.

'Wherever did you hear that?' His voice is low. A flicker of fear crosses his wee features. His thin wings fan slowly, his halo darkens.

I frown. 'Kiaran mentioned it.'

Derrick remains entirely silent despite hearing Kiaran's name.

Another secret. No matter how much Derrick might despise Kiaran, they share a past that I fear I shall never know fully. Faeries might be incapable of lying, but that has only forced them to develop more inventive ways of circumventing the truth.

Derrick turns from me. 'It's someone who hunts with a trained falcon, of course. What else could it mean?'

'Right,' I say, not without a hint of sarcasm. He won't give me the truth, not tonight. I'll have to wring the rest out of Kiaran when I see him. I set my clothes next to the fireplace to dry. 'I'm certain that's what he meant.'

A lie in exchange for his half-truth.

Chapter 11

I primp and dress myself to receive visitors the following morning, so Dona won't see my injuries. Silk gloves hide the cuts on my knuckles and fabric tied at my neck conceals the faint bruising on my skin. The bow rests at my nape, below the loose chignon I managed to pin up by myself. It matches my day dress of soft green, one of the only colours in creation that complements my freckled skin.

I walk downstairs, inappropriately carrying a cup of tea from one room to another. Sunlight – a rare thing in Scottish winter – shines through the drawing room windows and into the large hallway. It's late morning, but the sun is already low on the horizon. Its light catches the chandelier, and tiny rainbows dance over the blue urn-and-coral-patterned wallpaper in the hallway.

All I can think of is what Derrick told me last night. I have to find that blasted seal before more redcaps escape ... or worse. When Kiaran shows up, I'll wring the information out of him. The *daoine sìth* would have been the most powerful of the creatures trapped inside, and I can't come near to besting even Kiaran. If he won't help me fight them, I'll convince him to tell me what I need to know to defeat them. I'll do what I have to.

The desire to kill again uncoils inside me, so strong and relentless that for a moment I can't breathe.

I set the teacup on a table and reach into the pocket of my day dress. My fingers fumble over the tiny parts inside until I find my turnscrew and the small automated valve I've begun to construct for a fire-starter. I place a screw and twist.

Tinkering like this helps me think, but the release from a kill would allow me breathe again. It would ease the ache in my chest. Find the seal, then continue to track and prepare to kill the *baobhan sìth*. The same as every night.

No. Not yet. I place another screw, twist it. I must remain focused. It's time to socialise, to act the perfect lady. Time for *sit up straight, shoulders back, smile.*

'Lady Aileana?'

I jump and my hand knocks the teacup from the table. It hits the Persian carpet with a muffled *thunk* and tea spills onto the cloth. 'Oh my,' I say to my father's butler. 'That wasn't very well done of me, was it?'

MacNab smiles under a full sorrel-coloured beard. He leans his immense form down to pluck the teacup off the carpet. The china is dwarfed in his palm as he straightens. 'Not to worry, my lady,' he says. 'I had every intention of sending the carpet to be cleaned.'

'How very timely.'

MacNab bows. 'Is there anything I can do for you?'

'More tea would be wonderful, thank you.'

'Very good, my lady.' He nods to the table closest to the door. 'Some gifts arrived this morning from your gentlemen admirers.'

Prominently displayed on the drum table are four bouquets of various flowers: roses, violets, tulips, heliotrope, heather, wild flowers – expensive arrangements that can only be obtained from hothouses this time of year.

The antechamber has never been bereft of bouquets or calling cards since I came out of mourning two weeks ago. The controversy surrounding my mother's death has only increased the interest in me, though I'm not certain that would be the case if I lacked a substantial dowry.

I stare at those arrangements and quell the urge to throw them out the front door. They are part of a future I cannot control, where I exist as a wife whose foremost concern is producing bairns and being presentable on my husband's arm. My weapons will be replaced with lace fans and parasols.

It takes every ounce of careful control to return my attention to the fire-starter's automatic valve. I slip another screw out of my pocket. Insert, twist, repeat.

MacNab clears his throat. I didn't realise he was still there. 'Will you require anything else, my lady?' he asks. 'Shall I send some replies, perhaps?'

'Just the tea, please. I'll take it in the drawing room.' I pluck a calling card off the table.

William Robert James Kerr, Earl of Linlithgow. I'm fairly certain Lord Linlithgow's prerequisites for a wife do not include: *trained for battle, highly aggressive, slaughters faeries.*

The front door opens and my father, William Kameron, Marquess of Douglas, strides into the antechamber.

I straighten in surprise. Father has been away at our country estate for more than a month, with not even a letter to inform me of his intended return home.

I pocket the valve and grasp my skirts, forcing a smile. 'Good morning, Father,' I say.

My first instinct upon seeing my father used to be to embrace him. When I was young, I liked to imagine he would gather me into his arms and kiss my cheeks. I pictured resting my face against the broad wall of his chest and inhaling his soft scent of pipe smoke and whisky.

But Father never lived up to my daydreams. He always loved my mother more than me, and all his hugs and kisses and tender-hearted questions were for her alone. Those were the only times I ever saw him smile.

Now when he comes home, even those affectionate moments feel like a dream. What's more, he won't even look at me. The last time he truly did, I was covered in his wife's blood, a stained ghost of the daughter he once had.

The worst thing is that I think he believes me a murderess. His expression when he found me that night ... I'll never forget the combination of grief and quiet accusation. Later, when we were alone, he grabbed me by the shoulders and asked me what the hell had happened. I kept silent, even when he shook me so hard that my head pounded and my neck ached.

I never shed tears for the woman he loved so much. I never gave my father the answer he wanted most: some insight into what happened. He just left me with my maid, who helped me scrub off all the blood. And when he told the chief constable that my mother had been killed by an animal, I suspect he did it to save his reputation, not mine.

Father stiffly removes his hat and smoothes his dark, ruffled hair.

'Good morning, MacNab.' MacNab takes Father's hat and helps him remove his damp coat. 'Aileana,' he finally acknowledges me.

Father hesitates, then leans forward and presses a formal kiss to my cheek – so quick and brusque it feels more like a slap. I clench my skirts tighter and try to remain composed. It's best that I pretend I never wanted his affection, that we have always been a family consisting of an absent father, a broken daughter and a dead mother.

When MacNab's heavy footfalls disappear through the antechamber, my father and I stand in awkward silence.

Father clears his throat. 'Are you well?'

I nod. 'Indeed.'

Father removes his gloves and places them on the drum table. 'I saw the Reverend Milroy on my way here.'

I try to keep my face neutral. 'Oh?'

'He says you haven't attended services. Would you care to explain?'

I stopped attending services months ago, after the reverend preached about backward superstitions, faeries among them. He told us that such barbaric beliefs encumber progression and scientific advancement – because while knowledge makes men atheists, science brings them back to religion. Knowledge might have stolen my faith, but science will never bring me back to it.

'I've been busy,' I say, indicating the bouquets.

Father reaches for the cards tucked under each bouquet. 'Hammersley, Felton, Linlithgow.' He looks up. 'When you respond, I expect you to do so with the utmost decorum.'

I unpocket the valve and fiddle with it again. 'I shall, Father.'

'I need not remind you that when you leave this house, you represent the family name.'

'Aye, Father.' I slide a metal piece into position.

'Aileana. Put that contraption *down*.'

His voice is so cold and commanding, I can't help but drop the valve onto the table. 'Father—'

'Why did I arrange to have an entirely new wardrobe made for your season?' I open my mouth to answer, but he continues. 'It certainly wasn't so you could toil away on your inventions, miss services and neglect your responsibilities. So tell me – why did I do this?'

I lower my eyes, so he won't see my glare. 'You know why I invent.' I try to keep my voice soft, gentle. 'You know why it's important to me.'

It was what my mother and I did together, every day, that he was never a part of. When I build, it reminds me of her. He may have removed all of her belongings from the house, but I still have my inventions.

Father stiffens. 'I asked you a question, Aileana.'

I swallow. I hate this. 'So I might make a suitable match,' I whisper.

'Indeed. Under Scottish law, you are my sole heir. That sets you apart from every debutante in the city.'

Aye. The one thing I have that gentlemen want is more wealth. As if I needed to be reminded yet again.

'Indeed,' I say.

'A wedding would shift attention away from last year's ... unfortunate circumstance.'

I can't believe he just referred to Mother's death in the same way one might describe a couple caught in a garden tryst.

'Unfortunate circumstance.' I try not to sound bitter. 'We wouldn't want them to focus on that.'

Father lifts his chin with a scowl. He still won't meet my gaze. 'I hope you grasp the importance of this, Aileana. I'd like to see you matched before the season ends.'

'It might not be that easy,' I say.

'Then I will arrange someone for you,' he says simply.

Damn him. In the end, I truly have no choice – except perhaps the selection of whichever lord I'm best able to deceive. My future lies in a gilded prison of silks and balls and false politeness.

I can't help saying something. 'Are you so anxious to be rid of me?'

A flicker of emotion crosses his face. 'Don't interpret this as something it isn't.'

'Then what is it?'

He collects his gloves calmly off the table. 'It's quite simple. Part of your duty is to marry.'

'What if I don't want it? Marriage?'

He looks unconcerned. 'Of course you do. Don't be dramatic.'

I try to stay calm. 'I'm not being dramatic, Father.'

No response. Not anger or surprise or anything more than a single blink to indicate he heard me. 'What you want isn't important,' he says. 'Duty comes first.'

Something violent rises within me, but I press it down. I'm not meant for marriage. It isn't for someone like me. But Father doesn't realise that marriage would force me to suppress the part of me that still grieves.

'Of course.'

Father doesn't appear to notice the hint of anger in my voice. He passes me the calling cards. 'Send your responses.'

I resist the urge to crumple them in my fist. Instead, I accept them calmly. 'I shall invite Lord Linlithgow to fourhours.' When Father frowns in confusion, I tell him, 'Catherine is visiting for elevenhours.'

'Very well,' Father says. He glances at his watch fob. 'I'll have MacNab send Lord Linlithgow your reply, and shall return at fourhours to join you both for tea.'

I watch him walk to his study and try to calm myself. *What you want isn't important.*

In the drawing room, I flip the switch to light the fireplace. As the room warms, I sit on the red velvet settee and look out of the window, breathing in the scent of the burning wood crackling in the hearth. The sun peeks through the trees across the square. Thin white clouds drift overhead, carried faster by the wind. Ornithopters and airships float in the distance, wings fanning leisurely above the houses.

I lose count of how many cups of tea I consume as I sit there. I press the button and the electronic hand grasps my cup and pours the tea. Over and over.

It's a relief to be alone. Here, I can let my father's words wash over me with the crushing weight of a tidal wave. *What you want isn't important. What you want isn't important. What you want—*

'Lady Aileana?' MacNab pushes open the drawing room door. 'Miss Stewart is here to see you.'

Thank heavens. 'Do let her in, MacNab.'

A moment later, Catherine rushes in, her soft pink muslin gown rustling against the doorframe. Her hair is slightly windblown, her pale cheeks are rosier than usual, and her blue eyes are bright.

'Where's your escort?' I ask with a frown. 'Oh dear, don't tell me your mother came.'

'Good God, no!' she exclaims. 'I had to sneak out to see you. Do you have any idea what's happening out there?'

'Not the faintest,' I reply and press the button on the dispenser.

Hot tea pours into the cup I'm holding and I add a splash of milk and a sugar cube, as Catherine prefers. I nudge the saucer to her side of the mahogany tea table between us.

Catherine removes her shawl and settles on the settee across from me, smoothing her skirts. 'Princes Street is a complete disaster. Do you know half of North Bridge was destroyed?'

I wince. I had been hoping to escape all reminders of my destruction last night, but I suppose I should at least look surprised. 'How awful!' I reply. 'What on earth could have happened?'

She takes a sip of her tea. 'Apparently there was an explosion late last night, though what caused it remains a mystery. The force has been called in to investigate and inspect the damages.'

I freeze. I didn't even think to consider who might have been hurt as a result of my actions. 'Please tell me no one was injured.' I can barely say it.

'No one, thank God.' Catherine leans forward and takes my hand. 'I'm sorry. I didn't intend to distress you.'

I exhale in relief and give her a feeble smile. 'Thank you. Do continue.'

'There's not much more to tell. Everything between south Princes Street and Waterloo Place has been cordoned off.' She cringes. 'Traffic was so terrible, I nearly got out of the carriage and walked. I would have made it here faster if I had a blasted ornithopter.'

I nod. I'm one of the few individuals fortunate enough to own a flying machine. Though I built my own, it is an invention reserved for only the wealthiest families in Edinburgh. Only a few engineers in the country are qualified to manufacture them.

'I assume your mother responded in a panic, or else you wouldn't have slipped out of the house without an escort.'

Catherine nods calmly. 'She tried to use this as an excuse for me not to come to luncheon. Naturally.'

'Naturally.'

'And when that didn't work, she brought up what happened to Lord Hepburn.' She eyes me and sips her tea.

Oh dear. I had forgotten about poor Lord Hepburn. I do hope he's recovered from those nasty injuries without too much difficulty. 'What about him?'

'Have you not heard? The poor man was attacked during the assembly.'

I feign shock. 'Attacked? What do you mean?'

'Whoever it was cut up Lord Hepburn's chest, although he was found with stitcher sutures. Isn't that strange? As if his attacker changed his mind.'

I widen my eyes to appear as innocent as possible. 'My word! Does he remember anything?'

Such as an insane woman who fought off an invisible attacker and then stitched him up and left him on his bed? Does he remember that?

'No,' Catherine says. 'Inconveniently not.'

'Well.' *Good.* 'I hope they find the vile person responsible. Just think: the attacker might have been another guest at the ball. Can you imagine?'

Catherine sighs and plunks down her cup and saucer. Tea sloshes onto the tablecloth. 'For heaven's sake, I think I'm going mad.' She pinches the bridge of her nose and closes her eyes briefly. 'I can't believe I'm about to ask you this.'

'Ask me what?'

When she looks up again, her eyes are bright with unshed tears. 'Was it you?'

I almost can't breathe, my chest aches so much. '*Me?*' The word comes out in a croak. 'Why would you ask such a thing?'

'Blast it all, but I think the rumours are finally starting to influence me.' She hesitates, as though she's thinking very carefully about what she'll ask next. Deliberately, she says, 'I saw you in that hallway. You asked me to hold your reticule. You missed five dances and returned to the ballroom looking frightfully unkempt. What am I supposed to think?'

Our friendship has been steadfast since infancy. It was my only solace while I was in mourning, and is the only comforting relationship I have left. Despite that, I don't think I can ever stop lying to Catherine. I know she'll never understand how far I've gone from the person she believes I am, but I never once thought she doubted me.

'Do you think I killed her, too, then?' I ask quietly. 'My mother?'

'No!' She looks horrified. 'My God, I would *never* think that.'

'Then you must know that I would never have hurt Lord Hepburn.'

Catherine studies me. 'But you know who did. Don't you?'

I smile then. 'That would be an admission I was there. I was in the ladies' parlour with a headache, remember?'

Catherine doesn't return my smile. 'I don't know what you've got yourself into, but if it's serious, you should tell me.'

I'm tempted. Only faeries know my secret; most of them die after learning it. Catherine is my last connection to a normal life, to the one I had before I became … *this.* If only she knew how important it is that I have one thing left untouched by the fae. She grounds me in my humanity, what little remains of it.

'I can't,' I say softly.

She lowers her gaze. 'Are you safe, at least?'

'I promise I am.' It's so much better to keep lying than tell her even that bit of truth.

She wipes away her tears. 'I should never have let the horrid gossip get to me like that. I'm so sorry I doubted you.'

'There's no need to apologise. I doubt myself all the time.'

Nodding, she clears her throat. 'You must promise me that this headache will not return during Gavin's ball.' When I do nothing but stare at her, Catherine scowls. 'You did remember, didn't you?'

I return to sipping my tea. 'Aye. Your dear brother … who is at Oxford—'

'And who is returning tomorrow—'

'Of course,' I say brightly. 'How could I forget that?'

Catherine clearly sees right past my lie. 'We are hosting a ball in his honour and you assured me that you would save me from the clutches of tedium.'

'And so I shall,' I say. 'I wouldn't miss it for the world.'

I should be glad Gavin is returning. Before he left for Oxford two years ago, we had been good friends since childhood. Indeed, I once fancied the idea of us marrying someday. But now he'll just be another complication.

'And you will dance with every gentleman who signs your card.'

'I will dance with every man who signs my card,' I vow.

All a lady has is her reputation, and mine must be so questionable by now if even my dearest friend almost believed me capable of violence. I should try harder, as Father wishes. I should do my duty and put on my false cheerful face. No disappearing after a dance. I should go to the ball and behave like the lady I'm expected to be.

Unless, of course, a faery shows up and I have to save yet another elderly gentleman from its clutches.

Catherine beams. 'Now. I believe I was promised shortbread.'

'The primary reason you're here, I suspect.' I glance out of the window. 'Shortbread and lunch, then a jaunt to the park. We might not see the sun again until spring, after all.'

After luncheon, Catherine, Dona and I leave the house and set out towards the centre of Charlotte Square, where my ornithopter is parked. Mine is the only one still there, so the other families must have taken out their own flying machines to avoid the traffic.

I glide my fingers along the structure. When I built it, I made sure the metal boning was light and sturdy enough to flap exactly like bat wings. Spanning more than thirty feet when extended, the wings are positioned with interworking steel gears that revolve and twist to keep the machine in flight.

The steel and wooden-planked interior took the longest time to build. The small cabin has a retractable rain visor for inclement weather, though I prefer to fly with the top down. Two people can sit comfortably inside on the moulded leather seats, but Catherine insisted on bringing Dona along as our chaperone so we will be a bit crowded today.

'We mustn't call too much attention to ourselves or word will get back to Mother,' Catherine says as she tosses in her reticule. 'I'll be in enough trouble already with her as it is for not taking my maid with me. I just know she's going to lecture me on etiquette again.'

'No need to explain,' I say. 'Father already lectured me on that very subject.'

Catherine pauses. 'So, he's returned then?' She says it lightly, but with a hint of disapproval.

'Aye. Just before you arrived.'

'Oh dear. What did he say?'

What you want isn't important.

'Nothing of consequence.' I nod to Dona. 'Don't you think people will notice that Dona is a wee bit young for a proper chaperone?'

Catherine assesses my maid with careful scrutiny. Dona gulps and clutches her shawl tighter around her shoulders.

Catherine sighs. 'May I?' She plucks the shawl off Dona's shoulders. 'You know, this would be much easier if one of us had invited a female relative for the season.'

I lean against the ornithopter and close my eyes. By no means is it warm, but the sun feels so lovely on my skin. 'She would have to be one of yours, then. My family has generations of single children, and my grandparents are dead.'

'I have a distant aunt,' Catherine says. 'She claims the pigeons on her property wait to watch her undress.'

'Oh? Well, that's not surprising. Pigeons are quite dastardly creatures.'

Catherine plops the shawl on Dona's head and wraps it around so the lass's features are mostly obscured. 'There. That might be enough to fool people from a distance.'

'Let us hope we are not approached, then,' I say.

'I can't see, miss,' Dona mutters.

'All the better. You only need to be able to see your feet, so you don't trip over anything,' Catherine replies and pats Dona's shoulder reassuringly.

'Perfect.' I open the ornithopter door. 'We've rendered Dona mostly blind and partially disguised her as an old woman for the sake of a bloody walk in a public park.'

Catherine nods, not at all fazed by my horrid use of the English language. 'The things we do for sunshine.'

I step back to let Catherine and Dona inside, then stroll around to the driver's side and hoist myself in. Our skirts take up most of the free space in the cabin. Dona is squeezed in the middle, her tiny frame huddled even smaller.

'There now,' I say. 'Is everyone ready?'

Dona gulps. 'Lady Aileana, are you certain this is safe? I've heard stories—'

'Safe as houses,' I interrupt cheerfully. 'I built it myself, remember?'

Dona sinks back with a weak, 'Aye, my lady.'

I smile and flip the switches to turn the machine on. Steam rises from the front vent and Dona jumps. I bite back a laugh and settle into my seat. At least she isn't aware that she's sitting on the hidden weapon cache.

I rest my hands on the helm, salvaged from a schooner ship just like the one in my bedroom. The wings extend outward from their resting position to their full length, flapping in loud, smooth *whooshes*. We begin to hover just above the ground as the wings beat faster and faster. Then I shift the gear lever next to me and push my foot down on a second pedal. The machine rises smoothly and flies over the houses in Charlotte Square.

'Would either of you like some tea?' I ask. Both ladies shake their heads. I turn the ornithopter in the direction of the castle. 'Well, I would. Could you get me a teacup from the compartment beside you, Catherine?'

Catherine opens a wooden panel and removes a porcelain teacup. She passes it to me and I place it under the steel spout in front of Dona. I press another button and warm, already steeped tea pours into the cup. The scent of heather fills the cabin.

I pick up the cup and sip. Perfect.

'Oh my,' Catherine breathes. 'Look there.'

She points just over my shoulder. I turn and gasp softly. From the skies, we can see every bit of the destruction of North Bridge. Half of it has fallen into the valley below, with a broken portion still left hanging.

A large throng has gathered, lining the streets to view the bridge. Steam-powered carriages crowd the road, hardly any room between them. On the Old Town end, just beyond the bridge, traffic is being redirected to New Town via Lothian Road – no small detour, that. The whole city is a mess of traffic and pedestrians. All because of me.

'What do you think could have caused that?' Catherine asks.

We pass an automatic flying machine with a banner advertisement waving behind it. I focus on the words, to concentrate on something other than my destruction. *Bass's East-India Pale Ale ... This season's ale is in excellent condition, both in bottle and cask ...*

'I have no idea.' I hope they don't notice how my voice shakes, how intently I'm staring at the sign rather than at the sight below.

'Do you think it could happen again?' Catherine asks.

I return my attention to Catherine. 'Of course not.' I sound false, the way Kiaran does when he pretends to be concerned. 'Perhaps it has something to do with a malfunctioning carriage. Combustion is a tricky thing.' I smile at her. 'Fear not. We won't be blown to bits.'

Catherine and Dona appear satisfied with that. I steer us past Castle Rock. Even in sunlight the castle is dark and imposing, a startling contrast to the greenery below. The park is mostly empty, a surprise on such a lovely day. I'm stricken by the realisation that everyone must be gathered on Princes Street to gawk at the disaster.

I find a clear patch of grass towards the east end of the Nor' Loch, just below the cliff. The wings give a single, quick flap as the ornithopter lands.

'Thank heavens,' Dona mutters.

After a last sip of tea, I grab my parasol and open the door. The three of us stroll from the ornithopter, through thick trees that surround the base of Castle Rock. Damp grass squishes with each step we take.

The breeze here is brisk, but not terribly cold. This is one of the few winter days we will have when it's bearable enough to take an afternoon walk. The sun sets too early at this time of year for many outdoor activities. Already it's dipped below the treeline. Shadows behind the trees are growing longer and noticeably colder than the bright patches between them. The park is quiet, not even birds or other animals about. The three of us are completely alone.

'I wanted to speak with you about something,' Catherine says suddenly.

I open my parasol and rest the pole lightly against my shoulder. Distant rain clouds have begun to blow our way. We don't have much daylight left. 'Hmm?'

Catherine hesitates and glances at Dona. Dona lowers her head and immediately slows her pace to give us more privacy.

'If Dona hears anything,' I say to Catherine, 'she will be perfectly discreet.'

Catherine blushes but nods. 'I know you don't like to discuss it, but have you at least thought about marriage?'

What you want isn't important.

I look down at my feet. The tops of my slippers are stained with mud. 'Aye,' I say. I smile ruefully. 'I've concluded it isn't for me.'

Dona gasps from behind us. At my surprised look, she drops her head. 'Quite sorry, my lady.'

'That's all right,' I say. 'Unfortunately, my father feels differently. He says I am to be engaged before the end of the season. When I brought up potential difficulties, he claimed I was being dramatic.'

'Well,' Catherine says drily, 'he has all the sensitivity of a tea table, doesn't he?'

'Duty first, remember?' Father's oft-stated precept.

Catherine lets out a breath of disgust. 'So he's decided to be interested in your life now? And to think, it only took him a year to acknowledge you.'

I dislike her mother, she dislikes my father. Unlike my own, Catherine's father loved her – and he showed more affection towards me than I've ever received from mine. He died four years ago, when I was fourteen and Catherine was thirteen.

'My darling friend, your sarcasm is beginning to show.'

She smiles grimly. 'He deserves it.'

'No arguments from me.'

We continue walking, passing the ivy-covered ruins just below Castle Rock. The cliff face blazes orange from the setting sun peeking through the trees. The clouds are surging ever closer. As I breathe in, I smell the first hint of damp air that indicates it's going to rain soon. So much for our pleasant, sunny walk.

'I must know,' Catherine asks. 'Would you think less of me if I said I *wanted* to marry?'

'Not at all,' I say softly. 'I wanted it, too, before—' *Before I became what I am.* 'Do you have a particular gentleman in mind?'

Catherine flushes. 'Well, Lord Gordon and I have danced a few times, and he recently visited for fourhours.' She sighs. 'I find him most agreeable.'

If I were still the girl I used to be, this would have been my life. Courtships, deciding my best match, wondering about when I'd marry.

For a small, petty moment, I envy Catherine. She can share

her life wholly with someone, completely fulfilled. She won't need to lie to her husband, or slip out of the house at night to quiet a need for violence. Unlike me, she can love someone without pretence.

I try to sound more cheerful than I feel. 'That's wonderful. And your mother?'

'Mother considers him unsuitable.'

I snort. 'That's preposterous. He is an earl, after all.'

'It's not his title. It's because he's ...'

'He's what?'

She looks around, as if to be certain there is no one but my maid in the vicinity to hear us. 'He's English.'

I feign shock. 'My God! Someone call the magistrate immediately. An Englishman in Scotland, you say?'

Catherine laughs. 'I'm well aware how ridiculous it is, but my mother is adamant that I marry a Scot. She believes the English are heartless and deranged.'

With a snicker, I hop over another patch of mud and nearly slip when I land. Blast. Grass is quite treacherous in winter. After regaining my footing, I ask, 'Did she mention where she might have garnered this bit of intelligence?'

'I wish I could tell you. She called Lord Gordon a Sassenach. Can you believe that? It's the first time I have ever heard her say such a vile word.'

A breeze picks up. The leafless trees shake and the branches groan. A frigid draught knifes right through my thick cloak. I shiver and pull it tighter around my shoulders until the mink-lined collar is snug beneath my chin. My cheeks are already burning from the cold.

'At least Lord Gordon only needs Gavin's approval. His return home is more than convenient.'

Catherine brightens. 'Then Mother can finally focus on finding him a match, instead of expending all of her efforts on me.'

I bite back a laugh, imagining how her brother would respond to that. My goodness, he'd be horrified. 'Poor Gavin. The dear fellow has no idea what's in store for him when he arrives.'

She regards me briefly. 'I remember a time when *you* intended to marry him.'

I make a choking sound at the back of my throat. 'Really, Catherine. You're misremembering.'

'What nonsense! You used to write in your invention sketchbook: *Lady Aileana Stewart, Viscountess of Cassilis.*' She smiles slyly. 'I suppose you'll have to change that to reflect his new title now, won't you – *Countess of Galloway*?'

'Oh, do be quiet. That was a lapse in judgement,' I say, waving a hand dismissively. 'I was young and foolish.'

'You did it for four years.'

I glare at her. 'It was a very *long* lapse in judgement.'

'He's ... well ... some women say he's charming. And he's rather handsome, I suppose.' She turns innocent eyes on me. 'Is there someone else you consider more suitable?'

For no reason I can fathom, I think of Kiaran first. He's not remotely suitable, and I'm certain he's never to be trusted. But he is the only man who has ever seen the rage inside me, who accepts and encourages it. I can never forget the overwhelming taste of his power, so wild and strong. If I picture him clearly enough, I can still taste it at the back of my throat, as if he's actually here.

As if he *is* here.

My head snaps up and I almost gasp in alarm. There's Kiaran MacKay, sauntering through the trees towards us, garbed in the fine clothes of a wealthy gentleman. The rough raploch he usually wears has been replaced with finely tailored trousers, a black waistcoat and a frock coat that billows behind him. His dark hair catches the fading sunlight, the sunset glow a blazing halo around him. He looks as tempting as the very devil, and damn him for it.

I'm speechless with shock. This is a betrayal. This goes beyond our unspoken pact for privacy during our daytime lives.

Kiaran simply smiles.

Chapter 12

I try not to let my distress show as Kiaran approaches. Catherine notices something, though, and glances over at Kiaran … She freezes, gaping in shock.

He isn't even bothering with invisibility, then. I bite my tongue to restrain the vile oath that threatens to slip out. When he said we would finish last night's conversation, I didn't think that meant he'd accost me in a public garden.

Kiaran stops next to me and doesn't bother to acknowledge Catherine or Dona. His amethyst eyes bore into mine, challenging me. Now that I see them in full daylight, I can't help but notice how piercing they are, how unyielding.

'I need to speak with you,' he says.

Catherine and Dona gasp at his presumption. A gentleman never approaches a group of ladies and says something so forward. And Kiaran is already looking at me in a way that betrays far too much familiarity.

My private life is now exposed to him, and here I am. Not a huntress. Not the violent creature who slaughtered two redcaps just last night. A mere lady: fine garments, parasol and all.

And now I must act the part or risk losing my reputation. I raise my chin and attempt to impose some order on the situation. 'Miss Catherine Stewart, will you permit me to introduce … erm –' I swallow hard '– Mr Kiaran MacKay?'

Catherine stares at him, an odd expression on her face. 'How do you do?'

Kiaran finally averts his attention from me and acknowledges my companions. He blinks, as if surprised they're still there. Then he regards them both with a narrowed, fixed glare.

'Kam, I'm not here to socialise.'

'Don't you *dare* embarrass me, you oaf,' I hiss through clenched teeth. Then, more loudly, 'And this is Miss Dona MacGregor.'

He chose this moment to approach me, and I'll force him to observe the proper etiquette for greeting ladies in a park, the cad.

Dona doesn't speak. Her shawl has slipped from around her face and her eyes are wide and frightened her skin even paler than usual.

She can only sense me on occasion, Derrick said. Not that it's at all difficult to guess Kiaran isn't human, since he's terrible at playing the part. His fae nature is evident in his uncanny beauty, in the way he moves and breathes. He would never look entirely normal, even if he cared to try.

Damnation. I should have sent Dona away instead of listening to Derrick. Rose-scented cleaning solution, indeed.

'You,' Kiaran says to Dona, very softly, 'know exactly what I am, don't you?'

Dona trembles. 'I'm … I don't understand.'

'You understand perfectly well,' Kiaran says. 'But maintain that pretence. It might save your life one day.'

I step in front of Dona, glowering at Kiaran. 'Couldn't you even attempt to be human?' I ask. 'For a mere five minutes?'

Kiaran sighs and mutters something in that language I don't understand.

Catherine doesn't appear to notice my maid's panic, or the strangeness of our conversation. She stares at Kiaran in silent, unabashed awe. Then she blinks rapidly and puts her hand out, palm down, as though she had forgotten that part of a proper greeting.

Kiaran takes her hand. 'What am I to do with it? Kiss it?'

Dona shivers and Catherine looks to be on the verge of swooning. 'That would be wonderful,' she whispers, in a dreamy way that sounds completely unlike herself.

I gape at Catherine with dawning horror. Oh, hell! She's been faestruck. Kiaran told me about the terrible effect the *daoine sìth* have on humans. People willingly become victims for a single touch from a faery, for a moment of closeness. Before the *daoine sìth* were trapped underground, many humans had died because of it.

'I've changed my mind. Stop inadequately playing human,' I say. 'Drop her hand and step away. Take a very big step.'

Kiaran leans against the tree next to me. 'Are you quite finished, then?' he asks. 'We must discuss—'

'Forgive me, Mr MacKay,' Catherine says, shaking her head as if to clear it, 'but I must say, you're so very beautiful.'

Kiaran regards her calmly. 'I see this is not going as well as I had hoped.'

My goodness, what an insensitive buffoon. Just when I think he can't be so at sea when it comes to being around humans, he goes and proves me wrong. 'This is what happens,' I tell him, 'when you decide to make yourself visible. Are you *mad*?'

'It seemed … convenient at the time,' he replies, apparently unconcerned about the effect he's having on my friend.

'To the devil with you, Kiaran MacKay.'

Dona clutches Catherine's shoulder to keep her at bay. 'My lady,' she whispers, 'we should leave. This … something isn't right.'

'I don't want to,' Catherine says, wrenching out of her grip. 'I'm not ready.'

Catherine grasps the sleeve of Kiaran's frock coat, twisting the fabric to pull him to her, her eyes dazed. The faestruck will rip and tear clothing for another touch of a faery's skin. She hasn't reached that point, not yet, but any further contact with him and she might.

I yank her back and insert myself in front of her, grasping her shoulders. 'Catherine?'

Her fingernails dig into my coat, her movements uncoordinated and unfocused. 'Beautiful,' she breathes, never taking her eyes off Kiaran.

'Fix this,' I snap at him. 'Or I shall never forgive you.'

'Leave,' he tells my companions without averting his gaze from mine. 'Now.'

The burst of power that comes from him – usually so tempting and magnetic – cramps my stomach, a nauseating churn that doubles me over. It's a taste so heavy that I almost heave from it.

Without hesitation or a word of farewell, Dona and Catherine turn and stroll across the grass, in the direction of Princes Street. Their movements are calm, as if nothing is amiss. They wander through the trees and out of sight.

'What did you do to them?'

'I compelled them to return home,' he says. 'They won't remember me.'

'Is Catherine—'

'She's fine. The effects of seeing me will wear off.'

I throw my parasol onto the ground and scowl at him. It takes all my effort not to strike him. 'What were you thinking, coming here?'

Kiaran tilts his face to the sky. The final remnants of sunshine lights his skin with a golden glow both strange and lovely. 'Such magnificent weather, is it not?'

Stop staring at him, you ninny. I tear my gaze away. 'How dare you do this? We had an agreement.'

He pushes away from the tree and circles me, as if cornering his prey. His feet are silent on the grass. 'I don't recall ever speaking a vow.'

'It was understood.'

'I don't deal in implied negotiations.' Kiaran glances behind me. 'Am I to understand you don't want us to be seen together?'

I snort. 'Of course not. Especially now that you've deprived me of my chaperone.'

Kiaran clicks his tongue and gestures behind me. 'So you should be concerned about *them*, then.'

I whirl. A couple strolls in our direction, a chaperone not far behind. They have yet to see me, but a lady of my reputation and social standing should not be alone in a park – and being spotted alone with a man would surely make things worse.

With a gasp, I tear off a glove and grab Kiaran's bare hand. 'Hide us,' I whisper.

'I'll consider it. Shall we bargain?'

I'm tempted to pick up my parasol and beat him with it. 'You've ruined my afternoon. At least do me this service.'

Kiaran smirks and laces his fingers through mine. I'm amazed at how smooth they are, how warm. 'There now.' His words are low, barely audible. 'You're hidden.'

His eyes are depthless, as though they hold an endless expanse of space, deep and dark. Except for the gold flecks, cinders burning within the infinite abyss. Kiaran's age is reflected there. He has seen centuries come and go, seen countless people live and die, the birth and destruction of whole civilisations. He is a living relic.

The couple pass by us, laughing and chattering. I'm struck with sudden shame that Kiaran has to hide me from my peers, and that I even need him to. When did I come to care so much for his opinion of me? I want so badly for him to see me as the huntress and not the lady – *never* the lady. The nights we hunt are the only times I've ever felt on equal terms with a man – even if he isn't one.

I should be angry at him. I should scold him again for coming to me like this, for forcing me to reveal the side of me I didn't want him to know about. Instead, I blush with embarrassment, and I can't even begin to comprehend why.

Unable to meet his eyes any more, I look away. 'I never wanted you to see me like this.'

'Like what?'

'Me in this blasted dress. I'm the highborn daughter of a marquess. I must look like I've never touched a weapon in my life.' I shouldn't have told him this. Now I'll appear weaker than ever.

I am the wild creature he saw fight, kill and survive only last night. Dresses conceal my brokenness. They cloak the savage creature that lives inside me and thrives on anger. I am a wolf in sheep's clothing.

His response surprises me. 'Trifling matters, Kam. It changes nothing. Do you think these clothes hinder my ability to use a blade? They're no impediment.'

I almost laugh. 'Try fighting in a corset and petticoats.'

He smiles wryly.

I scan his undeniably expensive outfit. I know quality fabrics when I see them. 'Where did you even find those?'

'The shopkeeper gave them to me,' he says.

'Under the influence of faery powers, I presume?'

'*Sìthichean.*'

'Faeries.'

Kiaran smirks. 'I wanted the clothes. He had them. I asked for them – nicely – and he tailored them for me. Now they are well fitted. Must we discuss the morality of it?'

Morality. In all my worry over him finding me this way, I had completely forgotten the real reason he needed to speak to me, and I go cold again. Our genial moment has passed.

'Aye, MacKay,' I drawl. 'Let's discuss morality. Like the morality of failing to tell me about a seal that, once broken, will unleash faeries that could slaughter thousands of humans?'

Kiaran at least has the decency to look a bit uncomfortable, though his only tell is a slight shift of his gaze. 'Someday, I'll cut out that pixie's tongue,' he mutters.

'At least he was honest with me.'

I look around. There is no one else in sight, just Kiaran and me standing in the middle of a circle of trees. Good. I release his hand and put my glove back on.

'The seal breaking is an inevitability,' Kiaran says, stuffing his hands into his pockets. 'It'll happen when the lunar eclipse occurs on midwinter. In six days.'

'Six days,' I whisper, almost unable to say the words.

I go cold and it's hard to breathe. That's too soon. If the fae manage to escape, how will it be possible to save the city? An entire human army couldn't defeat the fae. Even a few more escaped redcaps could wreak untold havoc. I can't stand against them if that happens, not on my own. I can't save everyone.

'We have to find the seal before that happens,' I tell him. 'Reactivate it somehow.'

He shakes his head. 'The seal can only be reactivated during the eclipse. All the *sìthichean* will have slipped through by then.'

'Surely there must be something we can do,' I say.

'We have one chance.' He is so quiet I can only just hear him over the breeze. Around us, the trees rattle and dead leaves tumble through the grass. 'You have to be there to reactivate it,' he says. 'You're the only one who can.'

Chapter 13

Surely I must have heard him wrong. 'I beg your pardon?'

Kiaran shifts closer, removing his hands from his pockets to brush his fingers against mine. His power tingles through my glove, warm and soft. It would be a reassuring gesture if it hadn't come from him. Kiaran doesn't comfort. He never has. 'Last night you asked me a question. Do you remember?'

'What is a Falconer?' I whisper.

Maybe I shouldn't see where this path leads. Perhaps it is best to keep it simply a word and not learn the truth behind it. Let myself pretend that a Falconer is precisely what Derrick said it was, that he didn't half-lie.

No, I can't do that. Father may think that I play with my inventions and neglect my responsibilities, but he's wrong. *This* is my responsibility, my burden. I won't run away from it. I *won't*.

Kiaran lifts my chin. 'Kam. *You* are a Falconer,' he says.

'But what does it mean?'

He shakes his head. 'Tell me what you feel and I'll tell you what it means.'

Kiaran's palm presses against mine, warm enough to be felt through my glove. The backs of his fingers stroke my cheek and traces of his power glide along my skin and roll off like drops of warm water. The taste is exquisite, like silk flower petals that brush up and down my tongue. My breath hitches and I lean into the warmth of his touch.

'Tell me.'

'I-I don't—'

'You do,' he says. 'You feel power.'

'Aye,' I sigh.

'And you've sensed the *sìthichean* since the first one you ever saw, haven't you?'

The first faery. The first one the first one *the first one*—

I shove away from his touch, so hard that I almost lose my footing. Cold puddle water soaks through my stockings. *I won't remember. I won't remember.* But I can't stop the memories that gather and crash against me.

Blood. Blood coats my white dress, stains and slicks my skin from fingers to elbows. Lying prostrate in a thick pool of it on the cobblestones. I'm baptised in it, created, reborn. My stomach constricts with the thick, painful taste of iron.

Crimson suits you best crimson suits you best crimson suits—

'No.'

I slam the palm of my hand into Kiaran's nose with so much force that I hear bone crack. I have to escape that memory before it consumes me. Before I become that helpless girl who let it all happen.

I run. I dash past the nearby stand of trees and begin to round the base of the castle's cliff. The once-distant clouds have gathered swiftly overhead and rain begins to mist around me. My feet ache with cold through my slippers but I ignore the pain.

I'll never be weak like that again. *Never*. I can't let myself.

Hands grab me from behind, pulling at my cloak. I stumble and nearly fall in my attempt to escape. My feet falter as Kiaran roughly turns me around. 'Kam,' he snaps, gripping my shoulders. Blood drips from his nose to his lips. He's bleeding.

'Your nose,' I manage.

He touches his fingers to his face. His eyes meet mine and some emotion I can't name flickers in their depths. Approval? 'Don't you understand?' he says. 'You're the only one who could do this. No other human alive is capable of it.'

I twist out of his arms. 'I have no idea what you're talking about.'

'You do,' he says. 'Think back to—'

'I don't want to!' My emotions are out of control and if I don't rein them in, I might hurt someone. I might hurt *him*. I breathe deep. 'I don't want to remember. Don't force me to do that.' My voice is despicably thin, high-pitched. It sounds as if I'm begging him.

His depthless eyes search mine. 'Kam, this is what you were born to be. *Seabhagair*,' he says. 'Falconer.'

I shake my head and swipe at my cheeks, now dampened by the mist. The word should have stayed a word. I can accept being made into a faery killer, but that I was born to do it? That it's a gift I've had all along and never knew about? Believing I was weak that night last year is easier than knowing I might have had the strength to save my mother and didn't know it. That I let her die.

Kiaran sighs. With exasperation or pity, or perhaps a combination of the two. 'You sense fae power. You fight almost as fast as I do. You're stronger than other humans, and you heal more rapidly.' He touches his nose. 'You did this. With more training, you could again. And when you kill a faery,' he continues, relentlessly, 'its power goes through you.'

'How do you know that?' I whisper.

'You're not the first Falconer I've met.'

His gaze softens and for the first time since I met him, I see sorrow there. Who has Kiaran lost, that he should feel so strongly? He drops his eyes and the sadness is gone. 'But you are the last.'

'The last?'

'There were only a certain number of humans born with the ability to kill the *sìthichean*. Always women, always passed from mother to daughter,' he says. 'Your line is the only one left.'

'Don't you think that if my mother were a Falconer, she would have known about it?' With both hands, I try to shove him, but he doesn't even budge. 'Don't you think I would have?'

'No,' he says. 'Your line's power became latent. Generations of women would not have known. That ignorance saved your family from being killed but made your abilities more difficult to trigger. That's why I'm not naturally visible to you.'

'I see.' I say the words faintly, because I don't know how else to respond.

'Do you?' He pins me with a hard stare, one that I swear sees right through me. 'Kam, the Falconers have been tracked and slaughtered for centuries, even with their powers inactive. When you began to hunt alone, your kill signature became obvious to any *sìthichean* who knew what to look for.'

My spine prickles with dread, raising the hair along my skin as if I were brushed by cold fingertips. *Generations of women. Generations. Tracked and slaughtered.* My mind repeats his words, over and over.

'Are you listening to me? Now they know you're the last of your line, the only one left who can reactivate the seal. If you go out again, you have to take the pixie with you, so they can't find—'

'Stop,' I breathe.

Kiaran frowns. 'What?'

My fingernails dig so hard into my leather gloves I feel them against my palm. 'I told you my Mother was murdered by a *baobhan sìth*,' I say tightly. 'This is why. Isn't it?'

Kiaran stiffens. 'Aye.'

I straighten, pull my shoulders back and yield to the anger

again. It steals my grief. It absolves my guilt. I put the memories where they belong, in the empty place inside my heart. Just like that.

'I need to leave.' *Time to go and plan a slaughter of my own.*

I think I'll take the *baobhan sìth*'s head when I find her. Make a trophy out of it, just like Derrick always encourages me to. After all, she must have taken my mother's heart for the same reason. That's why she never killed her other victims that way. None of them were Falconers.

I step away from him then, in the direction of my ornithopter. The sun is almost gone now and the storm clouds fill the sky, thick and dark. The soft mist has turned into a light rain. My clothes are damp already. By the time I return home, I'm certain they'll be drenched.

'Kam—'

'Whatever you have to say can wait.' I'm surprised by how calmly I speak. My voice doesn't break, or betray my anger. 'I have an appointment at fourhours with one of my suitors.'

'Don't,' he says. 'Don't do this.'

'Life of a lady, MacKay. Full of tea parties and dancing and husband hunting.'

He looks me up and down. 'Do you think me so foolish that I can't see what you intend to do?'

My cheeks burn. 'You don't want to get in my way, MacKay. If what you've said is true, that bloody nose is the least I'm capable of.'

I stride away from him then. I pause only when he calls my name, but I don't turn around.

'At least take the pixie with you if you go out again. A *sìthiche* powerful enough can track you if you don't.' And I think I hear him whisper, 'Be careful.'

Chapter 14

'Aileana, I was going to tell you,' Derrick says. 'Really I was.'

I pull my legs under me as I sit at my work table. Metal components of one sort or another are strewn all around me. I place the final screws into the valve for the fire-starter I began making yesterday. My mind is almost entirely focused on my tasks, on preparing to kill the *baobhan sìth*. As for when the seal breaks ... one thing at a time. I have a lot to do before then.

Fourhours with Lord Linlithgow had been incredibly strained. I sipped tea and sat with the perfect poise I had been taught since childhood. Father nodded at me with approval, because I spoke only when necessary, like a good gentlewoman.

We discussed things that took little effort for me to lie about: watercolours and dancing and stitching. That I enjoyed reading – but of course not too much, because I mustn't imply I'm a bluestocking. We discussed our plans for Hogmanay, which Lord Linlithgow said would be spent with his sister in the country so they could celebrate the New Year together.

Lord Linlithgow said all the appropriate things and listened politely. A perfect gentleman, the product of what must have been impeccable etiquette lessons. The Aileana of last year would have considered how he'd age, and if we married how we would get on, what our children would look like. She would have found him an attractive match, certainly worthy of a second visit.

The Aileana of last year was a complete and utter ninny.

When afternoon tea was over, Lord Linlithgow left with a smile. I left and screamed into my pillow.

'Aileana?' Derrick's wings flutter once.

'If you'd wanted to tell me that I'm a Falconer,' I say, 'you've had every opportunity to do so. Indeed, I asked you directly just the other night and you expertly evaded the question.'

Derrick flutters to my work table and sits on my bundled jacket. Behind him, the light from the fireplace casts him in a glow of orange flame. I can see his face, the guilt there.

'I was keeping you safe.'

'In what way could keeping me in ignorance be construed as *protection*?' I straighten a piece of wire to add to the fire-starter. 'God spare me from such protection, especially when it involves safeguarding my poor feminine sensibilities from life-saving information.'

I connect the wire to the valve and twist to lock it into place.

'Aileana—'

'Furthermore, I can't believe I had to hear it from Kiaran rather than you. You live in my bloody dressing room.'

This time, he doesn't spew his usual tirade of insults about Kiaran. He simply says, 'I'm sorry.'

When Derrick says it like that, as if he's rather ashamed of himself, I begin to soften. He changed me after my mother died. When I met him, it was the first time I realised that some faeries might be good. That some are worthy of friendship. I can't stay mad at him for long.

I release a resigned breath. 'I forgive you.'

He lands on my wrist, tiny feet warm against my skin. I brush my fingers over his wings once and he flashes a smile that's gone so quickly. 'I have more news.' He speaks tentatively, as if gauging how I'll respond.

My urge to fight rises, an impulse I've never been able to quell no matter how often he tells me that she's killed again. The looming battle with the underground fae should be my priority – should scare the daylights out of me – but it's difficult to suppress the instinctual urge to hunt for her and only her. Until now, nothing else mattered.

I stand and Derrick follows me to the wall, watching quietly as I press the button to reveal the map. 'Where?'

'Glasgow. Two this time.'

So close now. At the rate the *baobhan sìth* migrates, she'll be here within a few days, before the midwinter eclipse. God, if I can kill her before then, I won't have to choose which fight takes precedence. I could go up against all those fae with her defeat so fresh in my mind that I'd feel invulnerable.

I remove a pin from the leather pouch and stick it right beside the other already marking Glasgow. A pin from more than a year ago. She's done nearly a full loop around the country, with only Edinburgh remaining.

I knot two ribbons around the pin. One hundred and eighty-six kills now. I can only hope these will be her last before I find her.

Returning to my work table, I resume my task of completing the fire-starter, more focused than ever. I attach one end of the valve to a metal plate and the other to the fuel reservoir. 'Can you light a wee bit of fabric and bring it to me?'

Derrick stares at me a moment, wings fluttering. A golden halo has begun to spread around him again. He flies to the fireplace, pulls some ribbon from his bag and dips it towards the flame. I set the plate on the table and twist the small fuel reservoir's control button a touch.

'Hover it above the metal plate,' I say.

He lowers the flaming fabric, and just before fire touches metal, a small flame ignites in the centre, where the gas escapes. Derrick tosses the ribbon onto the coals and flies back, to study my invention with fascination.

'What is that?' he asks.

I twist the button a bit more and the flame grows even higher. 'My next weapon.'

'Faeries don't burn,' Derrick points out. 'What's your plan?'

I remove a sprig of *seilgflùr* from the compartment beneath my desk. I'll test a much smaller amount with this device than I used in the explosive watch fob. Another disaster of that nature would surely send the city into a panic.

Naturally, Derrick retreats from the thistle.

'Let me ask you something,' I say. 'What do you think would happen if I mixed *seilgflùr* with whisky and set it on fire?'

Not just any whisky. My father's *best* whisky. Several bottles of old Ferintosh that he only pulls out in exceptional circumstances. *Ah, sweet revenge ...*

Derrick grins. 'Clever.'

I twist the button again to extinguish the flame. Next I set to work constructing an arm-mount for the weapon. Whether a few minutes or an hour go by, I'm so deep in my work that I jump when Derrick says my name.

'There was another reason I never told you.' He glides to my shoulder and tangles himself in my hair. 'I worried about you, when we met. I could never place such a burden on someone so young and anguished if I didn't have to. I *still* worry about you.'

'Worry about what?'

'That you would do whatever it took to kill the *baobhan sìth*, no matter the cost.'

'Why help me track her, then? Why not lie about that, too?'

'Because you deserve vengeance,' he says quietly. 'I would never take that from you.' He hesitates, wrapping strands of my hair around his hands. 'Did I make the wrong choice? Does knowing what you are make your mother's death any easier to bear?'

I wish it did. I'm supposed to be destined and naturally gifted to hunt the fae – a Falconer – and I couldn't even kill one when it mattered most. Some gift. I almost tell him that knowing makes it worse.

I turn my head, close enough that his wings fan my cheek with a soft, comforting breeze. Instead of answering, I say, 'Kiaran said to take you when I leave the house. Why is that?'

'I can shield you,' he says. 'So the others won't know where to find you.'

'Then come with me to the ball tomorrow, and you can worry over me there.'

'A ball?' Derrick brightens. 'I thought you'd never ask. I *love* dancing!'

I laugh and continue my work. I build through the night, determined to finish my project. The hours tick by and I'm so consumed that I don't prepare for a nightly hunt. I don't want to see Kiaran again yet, anyway. The repetition of building is so much easier than dealing with what he told me. I find comfort in placing the metal components, in watching the fire-starter take form with each piece I add. Even when the flame singes my fingers, I continue working, determined not to think of our conversation in the gardens.

As I grow more and more tired, my resolve fails. My eyelids begin to close. And Kiaran's words play again in my mind, a painful reminder that I was always fated for this. To be a killer. *This is what you were born to be. Falconer.*

Chapter 15

The following evening, Derrick escorts me to Catherine's ball. I dance with my partner in a dress of silver-blue covered in pale French tarlatan, devoid of the sewn-on flowers that have become so popular at assemblies. My sleeves are delicate, slightly transparent and drape loosely down my arms. White gloves reach to my elbows and my hair is pulled back in curls that rest on one shoulder. My dress swishes with every step.

'Good God,' Derrick says. 'I cannot believe I agreed to accompany you. I take back my words. Human dancing is dull! When is he going to throw you over his head?'

I smile at my dance partner as I grasp his hand in the reel. I've already forgotten his name – Lord F-Something. He has barely spoken to me, even when I tried polite conversation. His long face appears stuck in a perpetual scowl.

'And when are they going to serve the bloody food?' Derrick's wings tickle my ear as we form a circle again. 'Your friend intends to starve us, doesn't she? How can she starve the guests at her own ball?'

'Shut up,' I mutter out of the corner of my mouth. I regret bringing him as much as he regrets being here.

'I beg your pardon?' asks the woman next to me in the reel, blinking wide blue eyes.

'Lovely dance,' I remark cheerfully. 'Isn't it?'

I grasp Lord F's hand and twirl away, my slippers whispering over the hardwood floor. The walls are decorated with beautiful tapestries of scenes from the Scottish Highlands, and candles atop extravagant candelabras light the room.

Though electricity and floating lanterns are commonplace among the rich, Lady Cassilis has always shied away from technology. The steam-powered carriage is the most advanced invention on her property.

The dance ends and Lord F escorts me from the centre of the room to the refreshment table, where Catherine is standing.

He bows. 'Thank you for the pleasure of your company.'

Then he turns on his heel to go and scowl at someone else. I breathe a sigh of relief.

'Well,' Catherine says brightly, 'Lord Randall certainly appears … agreeable.'

Lord Randall? I wonder why I thought his name begins with an F. I'll remember that and make sure never to accidentally accept any of his invitations to tea, should he send them. He'd probably glare at me until I'm forced to feign illness.

'He acted as if he didn't want to dance with me at all.'

'Oh?' Catherine says, a bit too innocently. 'That's unfortunate.'

'You asked him to, didn't you?'

She flushes. 'Lord Randall had pulled out some snuff near the balcony, and this was your only unclaimed dance. You know Mother can't bear snuff.'

I open my dance card and study the array of signatures scrawled across the paper. 'Mmm. And you can't bear to see me sit through a single dance, apparently.'

Every dance is filled, just as at the Hepburns' ballroom. I suppose it didn't matter that I missed several dances there and disappointed those gentlemen.

I look up from my card just in time to catch glares from a group of ladies across the room. They whisper to each other.

I wonder if they're talking about Lord Hepburn's ball and my five missed dances. To them, I can't be counted on to fulfil even the most basic of my social obligations. That makes me a failure, a woman unworthy of any man's attention, let alone a full dance card.

Catherine follows my gaze and grasps a cup of punch. 'It's best to ignore them, just like you told me to.'

'Ask her. Why. She is starving. *Meeee!*' Derrick wails.

'*Fine,*' I snap, startling Catherine. She stares at me in concern. 'Forgive me, but do you have something small to eat? I fear I might not last until supper.'

'Of course,' she says. 'I believe cook is preparing more refreshments in the kitchen. They should be out soon.'

'Oh, thank God,' Derrick says. 'I'm away to the kitchen to steal the refreshments. Don't do anything foolish while I'm gone.'

He flies off in a blur of light. Thank heavens. When Dante described the circles of Hell, he clearly forgot the one where a hungry pixie sits on one's shoulder for eternity.

'So what happened yesterday?' Catherine says.

'Yesterday?' I say warily.

'At the Nor' Loch,' Catherine says. 'I really didn't mind the walk home with Dona.'

Damn Kiaran MacKay and his meddling. Either he didn't clear her memory, or he shoved some new events in there. Who knows what I'm supposed to remember?

'Aye. It was enjoyable,' I say hastily. Did he make her think we all walked home together, then?

Catherine frowns. 'You walked home by yourself? My goodness, you should have let me stay with you. So you weren't able to fix the ornithopter?'

For God's sake, what did Kiaran do to her? 'It's fixed. Fit and ready to fly.'

'But you just said—'

'Everything is quite fine,' I say, with a wave of my hand. 'So what did your mother think of your little unescorted outing yesterday?'

Catherine shifts her gaze and takes a sip of punch. Even the gold lighting from the candles betrays the flush that creeps up her neck. 'Well,' she says carefully. 'Well. She—'

'Wait! Let me guess. She called you an insolent girl and had you read from *Miss Ainsley's Book of Etiquette and Reflections on Societal Conduct?*'

She scrunches her nose and drinks again. I'll wager she's the one wishing the punch had whisky in it this time. 'Yes to both. Then she had me recite chapter nineteen entirely from memory.'

'Ah,' I say. '"Appropriate Behaviour Inside and Outside of the Home." But surely that's the most *exciting* chapter.'

'You think so only because you've broken every rule stated there.'

I glance at the kitchen door. What could Derrick possibly be doing in there that's taking so long? The pixie could devour a whole table of food in a few short minutes. 'I admit nothing.'

'At least Gavin was there to save me.' Catherine shakes her head. 'If he hadn't interrupted, I'm sure she would have had me recite the whole blasted book.'

'Speaking of,' I say, looking behind her, 'where is your brother? I thought I saw him briefly before—'

'He's right behind you,' a low voice murmurs in my ear.

I jump and Catherine laughs.

Oh, my. Gavin's blond hair is slightly mussed. His wide blue eyes are as lovely as ever. In a mere two years, he has managed to grow much taller than I remember him being, almost Kiaran's height. I have to tip my head back to look at him.

His smile is slow and rather charming. 'All grown up, I see.' His voice betrays a hint of an accent he must have picked up at Oxford.

I realise I've been staring and I blush. I hold out my hand. 'Gavin,' I say. I allow myself that familiarity. 'Or should I call you *Lord Galloway* now?'

A distant relative of Gavin's passed just last year, leaving Gavin with an earldom, a fortune to add to what he inherited from his father, and a few other properties in Scotland. It's strange to hear him referred to as the Earl of Galloway now.

'You can call me whatever you like,' he says, releasing my hand. He glances at his sister with a teasing smile. 'Though I rather think Catherine should use my title.'

Catherine scowls. 'Don't you dare bring that up again.' She looks at me. 'He took me shopping this afternoon and it was all *Lord Galloway* this and *Lord Galloway* that. I've never seen him look so smug.'

'I don't often get to abuse my new title at Oxford,' he explains.

'My,' I say with a smile, 'how unfortunate for you. You've been mistreated, you poor thing.'

Gavin smiles at me in the same charming way he always has, as though he never left at all. There's something comforting and utterly familiar about having him here, as though I'm back in a time before my mother died. Until now, I never realised just how much I missed him.

He leans against the back of a chair set up by the drink table. 'I sense you're not entirely sympathetic to my plight.'

'Of course we're not,' Catherine says. 'You vile man.'

'Do you see how she treats me, Aileana? She's downright vicious.'

'Vicious?' I laugh and ladle some punch into a porcelain cup. Lady Cassilis doesn't even have a dispenser like normal households. 'This from the boy who used to put ink in our tea.'

'I had almost forgotten that,' Catherine says. 'It was really quite awful of you.'

Gavin looks somewhat chagrined. 'I was twelve. You were girls, and therefore an entirely different species.'

'I went home with black teeth!'

'That was the worst part,' Catherine agreed. 'I couldn't smile the whole day.'

'You spoke much less, and Aileana could only visit again when the ink washed off,' Gavin says cheerfully. 'So, you see, goal achieved.'

'Really, Gavin. You are such a—'

'Catherine,' snaps the approaching Lady Cassilis. She looks as severe as ever, lips pressed into a hard line. She gives me a brief frosty glare – a look that clearly says she holds me responsible for her daughter sneaking away yesterday – then returns her attention to her daughter. 'I hope you were not about to insult your brother.'

'Especially when he controls your weekly allowance,' Gavin adds. 'Imagine walking past all those lovely shops without a farthing to your name.'

'You wouldn't dare.'

'Galloway, stop teasing,' Lady Cassilis says. 'You are not about to take away your sister's allowance.'

At that precise moment, Derrick barrels through the ballroom doors, bright as ever. He hovers above my shoulder and lands gracefully on my bare skin.

His wings graze my neck and he hiccups once. 'Glorious lady.' He stretches across my collarbone. 'I have consumed –' *hiccup* '– wondrous, splendid, beautiful honey. And it was –' *hiccup* '– magnificent.'

I almost groan aloud.

Gavin's eyes flicker to Derrick's perch on my shoulder. He

couldn't possibly have seen … ? Gavin's attention shifts to the couples beginning to congregate in the centre of the ballroom. No, I must have imagined it.

The first waltz of the night is about to begin. I place my cup of punch on the table and glance around for the gentleman who signed my dance card earlier.

Gavin bows. 'I believe I should like to dance this waltz with you. Would you do me the honour?'

'Galloway,' Lady Cassilis hisses. 'This is most improper. I don't recall the waltz being on the list.'

'I added it. My house, my rules.' He meets my gaze. 'You wouldn't deny your gracious host, would you?'

'I already promised the waltz to someone else.'

Gavin leans over and plucks open the dance card dangling from my wrist. 'Ah, Milton. You should definitely dance with me instead. He's never been any good at leading.'

'Galloway!' Lady Cassilis is apoplectic. 'That is exceedingly impolite. Let Aileana dance with Lord Milton and stop your foolery this instant.'

Derrick giggles into my ear. 'She's silly. So siiiiilly.' He pats my ear. 'Aileana. *Aileana!* Can you hear me? I know you can hear me. You can hear me. You're hearing me. Say something. Smile. Twitch. Cough once.'

Just then, Lord Milton approaches me and bows. 'May I have the pleasure?'

'Change of plan,' Gavin says, easing himself between Lord Milton and me. 'I'll take it from here, Milton.' He claps Lord Milton's thin shoulder as if they are old friends.

Lord Milton coughs slightly and straightens, looking quite shocked. 'I beg your pardon?'

Gavin smiles. 'I'll take this waltz with the lady.'

'*Daaaaaancing*,' Derrick cries. 'I love *daaaancing*! Tell him to toss you over his head!'

I resist the urge to reach up and flick him off my shoulder. My God, how much honey did he eat? When we get home, I'm going to lock him in that blasted dressing room until the effects wear off. No doubt he's had about a week's worth.

Lord Milton looks dismayed. 'But—'

'So glad you understand.' Gavin offers me his arm. 'May I?'

He drags me away from the group. I only concede so I don't attract more attention from the other guests.

We stand across from one another in the dance line. I glare at him, but Gavin simply flashes his disarming grin, bowing from the waist. He takes my hand and we begin our waltz.

Gavin must have practised while he was away. We used to dance around the drawing room of his house, he and Catherine and I. Gavin would step on my toes or twirl us into a table or cause me to trip over his feet. Now we move well together, each step smooth and graceful. His hand is firm against my back. I swear I can feel its warmth there through my dress and his gloves.

People are already staring at us, and I'm sure they're whispering about me again. I grit my teeth and try to focus on the dance, wishing it to end soon so I can excuse myself.

Gavin whirls me around and I look everywhere but at his face. His shoulder seems like a fine spot.

'I cannot believe you did that,' I finally say.

'I'm really sorry,' he says. 'I came off as an arrogant arse.'

'Indeed you did. Is that what they teach you at Oxford?'

He laughs. 'Direct hit.'

Gavin might be able to joke about this situation, but I can't. I have to behave properly for at least a few balls this season, before the gossip about me becomes even worse. This is an opportunity – perhaps my last – to have some control over my future, to match myself with someone I may grow to like with time. Who knows what kind of man my father would choose for me? My goodness, it might be some terribly overbearing lout twice my age.

'It's not funny, Gavin.'

'Forgive my impulsiveness, then.' Gavin flashes another smile. 'Your dance card was full and I wanted a conversation.'

Derrick giggles. 'Whirling! I love to whirl. Ask him to whirl faster! I see lights. Do you see the lights? Aileana? Do you see the lights?'

'Funny,' I say drily, ignoring Derrick. 'I thought we were conversing perfectly well before the waltz. Before you became – your words, not mine – an arrogant arse.'

He presses his body close to mine and I inhale the sharp, heady scent of soap and whisky that lingers on him. I love that smell. It reminds me of how we were before he left, when he used to tease me at afternoon tea and tug on my curls. It reminds me of everything I felt back then, when I wished he would see me as a woman and not a girl.

'Let's try again, then, shall we?' Gavin says. 'I haven't seen you in two years. How could I not steal you away?'

I laugh in spite of myself. 'A valiant effort. I suppose you don't care about the gossip?'

Gavin raises an eyebrow. 'Not at all. Since when did you?'

'More *whiiiiiirling*!' Derrick sings.

Gavin levels a severe gaze at Derrick. 'What the hell is wrong with your pixie?'

I almost stumble in shock. Gavin holds me closer and smoothly whirls us again. 'You can see him?' I whisper. 'You're a Seer?'

'Seer,' Derrick says in delight. His wings beat faster against my neck, then he giggles again. 'Can't fight like a Falconer. Can't do anything but see. Bloody useless, aren't you?'

'Is he ... my God, is he *drunk*?' Gavin says.

'On honey,' I say distractedly.

'Not drunk!' Derrick hugs my neck. 'I love you. Aileana, I love you. I love your dressing room. All of my things are in there. Beautiful things, nice things, things to mend, things to lie on. *Thiiiings!*'

Gavin does not look amused. 'Would he mind removing himself from your person?'

I'm still reeling from the knowledge that Gavin can see faeries. 'What? Why?'

'When the dance ends,' he says, squeezing my hand, 'meet me in my study.'

I can't. I promised Catherine I would stay and complete my dances. I promised my father I would behave properly and I can't afford any more blasted gossip. Gavin will want answers I won't be able to give. The pixie on my shoulder is the least of it.

'No,' I say, and shift my cheek so I can feel Derrick's soft, comforting wings.

'Please,' Gavin says, 'come when you can. Use the back entrance and go to my study. Leave the pixie.'

Chapter 16

I sneak out of the ballroom during the break for refreshments. Derrick remains perched on my shoulder as I descend the terrace steps into the garden. The night is moonless, and the garden is so scantly lit I almost trip over my feet. My slippers squish through wet, muddy grass. I wish, and not for the first time, that ladies would be permitted to wear sensible shoes to a ball and not these useless things.

I avoid a deep puddle as I approach the back entrance of the house. 'Wait for me here,' I tell Derrick.

'Hmm,' he says, plaiting a section of my hair. 'I have a duty. Don't I have a duty? This feels wrong.'

'I'll be fine,' I reassure him. 'I shan't be long.' I'll limit myself to ten minutes, just before the next dance starts. Surely a faery couldn't find me that quickly if Derrick leaves me.

'Well. All right, then.'

Derrick flies into one of the trees, his halo illuminating the branches around him.

I push the back door open and walk through the rear wing of the house towards the study before he can change his mind. When I reach the thick oak door, I take a breath before opening it.

Gavin looks over from where he's sitting on a leather settee.

A glass of amber liquid rests on the mahogany table next to him. 'Come in.'

It's a comfortable room. The carpet is so thick that my slippers whisper across it. I run my fingers along the detail of a tapestry hanging from the wall, tracing the stitched curves in the design of a thistle. I haven't been in this room since Gavin's father died.

The study is dimly lit, smelling vaguely of wood fire and cigars, the kind Gavin's father used to smoke. The furniture is all glazed mahogany and red leather. Three painted-glass windows face the garden at the back of the room. Next to them, a bookcase rises to the ceiling, stuffed full of the old nature volumes Gavin's father collected.

Gavin's mussed blond hair is shining in the firelight from the hearth beside him. He has removed his waistcoat and gloves, and the topmost buttons of his shirt are undone.

I try to avoid outright staring. I've never seen him so … informal. It isn't proper to be in such a state of undress with an unmarried gentlewoman. But then it isn't proper for us to be alone, either.

'I shouldn't stay long,' I say. 'I need to be back for the next dance.'

He picks up his glass and downs the contents. 'You know,' he says, 'it's been a while since I last attended a society function, but I don't recall ladies carrying around pet pixies.'

I'm once again startled by the reminder that he's a Seer. I've never met one before. Derrick told me they were so rare, he believed them all to be dead. 'He doesn't accompany me all the time. Too unruly.'

Gavin stands, opens a wood-panelled cabinet to remove a decanter and pours himself another dram of whisky. 'He has a loud voice for such a wee thing. Nearly deafened me.'

'You think *that* was loud?' I laugh. 'Pray you never hear him at his worst.'

'Well,' Gavin drawls, 'at least now I know what to do if that ever happens. I'll throw a jar of honey and run like hell.'

'I'll have to try that next time.' He appears to be taking this rather well. Then I notice his hands shake slightly as he sips his whisky. 'Are you all right?'

Gavin downs his drink in a single, quick gulp and pours another. 'The pixie startled me. I've never been that close to the fae before. I keep my distance from them.' He tosses down another glass.

It's unnerving to watch him refill it again, although it's completely understandable, given the circumstances. Gavin is trembling so badly that a dribble of whisky sloshes onto the carpet between his feet. He doesn't appear to notice.

Unable to bear it, I look away and continue tracing the tapestry stitching. 'Did you ... did you always have the Sight?

'No,' he says quietly. 'Not always. You?'

I shake my head. 'When did you know?'

'Shortly after I arrived in Oxford,' he says. 'Believe me when I say I regret ever leaving here.'

'What happened?'

He's silent for the longest time. 'Pneumonia, the physician said. I had the Sight throughout my illness.' His laugh is bitter. 'I thought it was hallucinations brought on by the fever, but when I became well again, it didn't go away.'

I know precisely what that means: Gavin died sometime during his illness.

In the Highlands, they call the Second Sight *taibhsearachd*. I've also heard it referred to simply as The Curse. The potential for it is quietly passed down the male line, dormant until the ability finally manifests – something that happens very rarely. The Sight can only be awakened when one of them dies and is brought back to life. Derrick once told me that when a potential

Seer dies, he is able to experience the other side, to see beyond the veil of the human realm.

If brought back to life, he becomes a *taibhsear*, a Seer. One of the cursed. I would never wish it on my worst enemy.

'No one even told me you were unwell.'

'No one knew.' At my frown, he says, 'I couldn't write. Not to you, Catherine or Mother. What could I say? That rather than studying, I spent half my time poring over superstitious nonsense to find out what was wrong with me?'

'Perhaps you should have come home.'

'Yes, brilliant idea,' he says, scowling at me. 'And what did I find? My oldest friend in possession of a pixie, despite the rather disturbing fact that the fae kill humans without remorse.'

I push away from the tapestry. 'Derrick is my friend.'

'The fae don't have friends,' he snaps, slamming the glass down onto the table. I jump, startled. 'That pixie will betray you. It's in his nature. They're monsters. I've seen—' He stops and shakes his head.

The silence between us stretches vast, filled only by the crackle of wood from the fireplace. I want to say that I know what horrors he's seen, because I've witnessed them all myself.

I sit on the leather couch across from him. 'Tell me why you asked me to come.'

'Aileana—'

'Tell me,' I say again. I almost reach out and grasp his hand, but stop short. 'It wasn't just to chastise me.'

'No.' His fingers trace the rim of the glass, along the pattern etched there. 'It was to caution you. If you keep that pixie, you're already too deep in their world. You should get out now.'

Get out now. It's too late for that. I'll never get out even if I decide I want to. They'll find me, hunt me down to the furthest reaches of this earth because I'm apparently the sole person alive who can fight them. Gavin doesn't know that I'm in this until I'm dead.

'What's it like for you?' I whisper.

He stares into the fireplace. 'I have visions of the kills before they happen, see the events as if I were there.' He finally looks at me. 'I feel what they do, over and over again. I die each time.'

I swallow the lump in my throat. I knew Seers had visions, but not how real they could feel. I've never seen Gavin look so haunted and vulnerable and utterly alone.

'All of them?' My voice almost breaks. I almost ask if he saw my mother die. If he was forced to live through what I witnessed that night. God, I hope not. Only one of us should be burdened by what happened.

'No,' he says. 'The visions are limited by distance.'

I should be relieved, but I'm not. The manner of my mother's death was but one example of the ways in which the fae kill, and they can be so creative in their torture.

'I'm sorry.' Such an inadequate thing to say.

Gavin refills the glass and sits down across from me again, saluting me with his drink. 'I appreciate the obligatory, unnecessary apology.'

'It's the best I can do, I'm afraid.'

I don't know how to comfort someone. I can't reassure Gavin with words or empathetic expressions. I don't have the words, and I've lost all ability to be gentle.

Gavin shifts closer, leaning over the table between us. 'Your turn.'

'I changed. After my mother died.'

When I'm calm, it's easier to distance myself from the memories. I can pretend my damage is less serious than it is. I can be simple. I don't have to tell him that if I let go even for a second, the guilt and pain from that night become so unbearable that they could crush me under their weight.

Gavin pauses, whisky halfway to his lips. His gaze softens. 'Catherine wrote and told me. My sincere condolences.' He drinks again. 'But you're evading the question. What the hell are you doing with a faery?'

'I told you. He's my friend.'

'Are you purposely being obtuse?'

'It's the only answer I have, Gavin.' He's been gone two years and I'm not obligated to tell him anything. My story won't fit into a ten-minute conversation, anyway.

Gavin's jaw tics. 'Fine. If that's how you want to leave it.' He throws his head back and downs another glass. I'm surprised by how sober he still is after all that whisky.

'Does that help?'

'Dulls the visions,' he says. 'Would you like some?'

I hesitate. I've had whisky many a time, but I'm not one to drink to excess. I always have to be alert and ready to fight at a moment's notice. But perhaps it could help soothe my anger, suppress it for just a while, so I can pretend I'm not really broken.

'Aye.'

Gavin pours more whisky and hands me the glass. The liquid burns when I drink, leaving behind a warmth that scorches down my throat. 'Oh, this is good,' I say. This tastes different from my father's stock. Stronger.

'Ideal for brooding.' He sits and crosses his legs. 'And it makes society events almost tolerable. It might even work for unruly pixies, too.'

I ignore his obvious attempt to shift the conversation back to Derrick. After all, Kiaran is a master at switching topics, and I have learned from the best. 'Best stock up. I foresee many more such events in your future.'

'Do you?'

'Indeed.' I take another sip. 'Lady Cassilis has plans for you.'

Gavin pales. 'What do you mean? What plans?'

'She intends to marry you off this season. Congratulations.'

Words that could strike fear in the heart of any bachelor with a title. 'She told you that, did she?'

'Catherine did. Your mother and I continue our reluctant tolerance for one another.'

'Mother reluctantly tolerates everyone. You just happen to be her nearest victim.' He leans forward. 'Tell me. Which poor lass has she deemed a suitable match?'

'None yet. Do you have any idea of your mother's requirements? I'd be shocked if she found anyone who fit them.'

'Just a moment.' He closes his eyes and takes a swift drink. 'All right, let's hear them.'

I take another sip myself, then put down the whisky and tick off each finger. 'Fluent in French and Latin; adept at the pianoforte; dances well; comes from a family of good breeding – preferably Scottish; stitches competently; possesses a modicum of intelligence – but not more than you; is pleasing to the eye; and – most importantly – sufficiently terrified of her future mother-in-law. Now I've run out of fingers. There you have it.'

Gavin blinks. 'You didn't include "wins every game of croquet", "reads to the orphan children" and "tames kittens".'

'If I had more fingers, they would have been, I assure you.'

'If this woman exists, I'm not sure whether to be impressed or apologetic.'

'Both. Definitely both.'

He laughs and his eyes meet mine. For a moment, he looks so much like the boy from my childhood that I fancied myself in love with. Then I see past the smile and realise he's not that boy, not any more. There is a sorrow that hasn't left his gaze since the moment I walked through the door. We'll never be the same, he and I. We've seen too much ever to be the people we once were. We can't go back. I'm beginning to wish we could.

'I missed you,' he says suddenly.

'I missed you, too. You never visited.'

'Fewer fae in England.' He rubs his eyes. 'The visions are worse the closer I am to Scotland. I visited Mother in York over a year ago and didn't sleep at all. I doubt I'll be here long.'

'Then why did you come?'

'To see Catherine properly matched. Mother convinced me to stay through the Hogmanay festivities, but I intend to leave after the New Year.'

I reach forward to grasp his hand. 'When you return to Oxford, write to me this time,' I tell him. 'Or I'll worry—'

A shrill howl pierces the air. As one, Gavin and I turn to the window. The howl wasn't normal, too high pitched to be an animal.

'What was that?' I whisper, moving to look through the window.

'I'd rather not find out,' Gavin replies. 'We should—'

The second howl is closer, louder than the first. The taste of smoke and dust settles quickly in my mouth. Dryness enters my lungs and I heave in air. I bend and cough until my throat aches.

'Aileana?' Gavin grips my shoulder.

'Get away from the window,' I try to say, but the words come out strangled, barely understandable.

Desperately, I shove him. He stumbles back and hits the tea table.

Then something smashes through the window and glass shatters around me.

Chapter 17

A massive creature with a gleaming black mane crashes into me. I grasp soft fur as my back hits the carpet and burns as I'm dragged along. Fallen shards of glass slice my flesh. I slam into Gavin's wooden desk and I bite my tongue so I don't scream.

A hound is on top of me, larger than any I've ever seen. If I were on my feet, it would have been as tall as my chest – standing on all four legs. Dark fur ripples and shimmers in the dim firelight, alternating hues of violet, green and red. Its eyes glow crimson.

A *cù sìth*. The seal has broken further and now the hounds have slipped through, just as Derrick said would happen.

I remain still as the hound carefully sniffs me, as if to make sure that I'm the very person it's looking for. The person it's been sent to kill.

'Aileana!' Gavin sounds so far away, as if he isn't in the room any more.

I grip its fur, digging my fingers in. I know it'll kill me as soon as it confirms who I am and I have to get it *off*. But the hound is too heavy, a good seventeen stone of solid weight on top of me. My corset, even loosely laced, is already restricting my breathing and the faery's heavy body makes it worse. My heartbeat fills my ears, the rhythmic thump growing ever louder, louder.

The *cù sìth* draws in one more breath, then opens its eyes and snarls. Now it knows who I am. *What* I am. Its teeth are pointed, sharp as blades at the tips. I hitch a breath, unable to move even if I wanted.

The hound's irises blaze a bright, burning red. Saliva drips onto my skin, those teeth scant inches from my flesh. My restraining hands digging into its neck are all that's preventing it from tearing into me, and only barely at that. I channel all the strength I have, drawing on the gift Kiaran's told me is my birthright as a Falconer. I close my fists in a harder grip. The heavy fur is tough, thick as armour.

Something slams into the hound and knocks it off me.

'Gavin!' I gasp.

The *cù sìth* shakes Gavin off its back, hard enough to throw him against the bookcase. It sways and volumes fall to the ground. Gavin slumps to the floor and tries to push himself up, but his shoes skid on glass from the broken window.

'Go to the door,' Gavin says. 'We can trap it—'

'And run?' I laugh, a low, throaty sound. Familiar anger burns through my veins now. I think of Kiaran's bloody nose, of the strength he says I possess. 'Not yet.'

The faery rises, stalking towards Gavin with a rumbling growl. Now it knows Gavin is a Seer, and it wants him, too.

'What are you doing, Aileana?'

'You told me your story,' I say. 'This is mine.'

Muscles in the *cù sìth*'s haunches bunch. As it leaps at Gavin, I throw myself at it, wrapping my arms around its middle. We crash hard to the floor. The wooden legs of the settee groan as we roll into it, collapsing onto its side. I reach for my skirts and push aside layers of petticoats, tarlatan and silk to find my *sgian dubh*. My fingers grip the hilt as the hound's snout comes down fast, teeth bared in a vicious snarl.

I strike, thrusting my blade into the *cù sìth*'s belly, where its armour-like fur is thinnest. I try to sink it to the hilt, but then I hear a hard metallic crack.

In shock, I pull my arm back. The *cù sìth*'s fur snapped my blade in half.

Before I can do anything, the hound lifts its snout and releases a shrill howl.

I stagger and almost fall as the thin, high wail resonates through my skull. I press my hands over my ears to muffle the noise but it doesn't work. Glass shatters. Shards from the other windows and the whisky decanter clatter to the floor.

My legs buckle. I sink to the carpet and glass cuts into my knees. I open my mouth to scream, but no sound escapes. Just when I think I can take no more, the howling stops.

I gasp and pull my hands from my ears. My gloves are wet with blood that must have come from my ears. In that second's distraction, the *cù sìth* leaps for me again. I throw myself to the ground.

I'm not quick enough. The hound's razor-sharp claws slash my back, tearing fabric and skin. *Bloody hell!* The hound careens into the desk behind me and the wood cracks under the impact, splintering right down the middle.

'Gavin,' I call, pulling myself into a crouch behind the fallen bookcase. He's hiding behind one of the overturned settees. 'Are you hurt?'

'My ears are bleeding. I have a nasty headache. I'm trapped in a room with a murderous faery and I blame you.'

'That's fair.'

I mentally curse myself for being so unprepared. I took Derrick's protection for granted and left my weapons stashed in Lady Cassilis's garden.

My fingers brush the *seilgflùr* necklace at my throat. This is all I have, the only object on me that can hurt a faery. As the *cù sìth* turns to leap again, I yank the necklace off.

'Aileana,' Gavin says. 'Don't—'

Before the *cù sìth* can move, I throw myself at it. We collide hard enough to squeeze all the air from my lungs.

Back on the ground, I try to get my arms around it, but the *cù sìth* bucks me off, strong paws hitting me square in the stomach. I double over and it rakes my shoulder with its claws. I bite my tongue, blood erupting in my mouth.

I go after it again, grappling with the creature until I manage to roll us so I'm on its back with the *seilgflùr* grasped tight in my fist. I wrap the plaited strand around the *cù sìth*'s neck and pull hard. The hound lets out a single gasp, then a tiny whimper.

The *cù sìth* bucks against me, trying to sink its teeth into my arm. *Seilgflùr* burns through the faery's thick mane and the stench of scorched fur and flesh fills my nostrils. I pull away and tighten my hold on the improvised thistle garrotte until its body begins to weaken. Its muscles relax as it gasps for air again.

When I'm sure the faery is too weak to fight me, I unwind the thistle and prise open its mouth. Before I can change my mind, I shove the necklace inside.

The moment the *seilgflùr* leaves my fingertips, the faery disappears from my sight. Invisible teeth slash open my gloves and scrape along my skin as I pull my hand out. I judge where its snout is and grip it to hold its jaw closed. The faery barely struggles before it dies.

As I slide off the *cù sìth*'s back, its power fills me. Release. It's like the light, joyous sensation of flying, of being lifted away from the world. Away from pain and guilt and death to a place where I'm convinced I'll never hurt again. I'll rise until the oxygen leaves me, until—

'Aileana?' a voice whispers.

If I had been standing, I would have fallen. The ache of anger settles in my chest, where my memories are, my guilt. They retreat inside the crevasse within me again and the lightweight flying joy is gone.

I open my eyes to see Gavin standing above me. He sighs with relief. 'I thought you were dead.'

'I'm a difficult lady to kill.'

He grasps my hand. 'I pride myself on being a calm individual,' he says, his breath visibly laboured, 'and I rarely resort to hysterics. But, when the situation calls for it – *what the hell was that?*'

'I killed a *cù sìth*. Surely you didn't miss it?'

'When you said you weren't running, I assumed you had a plan. I did not realise that plan was a fight to the death.'

'What else is there?' I hiss in pain as Gavin pulls me to my feet.

'You're hurt,' he says, drawing my forearm towards him to inspect my injuries. His fingers graze the spot where the *cù sìth*'s teeth scraped. These wounds will become my newest badges.

I scan the room and wince at the damage. 'Sorry about your study. I'm shocked no one came running with all the noise we must have made.'

Nearly every piece of furniture is broken. Splintered wood lies all over the floor, mixed with broken glass from the windows. Almost the entire collection of nature volumes is now strewn about the room. The only thing unaffected is the fireplace; logs are still aflame and glowing. I consider it a victory that I didn't end up getting burned.

'You can't hear much of what goes on in this part of the house,' he says, 'and I'm sure the music helped. I've never been so relieved that Mother insisted on hiring an orchestra.' He looks at our feet, where the dead hound would be if I could see it. 'At least they couldn't hear *him* – I was certain the damn howl would burst my ears.'

As Gavin inspects my injury more closely, I say, 'It's not

really a howl – that's its power. Our human ears just interpret it as sound— *Ow!*' He'd poked at my blasted cut.

'Sorry. This looks deep.'

'Well, don't poke at it,' I tell him. 'It hurts like the devil. Do you have any stitchers?'

'Mother doesn't keep them.'

I sigh. 'Of course not.'

'Aren't you the least bit concerned that some random faery attacked us, or that you're bleeding all over my study?'

'Not the least bit. And these are not the first scrapes I've endured, I assure you, nor are they the worst.'

He blinks. 'You know, I don't find that particularly comforting.'

'It wasn't meant to be.' I pull out of his grasp and wobble to an upturned settee to perch there.

'I told you my secret,' he said, 'but you kept yours from me. What else are you hiding?'

'You were gone two years and you returned yesterday. Why should I tell you anything?'

Gavin stalks over and grasps my gloved arm. I bite my lip to keep from crying out, because the bites hurt so badly. He reaches into a trouser pocket and produces a kerchief.

He regards me silently as he wraps the injury on my arm and ties the cloth. 'Isn't it a burden?' he asks. 'It was for me.'

He and I both have to play parts, to pretend to be the people we once were. Both of us might be broken in some way, but the difference is that I'm a killer. I have darkness to yield to that he doesn't possess.

'I can't think about it,' I say. 'If I—'

Gavin turns his head sharply towards the window. 'Oh,' he says. 'You.'

The faint taste of gingerbread and sweetness tickles my tongue. 'Derrick,' I say.

'I can't understand a damned thing you're saying,' Gavin says to thin air. He looks at me. 'He's your pixie. You speak to him.'

'Derrick, show yourself. I can't see you.'

Derrick appears at the same time as Gavin says, '*What?*'

The pixie flies to me. 'I was waiting in the garden and I thought I heard *cù sìth,* so I flew up and checked, and—'

He starts blathering rapidly in his own language, as if he's entirely forgotten he should be speaking in English. His wings whir, each word punctuated by heavy buzzing.

'Repeat that last part in English,' I say.

'There's an army of them,' he bursts out. 'And they're almost here.'

Chapter 18

The pain from my injuries dissipates instantly. All it takes is the promise of battle and a warm glow spreads through my body. Back to the hunt, back to the chase.

'How many?' I ask.

'Two dozen,' Derrick says. 'Maybe three.'

I shut my eyes briefly. The weapons I brought with me won't be enough to kill that many. 'Find Kiaran and tell him I need help. Try not to insult him while you're asking.'

Derrick doesn't argue, for once. 'What about you?'

I stride to the window, an easy escape route now the painted glass is shattered. Thank heavens Gavin's study is at ground level. 'I have weapons nearby, and more in my ornithopter.' And that's where I keep my spare *seilgflùr*. Kiaran might take it away during my training sometimes, but I've never lost it in a fight before.

Derrick flutters to my shoulder. 'They're on Princes Street and moving in this direction. Can you make it to Charlotte Square?'

'I certainly hope so, since I don't have any *seilgflùr* on me,' I murmur as I hoist myself onto the window ledge and prepare to jump into the garden.

'You don't have any—'

'Don't worry about me.' I let my cheek rest against his wings for a moment. 'Go.'

'Be careful, won't you?' Derrick's light glows brighter as he takes off.

I rip my already-torn petticoats and dress, until they stop just above my knees where the bottom of my pantalettes show, so the fabric won't hinder my movements. I toss the extra material to the floor and straddle the windowsill. My slipper brushes against some of the tall bushes below.

Rain falls steadily outside and dampens my leg. I shiver at the cold night air and the breeze on my bare arms. I'm about to drop down into the space between the bushes and the wall when a hand closes around my wrist.

It's Gavin, and he looks furious. 'You intend to go out there?' he asks. 'And you can't even see them, can you?'

I try to pull myself from his grip, but he only tightens his hold. 'I never said I could.'

'You implied it.'

'I'm un-implying it now.' I grin. 'I have other means.'

Gavin studies me intently. 'Did you choose this?'

Leaning in close, I press my cheek against his, a touch that goes against every social rule I've ever been taught. It's the excitement of the hunt that courses through me, a savage hum. I'm beyond propriety, beyond etiquette.

'I revel in it.'

I jump to the soft soil below. My slippers sink in and rainwater pools around my feet. The garden is misty, even darker than before now that the storm clouds have gathered thicker. Rain slicks my bare shoulders and the breeze only makes it more frigid. My heart slams in my chest and I want to run again, to give chase.

I'm about to sprint across the grass when I hear a thump behind me. Gavin. 'What do you think you're doing?'

He straightens, tall and elegant. 'I'm coming with you.'

'Don't be ridiculous.' I pivot on my heel and stalk in the direction of my hidden weapons.

He catches up to me and says, 'It's not ridiculous at all. You said yourself that you can't see them.'

'So?'

'Let me see for you.' His features are shadowed, his breathing ragged.

'No,' I say sharply. 'I won't involve you. I'm sorry I already did.'

'This is my choice, Aileana.'

'Why?' I ask. 'Why would you do that for me?'

He looks away from me, frowning, as if remembering something he's tried so hard to forget. 'I tried to help once,' he says. 'One of the people from my visions. The faery was so fast, it broke six bones in my body before I reached her.'

'Gavin, I—'

'I think you're foolish,' he says harshly. 'I think this is an exceedingly terrible idea that will probably end with both of us being killed. But if I'm to die, I'd rather do it knowing that I tried to help and didn't run.'

There's nothing I can say to that. I know that Gavin should go back inside where it's safer, where he isn't with someone being hunted by the fae. They'll hunt him too once they figure out he's a Seer in the company of a Falconer. I can't believe I'm doing this.

I sigh. 'Fine.'

God, I hope I don't regret taking him with me. As we round the house to the side garden, I listen for any indication of a faery nearby, but hear nothing. Instinctively, I reach for the reassuring thistle necklace but find it gone – then I remember in a rush that I can't see or hear them.

Swearing softly, I ask, 'Do you hear any howls?'

'Not yet.'

'Good.'

I crouch next to the hedges and pull my satchel out from its depths, reaching inside for my boots. I yank the blasted slippers off my feet and shove them inside in the bag, then lace the boots up. It's always best to be prepared in case I'm forced to run. If only I had thought to bring some spare thistle with me.

Next, the holster and my lightning pistol, two items I will never be without again. I slide the leather strap around my waist and pull the buckle tight.

'Do you always hoard your weapons in other people's gardens?' Gavin asks.

'Only when I don't want to be killed,' I say brightly.

The remains of my wet silk gloves stick to my skin as I tug them off and toss them into the bag. The crossbow comes out next. Then the fire-starter, which is now attached to a gauntlet of my own design. I slip it on and buckle the straps around my wrist and upper arm, where the fuel reserve rests.

I pick up the crossbow and check its interior chamber. It holds twelve slender quarrels, their tips dipped in a tincture distilled from *seilgflùr*. Designed to break on impact, the tips contain small wads of the thistle, enough to kill a faery almost instantly. The cranequin's reloading design loads and draws the quarrels automatically after each one is fired.

'Well,' Gavin says. 'You've certainly been busy.'

'A lady has to find something to do between painting landscapes.'

'You know, I'll never look at a woman in the same way again. I'll wonder if she's hiding weapons under the hedges.'

I grin. We edge around the bushes to the side gate, which opens with a squeak. I duck my head out and check the dark street for any people. Empty but for pools of light from the street lamps and a lone parked carriage. Gavin looks out with me and nods once to indicate it's clear of faeries, too.

The only noise filters from Gavin's house, where laughter and chatter and fiddles playing the Highland schottische drift through the open windows.

This is the first dance after the refreshment break, the one I had promised to return for. I've given away this dance, and the ones that would have followed. There will be no way to repair my reputation after this. Come tomorrow, it'll be in tatters. I'll be lucky if my father doesn't take the first offer he gets for me. This is my last chance to go back before that happens.

Gavin touches my shoulder. 'Are you all right?'

I make my choice. The same one I'll always make. I choose survival. I choose the hunt. Because Father would tell me, *duty first*, and *this* is my duty.

Gavin scans the road. 'Aileana. I hear them now.'

I reach for his arm and pull him along as I sprint past his neighbours' houses, shoving a low-hanging branch out of my way. I dodge through the gate into the public garden, which shuts behind me with a sharp clang as loud as a gunshot. We rush along the path between the trees inside. My boots slip and sink into deep mud.

'Where are we going?' Gavin asks.

'If we're quick enough, we might be able to bypass them on the way to Charlotte Square.'

Out of the garden and into the street. Our feet pound through puddles, our swift steps clack on the cobbles. As I enter St Andrew Square between the dim light of two street lamps, the rhythm of my breathing is strong, swift. I grip Gavin's hand, our fingers slippery from the rain.

He skids to a halt and I almost pitch forward onto the ground. 'Gavin?' I ask. 'What is it?'

'Something's wrong,' he says. 'I don't hear them any more—'

He sucks in a breath and turns, his eyes focused on something behind me.

I spin around but see only cobblestones, wet and gleaming. Then a smoky taste settles thick in my mouth. *It's here.*

Gavin shifts his grip to my wrist. I hold the crossbow tighter as he draws me in towards him. 'Steady,' he breathes. 'It hasn't seen us yet.' He moves to stand behind me, eyes level with the weapon's sight, and lifts my arm to aim it.

I tuck the stock of the crossbow against my shoulder and let him direct me. As he does, the abrasive aridity of the *cù sìth*'s power settles on my tongue, so potent that I can't gulp it down. So I inhale deeply through my nose, my focus on holding the crossbow so intent that the taste is but a mere niggling thing.

Gavin whispers a single word. '*Now.*'

I pull the trigger. A sharp yelp startles me enough that I barely notice the faery power coursing through me.

I heard it. I stare at the street and watch as blood pools on the cobbles.

Kiaran's soft voice echoes in my mind. *You're the only one who could do this.*

Seabhagair. Falconer.

Gavin tightens his grasp on my arm and rips me from my thoughts. 'Come on!'

I follow his lead and we race by the white stone residences in St Andrew Square, all of them dark save for a few lights in the windows below street level where the servants will still be working. Gavin pulls me through a break in the bushes that leads to the garden in the centre of the square. Branches tug and snap. My skirts rip even more. We race past the fluted column of Melville's Monument and back into the street.

Gavin stops again and I almost smack into him. He pulls me in front of him and repositions my arm to shoot. 'There,' he whispers. He's so close his breath tickles my ear.

I pull the trigger. A high wail resounds in the square and faery power crashes into me. I relax against Gavin. My chest expands and I arch my back. This time the sheer rapture of the kill is almost enough to overwhelm me. Almost.

Gavin wraps an arm about my waist and whirls me around, keeping his other hand tight on my wrist to direct the crossbow. 'Now!'

I don't hesitate, and the quarrel has hardly been released before Gavin turns me again. His foot slips between mine and he holds me firmly against him to direct me with more ease.

With his palm pressed against my stomach, he repositions me. 'Again.' I shoot.

We continue like this, Gavin indicating where to shoot and me pulling the trigger. Blood and rain glisten on the street. Street lamps illuminate the gory scene in an orange haze, obscured by thick mist. My damp hair falls into my face as Gavin aims my arm again and I fire. I'm breathless with exhilaration, with the power filling my lungs, my chest. We spin again and again – our killing dance. Our feet occasionally falter on the uneven cobbles, but my aim remains true.

Gavin's breath is soft against my neck. I can feel his every inhalation and exhalation. We move together even better than we did in the waltz. Our steps become cohesive and unified, smoother after each shot. Every kill moves us faster, hones my awareness of the fae. Soon I'm able to shoot before Gavin speaks, sensing exactly when he needs me to.

The overwhelming taste of smoke from *cù sìth* power dries my mouth, but I'm too sated to care. I feel light as air, invincible and strong …

Until the moment Gavin positions me once more and I hear a telltale click when I pull the trigger. I'm out of quarrels.

'Your pistol?' Gavin asks.

I step out of his embrace to sling the crossbow over my

shoulder. 'I need that to defend us on the way to Charlotte Square.' Smiling, I tell him, 'Don't worry – I have a surprise.'

I twist the button to activate the fire-starter and reach into the satchel for a glass bottle. I shove it into his hands. 'Here. A distraction. Toss it at the nearest *cù sìth*.'

For a moment, I think he almost smiles. Then he lobs the bottle three feet from where we're standing. The glass breaks on impact and a *cù sìth* yelps.

I reach towards the sound, palm out, and flick my wrist. The mixture of alcohol and *seilgflùr* flowing from the fuel reservoir ignites in an instant and fire explodes from the centre of my glove.

All around us, I hear the desperate baying of *cù sìth*. Their thin, high wails ring in my skull.

Gavin reaches into my bag and grabs for another bottle, but the howls shatter it before he can throw it. Damn! I hadn't expected that when I packed these. The stench of *seilgflùr*-laced alcohol and scorched fur stings my nostrils. My ears are ringing, bleeding from their cries. I don't think I can stand it much longer.

I push Gavin in front of me. 'Run!' I scream, though I know he can't hear me – his ears are bleeding too. Blood and rain-water stream down the sides of his face and stain the collar of his shirt red.

We run again, and the air is so cold, my breath exhales misty-white. The howls die down behind us. We race down George Street, occasionally skidding and stumbling on the slick cobblestones. My head aches so acutely that I'm struggling to see. As we flee, my wet, torn dress clings to my thighs, and each movement is stiff. My muscles burn with the effort.

'Are they close?'

Gavin grimaces and I know he must be hurting, too. 'Keep running,' he says.

New Town is laid out in a symmetrical, grid design. Easy for travel, but there are no narrow closes to hide in, no underground passageways, nor dark wynds to cloak us from view. That makes it exceedingly impractical for escape. The street is too long and straight to outrun them.

'We need to split up,' I gasp between breaths.

'What?' Gavin glances at me in surprise. 'No. That's—'

'Go down Young Street,' I say. 'Meet me at my ornithopter in the centre of Charlotte Square. They'll follow me.' I have to draw them away from Gavin before they surround us again. My lightning pistol only holds eight capsules – not nearly enough to defend us if that happens.

One glass jar in my bag was thick enough to survive the howls. I pour its contents in a line as far as it'll go across the road. Fire bursts from my palm to ignite it.

'That buys us a minute,' I say. 'Now go!'

I barrel off towards Rose Street.

'Damn it, Aileana!' Gavin calls after me. 'You can't see them!'

I don't need to. Kiaran told me that the *seilgflùr* would be a hindrance, that I needed to learn to fight without it. Now is the perfect time to test that.

But as I race down the street in the direction of my home, the dull smoky taste of faery power saturates the inside of my mouth and constricts my breath to a wheeze. They're close. And I'm not fast enough to outrun them.

That's when I see the clock tower, the electrical heart of New Town. In the absence of any narrow closes to duck into to slow them down, and without any *seilgflùr* on me to defend myself, it's the only way I can reach Charlotte Square alive. I hurtle towards the door and crash my foot through the wood, sending splinters of oak and dust flying.

I bolt inside and dash up the stairs. Each step is punctuated by the click of the rotating metal gears that generate New

Town's power. Electricity buzzes around me, like millions of agitated bees.

Think!

Up, and up, and up another flight of creaky wooden stairs towards the clock's illuminated face. I run through a plan in my mind, as quickly as I can. The clock tower has only two entrances – the one I already came through, and another on the side of the building that faces Princes Street at the bottom of the tower's shaft. If I can reach it, that'll split up the faeries and force them to take the long route around the road to find me. It might buy me a few minutes to run, and that's the best chance I have to make it to the ornithopter.

Over buzzing electricity, the clock's *tick tick tick* only makes me move quicker, more frantically. I shove through a door, over the bridge that connects the two sides of the tower. I have no idea how quickly *cù sìth* can run, but I'm sure I haven't bought myself much time.

Up another flight of stairs, and then I reach the top, finding the narrow wooden platform to be much smaller than I expected. I teeter on the edge and my arms flail. A *cù sìth* howls outside. *Calm,* I tell myself. *Be calm.*

With a narrowed gaze, I scrutinise the working gears below me, how they weave and circle each other in a regular pattern. The rope of the driving weight hangs from the ceiling to the bottom of the shaft. If I don't catch the rope when I jump, I'll have a few short seconds to fall and pray that I don't break something when I hit the lower cog. If I take longer ... well, that won't be a pleasant outcome either.

I look behind me. *Tick tick tick.* Time is running out. The taste of faery power is so pungent in my mouth that it hurts to swallow. I tear more fabric from my petticoats and wrap my single bare hand. The taste grows, a burning dryness that spreads inexorably down my throat.

Tick tick tick. I'm gasping for breath now. If I don't jump soon, the others will be waiting outside the other door to tear me to shreds by the time I get down there. I don't have a chance of fighting them blind; there are too many.

Something snaps at my dress. Invisible teeth or claws shred the material around my thighs. I cry out and kick reflexively. My boot connects with the faery I can't see and it yips in response.

Tick tick tick. Too late to change my mind and run back down the steps. So I whirl and throw myself off the platform.

Chapter 19

My grasping fingers close around the rope of the driving weight. Friction burns through the fabric wrapped around my hand and I grit my teeth as I slide down, coming to a halt above a massive rotating gear. My legs dangle in the air, toes barely brushing the thick metal below me.

The biting pain in the palms of my hands is almost enough to slacken my grip. The muscles in my arms bulge with the effort of keeping me in place as I stare down at the turning cog below my feet. It moves in and around smaller cogs, revealing a small opening during each rotation. Beneath it is another flat cog that spins.

In … around … out. There's the opening. I follow the pattern until I memorise it, until I'm certain I'll get the timing right. At the precise second the opening appears, I release the rope and let myself fall.

The moment I'm airborne, I close my eyes. The first person I think of – completely without reason – is Kiaran. Of his rare almost-smile, and those brief, extraordinary glimpses of vulnerability that he shows when he momentarily loses control.

My body crashes hard onto the metal cog in a graceless heap. *Hell and blast, it hurts.*

I struggle to my feet and stand unsteadily at the edge of the cog. As the cog rotates, I notice another opening below through which I can see the wooden floor at the bottom of the clock tower. Another drop, not terribly far at all. I scan the walls of the shaft to see if there is anything to help me climb down.

A series of metal bars project from the tower's interior wall. When the gear circles again, I leap. My hands close around one of the bars, and I swing my body to the next, then to another, and drop to the wooden floor in a crouch. My teeth click together hard from the impact.

For once, I'm grateful to Kiaran for the endless practice fights. If he hadn't trained me so ruthlessly, I wouldn't be at all able to plunge down clock towers or ignore the pain of landing. I get up, like he always tells me to.

The maintenance door is where I thought it would be. It takes me two tries to kick it open, until the hinges groan and the wood cracks. Dust flies into my face as I hurl myself outside and suck in the cold night air.

Across the road, I spot the scaffold-covered ivory monument in memory of Sir Walter Scott at the edge of the Nor' Loch. Princes Street, finally.

'Almost there,' I mutter.

The muscles in my legs ache in protest as I race towards Charlotte Square. The rain is falling even harder now, spilling from my hair onto my forehead as I pass blocky white buildings containing small stores. My breathing hitches when the smoky dryness overwhelms my mouth again. The hounds bay once more, so close. I never thought they would find me again this quickly, and my fire-starter won't be as effective in this kind of rain. But I still have my pistol.

I jerk the weapon from its holster. The conductor spines rise and the core rods open as I spin and aim for a spot that makes the taste in my mouth scorch my tongue. Praying my instincts are correct, I pull the trigger.

The invisible hound yelps and I grin in triumph, watching as the electricity snakes outward from an invisible point. I would savour the kill, but I don't have time.

I dash up the street, breath heaving, and the welcome sight of my ornithopter encourages me to run faster. Gavin is already inside.

'Aileana.' He sounds relieved to see me.

I sling the crossbow and satchel off my back and toss them inside. Then I jump into the leather seat, flipping switches to start the machine, and press my feet down on the pedals for an emergency take-off. The ornithopter lifts quickly with a strong flap of its wings.

On the ground below, the hounds howl, their frustration echoing across the square. I only hope that Derrick and Kiaran can kill them, since I couldn't.

Rain batters the metal-boned wings as we rise over Charlotte Square. I tilt my face to the falling droplets and exhale a long breath. My body relaxes.

We soar through the misty skies over Edinburgh. Clouds cloak the buildings in New Town, but the orange glow of city lights filters through. The air is colder up here, wetter. It seeps through my soiled dress and I shiver.

I stare at the hazy city below and let my muscles slacken, content to never move again. I long to close my eyes and let the flying machine take me far away, away from my responsibilities and a broken seal that threatens the lives of everyone I care about.

After a while, we rise up over Leith and the machine's rocking soothes me. The flapping wings sound vaguely like a heartbeat, soft and reassuring. *Whoosh-whoosh, whoosh-whoosh.*

'Thank you,' I tell Gavin once I've calmed my breathing. 'For helping me.'

'Always prepared to come to the aid of a lady in need,' he says. 'It's my gentlemanly duty.'

I glance at him in amusement and lean back in my chair.

'They were looking for you,' he says softly. 'Weren't they?'

It's so quiet up here, no sounds except falling rain and heart-beat wings. I swing the helm towards the Forth and study the masts of ships protruding through the fog.

'Aye.'

'You're not a Seer,' he says.

His features are unreadable. I wish I could understand what he's thinking. It would help me decide how much to tell him, how much danger I'm willing to put him in.

Gavin stares out at the calm sea fog, his breathing shallow. 'I don't know a damn thing about you any more, do I?'

It hurts to swallow. My throat tightens and I think I might choke on my response. 'I'm the same person I've always been.'

I don't know why I feel compelled to lie to him. Gavin has seen the fae, he knows what they do to people. He helped me at great risk to himself. Yet I want him to look at me the way he did earlier at the ball before Derrick came back from the kitchen, without a question in his eyes. With a certainty that I am precisely the same woman he left two years ago.

Instead, I'm sitting in a dark flying machine, wearing the torn remains of a gown that's covered with blood and dirt. I lost count of how many fae I just slaughtered. I'm a ruined girl who made her choice. This is who I am, a night creature who thrives on death and destruction.

'No,' he says. 'You're not the same person. So what are you, Aileana? I deserve to know after that.'

I unbuckle the fire-starter from my arm and jerk the gauntlet off my hand. I toss it into the back of the ornithopter. *What are you?* I don't even deserve to be a *who* any more. He must think I'm no better than the creatures I hunt.

'I'm human,' I snap. 'That's what I am. Just like you.'

'Like me?' Gavin says. 'I would never have been able to move as fast as they do. I can't fight like that. You killed those things without—' He sucks in a breath. 'I'm sorry, I didn't intend to sound accusatory.'

My anger fades. I grasp the hem of what remains of one of my petticoats and tear off a section to bind my injured hand. 'I understand. You've been quite calm, all things considered,' I say.

'A mere façade,' he says, waving a hand. 'It wouldn't be very manly if I screamed like a wee bairn, would it?'

'Not very.' We're both silent again. I continue steering the ornithopter, higher above the mist, closer to the stars.

'What happened?' he asks.

He shared everything with me, told me what it means to be a Seer. I responded by changing the topic and keeping my secrets. I treated him the same way I do Kiaran, the same way I treat Catherine. What kind of woman does that make me, that I don't trust anyone any more? Not even the people I love?

'My mother,' I say quickly, before I regret it or change my mind and lie again. 'She was killed by a faery. That's why.' *That's why I'm like this.*

I hear his breath catch. 'Not an animal attack, then.'

'No.' I try to stop the memories from resurfacing, to keep them in the empty space where they belong. 'Not an animal attack.'

'And now you enjoy killing them, don't you?' He says it so quietly I almost don't hear him.

My cheeks burn. 'Aye.'

I'm surprised by how ashamed I am of that admission. If this were Kiaran, that fact would have been a point of pride. But Gavin must be realising that his childhood friend has traded femininity for brutality. That the lass he knew is utterly gone.

'You're what the pixie called you – what was it?'

The word. The word that changed everything. 'A Falconer.'

'This doesn't change anything, you know. I still care for you.'

He sounds hesitant now. 'But you scare the hell out of me.'

Under normal circumstances, my chest might ache at his words. Gavin's childhood friend was the very epitome of proper. She had no secrets, experienced all the appropriate emotions. She would have run from the faery when Gavin had asked her to. She would have relied on him to protect her.

My apathy ought to be an impenetrable thing, a wall that keeps me safe and protected. I shouldn't care what he thinks. I want to pretend that he's a silly boy who simply doesn't understand me any more. Except he isn't a silly boy. And this truth is as sharp and painful as any blade.

'I don't blame you,' I say.

His gaze feels heavy in the darkness. 'This is going to kill you. Hunting them.'

'That may be,' I admit, 'but I can't go back to what I was. Planning for parties and marriage – that's not for me any more.'

Hunting is in my bones. The voice in my head that commands, the force that drives me. It is a part of me that will never leave, not until I die.

'I don't think,' he says, 'it's for me, either.'

I almost tell him *I'm sorry,* like I did back in the gardens. *I'm sorry for getting you involved. I'm sorry you feel like you need to protect me. I'm sorry you can't go back, either.* But I don't. I'm about to try something light and cheerful when Gavin grips my hand.

'Gavin?'

'There's something behind us.'

Chapter 20

I'm reminded immediately that I don't have the thistle necklace on any more. Thank goodness for the spare bundles in the ornithopter. I pull out a fresh plaited strand and knot the end. When it's secure around my neck, I look out behind us. My fingers dig into the leather seat and I gasp. Damnation.

Sluagh. A dozen of them.

The ghostly creatures sweep their enormous, graceful wings, mist gathering around them. They look almost dragon-like, with skin an iridescent, glimmering shade of pale grey, so thin that their angular, pointed skeletons are visible beneath. They're more powerful than the *cù sìth,* though not physically strong. The skin covering their necks and wings is thin enough to cut through with a blade.

'What are they?' Gavin asks.

'*Sluagh.*'

'That's impossible,' he says. 'The *sluagh* haven't been spotted for—'

'More than two thousand years,' I finish for him. 'There's something else I might have kept from you.'

'Really?' he drawls. 'I'm shocked.'

One of the *sluagh* shrieks and speeds towards the ornithopter, flapping its translucent dragonfly-like wings so fast they blur. The others flank the leader on both sides. As they draw closer, a cold, slick, heaviness slides along my tongue.

Gavin says, 'We should run this time. We really, really should—'

The middle *sluagh* opens its mouth and a breath of pale white mist bursts towards me with surprising speed. I grab the rain visor, throwing it up just in time to block the *sluagh*'s vapour. The heat of the blast is powerful, hot enough to incinerate flesh, and the metal visor burns my fingertips. Only after the *sluagh* flies past do I drop the visor, biting my tongue against the pain.

'What the hell was that?' Gavin says.

I pull myself to my feet, hands shaking. 'I should have mentioned they breathe burning mist, shouldn't I?'

'Your ability to communicate is atrocious, did you know that?'

I ignore him and sit in the front seat again, flipping the switch to increase speed. As the wings flap faster and faster, the machine begins to strain with the effort it takes to fly this quickly. I have never tested the ornithopter under such extreme conditions, but the engine should hold. The ornithopter shudders under my feet a little more than usual but continues to fly smoothly.

The acceleration puts us slightly ahead of the *sluagh*, but we're still not moving fast enough to outrun them. I shove the pedals to the floor with my toes. The machine jolts and the wings flap harder.

'Here,' I say, standing. 'Take the helm.'

Gavin slides into the driver's seat behind me. 'A few words of instruction might help.'

The *sluagh* are so close now. My heart slams against my ribs. I have to do something before they overwhelm the ship.

'Make us harder to hit and keep us over the water.' I spare him a fleeting glance. 'And I'll make sure you don't die.'

'Very considerate of you. A woman after my own heart.'

I kick a lever near my feet. The central compartment swings open and I pull out a massive crossbow. It's fixed to a swivel-stand, so I can pivot the heavy weapon freely and hold it more steadily than if I had to support its full weight. I've also added handles with a quick trigger mechanism. The inner chamber has the same reloading feature as my smaller design, only it shoots quarrels twice the size.

'So,' Gavin says, 'I take it we're not running, then?'

'Correct.'

I line up my eye with the sight, but just as I pull back the handles, the ornithopter dips. The crossbow's gears tick and the quarrel fires. A miss. *Hell and blast.* I've practised with the crossbow before, but never in these conditions.

'Steady, Gavin,' I say.

'I'm *trying*. Do you realise how long it's been since I've flown one of these?'

I smile grimly and focus my gaze through the sight again. The ornithopter shudders and swings, but I move with it. I breathe deep. On the exhale, I release another quarrel. It hits the *sluagh* right in the neck. A perfect shot.

The *sluagh* screams and explodes in a burst of light. The resulting mist surrounds the flying machine, swirling and coating everything in a blast so frigid that the raindrops on my arms freeze.

The *sluagh* let out angered, deafening squawks and begin to circle the machine in a frenzy, lustrous eyes bright and glowing now. There are so many of them. I swivel my crossbow to aim, but they're too fast. They clamour around the machine and I duck as one tries to claw at me with its talons.

Suddenly, they dive at us.

'Hard left!' I scream to Gavin.

The ornithopter lurches and I almost lose my balance. The

sluagh scream again and swoop towards us for a second pass. They are agile, swift. One of them blows more mist at me, and I barely duck in time.

I struggle to stay on my feet to stare down the crossbow's sight, aiming for the *sluagh* that tried to claw me. *Breathe,* I tell myself. *Steady.* I pull the handles again. The quarrel flies into the air, lightning-quick, and strikes the *sluagh*. The faery explodes and cold mist blows into me.

The *sluagh* dive again with piercing shrieks, wildly flapping their wings. Talons grasp at my clothes and slice my bare shoulders. I drop into a crouch. All I can see are veiny, flapping wings.

Before I can get back to the crossbow, one of them hurls itself at me. I brace myself for the heavy impact.

But it goes *through* me. And I feel as if my soul is being torn from my chest.

I try to draw a breath, but the inhalation becomes a gargle at the back of my throat. My throat closes and cold constricts my lungs, spreading under my skin and freezing my heart. The *sluagh* reappears above me, arcing its body to swoop down again.

Gavin.

I manage to turn my head. The faery is flying towards Gavin, who is turned away. Because he trusts me, trusts that I'll save him.

I move, biting back a scream at how much it hurts to move through the ice. I leap through the *sluagh*'s frigid body and slam into Gavin, pinning him to the floor of the ornithopter as the *sluagh* glides over us.

For a second, I rest my cheek against the slick, wet skin of Gavin's neck. My body aches and I shiver from the cold.

'Your knee is digging into my spine,' Gavin says.

'You're welcome,' I murmur. My tongue is heavy.

I pull myself to my feet and stumble, my muscles protesting the sudden movement. My vision is dotted, unfocused and blurry. I close my eyes hard and shake my head once. If Kiaran were here, he'd tell me, *Stand up* and *move*. A second spent dwelling upon pain is enough time for an enemy to regroup.

'Are you all right?' Gavin asks.

'Fine.'

I grab for the crossbow and swing the weapon around on its stand, blinking through the stars in my vision to take aim. I yank the handles back. Another miss. I swear softly and try to still my body, clenching and unclenching my freezing fingers to make them warm again.

Calming myself, I look through the sight. A *sluagh* screeches and heads straight towards me again, flying so fast I barely release another quarrel in time. It slices into the *sluagh*'s neck and the creature erupts into white vapour.

Faery power flows into me, warm and soft. My body is so charged, so energised, that my blood runs hot again. I aim the crossbow, swiftly firing one quarrel after another. I kill with such efficiency that the *sluagh* are unable to come near the flying machine. Gavin turns the ornithopter in circles and my wet hair whips at my face as I shoot another *sluagh*. My sodden petticoats cling to my thighs and rain slaps my skin. Ice from dying *sluagh* coats my arms.

And each time I kill, my agility improves. My mind becomes clearer. Murder is the simplest thing in the world, uncomplicated by emotions. It's just me and my victims. Hunter and prey.

My chest expands with triumph, with utter elation. My mind chants a single word as I kill. A benediction. A prayer. *More.*

Only one *sluagh* remains. It circles through the clouds, a wary ghost. My quarrels are gone and I have only my pistol left. My victim needs to be much closer for me to shoot accurately. I know what I have to do.

The *sluagh* sweeps underneath us, still cautious. I reach into the middle compartment shelf to pull out a canvas bag and draw my lightning pistol.

'Aileana,' Gavin says.

The *sluagh* rises towards us, preparing for an attack. I smile at Gavin, breathing so hard from my kills that I think my lungs might burst.

I pull my arms through the pack's straps. 'You take care of my bairn.'

He blinks. 'I beg your pardon?'

'My ornithopter.'

I step up onto the seat and fling myself into the sky. Air rushes around me. Gavin screams my name, his voice echoing through the clouds. What's left of my skirts flutters upwards as I gain momentum and I have to shove them down to see.

I hold the pistol out in front of me and point the barrel at the *sluagh*'s head as I plummet. *Steady now.* I pull the trigger.

The *sluagh* bursts apart in a cloud of electricity and mist. Cold, thick fog surrounds me as I fall through it, and ice adheres to my skin and hair.

I pull the cord attached to the pack on my back. Silk material billows above me and jerks me skywards. I close my eyes, shoving my pistol into its holster as I glide over the water. The sea laps below me, comforting, rhythmic. A soft breeze caresses my cheeks as I descend.

I take that last moment of calm to feel the faery's power wash over me, tickling along the inside of my skin in a soft electric current that weaves its way through my body. I let myself relax in the comforting embrace of my parachute and listen to the waves, to the hiss of wind and patter of rain around me.

Until I have no choice but to land in the water. So I grab the latches attached to my parachute and sink as close to the surface as I dare before pulling on them to release the canopy.

I fall the last few feet and it's like hitting stone, so frigid that

I gasp and almost suck water into my lungs. Then I'm pulled under, dragged down and down by the Forth's ever-changing current.

I fight and kick above water to heave in air, opening my eyes to gaze up at the low, heavy clouds and the onslaught of rain. I can barely move my limbs, but I force my legs to tread, to stay afloat any way I can. I fight against the current. My legs buck and cramp. I swallow and the saltiness makes me gag as I'm sucked underwater again.

I kick myself back up and look around frantically for land. A short distance from me is a rocky beach.

Swimming there is excruciating. The heavy, waterlogged material of my dress floats around me and pulls me down. It is an encumbrance, a test of my strength. I endure it, swimming with the help of the incoming tide, until I can crawl on my stomach across the jagged rocks of the beach, on land at last.

I cough up the water in my lungs and roll onto my back. Rain sprinkles my face, sliding down my cheeks. I press my palm to my chest and feel my heart thumping steadily within. *Alive. Still alive.*

I watch the clouds glide overhead, their rapid movement dizzying. I'm uncertain how long I lie there. Time ceases to matter. All I care about is the organ beating firmly beneath my fingertips.

'Aileana!'

I turn my head slowly. My vision is hazy, but I recognise Gavin racing towards me. The ornithopter is parked on the beach behind him. I never even heard it land.

'Aileana, thank God.' He kneels beside me. 'Are you hurt?'

'No,' I croak, licking salt off my lips. 'But I'm just going to lie here a moment.' My words are slurred. 'See? Hard to kill.'

Gavin swears softly as he removes his frock coat and lays it on top of me. 'If death ever comes to take you, I imagine it will be due to your own stupidity.'

'Water's cold,' I say.

'That's because you're lying in it.'

He's trying not to yell at me, I think. The sensible, gentlemanly approach to a woman he no doubt believes to be absolutely insane.

I smile wanly and study the way his blond hair curls into the collar of his filthy shirt. A memory flashes, unprovoked, of the day he left for Oxford. The silly vow I made to myself that when he returned, he would never treat me as a second sister again.

The thought makes me laugh. 'Do you know, I wrote to you while you were away.'

Good heavens, why did I say that? My mind is muddled, unfocused, probably because I'm so cold.

Gavin glances at me, startled. 'I beg your pardon?'

'Letters. Five of them.'

'I never got any letters.'

I laugh again, rather drunken sounding, and shift my bottom on the sharp rocks. A wave barrels in and completely drenches my legs again, but I still don't bother moving. I think I'll pass out if I move. 'Never sent them.'

'What did they say?'

'Dear Gavin.' My teeth chatter around the words. 'Today I accidentally smeared ink across my mouth. I thought of you.'

'You did not write that.'

'I did.' I grin. 'If I wrote one today, it would say: Dear Gavin, today I saved your life. Please remember that before you reproach me.'

He pulls me into a sitting position. Another wave comes in and I begin to shudder uncontrollably. My teeth click together so hard that my jaw aches.

'As I recall,' he says, pulling his coat more tightly around me, 'you tackled me from behind.'

'So?'

'How do I know I was in any real danger? Maybe you just wanted a bit of a cuddle.'

I narrow my eyes. 'Indulging in fantasies now, are we, Galloway?'

'My fantasy at this precise moment is to enjoy a dram or two. I could use the drink.' He glances at the flying machine. 'I don't suppose you have any whisky in your ornithopter.'

'I don't drink and fly! And even if I had some, you wouldn't be allowed any.'

'Harpy.'

'Cad. I'm still sitting in water.'

'Would you like me to help you up?'

My legs probably won't work. The swim to shore took so much effort, I doubt my body will listen to me any more. 'Um,' I say, a little uncertainly, 'no, thank you.'

I plant my hands down on the devilishly sharp rocks and manage to stand on shaking legs. My legs buckle. *Oh, damnation ...*

Gavin grabs me around the waist. 'I have you,' he murmurs.

I raise my eyes to his, but it's too dark to see him clearly. He is so quiet, his breathing as slow as the waves that lap around my legs. As rhythmic as the rain falling around us.

How can he be so calm about all this? I was the one who brought destruction into his life. Now he'll never be able to hide again, not here. He'll never be safe around me.

If my shaking legs would have allowed it, I'd have released his shoulders then. 'I don't blame you if you never want to see me again after tonight,' I say.

'Why wouldn't I?'

'Because,' I say, a bit helplessly, 'because you've tried to avoid the fae and I brought them right to you.'

'That thought had occurred to me.'

I nod. He doesn't have the skill to fight them off. A Seer's energy is a boon to any fae that finds one. He'll be just as hunted as I am.

'But if I did that – walked away – what kind of friend would that make me?'

'An intelligent one,' I say.

'But not a good one. That's not the kind of man I am.'

I stare up at him. I wonder if he thinks me damaged, beyond saving. Whether he is only here out of obligation, because we grew up together. I may not be his responsibility the way that Catherine is, but he treats me as though I am. He always has.

'Gavin,' I say, hesitant. 'I-I think—'

'What?'

I need control. I shouldn't feel this vulnerable or exposed. It's exhaustion from the fighting, it has to be. 'I can walk the rest of the way on my own,' I say.

'Right. I'll let go of you, then.'

He gently releases his hold. I squeak as my legs collapse under me. I would have fallen if he hadn't caught me again. In the dark, I see the flash of his teeth in a wide grin. He's enjoying this.

I almost swear at him. The smug bounder. 'I don't suppose you could—'

'Shall we dispense with the preamble? You want me to carry you.'

'Do you have to sound so satisfied about it?'

'Why not?' he says cheerfully. 'It's not every day I get to carry a lady.'

I glare at him. 'I should have let the *sluagh* take you.'

'Ah, but then you would be left alone on this beach, cold and wet with no one to swing you up in his strong, waiting arms.'

'You're enjoying this, aren't you?'

'Immensely.' Gavin lifts me, shifting so I'm cradled against the front of his body. I'm surprised, he did it very well. I wonder how many ladies he's carried away from freezing beaches.

My spine remains entirely straight and stiff as I rest there. Where am I supposed to put my blasted hands? I clumsily pat his shoulder and settle on grasping the fabric of his shirt. What do other women do when they're held? Swoon a bit?

'Er,' I say, a bit awkwardly, 'thank you?'

Gavin's finger brushes the outside of my arm. A reassuring gesture, but it feels intimate, utterly familiar. I tense at first, then relax and settle more comfortably against his chest.

'You hate asking for help, don't you?'

For once in my life, I want to be honest with someone. What would it be like not to hide or pretend? I've kept too many secrets from him already and that almost got him killed. But I've already grown so used to lying, I don't think I can do anything else.

'I have to take care of myself,' I say.

Gavin pauses. 'I know.' He stares down at me, serious now. 'But you shouldn't turn down an offer to be cared for. Some people aren't fortunate enough to receive one.'

Chapter 21

'You know,' Derrick says from his perch on my windowsill, 'I think I have something of a headache this morning. I didn't think faeries got them.'

He glows softly in the morning light that filters through my bedchamber window. I notice him eye the shiny parts of my lightning pistol, which I've taken apart to clean after my swim in the Forth. If I don't watch him, he'll steal some of the pieces and I'll find them tucked away in random places around my dressing room.

'Perhaps it's a honey-ache,' I say. I put aside the ramrod and pick up the pistol's barrel to push a small bristle brush inside. 'That's the result of eating too much of what wasn't yours.'

I pause to massage my temples, grimacing when I catch my reflection in the far mirror. I look like I've been hit by a locomotive.

Worse, I'm the throes of a fever that hurts my head and makes my body ache. My injured hand looks absolutely disgusting under the gloves I'm wearing, with my palm all torn and blistered. I had to dress myself again to hide my various injuries from Dona. One more morning like this and the poor lass might think she's been sacked.

'But your friend offered it,' Derrick complains. 'So she might not have explicitly *said*, "Derrick, please eat all of the honey in my kitchen," but it was implied by the mere fact that she *has* a kitchen.'

'Do you know,' I say, 'I don't think there was a word of sense in any of what you just said.'

'I think I'm still fuddled.'

'Now *that* makes sense.'

'So,' he says brightly, changing the subject, 'how did our Seer do last night? I don't think I like him, you know. He's too well groomed. Never trust a man without some indication of chaos, I say.'

'You spent five minutes with him.'

'One can learn a lot in five minutes,' he mutters and squints at me. 'You have sand in your hair. It looks silly.'

I pat the top of my head and cringe as some grit falls to the floor. I've washed my hair three times already and apparently I still haven't got it all out.

Casually, I brush the sand off the table. 'Thanks for that.'

'You're welcome, precious.'

With a sweet smile, I ask, 'And how was your adventure with Kiaran last night? Nothing quite like killing faeries to form an everlasting bond, aye?'

Derrick glares. 'Could you possibly form a working relationship with someone who isn't so crabbit all the time?'

'What did he do?'

'Stole all of my intended victims! There I was, getting ready to fly around and collect my trophies, and he jumps in and swings his blasted glairy-flairy blades and kills everything.' Derrick snorts. 'Damn the *daoine sìth*. Smug, arrogant bastards.'

Someone taps at the bedroom door.

'Come in.'

Dona enters, her head down. She dips in a silent curtsy, as if waiting to be acknowledged. Her demeanour is rigid, even shyer than usual. She hasn't looked like this since the day she came to live here three weeks ago. I tilt my head to try and see her expression properly.

'I beg your pardon, Lady Aileana,' Dona blurts.

My maid isn't particularly chatty, but she usually offers me a tentative smile when she visits. 'Are you well, Dona?'

Dona flinches. 'Indeed. My lady,' she adds hastily. She sounds so formal that I wince.

'Bloody hell,' Derrick says and flutters over to Dona. 'Do we have to break her arms to get her to state her purpose? *Why. Are. You. Here? We. Are. Deconstructing. Weaponry!*'

At least Dona's sensitivity to the fae is inactive right now, or she'd hear him screeching in her ear and then we'd never get a word out of her.

'Is there anything I can help you with, then?' I ask.

Dona clears her throat. 'Lord Douglas requests your presence in his study.' She visibly swallows once and hesitates before adding, 'Directly.'

I straighten in my chair, immediately alert despite feeling hellish. I've been dreading this moment all morning. 'I don't suppose you could tell me what kind of mood he's in?'

Explosive anger, calm anger, deadly anger, or I'm-sending-you-to-a-nunnery anger? I wonder if I should escape through my hidden bedroom door and hide somewhere until he calms down.

Dona's head snaps up and she blinks those wide blue eyes of hers at me. Then she takes a step towards the door and fidgets. 'Um. Well.' She sounds unsure. 'My lady. He's ... I'm not certain I can describe it, exactly.'

Oh dear. I rise from my chair, ignoring the wave of dizziness that threatens to engulf me, and nod once. 'All right. I suppose I'll have to get this over with, then.'

'What's he going to do?' Derrick asks, flying out of the room behind me. 'Set fire to you?'

I walk slowly down the hall and cringe in anticipation of what Father will say. 'I'm sure he'd find that a very tempting proposition.' I keep my voice low, in case Dona is still close enough to hear.

'Well, if you want, I can eat his ears. I like ears.'

At any other time, I would have laughed. Now, all I can do is say distractedly, 'Not necessary.'

'The offer stands.'

I wave him off and he flutters back upstairs. I continue towards the door of my father's study. Father sits behind his thick oak desk, pen scrawling rapidly across his letter-paper. He doesn't look up when I stop at the doorway.

His study has never been warm and welcoming, not even when my mother was alive. The heavy, dark furniture looks too big for the room. Even with the large window and the curtains open, light never seems to brighten the space. I study the shelves crammed with massive law books and journals and the travel journals he collects. Next to the window is a dark brown leather couch, and on a table in front of it is a whisky decanter with a single glass next to it.

I glance at my father in surprise. It's not even noon and he's already drinking. This cannot be good.

Tapping the doorframe, I say, 'Father.' Drat. What were the first words of the excuse I rehearsed again?

He nods to the chair across from his desk. 'Sit.'

'Father—'

He puts up a finger to silence me and continues to write. I shut the door behind me and wait for him to finish. I try to control the tension in my body, inhaling and exhaling deeply. As he writes, I only grow more anxious and my head is already pounding.

Finally, Father puts down his pen and laces his fingers together. He raises his eyes and ... my word, they're harsh and intense.

'Do you know why you're here?'

I nod slowly, fighting my first instinct to watch my toes instead of meeting his gaze. So much for my rehearsed speech. How is it that, in the matter of a few minutes, he can make me feel like a mere child?

'Of course you do,' he says, his voice hard. 'It has occurred to me that I have been far too lenient with you since Sarah died.'

I gulp. 'I don't—'

Father stands, and his wooden chair creaks against the floorboards. I wince.

'I've indulged you,' he continues, without acknowledging my interruption. 'I've given you an allowance without any objections to your spending. Ignored the gossip about your unconventional hobbies and your improper behaviour.' He walks to the window and looks out. 'Even though you've shown little respect for what I've done for you, I've given you chance upon chance. I lied for you. I defended you. A wasted effort, was it not?'

My heart speeds up, painfully fast. 'I can explain,' I whisper.

I'm still not certain what he'll do to me today. This is the first true emotion my father has ever shown me, and it's terrifying.

Absent father, broken daughter, dead mother. I can't miss what I never had.

Father turns from the window. 'Oh, you can explain? You can tell me why you left the ball last night? Why you were nowhere to be found until this morning, when you apparently arrived home in your ornithopter and several people witnessed you in an indecent state of dress with Lord Galloway?'

I'm painfully aware of every second that ticks by, every movement my body makes. It feels like an eternity before my fever-addled mind processes what's happening.

Oh, God. *Oh, God.* I thought this was just about leaving the dance. I hadn't realised someone had seen me with Gavin when we came back. How could I have been so stupid not to notice anyone about?

If I had been in my right mind – if the damn fever hadn't started the moment Gavin set me in that ornithopter – I might have. I would have come up with a plan to get us both home unnoticed.

There's not even the slimmest chance of a gentleman offering for me now. I'm utterly ruined. My neighbours saw me dirty and wet and freezing, wearing a scandalously torn gown. I had clutched Gavin's shoulders once before stumbling into the back garden. The gossip must have spread like wildfire.

I could have explained my absence from the ball. I could have said that I wasn't feeling well and had to leave. But I can't give a reason for why Gavin and I were in Charlotte Square in the early hours of this morning, especially with me dressed like that.

I shake my head. The words won't form and I can't even think up a lie to save me. 'I-I wasn't—'

'Wasn't what? Dressed indecently? With Lord Galloway?'

It doesn't matter what I say. His opinion of me won't change. He's never had any use for me and now he's burdened with the daughter who let his wife die, who he'll never marry off now.

'Those things are true,' I whisper, closing my eyes briefly. 'Father, please. Gavin – I mean, Lord Galloway – he—' My voice shakes and I steady it. 'He has been nothing but honourable towards me.'

My throat is already swollen from the illness, so it hurts to swallow. I cough once, repress another. My eyes burn.

I should be relieved that I don't have to pretend to be proper any more. I shouldn't care. I shouldn't. But ruin is the thing all noble ladies fear the most. My future may not include surviving on the charity of others, but I've shamed my mother's memory. Father and I are stuck with each other now.

'Irrespective of that,' he says, 'Lord Galloway has graciously offered for you. I have accepted on your behalf.'

I barely register his words, unable to properly piece them together amid my fevered thoughts. It can't be true. Surely it can't. 'Pardon?'

'I accepted his offer,' Father says. 'You are to be married forthwith, before the talk intensifies.'

'No.' I say the word before I can stop it. This isn't right. Gavin doesn't deserve this, especially not after helping me.

Father leans forward. 'Understand this, Aileana. Galloway has agreed to wed you in a fortnight. You *will* marry him.'

I stand and have to grasp the arm of the chair so I don't fall. 'This is *my* future, not yours. Am I to have no say in the matter?'

'The only other choice I had,' he says coldly, 'was to put a bullet in his heart from forty paces.'

'If my honour needs defending,' I say, 'I can do it myself.'

Father looks tired. 'Do you think this is only about you? *Your* honour?' He closes his eyes. 'One night of thoughtless frivolity and you have managed to tarnish our family name, my standing, and your mother's memory. What would *she* think, Aileana?'

My resolve almost shatters. 'Please don't. Don't make me do this.'

Father returns to his papers, picking up his pen again. 'Marriage to Lord Galloway is the only option you have.' He looks past me again, same as always. 'Now, I'll be busy this week making the arrangements. In the meantime, I expect you to conduct yourself in public in a manner befitting your future husband. Duty first.'

'And what I want isn't important,' I whisper to myself.

Chapter 22

I stare through the window of the drawing room, listening to the pattering rain outside as heat from the fireplace warms the back of my neck. Raindrops fall onto the windowsill and splash onto the carpet. I don't care how much the cold draught from outside makes me shiver, even with the fire roaring in the hearth. Because I feel nothing, empty. For once, I relish the lack of emotion. Every pretence I've built around myself is perfectly intact.

A couple walks by the steps leading up to the front door, their umbrellas dripping. They stop and the woman whispers into the man's ear, discreetly nodding to our house. They both shake their heads. Society, it appears, is more accepting of a rumoured murderess than a ruined woman, whether she's reported to be engaged or not.

I rub my moist temples. The dull headache has returned, exacerbated by the fever that continues to burn. Absently, I reach to my shoulder blade to scratch the wound the *cù sìth* gave me. It doesn't hurt any more, but it itches like the devil.

Only then do I notice the taste of earth and nature that has become so familiar. Then there's a knock at the door. 'Kiaran?' I say in surprise.

Kiaran saunters in and shuts the door behind him. I might

have been more shocked if I weren't so ill. First, that he came *here* to see me, and second, that he doesn't even have the decency to announce his arrival in the proper fashion.

'Still alive,' he says, leaning against the door. 'I'm impressed.'

He has a different wardrobe from when I last saw him at the Nor' Loch, but it's still expensive gentleman's clothing. Immaculate black trousers, white dress shirt, black overcoat. No hat. That might be too proper for him. All his clothes are soaked through, his hair clinging to his forehead, but he doesn't even appear to notice.

'What are you doing here?' Rethinking that, I put up a hand before he can respond. 'Actually, don't answer. Just get out, MacKay.'

I should be more furious than I am that he kept my heritage from me, that he never told me about the seal or the danger the city was in. But I can't summon the anger I would have felt. My father has just laid out my entire future for me, and stolen what little choice I had left. I'm in no mood to deal with Kiaran right now.

He doesn't appear to be at all surprised by my reaction. 'I came by for a visit.'

'I don't want you here.'

Without any preamble, he strolls over to the fireplace, picks up one of the small vases from the chimneypiece and inspects it. I almost tell him to put the bloody thing down and explain himself, but I bite my tongue and watch him. He doesn't look remotely uncomfortable being in my home, or touching things without asking permission.

'That's unfortunate,' he says. 'Your pixie told me you accept visitors during the day.'

Damn Derrick. I should never have sent him to Kiaran last night while under the influence of honey, the little traitor.

I sip my tea and watch him study the ornaments as though

he's never seen such things before. 'I recant what I said. I give you permission to cut out his tongue.'

'What a generous offer,' he murmurs.

'Didn't it occur to you,' I say, 'that I have a butler who will happily announce your presence? Being invisible doesn't give you leave to sneak inside someone's home. It's called courtesy, MacKay.'

Kiaran sniffs one of the vases. I frown. What is he doing? Is this some strange faery habit I'm not familiar with?

'Your butler,' he says. 'Large chap with the beard? I introduced myself to him, told him I was here to see you, and then I compelled him to go away so he wouldn't interrupt us.'

'I've noticed that's becoming a habit of yours.'

Kiaran holds up the vase. 'Why do you have empty pots on your chimneypiece?'

'They're decorative.'

He regards it with what might be disappointment, but it's too difficult to tell with him. 'Seems a waste. Do you know, they're quite useful for storing viscera.'

I choke on my tea and cough. Then, unable to stop myself, I bend over and keep coughing. My throat is thick and swollen and it's painful to swallow. I put up my hand in indication of an apology.

'Are you ill?' Kiaran asks, setting the vase on the chimneypiece.

I nod and recline against a pillow when the spasm passes, wiping the dampness from my burning forehead with a kerchief. 'I fell into the Forth.'

'That doesn't sound like a well-thought-out plan.'

'There were *sluagh*.'

Kiaran is quiet for a moment. 'Ah.'

'Ah?' I snap. 'I nearly die and that's how you respond? *Ah*?'

Kiaran shows no response to my outburst. He regards me

calmly, detached as always. 'I told you to keep the pixie with you,' he points out, sitting on the settee across from me. 'You look terrible.'

'We don't all possess indestructible fae skin,' I say.

I almost expect him to smile. He taught me to wear my cuts and bruises with pride, was the first one to call them my badges of honour. Instead, I see the briefest flash of ... *something* in his eyes. Guilt? It's gone before I can truly tell.

It's odd and uncomfortable when Kiaran displays any kind of emotion. I've become used to him as cold, impassive. But every so often he expresses something deeper and I wonder if his emotions are really that fleeting, or if he just wants to deceive me into believing they are.

No, I can't think about that. There I go, treating him as if he experiences emotions the same way humans do. 'Why are you *really* here?' I ask bluntly, despite how impolite it is. 'It isn't just to visit.'

'If you must know, I came to make sure you weren't dead.'

I almost cough up my tea in shock. 'My goodness, MacKay. Were you worried about me?' *Please say no like you always do, so I won't make the mistake of humanising you again.*

Kiaran's expression betrays nothing. 'Do you pine for my concern?'

'Certainly not.'

He looks amused. 'No? Then what *do* you long for?'

Vengeance is what I desire most, the only thing I've craved strongly enough to kill for. After all, it's the oldest motivation in the entire world. People might think it's love, or greed, or wealth, but vengeance gives you life. It strengthens you. It makes you burn.

I don't answer him. Instead I ask, 'What about *you*?'

Kiaran smiles. This time I can't tell if it's genuine. 'Looking for something redeemable in me, Kam?'

'Looking for the reason you hunt.' *What stirs those fleeting emotions that I so rarely catch?*

'Shouldn't my enjoyment of it be reason enough?'

Except that's not it at all. I've watched Kiaran kill. This is as personal for him as it is for me. But if he doesn't want to tell me why, we have far more pressing matters to attend to than our own vendettas.

I reach for the tea and sip to soothe my aching throat. 'We need to find the seal before Tuesday, MacKay.'

Kiaran moves to sit next to me, alarmingly close. Though I know he doesn't care at all for the rules of society – indeed, he doesn't even appear to be aware of them – I can't help but be a wee bit startled when he acts with such familiarity. Old habits die hard and all that.

'We'll find it,' he says. 'But make no mistake, we'll have to fight to close the seal again. We'll have to prepare for war.'

I almost stop breathing. To the *daoine sìth,* conquest is never their only goal. Kiaran told me that they were known for slaughtering the strongest of their enemies, keeping the rest alive to feed on. They call it the Wild Hunt, and it almost drove humans to extinction thousands of years ago. If the *daoine sìth* are released, the fae have the power to decimate us all until only ashes and ruin and the weakest humans remain. I don't imagine it was easy to trap them in the first place.

I can't focus on finding the faery that killed my mother now, especially not after last night. The number of fae in the city will only grow.

'War,' I whisper. 'How many will leave the mounds during the eclipse?'

'There were thousands fighting in the battle before the Falconers activated the seal to trap them.'

It sounds as if— 'You were there,' I say, suddenly realising. 'Weren't you?'

If I hadn't been watching him so carefully, I might have missed the emotion that flickers in his gaze, something almost sorrowful. 'I was there,' he says, very deliberately. 'For most of it.' And just like that, he relaxes, as if he's realised exactly how much he's given away. 'The Falconers killed many, but I expect hundreds will escape from the mounds on Tuesday. Maybe more.'

Kiaran's voice is as calm and dispassionate as ever. I almost ask about that battle two thousand years ago, how he escaped the same fate as the rest of the fae who fought. But he's back to being closed off, and I'm certain he won't tell me.

'You're just being pessimistic with that figure, aye?' I ask.

Kiaran blinks. 'No.'

I plunk my teacup on the table and almost spill its contents. 'Isn't that going to make this a rather one-sided fight? Two against hundreds? Good heavens, I'd think with the amount of power you all possess, faeries might observe some of the niceties of battle.' I wave a hand. 'Fight fairly and all that?'

It's a stupid thing to say. I know the fae will do whatever it takes to destroy and conquer, and they do nothing fairly. But Kiaran doesn't realise I'm trying so hard to pretend that I have hope, that I'm wishing for a different outcome for us all. Because for us to survive, we'll need an army of our own. And we don't have one.

'We did not gain dominion over every continent by being polite,' he says coldly. 'Make no mistake, when the *daoine sìth* come, they will annihilate everything in their path. People will die. Your friends, your father, that blasted pixie included. They will tear this city apart and, in the end, they will burn you from the inside out. I never said a thing about fairness. I taught you better.'

God, how Kiaran brings out the monster in me. All he has to do is imply that I'm naïve and rage burns me hotter than my fever.

'*You* make no mistake,' I say. 'I won't let any of that happen.'

Kiaran's lip twitches. His usual almost-smile. 'Train to survive, Kam. Else you'll lose.'

'We've been training for a year!'

The almost-smile is gone. He's back to looking at me like I'm a complete idiot. 'You've made me bleed once. The other Falconers would have prepared their entire lives for this battle.'

My head starts to pound. I swipe the sweat off my brow. 'Do you see anyone else here, MacKay? I'm all that's left. And I'm as prepared as I'll ever be.'

I've failed at doing everything expected of me. My reputation, my future – both are out of my hands. I won't allow Kiaran to let me doubt the part of me that seeks vengeance. That part will stop at nothing until the fae are decimated.

He leans towards me, eyes never wavering from mine. 'Then show me. Prove it.'

In an instant, I forget all etiquette and manners. I disregard my illness. Kiaran has challenged me. He wants proof? I'll show him.

I attack. Our bodies collide and we're on the floor. We crash into the legs of the table and teacups clang together. I shove aside my petticoats for the *sgian dubh* at my thigh, and strike right for his throat.

Kiaran smacks the blade out of my hand, sends it careening across the carpet. *Damn him!* 'Try harder,' he tells me.

Try harder? I smash my fist into his face. I roll off him and scramble for the blade. Friction from the carpet burns my elbows. Before I reach it, Kiaran drags me back.

I deliver a hard kick to his shoulder and lunge for the blade again. My fingers close around the hilt and I launch myself at him. We slam into the wall and the bookcase next to us shakes. My blade is firmly pressed against his throat. 'You wanted proof.' My voice is raspy. 'There it is.'

We breathe together, our bodies so close. I can feel the pulse at his neck and its cadence matches my own. His gaze meets mine and I swear there's pride in his eyes. Kiaran is proud of me.

My vision clouds then, and dots flash in front of my eyes. I stumble. My grip on the blade falters and it clatters to the floor. My skin is blazing so hot that it hurts and my legs barely hold me. I cough and cough and cough, so hard that my entire body shakes.

Kiaran steadies me, his hand pressed firmly against my back. 'Kam? Your skin is burning.' He lifts the hand from my back and his fingers come away bloody. 'And you're bleeding.'

I lick my scaly, chapped lips and manage to speak. 'We just fought. Of course I'm bleeding.' My words are slurred, as though I've downed a quarter bottle of whisky.

'This isn't something I did,' he insists. He tries to turn me, plucking at my day dress to get a peek at my back.

I push at his chest. 'What are you doing?'

'Stop being ridiculous and turn around.'

'No.' I smack his hands. 'Stop this at once, MacKay.'

'You're being difficult.'

'You're grabbing at me like a vile drunkard.' I smack his hands again. 'What do you intend to do? Use your faery wiles on me?'

Kiaran glares at me. 'Let me see it, Kam.'

'I'm perfectly all right. It's just one of my injuries from last night.'

'It's bad enough that blood is soaking right through whatever it is you're wearing. Now turn around.'

I sigh with exasperation and walk to the couch. I sit with the back of my dress facing him. 'Fine. There. Are you happy now?'

Kiaran settles on the couch with me, his body warm behind my own. 'I need to unbutton your dress.'

'I *beg* your pardon?' My cheeks burn, from either the fever or embarrassment – it's hard to tell. Thank goodness he can't see my expression. 'You must be joking.'

'My powers do not extend to seeing through a lady's clothing.'

I say a mental prayer, hoping that this ends quickly. 'Fine,' I relent. 'If you must.'

When he unfastens the first button, I begin to shake. This is too intimate. Just when I think I have myself under control, that my façade is impenetrable, he does something new to shatter it. To remind me that I'm still human, and that no man has ever touched me like this.

But he's not a man, I remind myself.

Another button, another, then another. I try to slow my racing heart but I'm unsuccessful. I have always been taught to keep a strict, physical separation from men. Even while dancing, gloves and clothing are a shield.

Hell and blast, I should have worn a corset and chemise, but the wound had scabbed over and the fabric made it itch. Without Dona to help me dress, I was too tired to bother with the necessities.

I hold my breath as he spreads the fabric apart. His smooth, warm fingers brush my skin and I close my eyes. I hope he doesn't notice how his touch makes me shiver. God, but I want to lean into him, to have his hands press against me. A small relief amid the pain.

He's not a man. He's not a man. He's not a— Damnation, he certainly feels *like a man.*

'Does it hurt?' His voice startles me. I shake my head, not trusting myself to speak. 'Then you're not immune to the poison.'

'The *what?*'

'Hold still.'

I try not to let myself become overwhelmed by his touch. Is this what it's like to be faestruck? To experience one moment of intimacy, no matter how inconsequential, and want more? I can't forget what he is. That even if he feels like a man, he isn't one.

Time to distract myself. 'MacKay?'

'Hmm?' He sounds indifferent. Impersonal, as usual.

'Tell me about the Falconers. Why are they called that?'

His fingers are picking at something on my skin, but I can only just feel it. The area around the wound is too numb. 'They had the ability to connect with falcons,' he says. 'Each woman had one, her personal companion, and could see through her falcon's eyes during a hunt.'

'Why falcons?'

Kiaran strokes my skin, leaving a damp trail of what I guess to be blood. 'You may see them as mere birds, but they are capable of travelling between our worlds, because they belong to both – just as a Falconer does. They are the only animals capable of seeing past our glamours, and are impervious to mental influence. It made them the perfect spy for your kind.' He clears his throat. 'And when Falconers began using them, the *sìthichean* attempted to slaughter them along with their owners.'

Under his formal tone is a hint of sadness. I wonder what memories haunt Kiaran, what could possibly have affected him so much that he should show any emotion at all. I would give anything for him to tell me.

'And where were you when all this happened?'

When his hand pauses against my skin it's no longer warm. It's freezing, cold enough to burn. The strong taste of earth and honey, so pleasant before, now coats my tongue so strong. 'That,' he says, 'is not what you truly desire to ask.'

I keep myself still. Sometimes it's best to treat Kiaran as a feral animal, a creature I've accidentally encountered in the wild. One mistake, a single sudden movement, and he'll respond as if I'm prey. I must never forget that.

'Is it not?' I say carefully.

'Don't play games with me.'

I say, very carefully, 'I want to know what manner of man I'm about to die beside on the battlefield.'

Only then do I realise my mistake. I called him a man again.

Kiaran leans in closer to me, the palm of his hand pressing into my shoulder blade. So cold. 'And there again, you make the human error of so foolishly valuing honour,' he breathes in my ear. 'Do you not remember what I told you the night we met?'

The night we met. What I recall from that night, the night after my mother's death, is my vivid, blood-pounding need for vengeance. I went into the city with the *seilgflùr* still woven through my hair – still believing it to be nothing but a pretty little adornment, the last thing my mother ever gave me. I carried an iron blade and went out to hunt for the faery who killed her.

When I couldn't find her, I tried to kill the first faery I met. It was an *each uisge*, the most dangerous breed of water-horse in Scotland.

It nearly drowned me. I remember struggling to breathe, coughing, gasping for air as I tried to free myself from the adhesive hair on its back. I must have gone unconscious, because the next thing I knew, Kiaran was holding me as I coughed up water. When I realised what he was, I tried to sink my knife into his shoulder. My blade shattered.

That day, Kiaran made me a vow. So long as I trained with him, he would never prevent me from seeking vengeance. He told me that some of what I would have to do on my path for retribution wouldn't be honourable, but it would be necessary. *Necessity before honour. Always.*

'Aye, I remember,' I whisper.

He slides a finger along my spine, over the upraised scar from that night. My first badge. My first test. The one that bound us together.

'You asked me what manner of man I am.' I close my eyes, wishing he hadn't noticed I'd called him that. Kiaran is so close now, pressed against me, his breath soft against my neck. 'I'm someone who has slayed for you, who pulled you from that river, saved your life and taught you all the ways to kill me and mine. But never make the mistake of thinking I'm a man. I aid you because I've deemed it necessary to do so. But I don't value honour.'

I swallow. 'Then what *do* you value?' I ask him. 'Isn't there anything you're willing to die for?'

Kiaran doesn't answer. His arm reaches around me. 'Look at this.'

Nestled between his thumb and forefinger is a tiny black barb, dripping with my blood. 'What is it?'

'A *cù sìth*'s claws are covered in these. It sends a paralysing poison into its victims, so they can't run.'

'You never told me that.'

'I must have forgotten.' Kiaran doesn't sound at all apologetic. He turns me to face him and touches my forehead. Instinctively I recoil, but he keeps his hand there. His fingers caress my hairline, feather-light. 'You're only immune enough to prevent it from paralysing you,' he says. 'It's still making you sick. Killing you.' He removes his hand. 'I'll have to take out the rest of the barbs.'

'Right now?' *Do his eyes have to be so intense?*

'I need to gather a few items first,' he says. 'I'll return tonight.' Before I can protest, he adds, 'No one will see me come inside.'

I realise how close our faces are, a whisper away. I hold my breath, uncertain if I should pull back, or if he has noticed it, too.

'Aren't you frightened?' I ask. 'Of the *daoine sìth* escaping the mounds? Of dying?'

I don't know why I ask him. It's foolish, and yet I have to know if he fears what will happen as much as I do.

He frowns. 'No.'

'Isn't there anything you fear?'

I want to understand him, to prolong this. He's always dauntless and inscrutable, yet his rare flashes of emotion betray something deeper, a part of him as yet untouched by apathy.

'Aye,' he says. The back of his hand slides across my cheek, cooling the skin there. I move closer. *Tell me. Tell me. Tell—*

Before he can say what he means, a sharp voice cuts through the silence. 'Get the hell away from my fiancée, you bastard.'

Chapter 23

Gavin stands in the doorway, blue eyes blazing. Until he looks at Kiaran – really looks – and all the blood drains from his face. A very bad word slips softly from his lips.

Dash it all. It's one thing to catch me carrying a pixie around, but quite another to find me in a rather compromising position with a *daoine sìth*. I shift my body to make sure Gavin can't see that my dress is open at the back. That would make this situation a great deal worse.

'Fiancée?' Kiaran repeats with a raised eyebrow.

'Oh, hell.' Gavin breathes the words and I only just hear them.

I glance from Gavin to Kiaran. My face burns. 'Well,' I say. 'Well. This is awkward.'

Kiaran's lips curve into a smile. Not the genuine almost-smile I've come to recognise, but one that scares the daylights out of me. Gone is the impassiveness of mere moments ago. 'And he's a *Seer*.' His statement holds a hint of a threat, spoken in that melodic tone I've come to dread. He laughs, and all the fine hairs on my arms rise. 'Such a rare creature to find these days.'

Gavin takes a single step back, face pale and awash with sheer panic. For a moment, I think he'll run, until he looks over at me. His body goes still. And I know then that he won't leave me alone here, even if I wished it. Damn him for trying to protect me again.

He meets Kiaran's dark gaze. 'Don't get any ideas, faery,' he says. 'I would be of no use to you.'

'Gavin,' I say. 'Please just—'

'On the contrary,' Kiaran says, ignoring me. 'This is an opportunity I never anticipated.'

In an instant, he rises to his feet and grabs Gavin by the throat, lifting him off the ground so his legs are dangling.

'MacKay!'

I move to help Gavin, but Kiaran's power freezes me in place. My limbs are heavy and unresponsive. The stark taste of earth saturates my mouth, sliding thick down my throat. Gavin chokes and gasps for breath.

A memory flashes. My mother, coughing up blood just a moment before death. All while I stood there and watched, too petrified to move. I did nothing then, the same as now.

I fight against the power that holds me. My fingers dig hard into my gloved palms, until my hands are stiff and aching. I try to curse at Kiaran but can't. My body can make only the barest of movements against his abilities.

'How very timely this is,' Kiaran murmurs. 'I thought every Seer was either dead or in hiding, and yet here you are. Now, what visions do you have for me?'

He touches a finger to Gavin's temple. Gavin gasps. Then his eyes glaze over and his head lolls back.

I will my tongue and lips to move. 'Let. Him. Go.'

Kiaran doesn't even spare me a glance. This is the terrifying Kiaran, the monster under his beautiful skin. 'Means to an end, Kam. I told you – necessity before honour. Have you learned so little?'

Kiaran's power is growing stronger, becoming a heavy presence in the room. The temperature has dropped noticeably, and soon I'm breathing white air and my fingers are numb. His power forces its way inside me, a heavy combination of dirt and mud and the overpowering tang of iron. Dots pulse in front of my eyes as I struggle to draw breath.

'I know there's at least one vision that keeps a Seer awake at night,' he says. 'It will tell me everything I need to know. Show it to me.'

The furniture has begun to lift into the air. The vases on the chimneypiece float away from their places and the settee I'm on is suddenly weightless. My feet leave the ground as it hovers above the Persian carpet.

Gavin has gone limp in Kiaran's arms. *Please be all right. Please be all right.*

'Stop resisting,' Kiaran murmurs, pressing his fingers more firmly against Gavin's temple. 'You're trying to distract me.' Then, he smiles. 'How sad for you. You couldn't have saved the girl, you know. That is a certainty. Now give me the real one.'

I watch him, curious now. What is Kiaran looking for? What vision could Gavin possibly have that would interest him?

'Ah. There it is.'

Everything in the room is silent. Kiaran's eyes are wide and sightless, watching Gavin's vision play out. The furniture in the room sways gently in the air. Books float off their shelves and the entire tea service drifts past me. The taste in my mouth is so thick that I can barely swallow.

Finally, Kiaran says, 'I see.'

He releases Gavin. The settee drops to the floor and almost throws me to the ground. My chest and throat ache from the deluge of power. Vases shatter at the back of the room. Teacups fall around me, a few saved by the thick carpet. Books lie scattered all over the place.

Gavin gasps for breath on his hands and knees. 'You bastard,' he manages.

Finding my body back under my control, I go to Gavin and grip his shoulders to steady him. When I look at Kiaran, I'm surprised by his expression. It isn't smug or arrogant or proud. His brow is furrowed with a hint of concern, quickly gone, replaced by his usual indifference.

Gavin shakes me off and rises to his feet. He snarls a word at Kiaran that makes my eyes widen. 'If you touch me again,' he says, 'I'll kill you.'

Kiaran slowly looks Gavin over, head to toe. 'You're just a Seer.' He smiles that unpleasant, terrifying smile. 'I could snap your neck before you raised a hand against me.'

'MacKay, *stop it.*'

I'd hit him. If I weren't so blasted sick, I would never have let this happen.

'Do you love him, Kam?' Kiaran asks. 'Does he fit your ridiculous notions of honour? Is he someone worthy enough to die next to?'

Gavin lurches forward. 'I can't imagine why she hasn't killed you already. Trust a faery and die. Every Scot knows that.'

'Find a Seer and cut out his eyes,' Kiaran says. 'Every *faery* knows that.'

'Enough!' I step between them. 'Sit down, both of you.'

Surprisingly, they sit across from one another in silence. Gavin scowls at Kiaran; Kiaran simply stares back. At least a minute ticks by and they both remain quiet. Neither one of them is going to tell me a thing.

'What was in the blasted vision?' I'm finally forced to ask.

'It's pointless to ask him, Kam,' Kiaran says. 'A Seer's mind – a feeble thing such as it is – has difficulty piecing together visions too far in advance. Too many outcomes and choices that have yet to happen to see it clearly.' He looks at Gavin. 'I knew which connections to make to view the whole thing. Yours is a gift wasted on the useless.'

Gavin leans back on the settee, crossing his legs. Sheer bravado, but he's quite convincing. 'Tell me, are all the fae raised to be such arrogant cads, or does it come naturally?'

'Try not to provoke me,' Kiaran says. 'Any use you might have had has now expired.'

Gavin looks at me. 'Why is he here?'

I swipe a hand across my damp forehead and sway on my feet. If I weren't leaning against the settee, I might have fallen. The illness is getting worse. It's something I can feel in my bones, a heaviness underneath my burning skin.

When I don't respond, Gavin studies me intently. 'Are you all right?'

'I'm fine.' I want to know what Kiaran saw, but I'm having trouble forming the words. I shiver and wrap my arms around myself. 'MacKay, what—'

'Not now, Kam,' Kiaran says abruptly. 'I'll take my leave.' He's already walking towards the door.

Oh no you don't. 'Will you excuse me for a moment?'

Without waiting for Gavin's response, I follow Kiaran out of the room, careful to turn slightly from Gavin so he doesn't notice the blood on the back of my dress and the undone buttons.

Kiaran is halfway down the hall. I hurry to catch up, ignoring how the quick movement nauseates me. 'Stop right there, Kiaran MacKay.' I reach out to grab him. His muscles tense under my fingertips.

'Aye?' He sounds so formal, so polite.

'Tell me what you saw.'

He hesitates, reaching for me as if to touch my face. At the last second, he drops his hand. 'Your friend's head was full of a great many uninteresting things.'

Kiaran can come up with a better version than that. He's a master at the faery half-lie. What could he have seen, that would affect him this way?

'That's not an answer,' I say.

Wordlessly, Kiaran steps behind me. Before I can ask what he intends to do, he begins to button up my dress.

It shouldn't affect me the way it does. Kiaran's behaviour is no different from usual. Still, there was that moment before Gavin came in when I swear he was going to say ... *something*. Kiaran MacKay is a mystery I wish I could solve.

He's so quiet, nothing but the whisper of his breath to indicate he's there. Finally, he says, 'I saw a lot of death.'

I go still. 'What else?'

His fingers linger in a feather-light caress at the nape of my neck. 'Do you think knowing makes it easier?' he whispers. 'You would try so desperately to prevent it, and every conscious decision you make would only help the vision come to pass.'

Kiaran speaks the last words so softly, I barely hear him. I've grown so used to the formal, passionless Kiaran that even the slightest indication of remorse is so clear: Kiaran tried to prevent a Seer's vision once and failed.

I have so many questions, but I decide on the one I'm only vaguely sure he'll answer. 'Then why did you want so badly to see it?'

'A decision made just before the vision is complete can alter the outcome.'

'And what if it doesn't?'

'That would be unfortunate.' Kiaran fastens the last button and turns me to face him. Any hint of emotion is already gone. 'I need to go and fetch my supplies before you die. I'll be a few hours.'

My God, it's as if he deliberately ruins every opportunity for an intimate moment between us. 'Well. I'll certainly try to survive until then.'

I think I hear his breath hitch. '*Gabhaidh mi mo chead dhiot*,' he murmurs. He's said that to me so many times before. His goodbye.

Kiaran strides past me down the corridor. I don't watch him leave. I step into the drawing room and grope for my shawl. It'll do for covering up the blood on my dress.

I wince at the state of the room. The floor is littered with books and broken teacups and shattered porcelain vases. A statue of Venus lies on the carpet with its arm lopped off. If I get all of the broken items cleaned up and thrown away, perhaps Father won't notice they're missing. And maybe he'll think the armless statue has character.

'Well, I can safely say that I've never experienced a more exciting two days,' Gavin says, jarring me from my thoughts. 'I suppose I should send a note before visiting again. "Are you in the company of any creature liable to attack me unprovoked? I can visit later."'

I leave the door open an inch out of habit. Some etiquette rules are hard to forget even when a certain faery doesn't bother to observe them. 'It would help if you didn't barge in unannounced.'

Gavin leans against the arm of the settee and picks up a book that has fallen there. He tosses it to the floor, apparently not the least bit interested in the wreckage. 'The front door was open, your butler was nowhere in sight and I heard voices. Who the hell was that?'

'Kiaran MacKay.' I sink back onto the settee. 'Most of what you saw last night I learned from him.'

Gavin pulls out a small flask from his coat pocket and takes a deep drink. 'Is that right? The fellow teaches you to slaughter his own kind and you don't believe that's a wee bit worthy of suspicion?'

Thank God the tea dispenser has survived its plummet to the floor. I right it and press the button to brew more tea, then fill one of the few unbroken teacups. 'If you're asking me whether I trust him, the answer is no.'

'Now *that's* reassuring. But it doesn't change the fact that you have a pixie who ate all my honey and a faery visitor who very nearly throttled the life out of me. Has anyone ever told you that you keep truly terrible company?'

I can't help but smile. 'I hope you realise that includes you?'

'At least you can count on me not to threaten your guests.' He takes another pull from his flask and smirks. 'Unlike your bad-tempered faery friend. So what *were* you doing with him when I arrived? It looked cosy.'

'Kiaran was ... helping me.'

'Was there something near your mouth that required such focused attention?'

I all but choke on my tea. 'Don't be absurd.'

'You were about this close –' he holds up two fingers, a hair's breadth apart '– from rubbing noses.'

I glare at him. 'Are you going to tell me anything about your vision? Surely you must have seen something of what Kiaran saw. Or are you going to pretend it never happened?'

Gavin's body goes still. A muscle tics in his jaw. 'You know,' he says carefully, 'that's a capital idea. Let's pretend, shall we?'

'Gavin,' I say softly.

'Don't,' he tells me. 'Just don't. I haven't seen much yet. And if I'm to be entirely honest with you, I don't want to. What little I have seen—' He downs more whisky.

'Is it about me?' I ask quietly. 'I think I deserve to know that much, at least.'

'No.' He shakes his head then. 'I don't know. I can only see the end of the vision now, not what leads up to it. The faery was blocking me from viewing it with him.'

Of course Kiaran was. 'Then how does it end?'

'I have nightmares about it. It's kept me awake nearly every night for the last week, and it's not something I want to discuss.' He sighs. 'It's my burden, Aileana. I shouldn't share it with you.'

Both of us are silent then. I look over at the window and watch as the sky grows darker and darker. The clouds are gathered thick and dark above the trees, swathed in the vivid colours of the setting sun. The rain continues to patter hard on the windowsill, the carpet beneath it soaked through now.

Across from me, I notice Gavin shiver and move over on the settee, closer to the fireplace. I don't feel the cold. My head is burning and I swipe more sweat from my brow, ignoring the dull headache pounding my temples.

Finally, I bring up the topic I've been dreading. 'You called me your fiancée. You offered for me.'

'I did,' he says softly.

I reach over the table between us and take his hand. 'You were under no obligation to do that.'

He doesn't look at me. The dark clouds are reflected in his eyes as he watches the rainfall. 'I was in a position to save your reputation, so I did. It infuriated Mother.'

The way he says it annoys me. 'You pitied me, didn't you?'

Gavin shakes his head and absently strokes a finger across my wrist. 'Is that what you think? That I did this out of pity?'

'What am I supposed to think?'

'You're my friend,' he says, eyes searching my face. 'Do you truly believe I could leave you like that? Wouldn't you have done the same for me?'

He would risk his life for my reputation – that fragile, superficial thing I've managed to shatter beyond repair. He knows the implications if we marry. As a lone Seer, he could go into hiding somewhere, the way the others did. By staying with me, we would never be free of the fae. Gavin's Sight doesn't come with the Falconer skills I have to defend myself, and I won't always be around to protect him.

'If we ever have a bairn,' I say quietly, 'you know what would happen. Our daughter ... she would be like me. A Falconer.'

Gavin grasps my hand hard then. 'And our son would be a Seer.'

We stare at each other, with the full weight of our circumstance weighing down on us. I want to be the last of my kind, so I never have to pass such a burden on to a child. How could I possibly marry and bring a child into this world, knowing it will be hunted?

'Gavin, I—'

Lady Cassilis's shrill voice resounds from the hallway. 'What do you mean, my son is not here?'

Gavin groans. 'Dear God,' he says. 'Save me.'

'Mother,' I hear Catherine say gently, 'I'm certain there is an explanation for this.'

'I know he came here,' Lady Cassilis says, ignoring Catherine. 'I demand to speak with my son at once.'

There is a rap on the drawing room door and MacNab pokes in his bearded head. His eyes widen at the mess Kiaran made, but he wisely remains silent about that. 'Lady Aileana. There is—' He sees Gavin and breathes a sigh of relief. 'Oh, Lord Galloway, I hadn't realised you were here. Do forgive me for not welcoming you.'

'Not of import,' Gavin says. 'If you tell my mother I'm not here, I won't hold it against you.'

'Hush,' I tell him. 'MacNab, please show in the viscountess and Miss Stewart.' Might as well get this over with now.

I glance around in dismay. It's not at all proper for the viscountess to see the room in such a state, but I don't think I'll be able to escort her elsewhere. My body has begun to ache, and the pounding in my head is growing worse by the minute. If I stood now, I don't think my legs would hold me.

MacNab nods and leaves. Gavin takes this brief reprieve to shove his flask into his jacket pocket.

Not a moment later, Lady Cassilis sweeps into the drawing room, heavy silk skirts billowing behind her. A large, feathered hat slants across her brow. Catherine follows her with an apologetic smile. She looks beautiful, as always, in her light blue day dress, with her blonde hair in loose curls.

'Galloway,' the viscountess says, eyeing her son with disapproval. 'Here you are, when I specifically requested a conversation with you earlier this morning.'

I try not to blanch. As I am the lady of the house, the viscountess should have spoken to me first. Failing that, it would be common decency to acknowledge me with a nod.

'You did,' Gavin says. He reclines with an amused expression. 'I was avoiding you.'

'Obviously.'

The viscountess still doesn't look at me, instead inspecting the state of the drawing room. I watch her take in the broken vases, the shattered teacups at her feet, the books strewn about the room. She blinks.

'Is this the permanent state of the drawing room,' she asks drily, 'or have we walked in on another of my son's renovations? This matches the appalling state of your study, Galloway.'

'We were balancing,' Gavin says quickly. 'First the vases, then the books, then the teacups. On our heads.'

I glance at him. What the devil? Who on earth would believe that?

'Balancing?' Lady Cassilis looks positively horrified.

'A new parlour game,' Gavin explains. 'Balance an object on your head, and whoever holds it there longest wins.' He glances over at the broken objects. 'Perhaps, in retrospect, a rather messy pastime.'

I suck in air as a wave of nausea hits me. I'm determined not to let the viscountess see how vulnerable I am. 'Lady Cassilis,' I say through clenched teeth. 'Would you like to sit?'

'That's quite unnecessary.' Her gaze finally settles on me. 'I'll endeavour to be brief.'

'Here we go ...' Gavin mutters.

Lady Cassilis glares at him sharply before continuing, 'I hope you realise this situation with my son has put me in quite a precarious position.'

I can barely concentrate on her words. The illness is now a storm inside me. Heat swirls along my veins as my heart pumps venom through my system. My heartbeat roars in my ears. God, can nobody else hear it? It's so loud, so slow. *Thump. Thump.*

'Lady Aileana,' the viscountess says.

'Aye?' I dare not say much, struggling as I am just to catch my breath. Black dots dance in my vision and I try desperately to blink them away.

'*Yes,*' she corrects.

I don't respond. I concentrate on my laboured breathing. Gavin looks over at me and I attempt my best reassuring smile.

Lady Cassilis continues, 'As my son is a gentleman—' Gavin's loud snort interrupts her, but she ignores it. 'He has decided that the best way of resolving the situation is to wed you.' The viscountess regards me grimly. 'I agree with his decision.'

'Splendid,' I whisper.

Catherine frowns and mouths, 'Are you well?' I nod, a mere shift of my head, because that's the only movement I can manage. Catherine doesn't look convinced. The viscountess goes on and I try to listen, but I must appear distracted.

'Aileana, have you heard a word I've said?'

'I beg your pardon, Lady Cassilis.' I swallow and offer the viscountess a wan smile. 'Please, do continue.'

The viscountess draws back her shoulders. 'As I was saying, I also agree with your father that this will have to be settled quickly. The Stewart name is old and renowned, and as you have an impressive dowry and lineage, I'm willing to concede to this match. After all, I refuse to see my family's reputation tarnished because some … some foolish girl seduced the only remaining Stewart heir.'

My head snaps up at that. *Foolish girl?* Rage simmers inside me and my defences begin to crumble. That carefully composed and maintained façade of calm is failing me. My polite pretence almost slips.

'Mother,' Catherine says, aghast. 'That is not at all appropriate.'

'Is that what you think happened?' I speak carefully, with more control than I feel.

Over on the settee, Gavin turns his head to me. He must hear the change in my voice, the undertone of anger creeping in. His eyes widen a fraction – in fear, I realise. He knows what I'm capable of.

You scare the hell out of me.

Last night, it hurt to hear him say that. I find those same words empowering now. To be feared is an elixir. I can be terrifying, strong, untouchable. In that world, I don't have to worry about reputations or marriage.

'I think we are far past what is appropriate, Catherine,' Lady Cassilis replies. 'Aileana has already attracted excessive attention, so my motive is to mitigate the inevitable gossip as much as possible. If we have the ceremony in a fortnight, there will be less talk if a child is born early.'

Gavin chokes low in his throat and stares at his mother in shock. Catherine perfectly mirrors his expression.

I stand. My cheeks burn with the fever and anger I can no longer suppress. '*Out.*'

Lady Cassilis's jaw drops. 'I *beg* your pardon?'

'Was I not clear? Get. The hell. Out. Of my home.'

Even Catherine turns to me, mouth agape. 'Aileana!' she gasps.

I never show this side of myself in public, but I can't hold it back one moment longer. My body trembles from the venom in my blood and my carefully maintained mental control is disintegrating. My rational thoughts are fading ... gone.

There is only anger, my hot skin, my pounding head, my roaring heart, and people in the room who need to leave.

'*Go. Now.*' I say it with more force.

Lady Cassilis draws herself up. 'I was willing to set aside our differences for the sake of my son. But I see I was not at all wrong about you.' She strides to the door in a flurry of silk skirts. 'Catherine,' she snaps, before exiting the room.

'Aileana.' Catherine's hand on my arm is so cool that I flinch. 'That wasn't— Good heavens, you're burning up. Are you ill?'

'I'm fine.' I swallow and shut my eyes hard.

'I can stay, if you need me. If you're—'

'*Catherine!*' Lady Cassilis's voice comes from the hallway.

'No.' I need to lie down. Just as I suspected, my legs can't hold me. I grasp the arm of the settee to keep me upright. 'Please. Go with your mother.'

'If you insist.' Catherine sighs. 'I'm terribly sorry for some of the things she said. She was much too harsh with you.'

I almost open my mouth to agree, but decide against it. As much as I dislike Lady Cassilis, she *is* to be my future mother-in-law. It's best I learn to accept that now. 'Her only son was just caught in a scandal with a girl she considers utterly unsuitable,' I say carefully. 'I understand why she was harsh. Tell her I'm sorry for everything.'

Catherine nods. 'I shall. Please send word when you're better. I'll worry otherwise.'

Her dress rustles as she leaves. It's the only sound I can hear, other than my violent heartbeat.

Gavin's hands are on my shoulders then, as he gently turns me to face him. He stares down at me, his eyes so blue, fierce and concerned. He slips an arm around my waist and draws me against his chest. I let out a soft groan of complaint as he places the back of his hand against my forehead.

'Shall I send for a doctor?'

'It won't help.' I turn my head and his fingers graze my cheek and rest on my collarbone, below my *seilgflùr* necklace.

'It's from a faery, then. Isn't it?'

I let myself rest against him, because there is nothing else I can do. I'm too weak to push him away.

I nod. 'One of the hounds.'

'I see.'

What does he see? He has offered marriage to a woman who will always be injured or bruised or bleeding. I will never be rid of my scars, and I'd never want to be. They will always be there, burned into my skin. Brands of my success, of my kills.

I lean back and meet his gaze directly. 'I don't want to marry you,' I whisper. 'Is that awful of me?'

'Not at all,' he says softly. 'I don't want to marry you either.'

Chapter 24

I wake with a start and gasp for air, flailing in sheets soaked through with sweat. Hands grab my shoulders roughly and hold me firmly against the pillows.

I stare up in shock at Kiaran. The taste of his power settles softly against my tongue, not at all overwhelming. His features are shadowed, barely visible in the glow of the street lamps filtering through the open window. He smells so strongly of heather and spring, with a hint of rain from the wet clothes he presses into mine.

'What on earth are you doing?' My mouth is dry. It hurts to speak, or move my lips.

'I said I'd be back.'

I swallow. My throat feels as though it's lined with blades. 'You said visit, not *attack*.'

Kiaran releases me. 'I tried to wake you. You were thrashing in your sleep and scratching your wounds.'

I reach for the button near my bed and the lights near the door turn on with a click. A soft glow illuminates the room and Kiaran's shining skin, swathing him in a gleaming halo of gold.

My gaze drops to his lips and I think about this afternoon. The way he stroked the scar running down my back, my body pressed against his after our fight—

No, don't think about it. I should move away from him. Further away. I whip the counterpane off my legs and try to stand. It takes two attempts. I stumble, but manage to catch my fall by gripping the bedside table.

'Well,' I say, my voice shaky, 'here you are.' I look at him again and lose all rational thought. 'In my ... bedroom.'

Oh, hell. Oh, *hell*, I did not consider this thoroughly when he told me he'd come here. This isn't something my etiquette lessons covered. Miss Ainsley's book has no chapter titled 'What to Do When a Gentleman Visits a Lady's Private Quarters'.

Kiaran settles on my bed – *on my bed* – and regards me with his usual inscrutable expression. He shouldn't be here. Surely he knows that people don't just *sleep* in—

'Are you feeling all right?' he asks.

'I'm fine.' Is he supposed to be that beautiful? Damnation, my head hurts. 'Tea!' I blurt, grasping the first fragment of Miss Ainsley's lessons that I can think of. 'Do you like tea? Would you like me to brew some? I have it all the time with visitors.'

Oh my goodness, what is *wrong* with me?

'Kam.'

'Which is not to say,' I continue, unable to stop now, 'that I have visitors to my bedroom all the time. Who are men. Um. I mean, faeries.' I wave a hand at the dressing room. 'Except Derrick, who is ... out.'

Dash it all, I should never have sent Derrick away. In anticipation of Kiaran's arrival, I told him to see if his contacts had any new information on the *baobhan sìth*, a task that generally keeps him out all night. He could have been right here, telling Kiaran to get off my damn bed and stitch me up already.

'And he won't be back for a while, you know.' I grip the table to steady myself. 'So—' Blast. I can't even think properly any more. 'Terribly sorry, I forgot what I was talking about.'

Kiaran is lounging on my bed looking downright entertained.

'We're alone, without the bothersome pixie,' he says. 'And you're asking me about tea for a reason I can't fathom.'

Alone. Who knows what I'll do, considering what's wrong with me. I might do something ridiculous, or say something regrettable. Well, more regrettable than what I've already said.

A sudden onslaught of cold strikes me. I hug myself and stumble to the fireplace with my teeth chattering. Warmth. That's what I need. That will make everything better. I fumble for the switch to light the fire, but my fingers are too numb to work it.

My legs buckle, but Kiaran is there. He wraps his arms around my waist and stares down at me, his body motionless. God, but his eyes are magnificent. I can see every fleck, every star shining within them. 'Your eyes glow,' I murmur. 'Do you know they glow? Like a bloody street lamp.'

'Shall I take that as a compliment or a criticism?'

'An observation.' A soft sigh almost escapes my lips, but I catch myself. What in the blazes? Am I faestruck? 'Let me go,' I tell him before I can stop to truly consider it. I try to push him away. If I'm struck, I'd rather not be so close to him. What if I become some mindless beast and start pawing at him?

'Your legs don't appear to be working,' he says. He presses his palm briefly against my forehead. 'Your fever is worse than before. I should take out the barbs now.'

How can I have a fever when I'm this cold? I want so badly to lean into him, to wrap my arms around him. He's so warm. I should pull away. I should. I don't. 'You can't be near me right now,' I tell him. 'I think I'm faestruck.' Why did I *say* that? Have I been robbed of all my blasted senses?

He stares at me. 'No, you're not.'

'Aye, I am.'

Kiaran's gaze is dark and glittering as he leans in. 'Is that what you think you feel? Faestruck?' His lips brush my cheek and my breath catches. 'Do you crave me, Kam?' he whispers. 'Do you ache for me?'

I shiver. I almost grasp his shirt and press my lips against his, just to see if he'll kiss me back. *No*, I tell myself. That would be a mistake.

I pull away from him, as much as I can with his arms still around me. 'Are you trying to make this worse?'

'The fever might have lowered your inhibitions, but you're not faestruck,' he says. 'If you were, you certainly wouldn't be lucid enough to ask about it.'

'Why do I feel like this then?' I whisper, mostly to myself. Why else would I want so badly to be close to him, despite everything I know he's capable of? I shouldn't be thinking about kissing him or touching him. I should be thinking of the best ways to guard myself against him. 'Are you certain you haven't accidentally done something to me? Like with Catherine?'

'You're a Falconer. I would have to force you under my influence.' He looks down at me then, unreadable as ever. 'And that is a line I would not dare cross with you.'

'You froze me earlier,' I remind him.

'I only prevented you from moving,' he says, his voice soft. 'You were defiant the whole time. The faestruck don't fight back, Kam. They don't resist. They grovel and beg for our touch. They waste away from it and still yearn for more.' His eyes are dark, so intense. 'When a *sìthichean* decides to take a human, it's not something they walk away from. Not ever.'

My breath catches. 'Have you done that to someone before?'

'I don't have an admirable past, Kam. I never led you to believe I did.'

Kiaran swings me into his arms before I can even protest. Unlike when Gavin held me, the fight leaves my body and I hang limply in Kiaran's arms, cold and aching. Not even his warmth can seep through my frozen skin. Damn it all. Just for now, I want to stop caring about how I should act, about the pretence of strength that I always put up when I'm around him. All I want right now is to be warm again.

So I rest my head against his shoulder and my fingers on his collarbone. There it is. A hint of heat under my dull, numb skin. I sigh.

'Better?' he asks.

I look up at him. I feel lethargic, as though I've taken a good dose of laudanum. I take a deep breath and whisper, 'May I tell you something?'

Kiaran shifts me in his arms, which only draws me closer. He seems unsure what to do with me. 'All right.'

I press my cheek against his rough raploch shirt. My sense of decency is lost. Warmer, I need to be warmer, to feel something through the numbness. 'Sometimes I almost forget you're fae.'

'Do you?' He sounds genuinely curious, maybe even a bit surprised.

'Aye.' I close my eyes. 'When you decide to be kind. Like you telling me that you would never faestrike me.'

'What about everything else?'

'I'm reminded of why I should never let myself forget.'

He places me gently into bed and eases the counterpane over my legs. 'Take your own advice, Kam. You'll find nothing human in me. Always remember that.'

Even with the counterpane covering me, the cold is unrelenting. I shudder under the silk sheets. Or at least I think I do. My body is hollow, numb. The only thing that tethers me to it is Kiaran's voice, our conversation.

I rub my cheek against the pillow to feel the fabric. Nothing. There are only my words. 'Are we agreeing with each other? This is a rare occurrence.'

Kiaran pulls my wooden work chair over to the bedside. 'Tomorrow we'll go right back to fighting.'

'A cherished pastime,' I murmur. My tongue is too heavy to speak properly.

His eyes meet mine, and for a brief second, I feel that connection to him again. An innate understanding. A likeness that I can't begin to describe or comprehend.

Tell me, I will him. *Tell me something, too.* I'm compelled to understand those parts of him that he keeps closed off and untouchable. Those brief glimpses into his soul that show how emotions have moved him somewhere in his vast lifetime.

Kiaran tears his gaze from mine and reaches for something beside the bed. He pulls up a brown leather bag and plucks out three small bottles, thread, and a curved needle.

I tense. 'What are those?'

'I have to stitch you up,' he says, as if it should be obvious.

My eyes widen. 'Are you mad? I have stitchers in my dressing room that could do a far better job, with less pain, than that thing you're wielding. Put it away.'

Kiaran regards me patiently. 'It's this, or you die. You choose.'

I suppose Kiaran wouldn't stitch me up by hand if he didn't have to. He'd consider it a waste of time. 'Fine,' I grumble. 'What's in the vials?'

He opens one bottle and holds it out to me. 'Drink this one.'

Inside is a milky blue liquid with what looks like thin slivers of glass floating in it. Surely he doesn't mean for me to drink glass. 'Am I going to regret consuming its contents?'

'No. But I imagine you'll still call me every expletive you can possibly think of.' He presses it into my palm.

'I don't like the sound of that.' I sniff the vial and scrunch up my nose at a sharp tang that burns my nostrils. Like something that might come out of my chemistry set. 'Ugh! What's in this? It smells vile.'

'I knew a human girl once. She was stubborn, like you. Refused to drink the paltry contents of that bottle, like you …'

He pauses for dramatic effect. 'And she died a horrible, painful death – torturous, really – because she wouldn't take my advice.'

I scrutinise him. 'There was no girl who died, was there?'

'There will be if you don't drink what's in that damned bottle.'

I prop myself up and scowl at him. Then I gulp in a breath, hold it and drain the contents.

The liquid burns, like potent whisky. It scorches my throat and races through my body much faster than I expected. I claw at the pillow and gasp pathetically. Intense, agonising pain follows almost instantly. I can't concentrate on anything else but how much it hurts, and I can't even say all the profanities that flash across my mind. My tongue is glued to the roof of my mouth, rendered immobile.

I meet Kiaran's eyes. His head is tilted, amethyst gaze studying me intensely. My God, has he poisoned me?

All at once, the pain ebbs. It slides off my skin in waves and leaves behind a strange, soothing current that drifts from my head all the way down to my toes.

Still, I glare at Kiaran and say, 'What did you do to me?'

'I gave you a mild sedative.' He studies me. 'It's supposed to calm you.'

'I'm sure it would work better if I weren't so annoyed with you,' I say. 'You could have told me it would hurt like the very devil.'

'What difference would that have made? You'd still have had to drink it and you'd still be miserable.' He shifts closer and motions for me to turn over onto my stomach. 'I have to remove your … whatever this is.'

'Nightdress,' I say, my cheek against the pillow. 'It's from Paris. You've been alive how long and still can't identify a woman's clothing?'

Kiaran plucks at my nightdress, as if trying to figure out a way to get it off me. 'Too many words over my lifetime for the same items. I really don't care to learn them all.'

'MacKay, stop fiddling around and just cut the blasted thing.' When he simply stares at me, I say, 'I have some dignity, however little you appreciate it. I refuse to let you remove my clothing.'

'If you insist.' Kiaran's blade appears from somewhere and he slices through the back of my nightdress. 'There. Your expensive French item is now ruined for the sake of some incomprehensible notion of propriety. I hope you're pleased.'

A heavy lock of that shining black hair falls onto his face. As he pushes it back, I let my gaze linger on him for longer than usual. I study those strong, high cheekbones and his square jaw, how his hair curls up at the ends. He dabs a bluish-grey paste onto his fingers from one of the bottles. Spreading apart the torn edges of my nightdress, he smoothes the paste along my wounds. Unlike the concoction I drank, this comforts straight away.

I close my eyes and – just this once, in my ill state – I allow myself to briefly take comfort in his touch, the way his fingertips linger along my spine. I begin to understand why people seek intimacy, why they long for it. Why it compels them to forget every awful, destructive memory they've ever had.

'What did you dream about?' Kiaran asks.

I'm so surprised by the question, I don't know how to respond. 'What?'

Kiaran plucks a pair of forceps from his bag. 'Your dream. The one you were having when I came in.'

Kiaran doesn't realise there is only *one* dream – one nightmare. A perpetual reminder of my failure. My weakness. 'I thought we weren't going to make this personal,' I say. 'Dreams are personal.'

'Kam, I'm picking barbs out of your naked back. It's already personal.'

I remain silent. Numbness is beginning to spread through my body, and I'm losing the reassurance of Kiaran's touch. If I close my eyes, I'll fall asleep. I'll have to relive the nightmare either way.

Before I change my mind, I whisper, 'My mother. I dreamed of her murder.'

Despite being unable to feel his hands, I sense Kiaran stiffen next to me. 'You saw it happen.'

'Aye,' I whisper. Now he knows my darkest secret, the memory that tears down every wall of carefully maintained control until all that's left is the dark part of me that kills.

I can't help but be drawn into the nightmare again. I spin in a white dress, in an assembly room filled with bright candelabras and lamps, surrounded by people in black coats and pastel skirts and puffed dresses. The fiddles play an upbeat schottische that I dance to until my feet ache.

Then I'm outside, breathing in the cool night air. I hear the sounds of a struggle, a muffled scream. I peer through the garden bushes that overlook the street. There's a figure lying in the rain, her white dress spread around her on the cobblestones, now soaked crimson.

Another woman is crouched next to the still body, her eyes bright and glittering an unnatural green in the glow of the street lamps. I watch blood slide down the long, pale column of her throat. Her lips peel back in a fierce smile of pointed teeth that I'll remember for as long as I live. Because I know immediately what this woman is, and that all the stories from my childhood are true: faeries are real, and they are monsters.

The faery uses her blade-sharp nails to cut into the dead woman's chest and she rips out her heart.

My eyes shut hard as I repress that memory again, shoving it deep inside me where it belongs. 'I'm sorry,' I say.

I'm not certain what I'm apologising for. I haven't told him anything, really. Not even how that night when he ripped out the redcap's heart brought me back to the part of my nightmare where the faery looks down at my mother's corpse and says something to her that I'll never forget.

Crimson suits you best.

Kiaran leans down and presses his forehead against mine. I don't pull away. *Make the thoughts stop,* I will him. *Tell me you're just as broken as I am.*

'*Tha mi duilich air do shon,*' he breathes, his lips so close to mine. 'Do you think we could exist without moments of vulnerability? Of regret?' He brushes a hand over my bare shoulder blade. 'Without them, you wouldn't be Kam.'

I never thought he would understand. The people who had been there after my mother's death – the ones who still spoke to me after it happened – reassured me that things would get better, that I'd get better. And with enough time, everything would be *all right*. But nothing is all right, and I am *not* better.

Time won't fix me. Time allows me to become more skilful at hiding how much I hurt inside. Time makes me a great liar. Because when it comes to grief, we all like to pretend.

Kiaran picks up the needle and dips it in the third vial. He must have touched my wounds again because he asks, 'Can you feel that?'

'No.'

'Good.'

He leans over me and begins the delicate process of sewing up my injuries. As the minutes tick by, I watch him from under my eyelashes. He frowns in concentration while he sews. Eventually, my eyes grow heavy, but I fight sleep.

'MacKay,' I say. 'What's the point in stitching me up to save my life when we're likely to die on Tuesday? Why are you on my side?'

Kiaran smirks. 'Ah, the pervasive idea of absolutes. When did I ever say my side was yours?'

'We hunt together,' I say. 'We save people. We're about to go into a war with unfavourable odds. It certainly looks like we're on the same side.'

We save people. I'm not even certain why I added that. It's my delusion that our nightly slaughter spares human lives, and that makes it acceptable, somehow. In reality, I'm selfish. I'm more consumed by a need to kill than to save another person. I wish I weren't.

Kiaran's laugh is sharp, abrupt. 'Tell yourself whatever you'd like, but don't speak for me. I'm not benevolent. If I've done anything good, it's because of my damned vow.'

I blink hard, trying to clear my clouding vision. 'Your *what*?'

His focused, patient demeanour is gone in an instant, and now his eyes burn, so exquisitely fierce that I can't look away. I have never seen such raw violence in a mere expression before.

Then, just as quickly, the wrath is gone, replaced with apathy. 'I killed humans every day,' he says coldly. 'Until I spoke a vow.'

I stare at him in surprise. A faery's vow is immutable and everlasting. To break one results in the worst pain imaginable, long and agonising, before the faery finally dies. It is not something to be taken lightly.

'Why would you do that?'

'You don't want to ask me about my past,' he says, voice low. 'Some things are best left buried.'

This vow, whatever it was, meant something to Kiaran. Something important. I have to know. 'If you won't tell me about your vow or your past,' I say softly, 'then tell me the real reason you hunt.'

His anger sparks again and I see something underneath it that I could identify anywhere: loss, hidden by centuries upon centuries of rage.

I know from experience what grief does. How it can transform us. That the only way to control it is by pressing it deep down inside ourselves where we hope no one will ever discover it. But it will always be there. Inevitably, something or someone will come along and dig up everything we've tried so hard to conceal. Kiaran did that to me. I just did that to Kiaran.

Now I'm almost certain I know the answer. Who Kiaran made his vow to and why he hunts the fae.

My eyelids finally flutter closed. I try to open them, but I can't. My mind has already started clouding. I fight against sleep one last time. I need to ask him. 'Did you love your human very much?' I ask.

He sucks in a surprised breath. His whispered response is so low, I strain to hear him before sleep takes me completely. 'I didn't love her nearly enough.'

Chapter 25

I wake at the sound of a chair scratching against the hardwood floor. I stir and open my eyes to see Kiaran about to leave my bedroom.

'Skulking out with no goodbye?' I ask.

Kiaran freezes and turns his head. 'I didn't want to wake you.'

'Liar.' I shift experimentally and am relieved to find the numbness gone. I feel … wonderful, actually. Not at all sore. 'How does my back look? Awful?'

Kiaran's heavy buckled boots are silent as he approaches the bed. He sits next to me. 'Feel for yourself.'

When I twist my arm to tentatively poke the wounds, I expect to find taut stitches lining the claw marks and flesh slick with blood. Instead, I find dry skin with smooth, upraised scars where my injuries had been but a few hours ago. New badges to accompany the many old ones that already line my back, and it feels as though they have been there for years.

I gape at Kiaran. 'What—' I shift to touch them again. God, but even my counterpane is clean of blood. 'How did you—' I stare at him. 'Some fae remedy?'

Kiaran shrugs. I ignore him and shove the pristine counterpane down my legs. All of the cuts I received from crawling on the beach rocks are healed. The raw skin and broken blisters on my hand are smoothed over. Even the injuries on my forearm, where the *cù sìth*'s teeth scraped me, are scarred. My bruises, aches and pains have vanished.

'Do you mean to tell me,' I say through clenched teeth, 'that you've had that concoction this *entire time*?'

'Of course.' His response is nonchalant.

I remember those nights I wandered home from our hunts covered in blood, most of it mine. When I barely made it there alive, and Derrick had to wake me every few hours to make sure I hadn't died. I endured my injuries in secret, dealt with the pain made worse by layers of clothing and corsets.

Kiaran could have alleviated that. Instead, he made me bear it. Just like that, my sympathy over his former human lover recedes and I'm left with the glaring reminder that he really can be a cold bastard.

'You never once felt the need to use it,' I say, voice shaking, 'during any of those nights I earned dozens of injuries?'

'This was a special case,' he says, 'since the poison would have killed you.'

'I'm surprised you didn't let it,' I snap.

There's Kiaran's anger again. It mirrors my own, except where mine is hot, his is the most frigid kind of cold. The temperature in the room drops and when I breathe in, I feel my lungs constrict.

'What would you have proposed for every other time?' he says. 'That I carry you away from every monster you face?' He moves closer, until he is practically nose to nose with me. 'Shall I smother you with my protection until you can't breathe or lift a damn finger to defend yourself?'

'Don't exaggerate,' I snarl.

'I trained you for battle,' he tells me. 'When we fight the *sìthichean*, do you think I'll have those vials with me? My needle and thread handy? Healing isn't one of my powers, so I taught you to endure pain.'

I'm beyond caring about his excuses. I have to know what else he's hidden from me. 'Tell me something. How long have you known the seal was going to break?' When he doesn't respond, I ask again. *'How long?'*

He clenches his jaw. 'Since before I met you.'

'Ugh!' I shove at his chest, scramble off the bed and sit at my work table. If I don't do something with my hands, I might be inclined to shoot him with my lightning pistol.

I snatch up the half-finished shoulder mount for my sonic cannon and shove a screw into one of the holes.

Kiaran doesn't even spare a glance at my project. 'Do you think it would have been better if I had told you? You were clearly grieving. You were untrained. When I met you, you couldn't even use a blade.'

'My, you are absolutely full of compliments today.'

His contemptuous gaze rakes me from head to toe. 'The *daoine sìth* will be at their weakest when they first escape the mounds. It's the best time to strike, and you're still not strong enough to fight them.'

I go still and the screw slips through my fingers onto the table. 'Not strong enough?' I ask quietly. 'I thought I proved myself perfectly capable earlier.'

'You bested me once, Kam. Do you honestly think you can defeat hundreds of trained *daoine sìth*?'

I barely understand anything he says beyond the sting of *not strong enough*. 'Not strong enough?'

Just when I think I have myself under control, he strips it all away and I'm left struggling with the creature inside me that wants nothing more than to fight him until we're both exhausted and bruised.

'No,' he says. 'Not yet.'

I snap. I grab the lightning pistol off the table. The core rods fan open as I aim for an extremity I know he can heal and pull the trigger.

Kiaran is much faster. He blocks the shot with his hand, grasping the capsule tightly in his fist. He stares at me calmly – for about a second. With a hiss of pain, he opens his fist and the metal capsule drops to the hardwood floor. A Lichtenberg figure forms on his palm, snaking up his wrist from a burn at the centre.

He stares at me in shock. A startling display of emotion for Kiaran.

I lean back in my chair, my anger sated. I believe I've proved my point. Again. 'My shot wouldn't have killed you, but I imagine that's still quite painful.'

I don't know what I expected from him. Annoyance, perhaps. Maybe for him to frown in displeasure and call me a fool again. What I didn't expect was for him to start laughing. Not the melodic, too-beautiful fae laughter he uses to intimidate me, but genuine laughter that dimples his cheeks and actually makes him look human.

'What's so funny?'

Kiaran straightens. 'When you picked up that pistol, I never expected you to shoot me.'

I smile and laugh, too. 'Didn't you always say never to draw a weapon unless I intend to use it?'

'So you *do* listen to what I say.'

'When it suits me.'

Kiaran surprises me by moving too fast again, shoving my chair back from the table. Then he leans in, his arms on either side of me. 'That might have amused me this time, but try it again and I'll break your pistol.'

I match his stare. 'Break my pistol and I have about fifteen other weapons that will do the same job.'

His grin is slow, downright seductive. 'I knew it since the day I pulled you out of that river.'

'What?'

'That you would always challenge me.'

Unable to bear the intensity of his gaze, I turn my head and study his injury. The burn on his palm is healing over, and the Lichtenberg figure is slowly disappearing back down his arm.

I frown as the fernlike pattern reveals a brand on the inside of his wrist. I don't remember ever seeing it before, or perhaps I've just never paid enough attention to notice. The design is burned into his skin, the scarified flesh upraised. An elaborate series of swirls, intertwined with each other, delicate and intricate. Whoever designed this had been painstaking in its detail. The shape is something I'm unable to identify, a symbol I've never seen.

Only fae metal can leave permanent scarring – and even then, only faintly. To make scars like these, the lines would have had to be traced over and over again with a sharp, burning-hot blade. It must have hurt a great deal while it was being carved. Compelled, I reach out to touch it.

Kiaran wraps his fingers around my wrist. 'What are you doing?'

'Your brand. What does it mean?'

Something flashes in his eyes, an emotion I can't identify. After a second, it's gone. He releases me. 'It doesn't mean a damn thing any more.'

I'm beginning to realise how much our secrets define us. A few days ago, he and I would have hunted together and returned to our respective lives, the same as always. Now our boundaries are fading, and we grasp those last few secrets we still do have, because baring one's soul is so much more difficult than pretending.

'All right,' I say calmly, tugging my hand from his.

As if realising he's betrayed some emotion, he straightens and stares down at me. 'Come with me.'

I blink. 'Where?'

'Must you question everything?'

'Aye,' I say. 'It delights me to annoy you whenever possible.'

His mouth quirks upwards. 'I've noticed.'

Chapter 26

Kiaran and I sit silently in the ornithopter as I fly us through the clear night sky. The cold air up here sears my skin and I pull my raploch coat tighter around me. I rest my hand on the helm and watch the ground slip by below us. We soar over the countryside beyond the city, where everything is still and quiet. Houses are sparse, identifiable only by the dim candlelight shining through occasional windows amid the dark farmland.

Kiaran hasn't spoken a word to me since we left Charlotte Square, as if he senses how badly I want to ask him about the girl he loved and what happened to her.

I look over at him, taking in his features, his pensive expression. I try to imagine him as an unrepentant monster like the fae I kill. What was it about *her* that made him change? I would never have thought the *sìthichean* to be capable of falling in love with humans. Predators don't come to love their prey.

Before I can ask, Kiaran speaks. 'Set us down there – by that dismal-looking residence.'

I peer over the helm. 'Dalkeith Palace?'

At his nod, I swing the helm, circling the clearing until I find the perfect place for us to land. *There* – behind a line of trees that should shield us from view of the palace windows, if anyone happens to look out while we're here. The machine settles softly onto the ground and I pull the lever to retract the wings.

'We're not going to break in, are we?'

Kiaran glances in the direction of the palace in disgust. 'I can't imagine there'd be anything in there worth trespassing for.'

'Perhaps His Grace has empty vases on one of his many chimneypieces,' I say drily, 'which you can steal to replace the ones you accidentally broke in my home.'

'That wasn't an accident. I decided I didn't like them.' He hops out of the ornithopter and begins to stride away.

I hurry after him across the grass, jogging to keep up with his long strides. We head through the trees and over the dirt drive in front of the palace. It's a tall, majestic structure – not at all dismal-looking to my eye – of sandstone brick with a generous assemblage of tall windows. Chimneys jut into the sky along the roof, a small indication of the many rooms inside, but smoke rises from only a single stack at the back of the palace. Someone must be home, then. The scent of burned wood lingers faintly in the air as I follow Kiaran through a forested area along the side of the east wing.

My boots squish into mud as I try to carefully guide myself around the tree roots. 'Any chance you might tell me where we're going?'

Kiaran's smile is visible even between the dark trees. 'You truly loathe being kept in suspense, don't you?'

'When you keep me in suspense, something bad always happens. Like me battling two redcaps.'

'There was no terrible outcome,' he says, glancing over at me. 'You survived with minimal damage.'

The night is brisk. Cold penetrates my coat and lingers on my skin. I cross my arms to keep warm. We walk without speaking, my breathing heavy compared to Kiaran's. As we continue further into the trees, fog begins to thicken around us. Soon I can't see more than a few feet in front of me and we're on no path that I can discern. It would be so easy to get lost out here.

Kiaran's voice startles me. 'Tell me about the Seer. Do you love him?'

'No,' I say. 'We're just to be married.'

I might have loved Gavin once, in my youth. I used to be convinced that he and I would be together for the rest of our lives. Now I've discovered that he's the perfect match for me – far more so than I could ever have possibly dreamed – but all I feel for him is platonic affection. No passion. No love, not any more. Sometimes I wonder if I'm even capable of love now.

'What, exactly, is the purpose of pledging your life to someone you don't want?'

'Duty first,' I say bitterly. 'That's what my father always says. Few ladies who shame their families are lucky enough to receive an offer from the gentleman who helped ruin her.'

He goes deadly calm. 'Ruined you, did he?'

'Of course not. He saved my life last night and fate was not kind to him for it.'

'Couldn't you choose not to marry him?' he asks. 'If you didn't want it?'

'Women in my world don't have many choices, MacKay. My life has already been decided for me.'

'Such a prison you live in,' he murmurs without a hint of sarcasm. 'I wonder how you breathe.'

The fog finally dissipates as we approach a clearing. We step through the long grass and I tilt my head back, studying the stars. *Can you name them, Aileana?* I hear my mother's voice, from those nights we spent in the garden reciting the constellations.

Clear skies are such a rare occurrence during Scottish winters, and I remember every single one from my childhood. Invention is my hobby, and astronomy was my mother's. Every time I look at a cloudless night sky, I recall her pointing to each of the constellations with her long, graceful fingers and repeating their names.

I realise I've stopped walking and hurry after Kiaran. 'Sorry.'

The moon is so bright, it illuminates everything as we advance through the clearing. A sudden taste bursts on my tongue, surprising me. It's not the overwhelming flavour of fae power that I'm used to, but something of a different kind. A subtle hint of terracotta, accompanied by the scent of spring and salt, as if we were closer to the sea.

I scan the clearing for the source of the fragrance, which only grows stronger as we walk, and my attention is drawn to the massive yew tree rising from the middle of the clearing. It towers over us, branches splitting off in every direction. Heavy roots stick out of the ground. It's the tallest tree of its type I've ever seen.

I peer into the branches. 'I don't remember hearing about His Grace having a yew tree of this size on his property. Surely someone would have mentioned it.' It isn't until I touch the trunk and the taste intensifies that I realise the tree is its source. Why on earth would a tree have such power?

'It's hidden from humans,' Kiaran says, stepping up beside me. 'You can only see it because you're wearing the thistle.' He lays his palm flat against the trunk.

'What are you doing?'

He almost smiles. 'You didn't really think I brought you all the way out here just to see a tree, did you?'

Before I can respond, he slams his fist against the trunk. A jarring boom resounds and the ground shakes under my feet. Lightning scatters wide across the cloudless sky, blindingly bright. A bolt strikes the centre of the tree with a vivid flash.

I stumble back, closing my eyes hard against the onslaught of light. A loud, reverberating crack startles me enough to risk opening them again. I watch as the tree trunk splinters right down the middle. Branches bow to the ground on either side, leaving a gaping hole in the heart of the tree. Roots pull out of the soil and curl around each other, shaping themselves into steps.

Between the two halves of the tree, a mirror forms and undulates like water. I see my reflection there, obscured by ceaseless ripples.

'What is it?' I whisper.

'The *clomhsadh,*' Kiaran says. 'Let me show you.'

A faery passage. My hand automatically reaches for the lightning pistol in its holster at my waist. Why would he bring me here, if not to fight? I meet his eyes then. I wish there was some indication of his intent there, no matter how small, but I find nothing.

With a shiver of anticipation running down my spine, I follow Kiaran up the rooted stairs. At the top, I pause to check my weapon once more before I step through the portal.

Beyond the *clomhsadh* is a loch. Kiaran and I are on a sandy beach surrounded by trees that tower so high they touch the thick clouds overhead. The loch itself is still as ice. Mist curls off the surface of the water to flow around my feet and up my legs and arms. The air here is electric, so alive I could swear I hear it whisper, but so softly that I can't make out the words. I watch the soft, pulsing glow of the loch as the surface gleams and changes colour, from aqua, to dark crimson, to glittering gold.

The stars are visible between the clouds – God, I've never seen them so bright. They glitter in elaborate, alien constellations, swirling as though blown by a breeze.

The air is fragrant, floral, sharp and sweet at the same time. And the taste here – it's like Kiaran's, with the same wild fierceness of his power.

'Where are we?'

Kiaran's eyes are luminous, even more uncanny than usual, and his exquisite skin glows softly, as though kissed by moonlight. It's as if I'm finally seeing him clearly, the way he *should* be. He has never looked more beautiful, or more inhuman. 'The *Sìth-bhrùth.*'

No wonder everything looks so different here. We're in the faery realm. I draw my lightning pistol, expecting hostile fae at any moment. 'Why would you bring me here?' I ask, scanning the line of trees for any movement with my finger firm on the trigger.

'There are several realms within the *Sìth-bhrùth,* Kam,' he says. 'This one used to be neutral ground, the only place where conflict was never allowed.' He looks out over the loch. 'You can put the weapon away. We're safe here.'

I'm not convinced. 'I know how this works, MacKay,' I say. 'I've heard the stories. Faeries bring humans here for what feels like a few hours, but when they leave, years have gone by in the human world.'

Kiaran almost smiles. 'I'll keep track of the time – you'll be home by morning.'

With a resigned sigh, I holster the pistol and step forward. My boots sink into the soft sand at the water's edge. 'Fine. So what's beyond the loch?'

'The two largest territories: Seelie and Unseelie. They've been abandoned for two thousand years.' He frowns, as if he's remembering something long forgotten. 'After the war, the only *sìthichean* left behind here were those from the smaller realms that had refused to fight. Most of them crossed into the human realm after the others were imprisoned.'

Those are the creatures I kill almost every night. With the strongest fae trapped, the weaker, solitary faeries had their pick of any humans they wanted. A veritable banquet. No wonder they didn't want to stay in the *Sìth-bhrùth*.

'What will happen to this place?'

'I imagine those in the mounds will return to their home realms if we're unable to trap them beneath the city again.'

If we fail, he means. I can barely allow myself to contemplate it. If I do, the burden will become more than I can handle, a terrible crushing thing. Two against hundreds, with no way of evacuating the city. We are all that stands between the fae and complete destruction. The very thought makes me want to run and never look back.

'Aren't you worried?' I ask. 'Shouldn't we be finding the seal or amassing weapons? We ought to be preparing, MacKay, not wasting precious hours in the human world by being here.'

Kiaran glances at me, detached as ever. 'I've seen my share of battle, and I've faced worse than what we are about to. Do you know the most vital thing I've learned?'

'What?' I ask, exasperated.

He inclines his head towards the beautiful scene before us. 'To take in all of this, every calm moment you can. Breathe in the sight so deeply that the memory becomes a fundamental part of you. Sometimes, it will be all that's left to ground you. I brought you here to give you that.'

I wonder what memories ground Kiaran, that he'd want such a thing for me. He's always been ruthless in our training, never once leading me to believe he held any reverence for serenity.

I almost enquire again about his past, about the woman he once loved. But as I watch him, I decide against it. He gazes pensively out over the loch, and there's a sadness that in him speaks to my own grief. Sometimes the memories we cling hardest to are the ones that hurt us the most.

'Why haven't you gone back to your realm?'

Kiaran stiffens. 'This beach is as close as I can go.'

'The beach?' I look at the inviting water, now glowing such a warm, vivid teal that it reminds me of descriptions of the Mediterranean. 'What happens if you go further?'

Sorrow flickers across his face. If I hadn't been staring at him, I would have missed it. 'I'll die.'

I'm surprised by his answer. 'What? Why?'

His mask slips back into place, stern and unyielding. 'It's a sacrifice I made, Kam. I can never go back there.'

I step away from him, before I ask anything else. I'm tempted to say something reassuring, but it feels patronising to console someone who has seen so much, who knows first-hand just how harsh the world can be. Sometimes words simply fail.

I lower myself to the sand and yearn to touch the water, but I don't want to be insensitive. It wouldn't be fair to Kiaran.

'Go on,' he says. 'I don't mind.'

I smile slightly and softly brush the surface of the water. It undulates under my fingertips, sending delicate ripples across the entire loch, lit up like lightning ferns. How strange and lovely. 'You never told me how you avoided being trapped under the city with the others,' I say.

Kiaran settles next to me on the sand and crosses his long legs. 'No, I didn't. It's an unremarkable story.'

The water is cool when I sink my hand in and wiggle my fingers into the smooth, lustrous sand beneath. I love the way it slips across my palm, how it glitters like starlight. There is a long silence between Kiaran and me as we watch the ripples cross the water. I do as Kiaran said to, and let myself remember the time before all of this, before we met.

I think of home, of my past. Naming constellations on clear nights. Spring when heather colours the garden. Travelling to my father's country estate outside St Andrews. Lying with Mother in the grass on lazy afternoons, watching clouds rush overhead so rapidly it was dizzying.

Mother used to see the shapes of flowers in the clouds. She'd spot snowdrops and primroses and irises – I think because those were her favourites. While she saw a garden in the sky, I only ever saw … well, clouds. Ever the realist of the two of us.

'MacKay,' I say, 'do you think … if I had never worn the *seilgflùr* that I'd be normal?' I trace my fingers along the surface of the water again. 'Like my mother?'

'Her abilities hadn't been triggered, so she never felt compelled to hunt the *sìthichean*.' Kiaran shakes his head. 'Unfortunately for you, the seal breaking would have interrupted any normal life you might have led,' he says. 'You would still have to fight. You never had a choice.'

Hunting the fae has always been the one thing I thought I had control over. I choose when, where and how they die. I choose my weapons and how long I allow myself to delight in us fighting before I finally end their lives. But now I know the truth, the real reason I hunt. *You never had a choice.*

I wipe my wet palm against my trousers and say bitterly, 'No choice at all, aye? Haven't any active Falconers ever stopped hunting?'

Kiaran leans back on his hands. 'A few tried. In the end, they couldn't avoid their true nature any more than you'd be able to.' He looks over at me, eyes swirling amethyst and molten silver, like nothing I've ever seen before. 'Unless I'm wrong. When you imagine yourself years from now, is it the Seer you're with? Or is it you and me, planning our next slaughter?'

I avert my gaze. I won't answer that. He already knows the truth. 'What's in the nature of a *sìthiche*, then?'

He stares at the water intently. 'The *sìthichean* have become consumed by their obsession with obtaining power. They've lost everything else they ever cared for.'

'Don't they have power already?'

'Ah, Kam. Power is immeasurable.' He breathes out the

words as if he knows from experience just how intoxicating it is. 'It's thrilling, seductive, a craving that becomes an ache inside. A need that is never sated or forgotten.'

Every faery I've killed brings me physical relief, respite against guilt. In the rapture of their deaths, my memories cease to exist and all that's left is the lightweight joy of power.

I'm no better than the fae. We both kill for a single moment of relief. How can I ever admit that to Kiaran? I live for the hunt now. It's not just about survival or vengeance any more – it's become an addiction, too.

When I close my eyes, I can so easily imagine power surging through me, as startling and blissful as the rush of it in those first few seconds following a faery's death. There it is – the same hard pump of blood through my veins, the electric current that raises the fine hairs all over my body. The feather-light feeling, as if I'm floating off the ground.

Except this time, I swear I can hear my mother humming under her breath, in the same light way she used to. I'm gripped by the memory, by the soft lull of her voice, by the power coursing through me that's so strong my chest aches with it.

With a smile, I murmur, 'I wish you could hear her.'

A ridiculous thing to say, but the words slip from my tongue with little resistance. The singing is so soothing, I could fall asleep to it, right here on the beach.

'Hear who?'

I nestle my cheek against my knees and ignore him. It's vital that I hold on to the memory – I'm afraid that if I lose it, I'll forget the sound of her voice.

'Kam,' Kiaran snaps, grabbing my shoulders.

A light, airy laugh shatters my calm. My mouth fills with the grotesque tang of iron and blood and it feels as if it's being forced down my throat. I cough and gag into Kiaran's shoulder, then shove him away so I can retch onto the sand. All that comes up is saliva.

'Kadamach,' a familiar silvery voice says. 'I knew I'd find you here.' She laughs once more. 'And you brought your Falconer with you.'

I freeze. The blood in my veins turns to ice and I can't breathe. I am the girl I used to be again, weak and helpless. My mother's corpse is lying on the cobblestones. My hands are coated with blood and I can't get it off and I scrub and scrub and scrub but it won't come off and my dress is ruined and I'm tainted and *crimson suits you best crimson suits you best crimson suits you best crimson suits—*

'*No*,' I growl.

Not that. I won't be taken back there. I won't become that girl again. I try to push out of the memory, but its grip is strong, so real and relentless that it plays over and over and I'm helpless against it. Then, all at once, it fades so quickly that I'm left gasping.

'So that's who you are,' the *baobhan sìth* says, so softly that I barely hear her. 'You belong to that Falconer I killed last year.'

Kiaran stands. 'What do you want, Sorcha?'

He knows her, just like he knew that redcap. I told him I was looking for the *baobhan sìth* the night we met. He knew it was her the whole blasted time. It's another sharp reminder that I should never let myself soften towards him. He's not trustworthy.

'What do I want?' she asks lightly. 'Why don't we start with a proper greeting? It's been a long time, *a ghaoil*.'

'Don't call me that again,' he says. 'Ever.'

I've never heard Kiaran so quietly enraged, no matter what I've said to provoke him or how much I've tried his patience.

Sorcha clicks her tongue. 'You might be content to forget our past, but I'm not.'

'I won't ever be content,' he says. 'Not until you're dead.'

'Don't bandy idle threats, Kadamach,' Sorcha says. 'You're still bound by your vow to me. *Feadh gach re.* Always and for ever, remember?'

Vow? He made her a vow? She speaks again, says something in their language. Her sickeningly saccharine voice draws me back to that night, to the moment I first heard her. *Crimson suits you best.*

Kiaran growls something in the same tongue and Sorcha laughs. I feel her eyes on me then, heavy and judging. 'Poor thing,' Sorcha murmurs. 'Is your Falconer afraid? Little girl,' she calls. 'Open your eyes.'

No, I can't bear to look at her. I can't.

'Didn't you hear me? I said *open your eyes.*'

Her commanding tone forces me to obey. I stare at the faery who murdered my mother.

The *baobhan sìth* is more frightening than I remember – and more beautiful. Sorcha hovers above the centre of the lake's icy surface, tall and pale and flawless as marble. Her white shift billows and flows around her in a breeze I don't feel, the material so soft and fine that it looks like smoke. Her eyes are unnerving, cold and unblinking, vivid as emeralds.

Then Sorcha's lips curve into a hellish smile – the one that haunts my nightmares.

My chest tightens and I can't breathe. Desperately, I try to suck in air. I feel Sorcha in my mind then, a determined and merciless presence.

I try to fight against her, but she's strong. She's a weight pushing me down, down, until my memories assault me and I'm nothing but the traumatised girl inside me who witnessed her mother's murder.

I am beside my mother's body again, and I can smell blood. Cold rain penetrates my dress, tinting it red where the fabric clings to my legs, chilling me to the bone. The blood smells and feels so real, so thick on my hands, that I swear it's stained my skin. I drop to my knees and heave, clawing at the sand to get it off, tears blurring my vision.

'*Sorcha,*' Kiaran snaps. He sounds so far away.

The memories stop. I'm in my own body again, out of the blood-soaked dress. I breathe hard and don't try to stand. It's taking all of my effort not to collapse entirely.

'So this is your champion,' Sorcha says contemptuously. 'She can't even withstand the most basic mental influence.'

'She killed every *sìthiche* you sent,' Kiaran says, raking her with his gaze. 'Bested by a girl of eighteen with only a year of training. How pathetic she must make you feel.'

Sorcha's eyes burn, the colour intense even from here. 'If you'll recall, *I* was the one who drove her kind to extinction. You've never been very good at keeping them alive, have you?'

Kiaran's knuckles are white around the hilt of his blade. 'Tell me why you're here.'

She ignores him and looks at me again, studying me, reading me so intently that I wish I could disappear. 'What a sad creature you are, nowhere near as strong as your distant ancestors. That's Kadamach's fault, you know,' she says sweetly.

'Don't,' Kiaran says. 'Now is not the time.'

'Oh, I think now is the perfect time. Shall I tell you why your mother couldn't see me, little Falconer? Why she couldn't fight back? He suppressed the abilities of the Falconers who survived the war, so their children's abilities never manifested and I couldn't track them. For centuries I looked, but in vain.' She smiles. 'Until I happened to see your mother. Weak. Helpless and untrained, because of *him*. She never stood a chance against me.'

Oh, God. I want him to tell me that it isn't true. That Sorcha is just lying because this is a game to her. But he doesn't. He won't even look at me.

'That's enough, Sorcha.' Kiaran's voice is a powerful thing. It resonates across the entire lake. 'Just tell me why you're here.'

'If you insist,' she says. 'I have a message from my brother.' At Kiaran's startled expression, her smile turns a bit smug. 'The underground isn't entirely closed off, Kadamach. Some of the walls are thin enough to speak through. Lonnrach wants you to know that he asked me to call off my soldiers. Apparently, he thinks your champion worthy of battle with him.' She pauses, and I can feel her gaze on me again, hot and probing. 'We disagree.'

I rise to my feet and seek the vengeance inside me and feel ... nothing. Not the destructive creature inside me that craves violence, or the need for release. Simply nothing. She's stolen it from me.

'She's certainly different from your other pet Falconer,' Sorcha says. 'A shame how that turned out.'

Kiaran's hand tightens around the hilt of his blade, but he doesn't draw it from the sheath. 'Is that all you came to say?'

'No, but I'd rather discuss this.' Sorcha smiles mockingly. 'What was that girl's name again? I never bothered to remember.'

'Finish your message,' he says with deadly calm, 'or I'll send my blade straight through your heart. Vow or no vow.'

'I see your patience hasn't improved.' Sorcha tilts her head. 'You hid this one well from me, Kadamach. I didn't realise she existed until a fortnight ago.'

I remember Kiaran's words to me then, that night on the bridge with the redcaps. The words that changed everything. *Now you've hunted alone and she knows there's a Falconer in Edinburgh.*

If I'd been paying attention, I would have noticed he said *she*. Not *they*. Which means any of the fae I've fought in the last fortnight could have been sent by her. No wonder these recent nights have been filled to the brim with faeries hunting *me*, and not the other way around.

Thoughtfully, she adds, 'Until I saw your memories, I never even knew you watched me kill your mother. How very sad for you.'

Vengeance rises up inside me, powerful as ever. My skin burns, my rage purifies, becomes a surging storm within me until I'm cleansed of memories and guilt. *Finally*.

Our gazes collide. 'Try me now,' I tell her. 'I'll make *you* bleed.'

Sorcha smiles at my words. 'She didn't sense me, you know.' She bares those elongated teeth I remember so well. 'I tore out her throat before she had the chance.'

I explode. I jerk the lightning pistol from my belt and pull the trigger before I realise Sorcha is too far away for the capsule to hit.

The capsule strikes the water as if it were solid ice. Electricity crackles along the surface and the scent of ozone wafts into the air. I'm surprised when I inhale that I can detect a hint of *seilg-flùr*, too. As if the thistle were more potent here.

Sorcha doubles over and gasps for air so hard that her entire body shakes with the effort. She barely manages to speak. 'What did you—'

She coughs then, deep and rough, splattering dark blood across her white shift. Smoke rises from her feet as if the entire surface of the water is saturated with the thistle, burning her.

Now might be my only chance to kill her before the battle. I want her dead for my mother. For *me*.

'Kam, *stop*.'

I launch myself towards the loch, pistol raised, but an invisible force knocks me back. I slam into one of the trees that line the water and hit the ground. Leaves fall around me. My pistol is still in my hand, but my grip on it is weak. Kiaran's power leaves a sharp, saturated tang of earth in my mouth.

It hurts to swallow. I rise to my feet and slide the pistol back into its holster. Kiaran stands between me and Sorcha. She's still gasping for air. It's the perfect time to kill her. 'Get out of my way.'

'No.'

'*Move!*'

I try to charge past him, but he smashes so hard against me that he knocks all the breath from my lungs.

'No, Kam,' he says, holding me close. 'I can't let you.'

I claw at his shoulders. Fabric rips under my fingernails. 'Damn you, she's weakened now! You told me that you would never get in my way,' I remind him. 'You *vowed* it.'

He leans in so close. 'I never spoke the words to seal the vow.'

Before I can respond, he brushes his fingers across my temple. The overwhelming taste of honey and earth saturates my mouth and my eyes grow heavy. I try to fight it but I can't. His power is too strong. Just before the emptiness takes me, he rests his cheek against my own. I think I hear him whisper.

'I'm sorry.'

Chapter 27

The weather matches my mood as Dona and I walk quietly along George Street towards the modiste's shop. My heavy green silk dress swishes and I squint up at the clouds from beneath my umbrella. Another cold, rainy winter day.

I can't help but mentally curse Kiaran with every step. Damn him for his meddling, for rendering me unconscious when I was so close to killing Sorcha, for ... *everything*. A dull headache pounds at my temples from his influence. I didn't even wake up until noon and Dona had to rush to dress me for our appointment with the modiste.

Derrick perches on my shoulder, wings moving animatedly as he rants. '—comes into the room and you're both soaking wet. Then sets you down on the bed – gently, I suppose, considering he's a right bastard – and calmly tells me that he will speak with you later. When he comes by, can I pull out his entrails?'

I can't help but laugh softly. Horseless carriages line the street and the traffic is heavy, still being diverted from Princes Street after the bridge disaster. I can't believe it's only been a few days since it happened. The street is lively with the sounds of steam engines purring, the laughter of ladies as they walk with gentlemen to their respective destinations. We stroll past the handsome white stone buildings with little hindrance, since people seem rather eager to step out of my way. They mustn't be associated with a ruined lady, after all. My reputation won't begin to recover until after I marry.

The residents of New Town are few in number, and everyone is either acquainted or known by reputation. Assuming one's reputation does not resemble mine, people are usually quite friendly and make a habit of greeting each other as they pass.

'Good day to you, Mr Blackwood,' I say.

The young gentleman simply nods and strides past without stopping.

'I suppose Mr Blackwood is in a hurry today,' I tell Dona.

'Why do we care about what these people think, anyway?' Derrick mutters. 'They're idiots. But, if you want, I can *make* them say hello to you. I haven't used my powers on anyone in a long time and now that I think of it, I rather miss it.'

'*We* should be polite,' I say pointedly through gritted teeth, though I don't feel amiable at all.

'Just being honest.'

Thankfully it isn't much further to the modiste's. I step into the shop and collapse my umbrella as I look around. The shop is warm and bright in comparison to the drab grey outside. Two velvet settees sit in the middle of the room, a tea service betwixt them already prepared. Beyond them are three mirrors framing a stool, where customers can view themselves from every angle. The wallpaper is a rich burgundy that matches the Persian carpet underneath the furniture.

Derrick snorts. 'No honey with the tea? What kind of establishment is this?'

Above us float the globe lanterns that are so popular these days. One hums a bit too close to my face and I nudge it gently back up towards the ceiling.

'Lady Aileana! I didn't hear you come in.'

Miss Forsynth, the modiste, bustles out of the back room. An older woman, about one-and-fifty, Miss Forsynth is the premier modiste in Edinburgh and Father has called on her to design my wedding dress.

'Good day, Miss Forsynth,' I say. 'Lovely to see you.'

'Please have a seat, my lady. May I take your coat? It's just us this afternoon.'

I remove the heavy, damp coat from around my shoulders and hand it to her along with my umbrella. She takes them to the cloakroom and returns with several swatches of fabric.

'Now then, let me show you some ideas.' Miss Forsynth sits next to me, clicking her tongue. 'I do wish I had more time to prepare your dress. We could work up something so much more elegant if we had another month.'

I sip my tea. 'I'm sorry about the rush.'

Smile. Nod. Be polite. Be proper Aileana, because proper Aileana apologises even when she doesn't have to. She's bland and dull and *nice*. I just have to survive the day without killing anyone.

Miss Forsynth pats my hand. 'Oh, my dear, I do *understand*. After all, Lord Galloway is quite handsome, isn't he? I can see why the hurry is necessary.' She eyes me knowingly. Good heavens.

I put down my damned teacup before I break it. Derrick snickers at me. 'No wonder you go out for a slaughter every night.'

Miss Forsynth picks up her swatches and hands them to me. 'Now, as I was saying, I have some lovely fabric choices for your dress before I show you some designs. This –' she holds up the one from the top of the pile '– is a delicate silk taffeta. Isn't it just lovely?'

'It's hideous,' Derrick says. 'Next.'

I stifle a sigh. There are so many places I would rather be

than here. Seeking out Kiaran and threatening him with my lightning pistol for a start. I still haven't processed the anger and shock I awoke to this morning after everything Sorcha revealed. Everything that Kiaran has been keeping from me.

'Lady Aileana?'

'Aye, quite lovely,' I say absently, plastering on a pleasant smile.

'Or look at this ivory silk,' she says, pulling out another swatch. 'It would go so beautifully with your colouring.'

Dona nods her approval, but Derrick buzzes near my head. 'Is she kidding? Ivory? Does she want you to look sallow? Why don't you just tell her to shove off and that you aren't marrying that bloody basta—'

'Blue,' I say firmly, interrupting Derrick's rant. 'I think I would prefer blue.'

Miss Forsynth blinks in surprise at my outburst. 'Blue? That's certainly quite … old-fashioned – ivory has become a popular choice among modern brides. Her Majesty herself wore it at her wedding and looked very beautiful indeed.'

'How splendid for Her Majesty. I, however, would prefer blue. Do you have this in blue?' I don't want to spend a minute longer in this place than I have to.

The modiste purses her lips, wrinkling the corners of her mouth. 'Of course. Marvellous choice.' She forces a tight partial smile. 'Shall I show you some design choices?'

Damnation.

She brings out some drawings and samples of other dresses. I nod at the appropriate intervals, barely comprehending her words. I must have agreed to something, however, because before I can make an excuse to leave, she escorts me to the back room to take my measurements and pin fabric on me.

I stand on a stool in the centre of the room and Dona steps up on her own stool to unbutton my day dress. She pulls the sleeves of my dress down my arms, revealing my chemise. I glare at Derrick, who's grinning wickedly. He sits on the chimney-piece and wiggles his fingers at me.

'Oh, fine,' he says as I shake my head subtly. His wings fan behind him as he turns away. 'Why must you always ruin my fun?'

I stand stiffly as Miss Forsynth takes her measurements. 'My lady, could you raise your arms, please?'

I lift my arms, a mute doll.

Three days. Three days until midwinter, three days until the world ends, and I'm doing this. I suppose it's appropriate. If I live through the battle, I will go right back to this – to being a plaything, a show horse for people to stare at and gossip over.

It will be as if nothing happened. I'll still have to marry Gavin in a fortnight. I'll still be forced into my neat little cage where ladies are never supposed to feel anger, where they must always be accommodating and complaisant no matter what grief they suffer under their pleasant demeanour.

What you want isn't important.

Miss Forsynth pokes at my upper arm and glances at me in surprise at the muscles there. Ladies are not encouraged to engage in the sort of physical activity that might make our bodies look less feminine.

By the time the modiste finishes measuring and pinning, I'm stiff from holding still for her. Before I leave, she says, 'In a few days time I shall stop over at your house for the first fitting.' She pats my hand. 'Fear not, my lady, you will make the most beautiful bride in Edinburgh. The blue is a lovely colour on you.'

I grit my teeth in a farewell grimace that I hope passes for a smile as I step out of her shop and into the rain. Most beautiful bride, indeed. If only that were my foremost fear. I wonder if I'll survive – if anyone will survive – to attend my wedding.

*

Later, at home, I stand in front of my hidden map of Scotland, studying the path of Sorcha's kills. One hundred and eighty-six kills. No one will know how they really died, except me and Derrick.

I brush my fingers over the ribbon that represents my mother's death, the first one I ever marked. God, I've planned for so long, trained and fought and killed and overcome everything I thought would weaken me if I ever faced this faery. I've built weapons, imagined myself slaying her in a multitude of ways. I planned. I tracked her. I practised. I waited.

In the end, none of it mattered. I was so consumed by my own memories, my grief, that she took advantage of it with little effort at all. I can place some of the blame on Kiaran for stopping me, and claim a small victory in hurting her for a brief moment. But before that, the *baobhan sìth* played with me. She broke into my mind, reduced me to that pathetic little girl who knelt in blood, too afraid to move. She could do it again if she wanted.

I grasp the bottom edge of the map and rip the paper off the wall with a sharp jerk, scattering pins and ribbons across the hardwood floor at my feet.

'Aileana?' Derrick sounds concerned.

'This is stupid,' I say, tearing the map into pieces. 'It was a waste of time.'

'No, it wasn't,' he says, flying around me. 'It's—'

I toss the paper into the fireplace and light it. I watch the map burn, curling and blackening at the edges. I let go of my hard work, all the effort I put into believing that I'd find Sorcha one day and slay her so magnificently.

'Aileana,' Derrick says from his perch on the table.

I sit at the window and stare outside. Only half-past four in the afternoon and it's already nightfall.

'You weren't there,' I say softly. 'After everything I thought

I was capable of – she made me watch her kill my mother all over again.'

I hear the flutter of Derrick's wings as he lands on my shoulder. 'I should have been there for you. When I heard she was in the city, I came home as fast as I could, but you had already gone.'

Laughing bitterly, I say, 'I'm glad you weren't there. She could have broken me so easily if she wanted to. I can't believe I let her—'

I stop, unable to say the words. *I can't believe I let her weaken me again. I can't believe I let her murder my mother again. I can't believe I let Kiaran get in my way.*

'I know,' Derrick whispers.

I watch the rain and inhale the scent of damp air. Soft fog lingers in the back garden. At moments like this, I appreciate how the weather in Scotland is never the same, and how swiftly it changes. How the rain itself seems to breathe, soft and slow. Right now, it falls in the same leisurely way feathers do. I open the window and let the wind carry the rain inside, to wet my cheeks and cool my skin.

I'm discovering a new kind of solace in being alone, in appreciating all the things I might never experience if I don't survive past midwinter. I've never been the kind of lass to seek stillness to find meaning. I find meaning in the simplicity of destruction. The calm before a squall presents a moment so profound and quiescent, when the entire world stops and waits.

'What are you going to do, Aileana?'

'About what?'

I lean out through the open window. Rain drops featherlight against my face. The cold air blows against me and the soft rain turns to wee pieces of ice that adhere to my hair.

'The *baobhan sìth.*'

I wince. 'For the first time in a year, I don't even want to think about her.'

'But—'

'Enjoy this with me,' I say. 'Help me forget about last night.'

His wings tickle my cheek as he tangles himself in my hair. 'Just one thing,' he whispers. 'Don't ever let her break you.'

If he were my size, I would have hugged him. Instead, I lift a hand and stroke the silky softness of his wings. His tiny cheek presses against mine.

Together, we sit and watch the rain fall.

Chapter 28

Past midnight, I am about to leave the house for a hunt when I sense the subtle tang of Kiaran's power emanating from the hallway. Blast! I hope he isn't visible for the servants to see him strolling about. I don't need another problem to add to my ever-growing list.

'I know you're there, MacKay, and you can go right back out the way you came in.'

The doorknob twists and catches on the lock. Kiaran swears softly. 'Open the door, Kam.'

Derrick dives from the windowsill, a red halo of light surrounding him. 'Oh, good. He's finally here. I believe I vowed to tear out his innards.'

'I swear, I am going to kill that damn pixie,' I hear Kiaran mutter. 'Kam. Let me in or I'll remove the door from its hinges. Your choice.'

I bite back my automatic reply: *You wouldn't dare.* Because he absolutely would, and I prefer to leave my door just where it is. I can't believe I'm doing this. I unlatch the lock.

Kiaran stands in the hallway, soaked through from the downpour, hands braced on either side of the doorframe. His dark hair clings to his pale cheeks and his shirt is nearly transparent from the rain, revealing his smooth chest rising and falling with his quick, ragged breaths.

I'm surprised to hear his breathing. Usually he is so silent, every part of him still. 'What do you want?' I ask bluntly. I have no energy for politeness.

Kiaran glances behind me. 'Are you going to invite me in, or shall I continue to drip all over your hallway carpet?'

I step aside to let him pass, and close the door behind him, then lean my back against it. 'Make this brief. I'm terribly inclined to shoot you again, and this time I'll aim for something vital.'

Derrick lands on my shoulder. 'Again?' He sounds indignant. 'How did I miss that?'

'You were out,' I say.

'Damn,' he mumbles. 'I should have loved to see it.'

Kiaran runs a hand through his wet hair. Water drips from his clothes into a puddle around his feet.

I have a hard time meeting his gaze after everything that happened last night. The only compliments I've ever received from Kiaran were for my battle scars, for how efficiently I can drive a blade through my enemy. Now he's seen how broken my mother's death has really left me, and when it mattered, he took away the thing I wanted most. His vow meant nothing, and worse: he made his own promise to Sorcha, and stopped me from killing her when I had the chance. That won't be easy for me to forgive.

Kiaran draws his shoulders back. He's so tall, he towers over me. 'I'm not here to apologise.'

'Wonderful. Thank you for confirming what I had already assumed,' I say. 'There are two exits out of this room. Choose one.'

Derrick chuckles. 'I'd say this is a rather glorious comeuppance.'

Kiaran's glare is scorching. 'Stay out of this.'

'No,' Derrick says.

'Careful, pixie,' he says. 'You forget what I am.'

Derrick swoops over to Kiaran and hovers in front of him. His halo is so bright now that none of his features are distinguishable. 'I've never forgotten. That's why I'll never trust you with her.'

Kiaran growls something in his language, and Derrick hisses a response with equal venom. I only comprehend a few errant words. The language is just similar enough to *Gàidhlig* to sound familiar, but not anything like I've heard it spoken.

Finally, Derrick snarls in English, 'I'm not yours to command. I never was.'

'*All right,*' I say, reaching for the pixie, but he's far too quick. I manage to insert myself between him and Kiaran. 'Derrick, could you go into the dressing room and give us a moment?'

He snorts. 'I think not.'

'Derrick,' I say, more firmly.

'Fine,' he retorts. 'But I still want his innards.'

He snaps another unintelligible word at Kiaran before barrelling into the dressing room in a stream of light. The door slams shut behind him.

Kiaran stares at the dressing room door. 'That pixie must care a great deal for you,' he says. 'I've never seen one cohabit with a human.'

He has quite an amazing talent for changing the subject. 'What happened between you two?'

'Nothing pleasant.'

'I already assumed that. You didn't answer my question.'

'I rarely do.' When I only glare at him, he says, 'Say whatever you're thinking. Get it out.'

I'm so tired of Kiaran's games, his vague answers. I'm tired of being manipulated. 'Your vow meant nothing – you let the *baobhan sìth* live.'

'Necessity, Kam. That was the first lesson I ever taught you.'

'Don't treat me like I'm naïve.' I rake him with my eyes. 'You speak of necessity to absolve yourself of any responsibility for your actions. Like failing to mention the part you've played in keeping my ancestors powerless. That you *knew* Sorcha. In fact, you appeared to be downright familiar with one another. Who is she to you? Old friend?' I step closer. 'Old *lover*, MacKay?'

Kiaran dips his head, his nose nearly touching mine. 'That's none of your damned business.'

I don't yield. I don't retreat from him or let him intimidate me. I meet his gaze directly and ask, 'What vow did you make to her?' When he doesn't respond, I speak more forcefully. 'Tell me. *Now.*'

How could he say a true vow to her and not me? His word was the one common ground we had. The one thing I could depend on him never to betray, at the risk of his own life. And in the end his vow was just another faery half-lie.

Kiaran's jaw tics and I wonder if he'll tell me anything, even another lie. 'My life is intertwined with hers,' he says. 'If Sorcha dies, so do I.'

My breath is squeezed from my lungs, leaving an awful ache in my chest. I turn away from him. My vision blurs and I'm horrified to realise that my eyes are filled with tears. It's been so long. I'd forgotten how much they burn.

'Why would you do that?' I ask. My voice is surprisingly calm.

'I warned you about the consequences of trying to prevent a Seer's vision from coming to pass,' he says quietly. 'This is but one of mine.'

Don't cry, I tell myself as he grasps my shoulders and turns me to face him. *Don't cry.* Too late. His body goes still, eyes searching mine. 'Tears, Kam?' he breathes. 'Whatever for?'

I don't acknowledge his words. I can't. 'You knew Sorcha is the one I've been searching for all this time.'

'Aye, I did.'

An awful thought crosses my mind, one that immediately dries my eyes. My fingers curl into fists. 'So did you let my mother die?'

He looks away from me then. 'By the time I tracked Sorcha to Edinburgh, she had already found your mother.' His fingers tighten on my shoulders, a seemingly involuntary motion. 'I had just enough time to tell her the truth about who she was. I advised her to leave the city, but she wouldn't abandon you. So I gave her the thistle and she put it on you that night. She wanted me to save *you*.'

I can barely remember my mother's words when she wove the thistle into my hair. I was so excited, only half-listening. She described how it matched my eyes. She warned me never to take it off, in a sudden sombre tone that might have unnerved me if I'd bothered to pay any attention at all.

I pull out of his grasp. 'Save me? Is that what you think you did, *Kadamach*?'

Kiaran's face hardens. 'Don't call me that.'

'Why not? That's your name, isn't it?'

He surprises me by resting a hand flat on my cheek. His fingers are warm, inviting. The connection between us is so intense that I might have been tempted to lean into that touch, but his gaze stops me. His eyes burn bright, uncanny and overwhelming.

'Shall I tell you about the one who answered to that name?'

His lilting accent is back. This is a voice born to compel, born to command. It is beautiful and ugly, terrifying and comforting, a million dichotomies I can only begin to describe. It's meant to remind me that beneath skin and bone he is a powerful, inhuman creature who could kill me with little difficulty. I almost forgot again.

I can't speak or move, can't look away. His fingertips trace along my collarbone, but his touch is cold now, growing ever more frigid. The hair raises along my arms.

'Kadamach lived for destruction,' Kiaran says. 'He would have ripped the soul from your body and devoured it. And that would have brought him rapture.' A flicker of fear ignites inside me as his lips brush my cheek. 'Names hold power, Kam,' he says. 'Don't use that one unless you'd like to see first-hand what it was once capable of.'

I don't step away, despite how much I want to. 'But you still cared for someone,' I say. 'A Falconer, like Sorcha said. Even Kadamach was capable of love.'

Kiaran flinches, a slight motion, barely noticeable, but it tells me how acutely he still feels the pain of her death. 'Don't make the mistake of believing you know that part of my past. If you think it humanises me, you're a sentimental fool.' He straightens and steps away from me, the trail of his cold touch still burning across my skin. 'It's time we found the seal.'

Before I can answer, he opens my bedchamber door and disappears down the hall.

Chapter 29

When I round the front of my house, I'm surprised to see my ornithopter parked in the middle of Charlotte Square again. 'You brought it back from Dalkeith,' I say to Kiaran. 'How on earth did you figure out how to fly it?

'I watched you yesterday.' Kiaran reaches into the front seat and pulls out my lightning pistol and holster. 'I thought you might want this.'

Gratefully, I take it from him and secure the holster around my hips before seating myself at the helm. 'So let me see if I have this right. We're looking for a two-thousand-year-old seal that's completely hidden from faeries—'

'*Sìthichean.*'

'Faeries. We have no idea what it looks like, how big it is, or even where it is—'

'It's in what is now the Queen's Park,' he interrupts again. 'The last battle took place there and it's directly above the prison.'

'So we have the general location, which happens to be approximately three miles in circumference? Brilliant. That's just brilliant.'

I start the machine. The massive wings deploy and flap, and we're soon airborne. I breathe in the rainy air and turn the ornithopter towards the south end of the city.

'You should be able to sense the device once we're close enough,' Kiaran says. 'When they activated it, the Falconers charged it with their power to ward off any *sìthichean* who happen upon it.'

'How can I be certain what to look for?'

Kiaran stares into the darkness beyond the ornithopter. 'You'll know when you find it.'

I sigh in frustration and gaze out over the city. Below, candlelight flickers in the tenements of Old Town and gas lamps cast deep shadows along the streets. Thin fog rolls along the ground and between buildings, coating the roads in ghostly white. The closer we get to Holyroodhouse and the Queen's Park, the more the light dims until there is only darkness below.

The faint outline of the rocky peak of Salisbury Crags comes into view. As my eyes adjust to the darkness, I focus on the steep hills across the valley. Arthur's Seat looms highest, its peak framed by clouds and mist. I steer the helm towards the dark meadow directly below it.

Rain beats against the machine's wings as we swoop down and land on the grass. The park is quiet but for the sound of the downpour, no birds or animals rustling in the trees.

My leather boots sink into the soft meadow grass when I climb from the ornithopter. 'Now what?'

Kiaran doesn't spare me a glance. 'We walk. You detect.'

He strides away across the dark grass. I dart after him and stub my toe against a rock. 'Could you please slow down for the girl with the useless human night vision?'

Kiaran stops. 'Apologies,' he says, though he doesn't sound at all as if he means it.

I feel his heavy gaze on me despite the darkness, and I still find it difficult to look at him, more so now than ever. He saw my tears. In a single moment I was forced to give up on vengeance, on ever killing Sorcha, or risk losing him. I never realised how much I had begun to care for Kiaran that it would hurt so badly.

I wonder what awful fate he tried to prevent by making that vow to Sorcha. What would be worth connecting his life to hers for eternity?

'What would you have risked to kill Sorcha?' he says before I can speak. 'And answer me honestly, Kam. Would you have given up your life?'

I glance at him in surprise. 'Of course not,' I say.

The lie rolls off my tongue with such ease. I've become so good at deception that there are moments when I almost believe my lies myself. A lie is best told with a single grain of truth, a factual hook on which to hang the falsehood. That's what makes them so easy to maintain.

'I saw your resolve,' he says quietly. 'I watched you decide that little else mattered to you except vengeance. And do you know what I thought?'

'What?' I whisper, almost afraid of what he'll say.

'I made you the same as me.'

I look away, towards the slope that leads up to the crags. Rain drops onto my face and I don't bother to wipe it away. My chest is so tight, my heart heavy. I had stupidly, inexplicably hoped he would tell me that I was strong, or magnificent. That he'd show the same pride in me that I saw the day before yesterday in the drawing room when I held the knife to his throat.

But he didn't. I'm like him. I'm a monster, too.

For the briefest moment, I wish I was the girl I used to be. I'd wear frivolous white dresses and attend dances and never worry about anything ever again. But I had to destroy the girl who wore white dresses because she wasn't capable of murder. And now I have to live with my choice.

My laugh is rough, bitter. I should resent him for everything he's done. His lessons have been branded inside me until I've become what I am now, this vengeful, destructive creature. But I can't. This is all I have, and there's no turning back.

'I made my own choice, MacKay,' I remind him.

'It was a choice I knew you would make,' he says. 'I saw your rage the night we met. I understood it all too well.'

We walk swiftly down the narrow path in the middle of the Queen's Park, both of us silent. I shudder against the cold and tug my coat cuffs down over my hands. Useless. My clothes are already sopping. I tilt my head to gaze at the sky, letting the rain slide down my face. The clouds are silver, low-hanging and dark at their bottom edges.

If I die, I think I'll miss this. I'll miss the stars and constellations my mother loved so much. I'll miss home. I wonder if Kiaran does, too.

'MacKay?'

'Hmm?'

'Do you ever—' I swallow once. 'Do you ever long for the *Sìth-bhrùth?*'

We skirt around a small loch, shining silver with reflected moonlight in the dark meadow. Kiaran's movements are stiff, as if he's startled by the question. 'Sometimes.'

'What was your home there like?'

'Beautiful,' he says. 'Brutal. No words in any language could ever adequately describe it.' When I stare at him expectantly, he looks reluctant to continue. 'I hated my home as much as I loved it.'

'But would you go back, if you could?'

'No,' Kiaran replies, his voice clipped, a bit angry. 'Never. It's not worth it.'

'Why not?'

He sighs. 'Because I didn't belong there any more, Kam. I don't belong here, either.'

He doesn't sound like he hates it. He sounds as if he misses it, as if he left a part of himself there that he'll never be able to reclaim. 'Too many painful memories there?'

I think about the Falconer he once cared for, what she might have been like. She managed to convince him to make a vow never to kill humans, to fundamentally change the creature he was born to be. What I wouldn't give to know how she took a faery, cold and hard and brutal as any other, and humanised him.

Just when I think he might be open with me, he shuts down. His jaw tightens and he stuffs his hands in the pockets of his wet trousers. 'Aye,' is all he says.

We're on the dirt path again. The soil crunching under my boots is the only noise other than the rain. The downpour has slowed to a soft, light mist that looks more like snow.

'After midwinter,' Kiaran says, 'will you still marry him? The Seer?'

I suck in a breath. 'My father wants me to.'

'But what do *you* want?'

What you want isn't important.

But it is. I want to leave the house without a chaperone. I want to be able to turn down dances and not smile and grieve without being judged for it. I want to feel again, the way I once did. I want … I want …

Hope again. To look forward to a day when my need for vengeance is pacified and I have a future. I know the truth. Even if I could kill Sorcha without condemning Kiaran to death, I won't ever change. I can't stop being what I am. This is my nature now, like Kiaran said, and I'll never be sated.

I can't say any of this aloud. 'I want to decide my own future,' I say instead.

Kiaran studies me, long and slow. 'Don't we all?'

A sudden powerful electric jolt shoots through my body. It happens so fast, my knees buckle and I stumble.

'Kam?'

'What *is* that?' It doesn't hurt, but the sensation isn't exactly comfortable, either. It invades me, alien and unwelcome. My skin tightens and aches and I resist the urge to scratch my arms. It's under my flesh, a persistent tingling. 'Don't you feel it?'

Kiaran shakes his head once. 'What's it like?'

'Something electric.' I shiver again. 'It's irritating. Like my skin is going to crawl off.'

Kiaran grasps my arm to pull me forward. 'We must be close, then.'

The sensation only grows more intense as we continue, but also becomes more tolerable. I can feel my blood pumping through my body, urging me to move faster. I close my eyes briefly and let the feeling lead me.

I leap over a rock in a run and bound across the grass, even though I can barely see. Kiaran races beside me.

The sensation becomes more acute, electricity more intense, a magnet pulling me in. I turn onto another rocky path and realise we're heading right for the remains of St Anthony's Chapel.

I race to the north wall of the stone ruins, where the chapel's entrance used to be. The energy drops to my feet before I reach the threshold and I fall to my knees in the mud.

Then I dig. With my fingers, my hands. I don't know what the bloody hell I'm doing. I just claw at the ground desperately, breathing so hard that my throat hurts. I dig and dig until my fingernails bleed and dirt cakes my skin. Somehow I know my body won't stop shuddering until I find the device. I have to find it. There's a buzzing in my ears, a low clicking that only makes me dig more frantically. I have to find it. I can't stop now.

My nails scrape against something metal. As I brush off the mud, something glows bright and golden underneath, warming to my touch. Something about uncovering it calms me. The clicking softens as I clear away the dirt that borders a luminous gold disc about the size of a carriage wheel.

The buzzing and electricity are gone and my trembling has stopped altogether. I lean over the golden cover for the seal, tracing the symbols carved into it. So beautiful and warm. There are five indentations near the edge of the disc, as if pressed there by fingertips. Compelled, I cover them with my mud-caked fingers.

The clicking stops, and suddenly I'm blinded by light.

Chapter 30

I close my eyes against the onslaught; images in negative and colours and dots pulse behind my eyelids. Soft warmth envelops me.

When I open my eyes, the golden light is still overwhelming. It blazes in a column up to the sky, surrounding me and illuminating the chapel ruins. Rain shimmers as it falls through the light, as if I'm surrounded by shooting stars.

I finally look down at the device, surprised to see that the top plate has slid open to reveal intricate golden gears inside. They are incredibly delicate, the metal thin enough to be slightly transparent.

I've never seen such detailed work. So many gears and pinions whirling smoothly around each other with tiny golden levers interspersed between them. Seven rings increasing in size from the centre of the circle outwards, forming an ever-moving mechanism covered in symbols, not unlike an elaborate clock face. The symbols on the gold rings nearest the middle are the most elaborate, evolving to broader swirls on the outer rings. I think of the brand on the inside of Kiaran's wrist, how similar it is to these designs, how utterly beautiful and detailed.

Gold markers are positioned at each of the cardinal points around the largest ring, with smaller notches between them.

It's both a compass and a clock, I realise, beautiful and mesmerising.

I feel power around me. Pure energy, soothing elation, a heat inside me that's like bathing in sunlight. This is the kind of device I long to make. Something that unifies me, calms me. And it's a part of my heritage I had never dreamed possible. It belongs to me.

Amid my elation, I look at Kiaran. He stands ever so still at the edge of the golden light.

'It's beautiful,' I say. 'Come over here – you should see this.'

He hesitates, gazing up at the aurulent light. 'I can't.'

'Don't be silly.' I push to my feet and reach through the light to grip his hand. 'See? Just come inside—'

When his fingers pass into the light, he sucks in a breath and jerks his hand from mine, clutching his wrist.

'MacKay!' I hurry to his side to see what's wrong. The column of light wavers, then settles into the ground. The power is gone so quickly and I shiver against the cold. 'What is it?'

'Nothing,' he says stiffly.

'Of course it's not nothing.' I try to peek over his shoulder but he shifts away. 'Show me.'

I pull his arm towards me, despite his resistance. When I see his hand, I let out a strangled gasp. There are blisters and torn red and black flesh at his fingertips, even bone peeking through, as if they have gone through fire.

'The device is warded against anyone who isn't a Falconer,' he says.

I feel a pang of guilt, then. He told me he couldn't come in and I didn't even bother to ask why. I watch the miraculous faery healing process spread across his hand. Gleaming pale skin is already peeking through the charred black, healing over the bones of his fingertips.

'I'm sorry,' I say. 'I shouldn't have—'

'Don't apologise – the light is meant to protect you against the *sìthichean.*' He nods to the device. 'Can you make it work?'

'I certainly hope so.'

As soon as I step back inside the circle, the light rises around me again. I crouch to the ground and slide my fingers along the gold rings. Power buzzes beneath my palms, an electric current that feels embedded in the smooth, silken metal. It's incredible craftsmanship.

Kiaran sits on a boulder and leans forward. 'What does it look like from above?'

'Complex,' I reply. 'Highly sophisticated. I don't recognise the technology at all. How could they possibly have built this two thousand years ago?'

Kiaran looks at me, rather pityingly. 'The *sìthichean* were far more advanced then than humans are now.' He inclines his head towards the device. 'That is *sìthichean* technology. A reverse-engineered and altered *iuchair* – the Seelie used it for confinement.'

Of course. I have never thought of the fae as innovators of any kind. It seems strange that such destructive creatures could build something so beautiful.

'How did the Falconers get hold of it, then?'

He looks away. 'They had help.'

I trace one of the swirls etched into the gold. 'From whom?'

'It doesn't matter. What do the symbols look like?'

I lean forward to get a better look. 'Complicated swirls. I don't really know how to describe the symbols they make. There's a star-shaped engraving next to the marker that indicates north, but the others are more obscure.'

'I suggest you take a good look and then cover the device again so no one disturbs it. You'll have to draw the symbols from memory.'

I look up in surprise. 'Can't we come back?'

'No.' He holds up his hand to forestall my inevitable question. 'Kam, for once just take my word for it. Can you remember the symbols as they are now and draw them later?'

I hesitate. 'I'm adequate at drafting, but I've never done so from memory.'

'Wonderful.' Kiaran rises to his feet. 'Then this is the perfect opportunity for you to try.'

Chapter 31

The echo of the electric charge lingers as I sketch the symbols. I swear I can still feel the heat beneath my skin, flowing through my veins. It sharpens my memory, which only grows stronger with each passing moment.

I keep drawing feverishly, obsessively. The charcoal scratches across the paper as if something beyond me is in control of it. My hand can barely keep up with the pace of my mind.

Someone grasps my shoulder and I flinch. The charcoal on the paper smears.

'Steady,' Kiaran says. 'You're shaking.'

'I'm fine,' I lie.

Rays of low afternoon light shine through the drawing room window and settle on the paper while I sketch. My fingers are stained black with charcoal and my hand is cramping, but I can't stop. The energy continues to pound inside me, symbol after symbol. I sketch a smaller swirl. The charcoal is so bulky compared to my memory of the delicate lines etched onto the metal, and I'm not nearly as adept at drawing something so intricate.

'Can't she activate the bloody contraption before mid-winter?' Gavin asks. 'Avoid the battle completely?'

Gavin came here under the pretence of elevenhours and

has been drinking tea like he does whisky ever since I explained what will happen on midwinter. Of course, he already had a vague idea of it from his visions, though he still hasn't told me how clear the premonition has become.

He shifts in his chair and recrosses his legs, one knee bouncing rapidly. His blasted teacup is empty again. I try to ignore him and focus on my drawing.

'No,' Kiaran says. 'We can't.'

'Could you try to be any less vague?'

'If we could avoid it, Seer, we wouldn't be here,' Kiaran says. 'And I'd imagine you'd be hiding in a hovel somewhere like the rest of your kind.'

'Well, if *your* kind weren't such—'

'Gentlemen!' I think my head will explode. 'I can't concentrate with you squabbling. At least Derrick is being polite.' I glance over at the pixie, who is perched on the windowsill. 'Make sure you stay that way.'

'I didn't say anything!'

'You were considering it. Don't think I haven't noticed you glaring at Kiaran the whole time.'

Derrick grumbles to himself and finally says, 'I suppose I understand why *he* is here.' He indicates Kiaran with a faint nod. 'But tell me, must the Seer be included in our little-end-of-the-world meeting?'

I begin another swirl, part of a new symbol that runs around the southward edge of the seal. I exhale with relief. Almost done.

'Gavin is here,' I say, 'because he's involved in this. I could have died the other night without his aid.'

A flash of guilt crosses Derrick's face. 'Ah. Aye.'

'Thank you for defending my honour,' Gavin says to me. He places his empty cup on the table. 'Where's your butler? I'm out of tea.'

'For heaven's sake,' I say, 'will you please sip the tea so I don't have to pour you another cup every five minutes?'

'We're facing an apocalypse,' he replies. 'There is not enough tea in the world to calm me.'

I draw the last symbol and the electricity tingling at my fingertips vanishes. My body stops shaking and I exhale a long breath, dropping the charcoal to wipe my tired hand with a kerchief.

'Finished.'

Kiaran leans in to inspect my work. His warm shoulder is so close to mine that if I scoot over only a wee bit more, we'd be touching. As I inhale his scent, I can't help but shift closer, closing the gap between us and pressing my side to his. The taste of his power only grows more intoxicating. He turns to look at me, and our faces are a mere breath away. Everything around me fades and blurs and my gaze drops to his lips.

'Does it look all right?' I whisper.

Gavin's voice sounds so very far away. 'Get back, faery. Now.'

Bloody hell. I recoil from Kiaran, suddenly aware of what I almost did. My cheeks flush and my heart speeds up in embarrassment. I swear, I was tempted to kiss Kiaran – and in front of Derrick and Gavin, no less. What is *wrong* with me?

'For once, I agree with the Seer,' Derrick says. 'Keep your distance, or I *will* bite you.'

Kiaran picks up my drawing. 'Try it and I'll pluck your wings off and feed them to you.'

Derrick hisses. Gavin just looks interested, as if wondering whether such a thing might be possible.

'Well,' I say brightly, 'we're getting on splendidly, aren't we? Glad to see you're all becoming friends over your mutually violent desires.'

'Not me,' Gavin says. 'I'm just here for the tea.'

'Not the company?' I put a hand to my heart. 'I'm wounded. I thought you liked me.'

'More often than not.'

Kiaran sets the paper flat on the table between us. 'Shall we discuss this, or would you prefer to socialise?'

I blink up at him. 'Please continue.'

'A clock and a compass were added to the *iuchair* design.' He indicates the symbols at each point. 'These are meant to correspond to a lunar event – an eclipse, in this case. The cardinal points keep the power intact wherever the device is placed. As long as the clock works, so will the device.'

'Why an eclipse?' I ask, leaning forward.

'*Sìthichean* are at our most powerful during lunar events, especially eclipses,' Kiaran explains. 'The symbols on the device channelled that power to imprison them. But no system is infallible. With each eclipse, those inside tried to break free, and the seal wore thin over time.' He glances at me. 'This wasn't supposed to be permanent. It was only put in place until they found a better solution.'

'So we're just going to implement this "temporary" solution again with only one Falconer remaining to activate it,' Gavin says flatly. 'Bloody brilliant, you are.'

Kiaran glares at him. 'It'll be different this time.'

'How?' I ask. I put up a hand before Gavin can say anything. 'We don't exactly have a wealth of options to choose from.'

Kiaran is closed off again, which means he's hiding something. 'You said it – we don't have any other choice.'

Derrick lands on the paper, his tiny feet delicately walking amongst the symbols. The slightly-too-long hems of his trousers drag behind him, smudging the charcoal here and there. He bends down to trace a line. 'For something impermanent, this is brilliant. A single *sìthiche* wouldn't be able to escape this kind of prison at all. Whoever helped the Falconers knew what they were doing.'

'Aye, she did,' Kiaran murmurs.

I frown in surprise. 'She? You knew her?'

Kiaran won't look at me. 'You could say that. She's my sister.'

Derrick cackles. 'Your sister! Not at all crabby, like you. She mixed my milk and honey once and told me I had the best sword swipe she had ever seen. Shared a trophy with me, she did.'

I glance between them. 'Have I missed something? No one told me Kiaran had a damn sister.'

'You never asked,' Kiaran says, with a dismissive shrug.

Oh, confound it. He knows perfectly well he never gave me any reason to ask. It's just another blasted secret of his. I'm considering keeping a tally of all the questions Kiaran evades, so that when each answer is finally revealed at some incredibly inopportune moment, I can look at the count and remember how much he hides from me.

Derrick bursts up into the air from the drawing, his wings buzzing as his body begins to glow silver, 'I still can't believe your sister designed this. She was far more wondrous than I gave her credit for. But the two of you really—'

'That's enough,' Kiaran snaps through clenched teeth.

'Really what?' I ask, thoroughly annoyed now.

Derrick flaps his wings once and casts a glance at Kiaran. Kiaran shakes his head once in reply.

'Nothing,' Derrick says brightly. 'Nothing of import.'

I'm going to add Derrick's evasive responses to Kiaran's tally, which will surely grow to fill whole volumes.

'Well,' Gavin mutters, 'that wasn't *remotely* awkward.' He reaches for my tea. Without asking my permission, he gulps it down.

If Kiaran wants to keep his secrets, then to the devil with him. 'Fine,' I say. 'Just tell me how to work the blasted device.'

Kiaran draws close. 'These symbols on the rings –' he taps them on the paper '– have to be aligned correctly.'

I examine the drawing for any discernible pattern to their current arrangement. 'Are they aligned now? Can't I just memorise this?'

'They're only partially aligned.' He studies the design intently. 'I remember some of how this works, but I can't be sure my sister didn't change the mechanism when she altered the *iuchair*. From what I know, these are the first lines of defence.' He gestures to the three outer rings. 'When they shifted, the *cù sìth*, the redcaps and the *sluagh* were able to slip the mounds. It looks like she saved the strongest symbols with the most power to contain the *daoine sìth*. They're the ones intact for now. But beyond that, she's the only one alive who would know how the rest are aligned.'

I consider every combination of the symbols but can see no repeating pattern on the inner rings. 'Well, where is she?' I ask. 'Can't you contact—'

Kiaran visibly stiffens. 'No.'

'Well, this has all been … enlightening,' Gavin says. He rises and waves a hand at the drawing. 'Look, I can't help you with this. I can't fight them like the rest of you can. I'll just be in the way.' His eyes flicker to Kiaran. 'You were right, you know. Ours is a talent wasted on the useless.' He strides out of the room.

'Gavin!'

I stand to follow him, but Kiaran grasps my wrist. 'Don't. You can't fix this, Kam. There isn't anything you can do for the Seer right now. Let him go.'

Reluctantly, I sit down. I hate every part of this situation. Sighing, I pick up the drawing.

'Focus,' Kiaran says. 'Once the *daoine sìth* are released, there won't be much time to reactivate the device.'

'I *know.*' I'm well aware of the consequences if we fail.

The city will fall because of me, because I'm too weak to save it. There are certainly times when I overestimate my abilities, reassuring Kiaran that I'm powerful enough, and if he tells me otherwise, I'll shoot him with my lightning pistol.

But saying I'm strong doesn't make it so. This isn't the time for a display of false mettle. I will either live to save us all, or I will die in battle and condemn countless innocents to death. Nothing else matters.

Seeing my expression, Derrick flies to my shoulder and presses himself against my cheek and strokes my hair, trying to comfort me.

'Let's discuss a plan, then,' I say. 'When, precisely, will the device fail?'

Kiaran leans forward. 'When the moon becomes totally eclipsed, a portal will open in the meadow under Arthur's Seat.'

'Right,' I murmur, picturing the Queen's Park in my mind. Arthur's Seat is the highest point in the park, overlooking the place where I landed the flying machine when we found the seal. 'How effective will the light barrier surrounding the device be?'

'It won't last long,' he says. 'A single *daoine sìth* could eventually break it down with a sustained surge of power. It'll fail much quicker if enough of them attack it together. Killing some of them will give you more time.'

'So we'll fight first. The meadow in the Queen's Park is flat enough ground for a battle,' I say, sipping the last drops of tea Gavin left in my cup. 'If we herd them into the meadow and slim their numbers, I can make a break for the device and work on the alignments while the light is still intact. Can you keep them busy on your own while I'm doing that?'

Kiaran looks doubtful. 'It depends on how well we do in the initial attack. How much time do you need?'

I study the drawing, running through the complex web of

symbols I need to piece together to make it work. 'Five minutes?' Good God, more like five years.

Kiaran shakes his head. 'I can give you two.'

Two minutes. I doubt I can solve this complex a puzzle in such a short amount of time, in spite of my natural aptitude for such things. Mother used to sit for hours with me while I tried to solve increasingly difficult challenges. It's how my love for engineering began: each machine became a different puzzle.

But this time I'll be working alone, in the dark, in the middle of a battle. The enormity of what's at stake is already making me feel queasy.

Perhaps I should lie again, tell them I'm confident enough to slay an army and live. But I can't. The words stick in my throat. Kiaran would see right through it anyway, as he usually does, and Derrick would only worry—

Someone knocks on the drawing room door. 'Lady Aileana?' MacNab says. 'Miss Stewart is here for fourhours.'

I feel my false smile settle into place. Perfect smile, perfect lie, perfect bloody life.

Chapter 32

Kiaran is at the door when Catherine enters. She doesn't see him standing next to her.

'I'll return later tonight,' he says before slipping out behind her. Catherine clearly can't hear him, either, thank goodness.

'Aileana?' Catherine's eyes are large with concern. 'Are you all right?'

I realise I haven't welcomed her. 'I'm quite well. Do forgive me – I'm just a bit … flustered.'

Catherine smiles sympathetically and sits on the settee across from me, arranging the skirts of her light yellow dress. Her blonde hair, the same shade as Gavin's, is pulled into a soft chignon. As usual, she looks fresh and lovely.

'Of course you are. I know this situation with Gavin can't have been easy on you.'

'Aye,' I choke out.

'Wonderful response,' Derrick says from my hair. 'Try to sound a little less forced the next time you lie.'

Catherine either doesn't notice my discomfort or has fallen back on Miss Ainsley's rules for handling awkward situations. 'I don't blame you,' she says wryly. 'I *am* glad that if you have to marry anyone, it's my brother, but the circumstances—' She pauses and takes a deep breath before asking, 'Might I be candid?'

I try not to shift uneasily under her gaze. 'Please do,' I say, though I dread what she might have to say.

'Were … were you and he *really* caught like … *that*?' From her expression, I can only imagine *that* has been warped by gossip into something utterly base and compromising.

'No!' My face burns. 'Not at all. I promise.'

She looks a little more relieved. 'What happened, then?'

'Well, it's rather awkward …'

Catherine waves her hands. 'Oh, never mind. I don't want to think about my brother kissing anyone.'

'There was no kissing!'

At that precise moment, MacNab enters with another tea service. Catherine blushes, and I feel like crawling under the blasted table.

'Thank you, MacNab,' I say, ignoring Derrick's snickering.

MacNab wisely betrays no indication that he heard what I said and leaves as quietly as he arrived. I press the button for tea and pour Catherine a cup. 'No kissing,' I say again.

Catherine takes the cup from me and sips. 'I passed Gavin on the way here. He looked upset.'

I clear my throat. 'This wedding business has been hard on both of us.'

Catherine nods in understanding. 'Of course. Are you feeling better?' Her brow furrows with concern. 'Mother was quite … distressed about yesterday.'

'I'm sure,' I say, a bit weakly. 'Aye, I'm better. I'll have to send an apology to Lady Cassilis.'

Catherine reaches forward and pats my wrist. 'I'm sure she would appreciate that very much and I'm pleased to hear your health has improved.'

God, sometimes I hate that Catherine trusts me so implicitly. I'm a liar, a deceiver, and my friend doesn't realise it.

When I attempt to speak about something inane, like the

wedding, nothing comes out. I'm asphyxiating on my lies, breaking under the pressure of this burden I've been forced to bear. If I fail to reactivate the seal, Catherine will die. This might be my last chance to save her.

Impulsively, I seize her hands, ignoring her alarm. 'I'm ready for you to ask me.'

Catherine tries unsuccessfully to extricate herself from my grasp. 'Ask you what?' She must see the desperation in my face, because fear and concern are reflected in hers. 'If there's something the matter—'

'You always wonder where I disappear to during assemblies,' I say. 'Do you really want to know?'

Catherine goes still. She looks at me as though she's waiting for me to reveal that I'm jesting. When I don't, she leans forward and takes a deep breath, pressing her hands into mine the way we did when we were children telling secrets. 'Yes.'

Derrick tugs on my ear. 'Aileana, I don't think this is a—'

'Show yourself,' I say to him.

Catherine frowns. 'What?'

'Are you quite sure about this?' Derrick asks me.

'I am.'

Out of the corner of my eye, I see the halo around him fade. He's fully visible, wee clothes and mischievous smile and all. Today's trousers appear to have been made from one of my soft green day dresses. His delicate wings fan softly behind him, tickling my ear.

Catherine gasps. Her eyes go wide and she jumps to her feet, dress rustling, all decorum forgotten. 'Faery,' she whispers.

'Now, that's just insulting,' Derrick says. 'I'm a *pixie*, you silly human.'

Catherine gapes at him. And then at me. And then at him. 'I-I think I need to stand,' she says faintly.

'You *are* standing,' I say with a smile.

'Indeed. Sit. Sit is what I meant.' She collapses onto the settee, her skirts and petticoats puffing up inelegantly all around her. 'Aileana,' she finally says, never taking her eyes off Derrick. 'Might I be candid again?'

'I'd prefer if you were.'

Catherine's hands flutter in front of her in distressed motions before she finally presses them to her chest to keep them still. 'I think I'm about to cast my accounts onto your carpet.'

'No, no,' I say. 'Let me call MacNab, he can bring us ... something. A bucket.'

'I may also faint.' Her chest heaves. 'Are you friendly, then?' she asks Derrick. 'Because I heard stories when Aileana and I were children.'

'I can assure you,' Derrick says with a sly grin, 'I'm *quite* friendly to lovely ladies like yourself.'

'Good heavens,' she whispers.

'Catherine,' I say. 'There's something else I must tell you.'

'Something more?' She laughs breathlessly. 'We might have to limit your life-altering revelations to one a day, you know.'

I smile briefly, almost apologetically. Catherine is taking this much better than I would have under the same circumstances. At least the first faery she'll remember is Derrick and not Kiaran. I don't imagine she would be so calm if she learned she'd been faestruck by him already and tried to paw his shirt off.

'I'm revealing Derrick to you now because I need to ask you to leave.'

Catherine's eyes widen. 'But I've only just arrived.'

'No. I need you to leave the city,' I say, trying to sound as calm as possible. 'Something awful might happen very soon, and if it does, I want you to be somewhere safe.'

'Something awful,' she repeats. 'Does it have to do with ... him?' She nods at Derrick.

'Not him, but other fae who would harm you, given the chance.'

'I see.' She's looking rather ill again. 'At Lord Hepburn's ball, you mentioned an evil faery. That's what attacked the poor man, wasn't it?'

'Unfortunately.'

'What about you?' she asks me. 'You still haven't told me what you do when you vanish.'

Uncertainly, I sip my tea. This time, I can't look at her. I don't want to see her face when I tell her. 'I kill them.'

'*Oh.*' Out of the corner of my eye, I see her lift a hand to her mouth. 'Oh,' she says again softly. 'I don't … I'm sorry, I don't quite know what to say.'

I nod in understanding. I don't know what to say, either.

'Will you leave, too?' she says faintly. 'Or will you …' She doesn't continue.

'One startling revelation a day, remember,' I say gently. 'I've already made two.'

Chapter 33

An electric lantern floats above my head in the garden, illuminating the prickly hedges that have lost their lush green leaves for the winter. I reach up and gently nudge it, so it casts light on the engine for the steam-powered locomotive I've been working on for months.

I put the gland and valve rods in position for the steam-chest, concentrating solely on the movement of my hands as I fit the pieces of metal together. If I don't keep busy, I'll be forced to think about the impossible puzzle of the seal that I've spent the entire day trying to solve, and about the consequences if I fail. If I allow myself to consider that even for a moment, I suddenly find it very difficult to breathe.

I'm taking longer than necessary to complete the steam-chest. No matter. When I finish here, I'll find something else to build. Something even more complicated that will help clear my mind for when I go back to figuring out the seal.

I wipe the back of my greasy hand against my cheek to brush back an errant strand of hair, then position a bolt in the engine. A few swift jerks of the spanner and it fits snugly in place.

The locomotive's body is a scaled-down version of the ones that grace the front of trains. It rests on four wheels, the rear pair larger than the front, both body and wheels attached to a manoeuvring mechanism I've designed to be effective over rockier terrain. The steam engine at the front uses fuel more efficiently than my ornithopter, so the vehicle is fast. Like my ornithopter, the vehicle's roof is entirely retractable. The interior boasts two leather seats with a standing platform behind them.

Stored underneath the platform is my latest invention: a sonic cannon. It launches a narrow, intense blast of sound that reaches beyond the human pain threshold and well past that of a fae. One shot should disorientate a number of them, a distraction we may need. I mentally thank the *cù sìth* for the inspiration.

'Kam.'

I jump and drop the spanner. The tool lands in the grass with a muffled *thunk*. I was so absorbed in my own thoughts that I didn't even sense him beside me, or notice the taste of his power. 'How long have you been standing there?'

Kiaran frowns, studying me. He's wearing rough raploch again, his hunting clothes. 'Not long. You look upset.'

'All things considered,' I say, 'I think I'm handling my impending death quite well, don't you?'

My words have no visible effect on Kiaran. He stares at the locomotive. 'What's this?'

'Transport,' I say. 'An alternative if the ornithopter is destroyed. It'll hold any extra weapons. Speaking of which –' I reach for the sonic cannon '– I'd like to test something on you.'

Kiaran raises an eyebrow. 'Are you planning to shoot me again?'

'You'll see.'

I slip plugs into my ears, then rest the barrel of the cannon on my shoulder and lower the intensity to give him just a wee blast.

I pull the release. Kiaran staggers most satisfyingly and his lips move in the shape of a *very* bad word. I bite back my laughter. I made Kiaran swear.

Smiling, I remove the plugs. 'I'd say that worked very well, wouldn't you?'

Kiaran moves too quickly for me to register. Suddenly he's standing so close to me that I have to tip my head back to see his face. 'If you wanted to fight, all you had to do was ask.' He lifts the cannon from my shoulder and puts it on the passenger seat. 'Try to best me again.'

'I'm not in the mood, MacKay.'

Kiaran ignores me. He moves and I dodge without thinking. His fist goes straight into the locomotive's passenger door, buckling it.

I mutter a curse of my own as I whirl to face him. 'Damnation, MacKay! I just finished fitting that door. What the hell are you doing?'

The street lamps behind him illuminate his dark hair with a golden halo and the scant light betrays a hint of a smile. 'Challenging you.'

'I don't accept.'

'I don't care.'

His arm shoots out and I'm sliding across the ground, grass burning my arms and my chin. I turn over and Kiaran picks me up by the ruff of my shirt.

'Fight me,' he growls.

'I said I don't want to!'

'Do you think that will matter when we're in battle? Will you tell our enemies that *you don't bloody want to*?'

With a growl, I launch myself at him. We trade blows. His are so quick I barely have time to dodge them. I block one blow with my upper arm and try to kick out at his knee. He manages to hook an ankle around mine and sweep my feet out from under me. I land hard on my bottom.

'*Stop it*, MacKay.'

Kiaran yanks me close. 'Tell me what happened the night your mother died.'

I shove at his chest. 'No.'

He tightens his hold. 'Did you even want to save her?' His eyes burn into mine. 'Is that why you just stood by and let it happen?'

I scream. I smash my forehead against his and slam my fist into his face. This time, I'm faster. I push against him with all my strength. I kick and claw him until his shirtsleeves are torn and his skin is bleeding. Even then, I don't stop. I shove him down to the ground and stand over him, ready to finish him off if I have to.

But he reaches up, striking fast, and drags me to the ground. He pins me under the heavy weight of his muscled body, clamping my arms against my sides as I buck against him. Confound it, I can't even throw him off of me.

'Damn you,' I snarl.

'You see how easy that was?' he says, looking down at me. His eyes are black and inscrutable.

I heave in frustration. 'What?'

'For me to say the very thing that would make you violent.'

I try to roll him off, but he's too blasted heavy. 'Because you were trying to!'

'Aye, I was.' He clamps my wrists harder and lowers his face towards mine until our skin is almost touching. I stop struggling. For an awful moment, I think he's about to kiss me. Perhaps even more awfully, I think I'd let him. I shiver at the thought.

'I know your weakness, Kam. What triggers you.' He leans in even closer, lips just above mine. 'After the other night, so does Sorcha. And make no mistake – she'll find some way to use it against you.'

He rolls onto his back. I lie there with the rough grass beneath me and press a hand to my chest. My heart beats rapidly beneath my palm, heavy thumps I can feel against my ribs.

'You know why I had to do that,' he says.

'I know.'

Above us, the clouds part to reveal the stars, bright and untouchable. Polaris. Alderamin. Gamma Cassiopeiae. I remember my mother pointing to each star as she named them. Her smile was so beautiful and warm.

Can you name them, Aileana? Here now, repeat after me. Polaris. Alderamin. Gamma Cassiopeiae. Crimson suits you best.

I flinch and pull myself out of the memories. I can't do it. I'm unable to remember my mother without recalling her death, without picturing her face flecked with blood. Without seeing Sorcha smile as she tore out her heart.

Now I'll never be able to kill Sorcha. I'll never find retribution for my mother's death. I'll have to let that disgusting faery live because I've come to care for Kiaran, far more than I ever thought I would.

I suck in a deep breath and Kiaran grips my shoulder, as if he heard my thoughts. 'Remember what I told you about cherishing these moments? You might lose them.'

I dig my fingers into the grass. 'Don't presume to tell me about loss, MacKay. What do you know of it?'

He deliberately brought that part of my memory back to teach me a lesson and show how it could be used against me. It's not my strength. It's my weakness, and it always has been.

Kiaran says, 'Lie still, Kam.'

He says it so calmly and rationally, and just like that my anger is shattered. I settle next to him and stare up at the sky again. The clouds are beginning to clear. Everything is so calm, so still. He's right – I need to appreciate this moment. I don't know how much my life will change after midwinter, if I'll even have one to return to.

'I'm sorry,' I whisper. 'I shouldn't have said that. You lost your Falconer.'

'Not just her.' There's a catch in his voice. I glance over at him, startled. But when I try to meet his gaze, he looks away. 'My sister, too.'

The sister Kiaran didn't want to talk about this afternoon in the drawing room. His sister, who built the device. Who can't be contacted ... *oh, no.*

I shut my eyes. 'She's imprisoned, too, isn't she?'

'Aye,' he says quietly. 'Aithinne fought alongside the Falconers. She made me leave in the middle of the battle, so I wouldn't be trapped with her and the others. Sorcha stayed out of the fight and had been tasked by her brother Lonnrach to slaughter the surviving Falconers if they won. My sister wanted me to ensure that didn't happen.'

'So she sacrificed herself.' I almost reach for his hand to squeeze it, to offer him some comfort, but I don't. I'm not certain how he'd take it. 'Do you think she's still alive down there?'

'The others aren't strong enough to kill her.' His jaw tightens. 'But that doesn't mean they won't find a way to make her wish they could.'

I shiver. Despite all that I've seen, I can't even begin to contemplate what methods of torture the *daoine sìth* are capable of. Even a faery as powerful as Kiaran's sister could be broken after two thousand years of it. God, what Kiaran must have gone through – must *still* be going through – knowing what his sister is enduring and being unable to do a thing to help her.

'We'll get her out,' I reassure him. 'She'll be free of that.'

Kiaran nods. 'Take care with her. She's the only one who can come up with a more permanent lock for the prison.' He's silent for a long time, and when he finally speaks again, I barely hear him. 'And I'll take her place with the others.'

I'll take her place with the others. All this time I've been dreading the consequences if I fail to activate the device. I've never considered what will happen if I succeed.

'Then you'll be—' He'll be imprisoned. And when his sister is safe, we'll be looking for a way to keep him there. '*No*, MacKay.'

Kiaran tilts his face to the sky. Moonlight bathes his skin in a lustrous glow. 'It's my choice.'

Something tightens in my chest and I can barely breathe. No matter what happens, I'll never see Kiaran again after mid-winter. Every option I have ends the same way: with me losing him.

I bite back a bitter laugh. I tried so hard to steel myself against him, putting so much effort into convincing myself of how unfeeling he is, how inhuman. I realise now that despite all my vows never to forget he's fae, it doesn't matter any more. Perhaps it never did.

'Please don't,' I whisper. I want him to tell me that he'll find some way to escape. That we'll make it out of this together.

'I have to.'

Anger flares inside me. 'You don't *have* to do anything. Staying out of this doesn't go against your damn vow.'

'This has nothing to do with my vow.' He looks at me then, with infinite sadness in his ancient gaze. 'I want to be there with you until the end.'

Chapter 34

When faced with the probability of death, hours speed by like minutes.

I've spent the night and morning building and bolting metal until my eyes hurt. My weapons are loaded, in perfect working condition, laid out in my dressing room. My arsenal is diverse, every weapon lethal to the fae, but it still isn't enough.

There's one more person I have to see before everything begins. My father sits at his desk, writing. It's such a familiar image, how I've always come to picture him. I take a moment to memorise his features. The dark hair that spills onto his forehead, his brow always creased into a frown of concentration. Those green eyes of his – the only thing we have in common – are narrowed as he composes his letter.

I wonder what he and I would be like now if he had ever shown me any affection, if he had let himself love me just a little. How different would we have become?

'Father,' I say.

He glances up without a hint of a smile. He looks surprised to find me there. 'Aileana. Come in.'

I sit in the leather chair across from him. 'What are you working on?'

'My accounts,' he says, putting the paper on top of a neat pile on the desk. 'I believe the earl will be quite pleased with your dowry.'

It takes me a moment to realise he's talking about Gavin and I almost wince. 'I'm glad.' The lie comes out easily. It has to. This is our goodbye and I want to do this right.

'I've sent word to have the country estate prepared for you and your husband after the wedding,' he says.

Your husband. I clasp my hands together so hard they ache. 'Splendid.'

'I appreciate you being reasonable about this.' He starts to write on another paper. 'Especially after our conversation the other day.'

What you want isn't important.

'Reasonable,' I say. 'Of course.'

Of course I'll be reasonable about spending the rest of my life with a man I don't love. He's the only possible choice that won't destroy my life and make me absolutely miserable. But what I want doesn't matter, does it, Father? Placate me with a country retreat, but we both know it doesn't mean a thing.

'I do want to apologise for my absence this week. I've been settling matters for Galloway.'

He makes it sound as though he's only been absent recently. The truth is, he's never been there for me. Not for my entire life. I certainly don't expect that to change.

'Since you are here,' he continues, 'I should tell you that I'll be leaving town today, so I won't be able to attend the ball announcing your engagement. I have some business to conduct in the country. I'm sure you understand.'

I clench my hand in a fist. He keeps speaking as if my opinions don't matter. As if *I* don't matter. God, doesn't he care about me, even a bit?

No. He's leaving, just like he always does. He probably sought out the first opportunity he could to get away from me again. I should be glad he's going. One less person I have to worry about if everything goes wrong. But I can't forgive him for never being there when I needed a father most.

'Oh, I understand.' I can't control the bitterness that creeps into my voice.

He doesn't even hear it. 'I shall return for your wedding, of course.'

'That would be *lovely*,' I say. This time, the acerbity of my comment is all too clear.

Father frowns and sits back in his chair. The leather squeaks under his weight. 'Are you well?'

No, I'm not. I'm close to breaking and screaming. I wish I could tell him that I don't give a damn about the wedding, and that I want him to look me in the eye just once because it might be the last chance he'll have.

'Do you ever think about Mother?' I ask, before I can stop myself.

Father inhales sharply and looks away. 'Not now, Aileana.'

'Why not?'

He shoves another piece of paper in front of him and scrawls violently. 'It's not an appropriate topic of conversation.'

My fingers clench harder. They're so red now. 'Why not?' I repeat.

'You may go.' Father never looks up. His pen scratches the paper so hard it's almost carving into the wood beneath. 'I don't care to discuss this with you.'

I stand and grip the chair's arm. 'But I do. Look at me.' When he doesn't, something breaks inside me. Desperation and hurt and an entire lifetime of being ignored by my absent father. 'Damnation, Father, *look at me*.'

For the first time in a year, Father raises his eyes to meet mine. They are cold and guilty and ... sad.

Just as quickly, he averts his gaze. 'You look so much like her.'

His voice almost cracks and I stare at him in shock. I've never thought about my resemblance to Mother. I'm a tall, awkward creature with a mop of copper curls that never stay put. My mother was beautiful. When she moved or walked, she glided, feather-light. Her hair was always neatly styled and her skin was perfect alabaster. She never had any freckles, unlike me. She called mine angel kisses.

He lost her and now he's left with a daughter who will never, ever be her. I'm a pale echo of the woman he loved more than anyone else in the world. I'll always remind him of what he lost. What we *both* lost.

I say the only thing I can. 'I miss her, too.'

'I know,' he whispers.

Our grief destroyed and recreated us. We should have grown closer after my mother died. Her death made me realise just how swiftly we can lose the ones we love, gone for ever in an instant.

I turn to leave, because if I don't, I'll try once more to run into his arms and grip him tight, the way I used to when I was a child. He'd always push me away. Always. 'Goodbye, Father,' I say instead, turning to leave. 'Enjoy your trip.'

Later that night, I sit with Kiaran beside the fire in my bedroom, he in the leather chair, me on the settee. I'm exhausted after hours spent trying to figure out the key to the seal as we worked on our weapons.

'Is this our goodbye?' I ask.

I've said too many goodbyes today. Earlier, I watched Father get into his carriage and leave, just as he said he would. I've never felt more alone.

'I don't say goodbyes,' Kiaran says, staring into the fire.

'Too difficult?'

His mouth quirks up. 'Only the ones worth saying.'

'What will they do to you?' I ask. 'If you're trapped in the mound with them, will they—'

'Kam,' he interrupts. 'Don't ruin this.'

I stare at him, watching a strand of hair slide onto his forehead. He reaches up to push it back with his long, graceful fingers.

Stay with me, I almost say. I don't know why the thought of losing him fills me with grief, but it does, and it won't abate. I've lost too much already. 'Leave the battle before I activate the device,' I say. 'Like you did before. I'll trap them, and we can hunt the others together – the same as we always have.'

'This is the downside of immortality, Kam.' He looks at me then, studies my face. 'Nothing stays the same. Everything changes. Except me.'

'There must be more than a few people who wish for that.'

'Because they don't understand what it truly means.' He stands and rests his hands against the chimneypiece. Firelight outlines his body, swathing him in golden light. 'Do you know why the *sìthichean* crave human energy above all else?'

No.'

'Because it burns so brightly. Humans pulse with vitality and an unending, compulsive need to cling to life. One taste lets us bask in mortality we have no other way of experiencing.'

'Have you ever wished you were human?'

He glances at me. 'Now *that,*' he says, 'is something I've never been asked before.' I wait for him to continue, but he straightens and says, 'I have something for you.'

'An answer to my question?'

He smiles. 'A gift.'

'A gift?' Kiaran doesn't give me gifts. I'm immediately suspicious. 'What is it?'

'Flowers.'

I blink. 'Really?'

'No. Shall I go and get it, or would you prefer to ask more questions instead?'

Two minutes later, he returns with a small trunk tucked under one arm and something shining in his fist.

He tosses the gleaming object to me. It's a lightweight gold disc in the shape of a star, only slightly bigger than my palm. Beautifully crafted, smooth metal with delicate etchings similar to the ones on the seal. My word, it's magnificent.

'Those symbols mean it's charged with my power,' Kiaran says. 'As long as I'm alive, you'll have my abilities at your disposal.'

I look up at him, surprised. He's giving me his power? 'Won't that weaken you? Why would you do this?'

'If circumstances had been different, you would have been properly trained to use your own innate abilities,' he says. 'As it is, we've run out of time. Don't worry about me.'

Kiaran holds out a hand and the disc rises from my palm and floats to him. With a wave of his fingers, power flares and the star transforms into two matching weapons, knives with long, narrow blades that look a lot like the ones Kiaran carries on our hunts.

I grip the knives, testing their weight and finding them surprisingly light. The blades are silver, thin and slightly transparent. The gold hilts are decorated with symbols that wrap around them in a vine-like pattern. I run my thumb carefully along a blade. Perfectly honed. They are the most exquisite weapons I've ever held.

He takes one from me and tosses it high into the air before catching it by the hilt. 'See how easily it can be thrown? It also blocks *sìthichean* power.' He throws it again, only this time it hovers in the air above his hand and compresses itself back into a star-shaped disc, identical to the original, but smaller. He passes it to me. 'Here – touch the other blade to it.'

I connect the star and the remaining knife. Power flows from the objects as they melt together to form the larger star. The metal is smooth in my palm again.

It's so astonishing that I almost forget myself for a moment. 'Thank yo—'

'Don't say it!' he tells me.

I let out a frustrated breath. 'I'll never understand why none of you likes to be thanked.'

Kiaran gestures to the star-shaped disc. 'That fits into your next gift.'

He opens the trunk and lifts out a cloth-wrapped bundle. Carefully, he peels the white fabric away to reveal magnificent gold-plated armour. There is a breastplate, a backplate, and two metallic vambraces decorated with what look like shining silver veins.

On the breastplate, over the spot which will protect my heart, is a star-shaped outline. Kiaran takes the disc from me and presses it into place. It clicks softly as it settles there.

The breastplate gleams in the firelight, and those silver veins shimmer. And humming through them, especially when I reach down to trace my fingers over the symbols on the star, is the unmistakable sensation of Kiaran's power. It tastes of the same sweetness and natural things and every element combined. Pure, beautiful wildness. And it's mine. Kiaran has given this to me.

'This won't protect your mind from *sìthichean* influence, so Sorcha can still use your memories against you. But the armour will amplify the connection to my power – you'll be as strong as me.'

'MacKay,' I say softly. But I can't continue. I'm so overwhelmed, I don't know what to say.

His eyes meet mine. 'Shall we practise using them?'

I nod. I know this will be his last lesson.

Chapter 35

The following afternoon, I stand in front of the oval mirror in my bedchamber and try to focus on donning my armour. My hands shake when I reach into the trunk.

I position the gold plates against my arm and buckle the leather straps underneath that run from my wrist up to my shoulder. The fae metal is warm through my long sleeves and so light and flexible that it's hardly noticeable when I move. When I strap on the other vambrace, Kiaran's power rushes under my skin, a gentle current at first, soon pulsing and strengthening inside me.

The breastplate fits smoothly over my chest, small enough to fit my shape. I slide leather straps through buckles at my sides – connecting the breastplate to the backplate – and the power intensifies again. My senses become so acute that I am aware of every muscle, vein, organ and bone – every part of me and all my new abilities. This is what it must be like to be fae – to have so much power at my disposal that a single flick of my wrist can cause a storm.

But I'm not one of them. I bend to retrieve my lightning pistol, snug in its leather holster, which I secure around my hips. The miniature explosives are next. Each little timepiece is fastened to a strap that runs across my breastplate. I grab my crossbow and sling the band across my shoulder.

A whistle comes from behind me. I turn to see Derrick hovering in the dressing room doorway, wings fanning softly. 'You look …'

'Ridiculous?' I guess.

'No.' He sighs. 'I had myself a wee lady of my own once, with armour like that. She was exquisite.'

'What happened to her?'

Derrick shifts uncomfortably. 'She left for Cornwall. With the other pixies.' He flutters upwards. 'Your *sìthiche* is waiting outside. Got all grumbly and told me not to go back out without you.'

I start for the door. As I pass the dressing room, a flash of colour makes me pause. 'Tell Kiaran I'll only be a moment.'

Derrick grins. 'I hope he's annoyed. I love it when he gets annoyed. But don't be long – the moon is getting redder.' He leaves in a flutter of wings and light.

In the dressing room, peeking from underneath a pile of soft, pastel silk dresses, is my mother's tartan. Derrick must have removed it from the trunk last night.

My eyes prick with tears as I bend to pick it up. I admire the plain fabric, the simple design of light and dark wool, as I draw it to my face and inhale its scent. I swear I catch the faint sweetness of my mother's perfume. Lavender with a hint of rose. I hug the tartan hard and shut my eyes. I drag in another breath, but the scent is gone. Maybe I imagined it.

Carefully, I fold the woollen shawl and place it back inside my wooden trunk. Though I'm tempted to take it with me, I'm still not worthy enough to wear it.

As I make my way downstairs, I try to ignore every detail of the house I grew up in, the house that contains so many reminders of my mother and father. But I can't. I pass the paintings of Scottish shorelines my mother hung in the hallways because she missed the sea. The scent of pipe smoke and whisky still lingers near Father's study as I walk by. I can't remain here, no matter how much I want to.

I close the front door for the last time and head for the centre of Charlotte Square. Derrick and Kiaran are waiting next to the ornithopter and the locomotive, glaring at each other. Apparently they've agreed on some kind of grudging truce.

I tilt my head to the sky. The clouds are thick, dark, except the ones that surround the moon. My senses are so enhanced that I can see every crater and mare that darkens its surface. The rust colour presaging the eclipse has begun to envelop its white glow. Soon, it will be consumed. A blood moon.

As I near the ornithopter, Kiaran scans me quickly, head to toe, and almost smiles. I know that look. He likes what he sees.

'Aileana!'

Gavin runs across Charlotte Square. He comes to a halt in front of me, clad in gentlemen's finery, with fitted trousers, waistcoat and a perfectly tied neck-cloth. I wince at the reminder – he's dressed for the ball at the Assembly Rooms, to which he's supposed to be escorting me. Our engagement will be formally announced to our peers tonight.

Gavin blinks at my armour. He's certainly not as appreciative of it as Kiaran. 'What the hell is that?'

'Armour.'

'Looks heavy.'

I smile and clear my throat. 'Catherine – is she—'

'She's fine,' he reassures me. 'In a bit of a shock, but she managed to convince Mother to leave town with her. I don't know if you're aware, but Catherine is a very skilled actress if the occasion calls for it.'

'Oh, I am. Why didn't you go with them?'

'I'm here to help,' he says. 'I'm at your disposal.'

Derrick lands on my shoulder. 'Oh, so *now* you're interested in helping?' he says. 'What was that business you were spouting yesterday about being useless before you ran off like a miserable coward?'

Gavin glares at him. 'Don't bother with the bloody lecture, pixie.'

'Gavin,' I say, 'you should leave Edinburgh. Any Seers in the city will be at greater risk than everyone else.'

He reaches out and clamps a hand around my vambrace.

'No,' he says. 'I know I can't fight for you.' My eyebrows rise at the way he words it. He must notice because he quickly amends, 'I can't fight *them,* I mean. But you can't expect me to go to that blasted ball alone and twiddle my thumbs all night.'

One more goodbye. The last one. But somehow, I can't bring myself to say the words again, not when I stare into his eyes. They plead with me, brimming with the same determination I saw the night he chose to leave the ball and stand by me.

My voice is shaky when I speak. 'All right.'

'Kam,' Kiaran says sharply.

I can practically hear his reasoning in his tone. If the faeries sense Gavin, they'll be drawn to him. They will kill him.

'Watch the battle from somewhere safe,' I tell Gavin. 'If this doesn't work out, I need you to try and save as many people as possible. Get them out of the city, if you can.'

'How?'

'Take my ornithopter. You can spread the word faster and cover more ground that way.' I step back from him. 'Kiaran and I will take the locomotive.' I reach to my shoulder and stroke Derrick's wings once. 'Derrick, you'll go with him.'

'What?' His wings flutter. 'I'm not leaving you.'

'Aye, you are,' I say. 'Stay with Gavin.' I swallow, so the next words don't come out choked. 'Protect each other.'

Protect each other, because I won't be here to do it myself.

Derrick flies to Gavin's shoulder and perches there, but he's far from happy about it. 'Fine. But this is against my better judgement.'

Before I get inside the locomotive, Gavin squeezes my wrist. I meet his eyes and am shocked by the fear I find there. 'Aileana,' he begins, but he doesn't continue.

I know what he means to tell me. When Cassandra foresaw the destruction of Troy, I imagine she felt similarly: ineffectual, terrified and desperate to prevent her vision from becoming reality.

'You've seen the whole vision now, haven't you?' I say. 'Everything that Kiaran saw.'

Gavin nods. Before I can say anything, he pulls me into a hard embrace, crushing me against him. 'I couldn't see it clearly before, what makes it happen. Last night I did.'

I bury my face into his shoulder, remembering Kiaran's words. *Every conscious decision you make would only help the vision come to pass.* 'Don't tell me.'

'I won't,' he whispers. He holds me so tightly, I can feel the shape of him through my armour. 'You can change it,' he tells me. 'If anyone can, it's you.'

When I speak, my voice almost breaks. 'I wish I had never brought you into this. If anything happens to you—'

Gavin gathers me even closer. 'Don't.' He presses his cheek against mine. 'Don't think, for one moment, that any of this is your fault.' He pulls back, eyes searching mine. 'I made my choice that night in my study. I'd make the same choice again.'

Tears mist my vision and I fight to keep them from falling. 'I still maintain that was a foolish decision.'

He smiles slightly. 'Yet infinitely preferable to another damn dance, don't you think?'

I return his smile. 'Infinitely.'

'Kam.' Kiaran says my name quietly from inside the locomotive, as if he doesn't want to interrupt but knows he must. If we don't leave now, we won't make it to the Queen's Park in time.

'Gavin, promise me you won't do anything stupid.'

'Only if you promise me you won't die.'

I can't reassure him that I'll see him again, that I'll survive this battle. I can't tell him that I wish he had come home sooner so we could have spent more than a few days together. I can't tell him that I regret the two years we were apart, because now they feel like seven hundred and thirty days' worth of wasted opportunities. I can't make promises to him that I'm unable to keep.

'Stay safe,' I tell him.

'And you.'

I step into the locomotive and settle next to Kiaran, then flip the switches to start the engine. It comes to life with a mechanical whir and steam rises from the stack at the front.

I shove the lever forward and we drive out of Charlotte Square.

The Queen's Park is very different seen through the filter of Kiaran's power. My senses are enhanced, my vision and hearing more acute. Every blade of grass is a thousand times sharper, and I can clearly see every branch on every tree, right down to the smallest twig. And the colours … It's a different spectrum from the one I'm used to, more beautiful and vivid. This is what it must be like for someone to use their eyes for the first time. I'm not certain what to focus on: the colours, or the grass, or the trees, or each individual falling raindrop. It's utterly overwhelming.

I glance at the clouds as I drive, and the moon shines through them again, almost completely red now except for the tiniest sliver of white at the bottom.

I stop the vehicle in the meadow, near where the fae will pour from the mound. I examine the cliff face below Arthur's

Seat, the calm trees resting against the rock. The park is quiet, everything still. Not even a breeze to stir the branches.

Now we wait.

I look at Kiaran and find him watching me, those strange and lovely eyes more vivid than ever. I see him the way I did when we were in the *Sìth-bhrùth*, uncanny and magnificent. 'You're stoic as always, MacKay.'

'I've had years of practice,' he says.

'What should we do about your sister?' I ask him. 'Should we get her out first?'

He shakes his head. 'She'll know to leave before the seal is reactivated. Focus on the battle, not her.'

I laugh once, low and forced. 'Be honest with me – do you think we'll win?'

Please say we'll be fine, I think to him. *Please.*

A flash of emotion crosses his features, something incomprehensible to me, as if he can read my thoughts. 'I don't know.'

Sometimes I wish faeries could lie as easily as humans do. Maybe then Kiaran might feel compelled to reassure me, just this once. I want him to tell me that we'll be victorious. I want him to tell me that I'll activate the device and find some way to save him from imprisonment with the others. I want him to tell me that I won't lose him the way I lost my mother.

I reach over and clasp Kiaran's hand. His soft intake of breath makes me pause, but after a moment, I thread my fingers through his, and he lets me.

When you lose someone, it's so easy to forget they're gone at first. There were so many moments when I would think to tell my mother something, or expect her at the same precise time each morning for tea. Those flashes are so fleeting, so joyous, that when reality surfaces, the grief becomes fresh all over again.

I can't go through that with Kiaran. I almost lost myself in grief the first time.

'I'm scared,' I whisper.

Kiaran looks at me, so still and quiet. I brace myself for his words, unsure of what he'll say. Terrified by what he'll say.

He doesn't speak. Instead, he grasps me by the collar of my coat and presses his lips to mine. Kiaran kisses me deeply, with an urgency I never thought him capable of. He kisses me like he knows he's going to die. He kisses me like the world is going to end.

I cling to his shoulders and tug at his jacket, bringing us closer. I want nothing more than to hold him and bury myself in his arms and forget everything. I want time to stop.

He pulls back and rests his forehead against mine. 'I'm scared, too.'

I never thought I'd hear those words. Not from him. I look up at the moon again and it's nearly consumed. 'Leave,' I tell him, suddenly more frightened than ever. I have to try one last time to convince him. 'You still have time. Save yourself—'

Kiaran's kiss is fierce, his breathing ragged. 'Have I ever told you the vow a *sìthiche* makes when he pledges himself to another?' He slides his fingers down my neck and his lips are so soft against mine that I barely feel them. '*Aoram dhuit*,' he breathes. 'I will worship thee.'

I come undone. I pull him hard against me, and bury my face into his neck. My tears are scorching hot against his skin. I press my lips to the wild pulse at the base of his throat. 'I'll save you,' I tell him. 'I will. I promise.'

Before he can answer, a piercing screech of scraping metal echoes around the park.

The ground beneath the locomotive shakes and I grab the helm to steady myself. Mist rises from the earth, soft and ethereal at first, then thicker, faster.

I look up at the moon. It's engulfed in red.

Kiaran grips my hand. 'Close your eyes.'

'What?'

I can't see him through the rising mist. It's thickened too quickly.

He shoves me against the seat and covers my eyes with his hand. Light filters through his fingers, through my closed eyelids. It's so bright, it actually burns. A dense, oppressive heat thick enough to suffocate me if I let it.

Then … power. Similar to Kiaran's, only magnified a thousand times. My mouth is inundated with sweetness and mud and dirt and crushed flower petals. I try to swallow it down, suppress it, but it keeps coming. It's crushing me, a flood strong enough to rip me to pieces. It's choking me, drowning me, and I can't breathe through it.

'Kadamach,' a powerful male voice says. 'It's so good to see you again.'

Chapter 36

'Lonnrach,' Kiaran says.

He takes his hand from my eyes and I blink against the bright mist. Swallowing the power is difficult. My senses are overwhelmed: the stark taste in my mouth, the scent of rain and something sweetly floral.

The dense mist clears to reveal a tall figure astride a steaming, muscled horse. A *metal* horse. Silver alloy with gold veins, the opposite of my armour, and beaten so thin that its organs are visible beneath. Shining metal bones and muscles of varying thickness glint in the moonlight. Everything is metal except for its heart – which is a real, fleshy organ that beats and pumps liquid gold through the horse's veins. Steam blasts out of its nose and swirls around Lonnrach's legs.

There are more riders behind him, dozens of them, and other faeries on foot, standing silently in the tall grass. No wonder their power is overwhelming – I've never encountered more than two fae together at the same time. All of them wear battle armour like mine. Beside them are a dozen *cù sìth* and redcaps, and looming on the rocks above us are *sluagh*. Their thin, semi-transparent wings are tucked in as they watch us, eyes glittering, but they're poised for flight.

My very first thought is to run. Run until I faint.

'So this must be the Falconer I've heard so much about,' Lonnrach says. He speaks gently, his words carried by the breeze.

I slowly raise my eyes to his. They're the most vivid blue I have ever seen. They stand out against his pale skin and salt-white hair. He is beautiful, magnificent. Power rolls off him like steam from his horse. I can't look away – and I don't want to.

'Come to me,' Lonnrach says.

His voice is soft but commanding. Compelling. I feel him in my mind, the same way I felt Sorcha's touch back at the loch. Only his power doesn't try to break me. It entices me. It steals through my veins and takes me over until the tension and fight leave my body and I can resist him no longer.

Too late I remember Kiaran's warning when he gave me the armour, that it wouldn't protect me against faery influence. *Damnation.* I buck against it, but Lonnrach's presence is too soothing, too strong.

I step out of the locomotive, but Kiaran's hand tightens around my wrist. 'I don't think so.'

Lonnrach remains focused on me. 'You've always been selfish, Kadamach.'

'And you're an arrogant upstart,' Kiaran replies calmly. 'This isn't selfishness. I just don't like you.'

Lonnrach smirks at him. 'You mean you don't trust your Falconer. If she's as powerful as you hope she is, she should be able to resist my compulsion. Let her come to me.'

I don't remember Kiaran releasing my wrist, or walking over to Lonnrach. Everything in my peripheral vision is hazy, tunnelled. I try to shake my head to clear it, but can't. I have to free myself. How did I break from Sorcha's influence? *Think.*

It's too late. I've already approached and the horse's heart beats at my eye level. Compelled, I smooth my palm over the creature's shoulder. How can metal be so soft? Like fur, but sleeker.

Lonnrach curls a finger under my chin. When my gaze

meets his again, it's as though I'm being dragged underwater by an inexorable current. My body isn't my own, and neither is my mind. I am in dark, cold water and my other senses are muted, dulled. There is only taste. Flower petals drag along my tongue and it's not unpleasant.

Lonnrach studies me. 'So you're all that's left,' he murmurs. 'How very brave of you to come.'

His voice makes my body feel light as air, millions upon millions of molecules floating weightless. I have to break his hold or he'll kill me, easily. I try to push against his presence again, but he only invades me further. His power is calming, not violent or brutal like his sister's. That only makes it worse.

'How old are you?' he asks.

'Eighteen.' I sound so far away, as if I'm hearing myself from the other side of the meadow. I have to kill him now. My hand shifts toward my blade, but his power stops me.

'So young.' He strokes my cheek. 'It's such a shame.'

He makes me lean into his touch. 'Are you going to kill me?'

'Eventually.' He bends down and whispers, 'You see, you have something I want.'

'What is that?'

Lonnrach's lips curl with the hint of a smile. 'Plenty of time for that.' He glances at my armour. 'Well done, Kadamach. She's quite exquisite.'

'You shouldn't underestimate her,' he says calmly. 'She'll cut your throat.'

When Lonnrach studies me again, his gaze rakes me from my toes to my face, long and slow. 'She looks tame enough now. But I always did love a Falconer in armour. Metal suits you best.'

Something snaps inside me. A torrent, a wave of awareness and everything comes rushing back.

Crimson suits you best crimson suits you best crimson suits you best crimson suits you best—

That's all I need to break his influence. Wrath rises inside me with the strength of a surging storm. Kiaran's powers strengthen it, intensify it, and the air around me becomes charged with it, mine and Kiaran's combined. It crackles with electricity and when the first drops of rain hit my armour, they spark like bolts of discharge.

Lonnrach stares at me in surprise. I feel his mind in mine, enticing. Weakening. I snap our connection – and smile. In an instant, my blades are in my hands. 'If I have something you want,' I snarl, 'you'll have to fight me for it.'

I jump and swing my arm up, slashing him across the cheek. It's a superficial cut. A warning. I smile as the blood trickles down his face.

Lonnrach's eyes narrow. He speaks again, calmly, but this time he faces his army. 'Destroy it all.'

Chapter 37

They've been waiting for this. Lonnrach has barely finished speaking before a *cù sìth* leaps at me with teeth bared, enormous claws extended. I throw myself under it and whip one blade up. It slices deep into the beast's left flank and blood splatters warm against my cheek.

There's no time to make sure it's dead. Horses surround me, *daoine sìth* raise their blades and *sluagh* circle above us, their piercing screams so stark amid the quiet.

Then a hand clasps mine. Kiaran.

There, amid the chaos, I want to tell him something. That I wish I had more time with him, or that I regret never saying just how much I care for him.

Kiaran nods, as if he understands, and turns from me. He slides his blades from their sheaths. I press my back to his and face in the other direction. We're ready.

The horses surge forward and I leap and swing my blades. Metal clashes against metal, loud and deafening. The air is still and charged with power, surrounding us with glimmering, brilliant colours. Power slices through me with such force that my muscles protest and ache.

I ignore the pain and slash a *daoine sìth*, slam my fist into another's face, dodge blade after blade. Fae-powered lightning strikes my shoulder and the current burns through me. Kiaran's power swells inside me and when I hold out my blades, light erupts from them and slams into a group of *daoine sìth*.

Another stretches out his hand and vines break free from the ground, wrapping around my arms and feet. Power bursts from me. The plants disintegrate and fall, naught but ash.

I leap forward and slice the faery's throat with my blade. Blood gushes onto my armour and into those tiny silver veins that run along the vambraces. The faery blood amalgamates with my armour. The rush from death is strong, a quickening energy that fills me up until I think I might burst.

My blades plunge through armour and slice into bone and sinew. I whirl on my toes and slam my metal fist into another faery's gut. The force of my blow sends her flying, but she recovers and throws up her hands. Power crashes into me, quick and forceful enough to bruise my chest through the metal breastplate.

The taste of dry earth slides down my throat and I'm suddenly surrounded by flames. Fire burns through my armour and scorches my flesh. But Kiaran's power is a current inside me and I feel it take over, healing and energising, resonating through the armour, through the faery blood that covers it, through my heart. I draw upon all that power and gather it together inside me, the strength of a storm, and hurl it at the wall of fire.

The flames dissipate around me and the savage part of me screams with victory.

The *daoine sìth* tries to throw more energy at me, but Kiaran's power is too strong. I sheathe a blade to aim the lightning pistol at the faery's head and shoot. So easy.

Surrounded by rain and bodies, I look towards the end of the valley, where the outskirts of the city stand. *Daoine sìth* are riding away from the meadow on horseback. Away from the battle and towards my home. I notice Gavin circling my flying machine there, watching to make sure the battle doesn't spill into the city. I won't give them the chance.

I sprint for the locomotive, holstering my pistol and touching my blades together so they revert to the star-shaped disc, which slides back into my breastplate. Once inside, I shove at a lever to open the weapons compartment, bringing out the sonic cannon.

As I feel around for earplugs, I shout, 'Kiaran!'

'Aye?'

He's in the locomotive behind me, covered in blood and dirt. His eyes burn bright.

I toss him another pair of earplugs. 'You'll be needing these.'

I slip my own plugs snugly into my ears and heave the canon onto my shoulder and flip the intensity level all the way up. For a brief moment, I savour a silence so thick that no sound can penetrate it. The calm before a squall. The sweet sound of peace just before the chaos.

Then I aim for the faeries and pull the release. The contraption shudders in my hands and I watch them fall to the ground as the wave of sound hits them.

I turn and aim again to incapacitate the larger group, which is already pounding fast towards me on their horses. I pull the release again. When the sound pulse hits, they fall in waves as though something solid has crashed into them. The faeries closest to me lie twisted on the ground, bleeding from their ears.

I pull out my earplugs and smile at Kiaran. 'Decent distraction, aye?'

Kiaran looks impressed. 'I knew there was a reason I liked you.'

I nod to the incapacitated fae at the far side of the park. 'Your kill or mine?'

'Mine,' Kiaran says. His smile is slow and terrifying. 'Definitely mine.'

He leaps out of the locomotive and sprints toward the others.

If I didn't have so many enemies at my back, I would have gone with him.

Instead, I throw myself at a circling *sluagh* and plunge my blade into its neck. Cold mist erupts and ice adheres to my armour.

I rush my enemies again. It happens so fast, there's no time to focus on any particular individual. When one comes at me, I kill it. Then another, then another. I use my explosives and rock and earth rain down on me. The meadow illuminates with power and the sky with flashes of light. Energy hits me and I endure the pain. I dodge, I slice.

I don't know how many faeries I've killed. All that matters is the rush of energy as they die, the sheer joy of it. I slash my blades into the air and watch my borrowed power burst out of me. It slams into more bodies and the shrieks are deafening.

Kiaran's abilities are intoxicating. The hunt should always be this way. The thrill, the victory. The fear. I need more.

'Kam!'

Kiaran grabs me from behind, spins me to face him. I nearly lurch into his body, so drunk with power that nausea is beginning to cramp my stomach.

He puts his hands on my face and forces me to look at him. 'Now,' he says. 'We've killed enough of them that the shield will hold a little longer. You have to go and activate the seal now.'

'Now?' I shake my head, trying to comprehend his words. The urge to fight is pulling me back into the fray again.

I briefly scan the meadow. Kiaran pulled me away just as the remaining fae were retreating to regroup, while those injured are still healing from their many wounds. Scraps of bloodied armour glint in the darkness. Kiaran and I cut through and slaughtered so many, their bodies litter the meadow.

God help me, but I *loved* it. What kind of person does that make me?

'Kam?'

'I can kill the rest,' I tell him, dismissing the horror over what I've done. Now isn't the time for guilt. 'I can.'

'No, you can't.' Kiaran's eyes hold mine, so intense I don't think I could look away if I wanted to. 'My powers weren't meant for you. If you hold them too long, they'll destroy you.'

'But—but what about—'

You. What about you? My throat closes.

'Don't,' he says. 'You have to let me go.'

That's what stops me cold, suppresses the urge to kill again. I can't help myself. I pull him to me and kiss him desperately.

'I'm sorry,' I say. It's all I can manage. 'I'm so sorry.' I kiss him again so hard, I think my lips will be bruised.

He takes hold of my shoulders, breathing hard as a flash of anguish, of regret, crosses his beautiful face. That look will haunt me for the rest of my days. 'Go, Kam.'

'But—'

'Damn it, I said *go!*'

He pushes me away, his expression carefully composed again, battle-ready. I'll always remember him this way. Strong, unyielding to the very end.

Against all of my instincts, I turn away and leave him there.

Chapter 38

I won't be fast enough, not with the faeries pursuing me on horseback. I sprint to the locomotive again, running so swiftly that I can barely breathe. I crash through puddles that soak through my boots. Rain slaps against my skin, cold and relentless. I leap over the bodies of fallen fae soldiers and try not to think about Kiaran's fate if I manage to activate the seal.

Out of the corner of my eye, something dark and gleaming leaps at me. I hit the ground rolling. The *cù sìth* vaults above me and lands in the grass. Instinct takes me over. Blades I don't remember drawing are already in my hands as I throw myself at the hound, slashing.

I don't even pause to enjoy the kill. I'm on my feet and running through the meadow again. I hear galloping horses behind me and know I haven't much time. The fae are beginning to recover.

Not much further to the locomotive. Every part of me aches with the effort to keep running. My legs burn. My throat is dry and every breath is agony.

I yank open the door and hop inside, already flipping the switches to start the engine before the door slams shut. 'Quickly now,' I whisper to myself, twisting the dial to enable the highest possible speed.

The engine purrs to life. Only then do I look back and see the fae on horseback heading straight towards me. I draw a blade, ready to fight again if I need to. But Kiaran is already there, leaping and cutting through the fae.

I return my attention to operating the locomotive, but it stalls. 'Come on,' I mutter, pushing the pedals with my feet.

'Hurry, Kam!'

Kiaran's power thunders around us. Power crackles across the meadow, a blinding, searing light that scorches my cheeks. I pump the lever, but again the engine stalls.

'Kam!'

'I'm trying!'

Just then, one of the *daoine sìth* on horseback reins in his mount and holds a palm out towards me, fingers splayed. *Oh, damnatio—*

Light bursts from his palm.

I throw the door open and dive from the locomotive, my body slamming into the ground. I yelp as my wrist cracks under my weight.

The locomotive explodes. I pull my knees to my chest and cover my head as scraps of glass and metal hit the ground. A large, sharp piece embeds itself into the ground right next to my face.

Get up, get up!

I push to my feet, ignoring the sharp pain in my wrist. Kiaran's powers are already healing it.

Ahead of me, I see a metal horse without a rider. I race across the meadow and leap onto the animal's back, settling myself astride in the saddle. The horse whinnies in protest and smoke rises from its nostrils. It rears, but I hold on tight to its fine golden mane. Kiaran's powers stream from my fingertips, glowing brightly. The horse calms.

'Go,' I command.

The horse takes off so fast, I can barely keep hold of its

mane. It pounds across the Queen's Park, through grass so wet water splashes high enough to soak my trousers. Beneath me, its hooves thump as loud and fast as its heart. Thump*thump*-thump*thump*thump*thump*. I lean my body closer to the creature's back, until we move together.

I don't dare look back. I'm afraid I'll turn and find Kiaran dead. I have to trust that our connection through the armour will let me know if that happens.

The galloping hooves behind me only worry me more, but I try to remain focused, tightening my grip on the horse's mane. I urge it faster, faster. Power snaps around me, blindingly bright.

A bolt of energy strikes the grass close by and the horse screams in protest. It rears up and I almost lose my seat. I channel Kiaran's power to soothe the beast, to coax it back to running.

The horse's front hooves hit the ground again and we're moving with even greater speed, crashing along the dirt path that leads to St Anthony's Chapel. I feel the buzzing of the device before we reach the archway. Then I'm out of the saddle and racing to the stones. I drop to the dirt and dig to uncover the device again.

I look up. There are more horsemen behind me, *sluagh* in the sky above me. No sign of Kiaran, but I can't think about that now.

My digging grows more frantic, the buzzing just as loud as before. Finally, the gold gleams through the mud.

I press my fingers into the indentations along the side of the metal plate, and light explodes from the device just in time.

A *sluagh* crashes into the light shield. I've never heard a scream like that before in my life, so full of agony. I watch in shock as the *sluagh* bursts into blue-white flames and erupts in a burst of ice and mist. Then … nothing. There's only frost on the ground to show the creature ever existed.

The faeries on horseback pursuing me come to a hard stop at the edge of the illuminated shield. They circle me eagerly, mist swirling around their feet. There's still no sign of Kiaran beyond the fae surrounding me.

Lonnrach approaches and regards the light shield calmly. 'That won't save you.'

He holds out his hand and gold power bursts from his palm. It hits the light, and ripples across its surface like water. The other fae join in, their powers mixing together to strike the shield. Soon, it will weaken and fall.

I brace my hands in the mud, on either side of the *iuchair*. The inner rings have changed positions, just as Kiaran said they would. I remember their correct arrangement from my drawing. I turn the inner circles of the compass and align the symbols with the clock. The etchings shine as they line up and click into place.

Now for the rest. The missing piece of the puzzle. My eyes rove over the symbols I've connected, searching for a pattern. Still nothing. What do the bloody things mean?

The clang of metal distracts me. I look up. Kiaran! He must have fought through the wall of riders. His clothes are torn and there are open cuts along his arms.

Kiaran thrusts his blade into a *daoine sìth*'s chest and glances at me. 'Hurry!' he says.

Lonnrach's power slams into the shield again as I return my attention to the *iuchair*. But the symbols still don't appear to be sequential. They're random. Just errant carvings in no particular order, like stars in the—

Can you name them, Aileana? Here now, repeat after me …

Crimson suits you best.

I shake my head against the memories. Images of my mother lying dead. A beautiful corpse of the person I once knew.

Can you name them?

Crimson suits you best.

I grit my teeth and thrust the memory of my mother's death back where it belongs. I open that deep crevasse within me and shove my pain inside. Those images of my mother's dead body are buried in a coffin to be sealed in my heart.

Can you name them, Aileana?

Polaris, the centre ring. I draw a finger to the arrow pointing south and turn the next one in relation to that in the device. Capella. The symbols that represent Pegasus. Orion.

North. I recognise the shape of Cassiopeia. The Plough.

I rotate the rings until they match, the way they would on a star map. How could I not have seen this before? So many old monuments correspond to celestial alignments. They are constant, like the moon.

Last ring. The eastern alignment of stars and the fae will be trapped again—

And Kiaran will be trapped with them.

I look for him and watch as he slices effortlessly through a *daoine sìth*'s armour. When he fights, he's pure grace. Movement that any warrior would envy. I'll never see it again.

But I have to do this. With my eyes closed, I click the last symbol into place. And wait. The clanging of metal and booms of power still echo through the park. I open my eyes and look down at the seal. Nothing happens. My God, is it broken? Did I do something wrong?

'Two minutes.' Kiaran fights his way into my line of sight, pausing only to run his blade through another *daoine sìth*. 'I said two minutes, remember?'

'Something's wrong,' I say, beginning to panic. 'It's not working.'

'Then you didn't position them right—'

Lonnrach swings his blades at Kiaran. Kiaran dodges. If he were anyone else, the movement would have looked smooth, easy. But I know better. Kiaran is tiring. He's already used up so much of his power by lending half of it to me.

Kiaran recovers with a small smile at Lonnrach. 'You've improved.'

'The benefits of prison, Kadamach,' Lonnrach says. 'All I had was time.'

They leap at each other, blades raised. Power ignites around them, so brilliant I can barely see them through it, just shadows of their bodies as they strike and slash at each other. The energy crackles so thunderously, I can barely hear the sounds of their weapons clashing.

When the light fades, they're both bleeding from various cuts. Kiaran has a serious injury on one arm, a deep gash that's bleeding copiously through his shirt.

'Don't you want to help him, Falconer?' Lonnrach asks. He finally takes his eyes off Kiaran and looks right at me. 'If you imprison him with us, there will be no end to his torture.'

I hesitate. I glance at Kiaran again and all I can think about is that look of regret and vulnerability, the promise of what could have been between us.

Kiaran throws himself at Lonnrach. 'Activate the damn seal, Kam!'

Power bursts around them and I focus again on the seal. Kiaran's right. I can't let myself be distracted. I have to do this.

I stare at the seal, wincing as another burst of fae power strikes the shield. It ripples around me, beginning to falter. I focus on the symbols. What am I missing?

'*Aileana,*' a voice whispers in my mind. I know that voice.

'Mother?' I whisper.

'Aileana.' I hear again. It sounds like her. That beautiful, calm voice. So tender, so familiar.

No. It can't be her. I lift my eyes from the device. Sorcha

is standing amid the dead bodies Kiaran has left in his wake, smiling her hellish grin.

Rage flares inside me. She doesn't deserve to be trapped alive with the others. She deserves to feel my hand tearing through flesh and breaking bone so I can steal the beating heart from her body just like she did my mother's.

No. I need to activate the device. I *have* to.

Sorcha grins, as if sensing my struggle. I try to focus on Kiaran, on how I need to keep my rage coiled tight so he stays alive.

I think of our kiss, how his lips lingered against mine. His whispered pledge. *Aoram dhuit. I will worship thee.*

I drag my attention back to the seal again, the positioning of the symbols. I glance up. The clouds have begun to blow away, leaving behind a clear night sky bright with stars. I study the constellations.

Perhaps Kiaran *was* mistaken, like he suspected he might be. If his sister had to alter the seal for this purpose, maybe she changed the sequence. The key to the correct placement of the rings might not have anything to do with a fixed position on the seal. Maybe aligning them to their position in the sky *now* is what relocks it.

I click the symbols into new positions, this time corresponding with the placement of the constellations in the sky. Once the first ring is completed, the seal begins to hum. I almost smile. I got it.

I click the second ring into place and the hum increases.

Sorcha's voice mimicking my mother's resounds in my head again. *Falconer ...*

I put my hands over my ears as if that could somehow muffle her. Now I know why Kiaran told me to focus on my memories of that night at the loch, to let them ground me. They cleanse me of my rage until I'm left only with my memories of us together. Us hunting together, running through the city in the night. Sparring until the early hours of the morning. Lying in the grass, Kiaran telling me that he wanted to stay with me until the end.

They all anchor me. I ignore the wavering shield around me and click the third and fourth rings into place. Then the fifth.

Another memory interrupts, flashing violently in my mind. Sorcha ripping through my mother's throat. Sorcha clawing open my mother's chest. Sorcha's wide smile as she holds my mother's bleeding heart aloft. *Crimson suits you best crimson suits you best crimson suits you best crimson suits you—*

'Stop it,' I say. 'Stop it stop it *stop it*!'

Make me, her voice whispers in my mind.

I try to rouse my memories of Kiaran again, but every time I think I've succeeded, I feel Sorcha in my mind. She drags me out of the calm space I want to be in and shoves me back into the body of the girl I used to be, weak and trembling and numb. She forces me to sit next to my mother's dead body again, and feel the slick, heavy weight of her blood all over me.

'*Stop!*' I open my eyes again to meet Sorcha's.

Sorcha speaks again with my mother's voice, the voice that used to soothe and laugh and comfort me. 'Then take my heart in return, Falconer,' she taunts. 'If you can.'

My memories of Kiaran cease to matter. There is only rising anger and the single image of one hundred and eighty-six crimson ribbons attached to pins on a map. All those people she killed. That's all it takes to silence the rational part of me.

I stand with my blades in hand, about to stride out of that light shield to kill Sorcha.

'Kam, *don't*! The Seer's vision!'

I look over. Kiaran's eyes catch mine as he blocks another blow from Lonnrach. I stop at the edge of the light, my foot poised to take that last fateful step.

And I can see everything so clearly, perhaps the way Gavin did. I see myself stepping through the shield. Maybe I kill Sorcha and Kiaran dies. Or maybe she kills me. In both versions of that reality, the city falls. The buildings are reduced to rubble and ash. Everyone I love dies. That's how the vision ends.

Sorcha would try to convince me that vengeance is worth risking everything for. But the dead don't come back. I know that better than anyone.

'No,' I tell Sorcha. I make the decision I hope will change the vision. I step back towards the seal and think of the words Derrick said to me after I destroyed the map. 'I won't ever let you break me.'

I ignore her efforts to scratch her way into my mind, to expose every memory, every nightmare, every rage-fuelled fight I've ever had. She tries to draw me back into that vengeful part of me again, into the irrational creature who would abandon the most important thing of all just to kill her.

I won't be that person for her. I click the sixth ring into place and listen to the pleasant hum of the device intensify again.

Glancing up, I look at Kiaran one last time before I align the final ring. The position of the blood moon. He and Lonnrach are still fighting, their power beginning to scorch the earth black around them.

'Goodbye,' I whisper to him.

Before I click that last ring into place, Lonnrach grabs Kiaran by the shirt and throws him into the shield.

The shield snaps and breaks with a tremendous clap, gold light cracking around me. Kiaran crashes into me and I end up sprawled on the ground beneath his heavy body.

'Kiaran?'

I manage to push him off me. Part of his face is scorched from the shield, skin blackened, bone showing through. His eyes are closed and he isn't moving. I frantically search for his pulse.

My fingers touch the blackened, withering skin at his throat and it nearly breaks me. Tears fall from my eyes.

'*Kiaran.*' I shake him. 'Kiaran, wake up.' He still isn't moving, not even breathing. I shake him harder. I hit his chest. I scream at him. '*Wake up! Kiaran!*'

Boots crunch through the dirt in front of me and I look up to meet Lonnrach's hard, crystalline gaze. 'He's alive, Falconer. Even a shield as strong as that isn't powerful enough to destroy him.'

My brief moment of relief is crushed by the dawning horror of what I've done. The seal. *Oh, God.*

I push to my feet, lurching back to the device so I can align the last circle and save us all, but Lonnrach seizes me. The bite of his blade is sharp under my chin and I feel a trickle of blood slide down my throat.

'You really believe me to be your worst enemy.' He glances over at Kiaran, an emotion in his gaze that I can't comprehend. Then he says something I'll never forget. 'You'll wish you had killed Kadamach when you had the chance.'

Bestiary

Aileana Kameron's Notes and Observations of the Fae

With some comments from Kiaran MacKay.

Not to be removed from the dressing room trunk by a certain pixie in residence …

Derrick, this means you.

As I have come to learn, the stories of the fae from my childhood are the result of several thousand years of diluted oral history.

What remains of the fae world now is but a shadow of its former magnificence. The Seelie and Unseelie – two warring kingdoms of light and dark fae – once conquered whole continents. Humanity was driven practically extinct by what the fae called the Wild Hunt, a systematic attempt to capture and kill the strongest humans, especially those with the Sight.

It was the never-ending war between the two kingdoms that nearly destroyed them, and the final war with the Falconers that finally finished them both.

After everything Kiaran has taught me, I've come to realise that only one truth has endured across time:

Never trust the fae.

Aileana Kameron, 1844.

Baobhan Sìth

Solitary fae (Possibly belonged to a kingdom in her past). She is related to the *daoine sìth*, yet distinct because of her strong telepathic abilities. She is magnetic, with long dark hair and the most vivid green eyes I've ever seen. Her smile is both haunting and terrifying, a thing of nightmares. Her power tastes heavy, as if blood is being forced down my throat. Aside from slaughtering the Falconers, she murdered any other *baobhan sìth* born so that her abilities would remain unmatched.

Strengths: She is highly intelligent and cunning, her ability to kill aided by mental powers that can deceive a person into meeting her on a dark road of her choosing where she drains her victims of blood.

Kills: ~~20~~ ~~36~~ ~~87~~ ~~103~~ Too many to tally.

Weaknesses: ~~No known weaknesses~~. I will find one.

Cù Sìth

Non-solitary fae, Unseelie. A faery hound nearly five feet in length, seventeen stone in weight, with fur that alternates in different colours (red, green, deep violet, as I've witnessed). Its place in battle was similar to that of the redcaps: to immobilise their enemies' numbers as quickly and efficiently as possible.

Strengths: A single burst of power that can render a person immobile (to human ears, it sounds like a piercing howl); dense, impenetrable fur, razor-sharp claws. They travel in packs.

Weaknesses: Thinner fur at the belly, but not by much.

Addendum: Power tastes of dry ash. It seems they also have poisonous barbs along their claws that can cause fatal illness. *Thank you* for not warning me about that, Kiaran.

Daoine Sìth

Non-solitary fae, both Seelie and Unseelie (light and dark fae). They are unearthly beautiful, a warrior race known for wreaking destruction and for driving humans to near-extinction (what Kiaran calls the Wild Hunt). The *daoine sìth* once ruled not only the faery realm (*Sìth-bhrùth*), but once managed to conquer nearly every continent on earth. Kiaran claims there was once a distinction between Seelie and Unseelie rule, but over time both courts became equally power-obsessed and ruthless.

Of course, Kiaran is being vague on strengths and weaknesses but I have managed to garner that their powers include the ability to command the elements.

Weaknesses: ?

Kiaran's power, at least, tastes earthy-sweet, floral, something wild. Which is indescribably lovely when he's being pleasant, and nauseating when he's not.

THEY ARE ALSO SMUG, ARROGANT BASTARDS.

Pixies

In *Gàidhlig*, they are referred to as *aibhse.*

Small, winged-fae fae, mostly non-solitary. Pixies, like other smaller fae, are only distantly related to the larger types of *sìthichean*. They once had their own realm, lands, and kingdom that was separately ruled somewhere on Skye, but mass-migrated to Cornwall sometime before the Falconer battle with the *daoine sìth*. Pixies' power shines in a halo around them, the colour of which changes depending on the pixie's mood. Can feed off of human energy, as do most other fae, but largely choose not to. Power tastes of gingerbread. Apparently cannot help but mend clothes and steal shiny objects. *I'm going to steal your favorite pistol when you aren't looking.*

Strengths: Extremely fast flyers; adept with small, sharp weaponry. *I am also quite handsome to the ladies.*

Weaknesses: Honey *not a weakness*, torn ballgowns *also not a weakness.*

Derrick: If you write in this journal again, the honey goes out with the rubbish.

Redcaps:

In *Gàidhlig,* they are referred to as *athach.*

Non-solitary fae, Unseelie. About the size of a revenant, but leaner. Their arms hang low and their hands are large, with long, tapered fingers. They wear masks of bones, and smear the blood of their last human victims over their foreheads. Redcaps were once the brawn of the Unseelie army. Using their war hammers made of fae metal, they could cut through opponents quickly, rendering the other army weakened.

Strengths: Agility, war hammers.

Weaknesses: Spot along the lower back that can be punctured by a mortal weapon. Much of their power is harnessed within the hammer; taking it away makes them vulnerable to attack.

Addendum: Power tastes of witch hazel and iron. And apparently one should not mix excessive amounts of *seilgflùr* with gunpowder and try to blow up a redcap – disaster will ensue.

Revenants

In *Gàidhlig,* they are referred to as *Fuath.*

Solitary fae. Massive, hulking creatures that average seven feet in height. Hideous, rotting-looking skin (apparently a natural deficiency of this type). They smell of decay because of their skin, but also because of their tendency to take deceased victims back to their underground dwellings as a sort of trophy. Their feeding pattern is much slower than other fae, as they wait until their last victim is fully decayed before they hunt again.

Strengths: Size, musculature.

Weaknesses: An opening along their thoracic cage; a soft spot along their abdominal cavity. They are exceedingly stupid.

Addendum: Kiaran was being kind when he described their scent. I shall attempt to hold my breath in the future. And, confound it, they taste like sulfur and ammonia – a more abhorrent combination I cannot conceive of.

Sluagh

Non-solitary fae, Unseelie. Flying creatures that resemble dragons. Skin is thin and iridescent. With their ability to fly silently and in large numbers, they once served the Unseelie the way falcons did Falconers: as spies from the air. They tend to use their powers from a distance during any confrontation, as they are among the most physically fragile of the fae. However, Kiaran tells me not to be fooled by their weak appearance.

Strengths: Well, their ability to incinerate anything in their path certainly sounds decidedly unpleasant; I'll be sure to avoid.

Weaknesses: Skin thin enough to cut through.

Addendum: Their power lacks taste, but instead feels cold and slick. And now I can say that I've experienced their incineration power firsthand and lived to tell the tale …

Acknowledgements

This book was such a labour of love and could not have been possible without the support and encouragement I received along the way. Thank you Dawn, Ewa and Suze for assuring me it was worth writing. To my incredible critique partner, Tess Sharpe: we made it. We did it. Here's to the last 12 years and many more to come! To the lucky 13s, thank you all so much for this year, and for listening. You guys are wonderful.

For all the people who helped me during the publication process, every step of the way. My agent, Russell Galen, who has been an amazing champion for this book and its sequels from start to finish. My foreign rights agent, Heather Baror-Shapiro, for being my advocate with editors around the world. And my esteemed editors, Gillian Redfearn at Gollancz and Ginee Seo at Chronicle Books, thank you ladies for helping to make this book the best that it could possibly be. I am so grateful to you both. To the team at both Gollancz and Chronicle, I am continually amazed by how much you love this book and all the work you've put in. Thank you, thank you, thank you.

Finally to Mr May: *Is to mo thasgaidh 's mo reìr*. I love you.